PRAISE FOR THE NOVELS
OF KATE HEWITT

"With lush coastal imagery and well-drawn characters, Hewitt immerses the reader in the deeply personal struggles and triumphs of Rachel and Claire. At turns introspective and exhilarating, this novel proves that it's never too late to start over." —*Booklist*

"Pulled me in and never let me go. . . . Hewitt writes about the complex emotions of family relationships with sensitivity and realism."
—Marie Bostwick, *New York Times* bestselling author of *The Second Sister*

"A moving look at what family can look like and how much it can mean." —Wendy Wax, *USA Today* bestselling author of *One Good Thing*

"Kate Hewitt skillfully weaves together two stories in this engrossing tale. A warm, wonderful, emotional read."
—Sarah Morgan, *USA Today* bestselling author of *Sunset in Central Park*

"As deeply satisfying as a fragrant kitchen, a warm cup of tea, and a heart-to-heart chat in the midst of a Cumbrian downpour."
—Emilie Richards, *USA Today* bestselling author of *When We Were Sisters*

"A lushly imagined, deeply moving story . . . stunning . . . the perfect book to lose yourself in!"
—Megan Crane, *USA Today* bestselling author of *In Bed with the Bachelor*

"Completely and totally charming. . . . I read this book straight through, in pajamas, eating brownies, on a rainy day in Oregon. I don't think I left my couch. That's how much I loved it."
—Cathy Lamb, author of *My Very Best Friend*

OTHER HARTLEY-BY-THE-SEA NOVELS
BY KATE HEWITT

Rainy Day Sisters

Now and Then Friends

A Mother Like Mine

KATE HEWITT

BERKLEY
NEW YORK

BERKLEY
An imprint of Penguin Random House LLC
375 Hudson Street, New York, New York 10014

Copyright © 2017 by Kate Hewitt Limited
Readers Guide copyright © 2017 by Penguin Random House
Excerpt from *Rainy Day Sisters* copyright © 2015 by Kate Hewitt Limited

BERKLEY is a registered trademark and the B colophon is a trademark of
Penguin Random House LLC.

Library of Congress Cataloging-in-Publication Data

Names: Hewitt, Kate, author.
Title: A mother like mine/Kate Hewitt.
Description: First edition. | New York: Berkley, 2017. |
Identifiers: LCCN 2016052127 (print) | LCCN 2016058521 (ebook) |
ISBN 9780399583797 (softcover) | ISBN 9780399583803 (ebook)
Subjects: LCSH: Mothers and daughters—Fiction. | Domestic fiction. |
BISAC: FICTION/Contemporary Women. | FICTION/Romance/Contemporary. |
FICTION/Family Life.
Classification: LCC PS3619.W368 M68 2017 (print) | LCC PS3619.W368 (ebook) |
DDC 813/.6—dc23
LC record available at https://lccn.loc.gov/2016052127

First Edition: August 2017

Printed in the United States of America
1   3   5   7   9   10   8   6   4   2

Cover photographs: women by plainpicture/Lubitz & Dorner;
Labrador dog puppy lying on the beach © manushot/Shutterstock
Cover design by Katie Anderson

Dedicated to my mother,
for always being there for me.
I love you, Mom!
Love, Katie

A Mother
Like *Mine*

I

Abby

"ARE YOU ALL RIGHT?"

The Cumbrian greeting that could have offcomers stiffening defensively made Abby Rhodes smile. The man who'd asked, another parent with a child in the Reception class at Hartley-by-the-Sea Primary, was waiting stony-faced for the expected answer: "all right," or *areet*, as a Cumbrian would say, and Abby was a born-and-bred Cumbrian even if she'd only been back in the Lake District for not quite two years.

"Areet," she said firmly, because standing in the school yard with the sun shining down, she knew she was. She hadn't always been, and even a few months ago she might have given a different answer, or at least her "areet" would have wavered a little. But not now. Now she was starting to finally feel as if she'd made a place for herself and her son.

The farmer nodded in apparent satisfaction and looked away, the conversation clearly over. Abby leaned against the stone wall of the school yard and gazed out at the village spread below her in a living map, the terraced houses and the whitewashed cottages giving way to a patchwork of rolling sheep pasture and fields of bright yellow rapeseed that led to the sea, a hazy gray-blue on the horizon.

It was a warm day in mid-June, a day of mild breezes and benevolent sunshine that could almost make Abby forget the freezing temperatures and slanting rain of just a few weeks ago. Everyone had been remarking about the weather; reaching sixty degrees in Hartley-by-the-Sea was considered a newsworthy event and definitely classified as a heat wave. On the way to school that morning, Abby had seen Eleanor Carwell in only half of her usual twinset, emphatically waving a fan in front of her face as she took her daily walk to the post office shop. "Isn't it red-hot?" she'd exclaimed, and Abby had, of course, agreed.

Now from her vantage point at the top of the village, she could just glimpse the tan strip of beach, visible since the tide was out, and the low, ramshackle building on one end of the concrete promenade that was the beach café as well as her home.

It had been nearly two years since she'd limped back to her grandmother in Hartley-by-the-Sea, drained and still grieving, not just for Ben but for everything she'd lost, clutching her three-year-old son, Noah, and needing a job as well as a place to stay. Two years that had seen her start to revitalize the shabby café by the beach, make a few friends, and begin to feel a wary, fragile happiness that could be blown away on the next sea breeze—God knew it had been before. But she was starting to think that maybe this time it wouldn't be.

Are you all right?

Yes, she really was.

"Mummy!"

Abby refocused her gaze on her son, who was barreling towards her from the front doors of the school's Infants' entrance, a blur of dark hair and pumping limbs. He tackled her straight on, skinny arms wrapping around her middle as his head burrowed into her stomach.

"Oof." Abby rolled her eyes good-naturedly at a few of the other parents who were smiling in sympathy at her son's exuberance. "Well, hello, Noah."

He tilted his head up to grin at her, silky hair sliding away from his eyes, his gap-toothed grin—he'd lost his first tooth a few weeks ago—like a fist squeezing her heart. She ruffled his hair, noticing how he jerked away, her baby already a little boy, starting to grow away from her. It made panic clutch at her insides even though she knew it was normal and necessary.

"Can we go to the beach? Please? Please?" he asked, his words tumbling over themselves. "It's so nice out—"

Abby managed one last ruffle of his hair before he was darting away, moving on his tiptoes, ever in motion. "I suppose we can."

She smiled at a few of the other mums whom she'd gotten to know over the last year; most of them were a decade older than she was, but Meghan Campbell was the same age as well as another single mum, and she gave Abby a cheeky grin as she led her own son, Nathan, by the hand down the steep lane that led to the high street.

"We're going to the beach," Abby called to her. "If you and Nathan want to come along."

"Why not?" Meghan called back. "Can't waste this weather, can we, Nath?" She turned to Abby. "You know this means it will pour rain the whole six weeks of the summer holiday, don't you?"

"Of course. This is Cumbria. We can't have that much good weather."

They kept up the banter all the way down the high street to the turning on the beach road; unable to resist the straight stretch of pavement with sheep pasture rolling away on either side, Nathan and Noah took off, and Meghan and Abby both watched with rueful affection.

"On a day like today," Meghan said as she tilted her face up to the sky, "I almost don't mind living here."

"Oh, Meghan. You like living here, don't you?"

Meghan lowered her head with a gusty sigh. "Since I haven't lived anywhere else, I suppose I can't really say." She glanced at Abby. "What about you, Miss Liverpool?"

Abby laughed wryly and shook her head. She'd once lived in

Liverpool, yes, but it felt like a million years ago now, as did the trappings of that life: an unfinished degree in veterinary science, a fiancé, a future. She'd been planning to apprentice at a vet's in the city; she'd seen herself and Ben living in a chic city center flat, pursuing their careers, living their carefree lives. So much had changed since those heady days, but right now she couldn't begrudge the loss of any of it. She had her son; she had her grandmother; she had a business she enjoyed.

"I'm all right here," she said, and they walked on.

They'd just reached the beach car park, the boys sprinting towards the playground on the field above the promenade along the sea, a few bright kites circling in the air above them.

"Slow down," Abby called, and then came to a halt herself when she saw her grandmother waving from the beach café's doorway, one hand clutched to her side, her face red with effort.

"Oh no," she muttered, and Meghan glanced at her.

"What's up?"

"Gran . . ." Abby nodded towards Mary. "Noah——," she called, but Meghan stopped her.

"Go on. Whatever it is, it will be better for you if Noah isn't underfoot. I'll watch them at the park for a bit."

"Would you——," she began in relief, only for Meghan to wave her away.

"Easier for me if Nath has a friend there," she assured her with a grin. "Really, I'm doing myself a favor. I'll drop him back in an hour or so."

Abby called her thanks as she started hurrying towards the café. Her grandmother had had a heart attack two years ago, which had, at least in part, prompted Abby's return. There'd been no one else to help Mary Rhodes run the place, and Abby had needed somewhere to go. Since then, she'd been gently taking over the management of the café; Mary wasn't one to let go of anything easily, and the beach café had been in her family since the 1940s.

"Gran," she called as she reached the cracked concrete steps. "What's wrong—"

"Nothing's wrong," Mary wheezed. "Just wanted to catch you before anyone else did."

"Okay. But you look like you need to sit down." Abby tried to speak mildly; Mary resisted any suggestion that she wasn't completely recovered from her heart attack.

"I'm fine," Mary answered, her words erupting in a cough before she fanned her face and took a few gulps of fresh sea air. "It's just you know how gossip spreads in this village." Mary's face was red and shiny even as she managed a wry smile. "Worse than measles."

"I didn't realize there was anything to gossip about." Abby took her grandmother's arm and attempted to gently steer her back inside, but Mary Rhodes wasn't having it. She shook her head, staying Abby with one hand.

"Abby, wait."

"It's no good standing about in the heat, Gran."

"I won't melt in what passes for a Cumbrian summer," Mary retorted. "Even if I'm doing a good impression of it." She took a well-pressed handkerchief from the pocket of her skirt and dabbed her forehead. "Abby, love, look. I know it will be a shock, but . . ." Mary paused, the hesitation so unlike her. She had always had a quick comeback or a sharp word coupled with a ready smile, and she had done her best to struggle back after a heart attack and bypass surgery. She took a deep breath, her ample chest expanding like a bellows. "Your mother's inside."

The words didn't immediately compute. Abby simply stared and Mary added, her voice choking a little, "It's true. Laura . . . my girl's finally come home."

Abby registered the look of tentative hope on Mary's face and didn't know how to feel. When had her mother last visited? Six years, at least. Abby had been pregnant with Noah. It had, as far as she could remember, been as awkward and tense as all the other sporadic visits. And yet *my girl*. Her grandmother seemed to be marking this visit more than any other. Mary had never seemed that maternal; like mother, like daughter, Abby supposed, although Mary had acted more or less as a mum to her since she was two, when Laura had left for good, her spurts of sentimental affection broken up by impatient cuffs and sharp words.

But Laura, back here, now? Abby simply stared, trying to probe how she felt about it, the way you would a sore tooth, anticipating that sudden lightning streak of pain if you touched a certain spot.

She felt nothing. She couldn't tell if it was a true emptiness of feeling or merely a thin veneer of numbness, and she didn't want to examine the lack of emotion too deeply. In any case, how could she expect to feel something for a woman who had barely been part of her life? Laura had left when Abby had been only a toddler, hightailing it out of Hartley-by-the-Sea for a hostess job in a nightclub in Manchester. She'd visited on rare occasions, once a year at most, and then, when Abby was twenty-one, pregnant and alone, Laura had moved to New York. At that point Abby had been too tired and jaded, everything about her life already too broken, to care.

"What is she doing here?" Abby asked, her voice coming out flat.

"She wants to see you—"

As if. "And give you another heart attack?" Abby finished. "Let's get you inside, Gran."

It was easier to concentrate on settling Mary than thinking about her mother. "I'm not an invalid, you know," Mary grumbled, but she didn't resist as Abby led her inside and to a chair at one of the café's rather rickety tables. She sat down with a heavy sigh and then looked up at Abby.

"You will go talk to her? I know it's been a long time, Abby, but it could be different now and I'm not getting any younger, you know. I'd like to see something good come of all this."

So her grandmother wanted to orchestrate some reconciliation? She'd always had a soft spot for sentiment, and yet the idea was laughable. Offensive, even, because when had Laura made any effort at all? A few presents and the occasional awkward visit were as far as she'd ever gone to forging a relationship. Her mother was, and always had been, a deliberate stranger. Abby bustled about, neither meeting her grandmother's eye nor giving her an answer. Mary wasn't fooled.

"Abby."

"I will, Gran. Talk to her, I mean." She let out a weary breath. "I will." Abby glanced around the café, taking comfort from its worn familiarity. Fairy lights strung over the door, and paintings by local artists adorning the walls. The community notice board she'd put up when she'd first arrived was full of advertisements and flyers for local events; admittedly most of them were a couple of weeks or even months old, but Abby liked seeing people scan the board as they waited for their teas and coffees, noting a toddler morning or a weekend ceilidh.

Right now the café was empty, save for a few pensioners at a table in the corner, lingering over scones and tea, and a handful of people at the ice cream counter. Sophie, a young woman Abby had hired for sunny afternoons such as this one, stood behind it, doling out the scoops. Her mother, thankfully, was nowhere to be seen, although perhaps Abby wouldn't have recognized Laura Rhodes if she saw her.

"Abby."

The voice she recognized. Low, melodious, attractive. Laura Rhodes had always worked at seeming attractive, always been confident that she was. Abby had recognized that even as a little girl, watching her mother spritz perfume and smile carefully at the mirror, her eyes narrowed as she assessed for lines, wrinkles. Cracks in the perfection. Once Abby had asked if she could try one of her mother's lipsticks. Her mother's smile had faded, her gaze still on her own reflection, and she'd murmured, "Let's not have you start all that."

Now Abby turned around and faced her mother. Laura stood in the doorway that led back to the flat adjoining the café, and Abby first saw the clothes: stiletto heels, a pencil skirt, a silk blouse, all looking expensive. Hardly the kind of outfit you'd wear in Hartley-by-the-Sea. Reluctantly she allowed her gaze to move up to her mother's face.

Laura wasn't smiling; she rarely did, since it caused wrinkles. Just one of the pearls of wisdom Abby had picked up during one of Laura's infrequent visits. Laura's dark hair, the same color as Abby's but expertly highlighted with blond and lighter blond streaks, was pulled up in some fancy style and diamond studs glinted on her ears. She'd certainly gone for the classy look. Last time, if Abby remembered correctly, she'd had more of a sexy thing going on: leather trousers and a camisole top that had shown her toned, tanned thirty-seven-year-old body to perfection. Abby, thirteen weeks pregnant and throwing up every half hour, had felt dumpy and ugly and fat.

"Well?" Laura lifted her eyebrows, her mouth curving in the smallest of smiles, the kind that didn't reach her eyes. "I know it's been a long time, but—"

"What do you want me to say?" Abby's voice came out sounding angry. And she wasn't angry. She didn't care enough to feel anything but indifference. Or at least that's how she wanted to feel. How she'd trained herself to feel over all the empty years. The last thing she wanted to do now was throw some hissy fit, but then her mother had often provoked this feeling inside her, helpless frustration and hurt that she wasn't important enough to stick around for.

"Abby," Mary protested quietly, reaching out to put a hand on her wrist. "It's your mother."

Abby almost snapped that Laura didn't deserve that title. If anyone did, it was Mary, who had raised her from toddlerhood and opened welcoming arms two years ago, when she'd returned with Noah. Now she looked down at her grandmother's still-red face, her mouth turned down at the corners, sympathy softening her eyes. "Please," she said quietly, and Abby knew that for Mary's sake alone she wouldn't cause a scene.

Besides, any kind of altercation would be all over the village in minutes, and the next time Abby walked up the high street, the comments would come: *So your old Mum's back, eh? Not so old, though, really. What do you think to that? She always was a looker.*

No, thanks.

She took a deep breath, letting it fill her lungs and steady her. First things first. "Let me get you some water, Gran. You need to stay hydrated in this heat." She moved to the kitchen in their private flat, brushing past her mother on the way to the sink. She felt her own body trembling. Why did she have to react this way, after all this time? Six years since the last visit and she still felt raw. Still hurt by her mother's absence, her deliberate disinterest.

Laura followed her back into the flat's kitchen, a tiny room with a wedge of countertop and a round table that fit the three of them for meals. No room for Laura. But then of course she wouldn't be staying. She never did. The realization brought the usual rush of relief mixed with an unwelcome shiver of disappointment that reminded Abby of her entire childhood, waiting for those rare visits, not quite daring to beg them to be longer or more frequent. Her nose pressed to the rain-splattered glass of the café, as she looked for that familiar, elegant figure walking down from the train station, a figure that never quite seemed to come close enough.

"Well, this isn't much of a homecoming," Laura remarked dryly, and Abby nearly slammed the glass on the counter. At the last second she managed to slow her hand. "I suppose I shouldn't have expected much, after all these years." Laura's voice was light, with a hint of humor, just as it always was. She always spoke as if she was looking down on everyone from her lofty, stylized perch, amused by the people who just couldn't seem to keep from inviting her into their lives time and time again.

"You know Gran's been ill," Abby said, her back to her mother. "She had a heart attack two years ago, not that you even called."

"Your grandmother is partly why I came back—"

"Partly?"

"I want to see you, as well, of course. And . . ."

This time Abby did laugh, a harsh bark. "Noah. Your grandson's name is Noah."

"I knew that," Laura answered, and now she sounded a little stiff. "Of course I knew that."

"Just took you a minute to remember?" Abby filled the glass with water and moved past Laura without looking at her. For the next few minutes she focused on her grandmother, conscious of the pensioners in the corner, who were drinking their tea with too much deliberation, ears straining to hear the gossip, or crack, as Cumbrians called it. And there was certainly some good crack to be found here. The Rhodes family had been providing crack for the village for generations.

Briefly Abby closed her eyes, regretting her outburst in the middle of the café. Sophie had gone still, the ice cream scooper dangling from one hand, as she watched their little domestic scene unfold. Abby knew she could gossip for the entirety of England. The news that Abby's mother was back and the reunion hadn't been a happy one would be known from here to Egremont, and once again the Rhodes women would be on everyone's tongue.

She should have been used to it by now. The tongues had wagged when she'd been a child, fatherless and virtually motherless, as well. And then again when she'd returned aged twenty-four, a child in tow and no man to speak of. History repeating itself yet again. People weren't unkind in Hartley-by-the-Sea, but they liked to talk. If they shook their heads in either pity or judgment, it didn't matter to Abby. They felt the same.

Mary covered Abby's hand with her own knobbly, arthritic one. "Go back there, love," she said. "I know it's difficult, and you're not best pleased to see your mam. I understand that. I do. But she's here and she loves you, and that counts for something, even if you don't think it does."

"I know, Gran," Abby said dutifully, even though she doubted her mother loved her. Love looked different to Abby, at any rate. The love she felt for Noah was all-consuming, almost frightening. It had been just the two of them against the world for so long that the possibility of losing him could wake her up in the middle of the night, air bottling in her constricted lungs. When she'd sent him off to Reception last September, she hadn't brushed a tear from her eye as some of the other first-time mums had; she'd put her hands on her knees and focused on her breathing, an icy sweat prickling between her shoulder blades, as she tried to stave off a panic attack. The experienced mums who had been happy to see their little ones toddle off had looked both amused and slightly pitying.

Now Abby tried to think of the last time she'd heard from her mother: perhaps a postcard from California when she'd gone there on holiday two years ago. *Having a lovely time! Hope all is well, Laura.* And Mary thought her mother loved her? Or was that just a desperate hope?

Wearily she patted her grandmother's hand and walked back into the flat. Laura was still in the kitchen, her back to Abby as she gazed out of the tiny kitchen window towards the sea. Abby closed the door behind her, just in case they raised their voices. Not that Laura had ever raised her voice. She'd never stayed long enough to get angry. And Abby was determined not to give in to that, or any, emotion.

"It's so beautiful, isn't it?" Laura remarked as she nodded towards the window. "On a day like today, there's nowhere else you'd rather be."

"Seemed like there were plenty of places you'd have rather been over the years," Abby replied, and Laura let out a sigh, as if Abby's snark had disappointed her. It annoyed Abby. She didn't want to snip at her mother, didn't want to give her that much power, but how was she supposed to be? Her mother had chosen to be a stranger. It wasn't something she could just gloss over or pretend hadn't happened. Yet she could at least be a little more adult about it.

"So what's brought you back, exactly?" she asked, trying to keep her tone interested or at least neutral.

"I thought it was time." Time for what, exactly? "Where's Noah?"

"Playing at the beach with a friend."

"He must be quite big now."

"He just turned five." Laura had never seen him. Never even asked for a photograph.

"Goodness." Slowly Laura turned around. The sunlight streaming through the window highlighted the crow's-feet by her eyes, the more deeply drawn lines from nose to mouth. "You've done some nice things with the café, as far as I can see. The art on the walls . . ."

"It's done by locals. We've sold a bit too, to the tourists mainly, although some residents buy them, as well. We had a party, a kind of gallery showing. . . ." She stopped abruptly, hating that she was acting as if she wanted to impress her mother. In any case, "gallery showing" was a bit of an exaggeration for what had been a handful of friends and a box of white wine. Still, it had been good fun.

"What a good idea," Laura said. "You've inherited my business sense."

Abby opened her mouth to say she hadn't inherited anything from her mother, save for a few unfortunate genes and maybe a propensity to get knocked up, but then she closed it and shook her head. "So what do you mean, it was time? Why are you here, exactly?"

"I wanted to see you all. And . . ." Laura trailed off, color appearing in her cheeks with their suspiciously sculpted cheekbones. Abby wouldn't put a little—or even a lot of—plastic surgery past her mother.

"And?" she prompted, an edge to her voice.

"And I thought it was time I came home," Laura finished, spreading her manicured hands, the tips shiny and pink and also suspiciously artificial looking, with an elegant shrug. Abby didn't think it was what her mother had been going to say.

"This hasn't been home to you for a long time."

"True." Laura sighed, as if this whole conversation was tedious but expected. "But it's still where I was born, Abby. Where I grew up."

"The place that you left."

"So did you, Abby." Laura's voice turned sharp. "I'm not the only one who wanted to escape Hartley-by-the-Sea, you know. Or the only one who decided it was time to come back. My mother's ill and I've never met my grandson. I came back for all of you."

The words were right, but they didn't quite ring true. Or maybe they did, and Abby had simply lost the ability to trust her mother. "That makes a first," she snapped, and then wished she hadn't. She wasn't *hurt*. Not after all this time.

"That's true," Laura answered. No apology, no remorse. There never had been.

"Okay." Abby needed to get ahold of herself. She was showing too much emotion, feeling too much pain. It aggravated her, especially because half an hour ago she'd been musing about how happy she was, how settled. Her mother's arrival didn't have to change any of that. "So, how long are you here for?" Abby kept her voice brisk as she moved around the kitchen, flinging dirty dishes into the sink. Laura moved out of her way, studying the Star of the Week magnet on the fridge that Noah had gotten at school.

Laura would most likely be here for only a few days. She'd never stayed for longer than that. And Abby could handle a few days; she had before. When she'd been little, her mother's departure had brought disappointment; now the prospect brought only relief. Almost.

"Well? A couple of days?" Abby turned to face her mother, hands on her hips, eyebrows raised. Laura was smiling faintly, but not in a good way.

"I'm not sure," she said after a pause. "A while."

"A while?" Abby stared at her, her stomach starting to churn.

"A good while," Laura said, and her smile stretched like an elastic band about to snap. She took a deep breath, that fixed smile still in place. "Actually . . . for good."

2

Laura

LAURA STARED AT ABBY'S appalled expression and told herself she shouldn't have expected anything else. She knew full well she wasn't going to get some kind of mother award, like Noah's Star of the Week magnet. No smiley faces for her when it came to the whole motherhood thing. No, her attempts at motherhood deserved a lot of red ink, angry cross-outs, and a scrawled *Needs Improvement*. She *knew* that, but Abby's look of blatant horror still put her on edge.

"Keep frowning like that and you'll have wrinkles," she said lightly, and moved past her daughter. She'd forgotten how tiny this kitchen was. It smelled like bleach and baked beans, and the mix of odors turned her stomach. She'd forgotten how the whole flat affected her, made her remember things she'd rather not. Her father lying on the sofa, his breath coming in awful, wheezy gasps, like a broken bellows. Abby screaming from the tiny bedroom, shrill, colicky cries that Laura had not known what to do with. Her brother, Simon, slamming the front door.

And now she was back. It was the right thing to do—she believed that; she had to believe that. It wasn't as if she'd had a lot of other options. And she'd known coming back was going to be hard, but knowing something didn't make putting up with it any easier.

"What . . . what do you . . . ?" Abby spluttered, clearly shocked by

Laura's announcement. She wished now that she hadn't said it quite like that. *Back for good.* It revealed too much need, and in any case she had no idea how long she was staying. She still had some savings. She could start over somewhere else eventually, as dispiriting as that prospect felt. But first she wanted to make amends, even if right now that felt utterly impossible. Her mother had been glad enough to see her, at least. Laura suspected Mary felt guilty over the way things had gone down when Abby had been two, although she knew her mother would never admit to it. But Abby was another matter entirely. Winning her daughter round was going to take more energy and conviction than Laura feared she possessed. "What do you mean?" Abby finally demanded. "You can't stay here."

Can't? That was a step too far. "It's my home too," Laura reminded her, trying not to sound too tart. So Abby could slope home with a toddler in tow, but Laura couldn't? At least she wasn't bringing a kid with her. She'd never been good with children, no matter that she'd had one of her own.

"Laura, you're forty-three. It hasn't been your home for over twenty years."

"Actually," Laura answered, and now she definitely sounded tart, "I'm forty-two. My birthday's in August. And I didn't realize there was a statute of limitations on calling a place home." She folded her arms, annoyed in spite of her determination to stay calm, distant. That was the only way she could handle coming back to Hartley-by-the-Sea. As if none of it really mattered. As if none of it could touch her or remind her of how she used to be. Fresh start, she'd told herself, but now she wondered if someone like her could have such a thing in a place like this. Cumbrians had long, long memories.

"Laura . . ." Abby just shook her head, and Laura suppressed another prickle of annoyance. Abby had never called her Mum or Mummy, not even as a toddler, when Laura had actually been around.

And after she'd left, from then on it had always been a careful, polite *Laura*, Abby always watching her warily with those sad, dark eyes, as if her mother wasn't someone to be trusted or even liked. And maybe she hadn't been, because God knew she'd messed up enough. But it would have been nice if Abby could have been a little more mature about things now. A little more enthusiastic.

"Don't throw a fit," she said. She shifted from foot to foot; there was no place to move in this kitchen. It was tiny and airless, despite the open window and the sun shining outside, children's laughter drifting on the sea breeze. "I don't actually mean *for good*, for good." She laughed lightly, the sound only a bit brittle. "I just meant for a while. Long enough to . . ." She hesitated, resisting anything that would sound sentimental, knowing Abby wouldn't take to it. One thing she'd never been was maudlin.

"To what?" Abby demanded.

"To get to know my grandson. And you. I could help out with the café, if you like." She smiled, trying to inject a note of enthusiasm in her voice. "You've done wonders with the place, but you could use a bit more help, I'm sure."

Abby stared at her, arms folded, mouth still puckered, eyebrows drawn together in a frown. *She should really get those plucked,* Laura thought distantly. Honestly, her daughter had never known how to make herself look a little better. Long, dark hair in desperate need of a trim and a highlight, kept back in a messy ponytail, sallow features without a scrap of makeup to brighten them up. It didn't even look like she was wearing *concealer*, for heaven's sake. She could use a serious makeover. Not that Laura was going to suggest that now.

"How long are you staying?" Abby asked. She'd ignored Laura's suggestion of help.

"I don't know. Until . . ." What? She found another job? Another place to live? Another life? "Until I feel like moving on."

"Until *you* feel like it?" Abby repeated. She must have realized how ungracious she sounded, because, with a sigh, she continued in a more measured voice. "It's just there's not a lot of room."

"I know how big the place is, Abby. I did grow up here." Briefly Laura looked away. She didn't want to start bickering.

"Noah has the smaller bedroom. . . ."

Which had been her brother Simon's. It was small, barely big enough for a bed and a bureau. "I'm sure you can double up with Noah for a bit," Laura returned, and then could not keep from adding, "That's what I did, you know. With you."

Abby's mouth dropped a fraction, and Laura was almost savagely glad that she'd gotten the better of her daughter in that particular exchange. Except it was all so petty, sniping at each other this way, and just being here at all was exhausting her utterly. She was starting to feel like the idea she'd had back in New York—when her life had fallen apart and she'd actually missed Hartley-by-the-Sea, had yearned for the family she'd turned her back on—was a terrible one, born in a moment of self-pitying desperation. Still, she was here now. And there wasn't another train until tomorrow. "I'll go get my suitcase," she said, and left the kitchen without looking back.

The low murmur of voices and the clink of cheap china cups and tin teapots ceased as soon as Laura walked through the door into the café. Her mother had retreated behind the counter, and was leaning heavily against it, her face still red and shiny. She glanced at Laura, apprehension and hope evident in her face, and Laura managed a small, tight smile.

"All right?" Mary asked, as if she thought one conversation would sort everything.

"I'm just going to get my things," Laura said, catching the eye of a beady old lady in the corner.

Her step faltered for a second; there was knowledge in that bright, narrowed gaze. The old bat probably remembered Laura from her youth. She'd most likely been coming to the café for the weekly ritual of tea and a too-heavy scone for decades. Mary had never had a light hand with pastry.

Laura looked away and kept walking, grateful when she reached the glass-fronted door, wrenched it open, and stepped outside. The air was fresh and tinged with salt and the view was Hartley-by-the-Sea's best: the sea glinting bright blue in the distance, the beach a lovely, long golden strip, with children and dogs racing over the damp sand. The red sandstone headland looked a little more crumbly than Laura remembered, but that wasn't all that surprising, considering the coastal path on its cliff top had to be moved inland every year because of erosion.

Above the headland, green meadows dotted with both buttercups and sheep rolled on to an impossibly blue horizon. You couldn't imagine a lovelier scene, and yet for years Laura had looked out at that beautiful sight and felt as if the sky and sea and cliff were all closing in on her. They had loomed, menacing, no matter how blue the sky or how pastoral the scene. And in any case, most days it was sleeting rain that blew sideways into your face and kept you from seeing anything at all.

Yet right now Laura wanted to forget all the hard memories of living here and simply enjoy the almost startling beauty. The air was so fresh it felt like drinking a glass of water, and the colors were all Technicolor-bright—yellow rapeseed, green grass, blue sky. It was like the drawing of a child who'd gone a little crazy with the crayons.

Laura picked her way down the cracked concrete steps to the tiny, rutted car park. Abby had done some good work with the café, but it still need serious amounts of TLC, or maybe just cash. It had been stupid to wear heels in this place, but she felt better in them. Stronger. Of course, most of her wardrobe would look ridiculous in Hartley-by-the-Sea. Pencil skirts and silk blouses didn't go down well when you were navigating sheep poo and mud puddles. Sighing, she opened the boot of her rental car and took out her one suitcase. Gucci, not that anyone would notice. Maybe she could sell it on eBay. She'd need the cash eventually; the nest egg she'd nurtured over the last few years wasn't going to last forever. Maintaining the lifestyle necessary to her profession had been expensive—and it was all gone now, every last bit of it.

The loft apartment in Soho, the designer wardrobe, the high-flying vacations, the jewelry, and the top-of-the-line phone and laptop—all of it, gone. The funny thing was Laura didn't even feel so much as a flicker of regret. Just a sense of emptiness, an internal spinning, because she had no idea what she was going to do with the rest of her life. She was forty-two, but she felt about eighty, ready for the end. And as far as her colleagues in New York had been concerned, she'd been as washed-up as all that.

Face it, Laura. You've had it. It's over.

A few well-meaning friends had given her some leads, suggested a sideways move into behind-the-scenes PR or marketing. And she'd considered it, because the alternative seemed worse. But in the end she simply hadn't had the energy to embark on something new. She'd attended one horrendous job interview where a smug and slightly leering twenty-four-year-old had demanded why he should hire her. Laura had stared at him, feeling tired, jaded, and as washed-up as a dirty dishrag. "I have no bloody idea," she'd said, and walked out. An hour later she'd booked a flight to Manchester.

Now she lugged the suitcase up the steps, wincing as it bumped on each one, scuffing the leather. Yes, that life was certainly over. She just hoped there was a beginning to be had in Hartley-by-the-Sea.

Back in the café the muted chatter halted for only a second before continuing, deliberately, a little bit louder. Mary was still at the counter, chatting with an elderly woman who was wearing a twinset, tweed, and *very* sensible shoes.

"You remember my daughter," Mary said, unfounded pride in her voice, as she nodded towards Laura, standing in the doorway with her scuffed suitcase.

The woman turned, clocking Laura with a bright, beady gaze. "Yes," she said. "Of course. I taught her English in Year Six." It was Mrs. Hampton, Laura realized with a jolt. She tried to smile, but her face felt stiff. "I always thought you had a lot of promise," she continued. "Your creativity was marvelous, but your spelling was atrocious."

"I've afraid it hasn't much improved," she said lightly, and the old lady cracked a smile.

"Well, it's good to have you back. I like to see families together."

Laura managed a smile in return and then stepped aside so Mrs. Hampton could stump through the doorway, aided by a knobbly-looking cane.

"Nothing much changes here," she remarked to Mary.

"That's why people like it. You can depend on Hartley-by-the-Sea."

Laura knew there was no point in remarking that she hadn't been able to, at all. That was her fault, she knew, for making some spectacularly bad choices. Hopefully coming back here wasn't another one. When she'd arrived, Mary had looked almost comically shocked, staring at her for a good thirty seconds in silence before Laura had finally said, her tone light and wry, "Hello, Mum."

Mum. It didn't sit all that well, after all these years. Never had, really; perhaps Abby had gotten that from her. Not a great track record, the Rhodes women, as mothers, but Mary seemed to be making up for it as a granny, or trying to, anyway.

Now Mary eyed her with a mixture of apprehension and apology that didn't sit well with Laura, either. "So." She rested the suitcase in front of the till and subjected her mother to the smile she'd perfected over the years, with only her lips, not the eyes, and touching the tongue to the back of her teeth. It kept her jaw from sagging and her eyes from wrinkling. She'd even practiced making it look sincere. "I assume I'll bunk in Simon's old room?"

"Noah's in there now. . . ."

"He can share with Abby, surely?" Laura let a slight edge creep into her voice, the tiniest reminder of days gone by. Sleepless nights with a teething toddler sharing her single bed and her fourteen-year-old brother slamming through the house, shouting how he couldn't sleep for "that effing kid." And then dear old Mum telling her accusingly that if she hadn't gotten herself knocked up, they wouldn't be having the row. Because of course it was always her fault. Always had been.

The surge of bitterness this memory caused felt like swallowing acid, tasting bile. Laura forced it back. There was a reason she didn't think about those two years in Hartley-by-the-Sea, a teenage mother to a daughter she hadn't known what to do with. There were a lot of reasons.

"I suppose," Mary said uncertainly. Her breathing was still coming in unhealthy-sounding huffs. "Did you ask Abby?"

"No," Laura replied. "I told her." And then, not wanting to feed the village's relentless gossip mill anymore, she grabbed her suitcase and walked towards the door to the flat.

Abby was banging around in the kitchen, getting out pots and slamming them onto the stove, and Laura bypassed her completely, heading for the stairs at the back. The stairs were particularly claustrophobic, tiny and narrow and steep, the walls with their pea green flocked wallpaper seeming to close in on her. If she ever had a chance, she was going to suggest some new wallpaper or, better yet, fresh paint.

Upstairs Laura shouldered her way into her brother's old bedroom, now decorated with lurid dinosaur appliqués on bright blue painted walls, and a toddler-sized bed with a duvet that also featured dinosaurs, these ones inexplicably wearing cowboy costumes. Laura stared at the bed in rueful dismay. Dinosaurs with ten-gallon hats aside, she was supposed to sleep on a bed that was a good two feet shorter than she was? Sighing, she hauled her suitcase on top of it, causing the bed to creak alarmingly.

Abby was right. She couldn't stay here. Not for long, anyway. When she'd decided to come back to Hartley-by-the-Sea, she hadn't thought through it all that carefully. It had been more of a visceral, gut reaction, a deep instinct that after twenty-three years, she couldn't run anymore. Couldn't live life as if it had started in Manchester, aged nineteen.

The trouble was, where else could she go? The hollow feeling in her stomach that had been plaguing her since she'd been fired two weeks ago emptied out a little more at the realization yet again of how few options she had. How few friends. Which is why she'd come back . . . because at least here people knew her. Whether that was a good thing remained to be seen.

With a sigh Laura sank onto the bed, next to her suitcase, a wave of fatigue crashing over and nearly felling her. Starting over in Hartley-by-the-Sea was going to be hard. She had to face her own memories as well as everyone else's, and right then she didn't know if she had the energy. Starting over somewhere else held a reluctant, depressing sort of appeal—yet what kind of job could she get now? She was middle-aged with no real qualifications and she was finished in the clubbing world. Too old, too wrinkled, too has-been. Night-clubs, as Tyler Lawton, the brassy new owner, had informed her, didn't want grannies carding them. Not that she'd actually carded anyone. She had bouncers and bartenders for that sort of thing. She had some class, unlike Tyler, a shiny-faced Harvard grad who reeked of new money and collected nightclubs like baseball cards.

The best job she could hope to get now was likely to be a manager of some tacky diner, a Little Chef in a poky market town, or, back in America, a weathered-looking Denny's or Applebee's. She no longer had the contacts for the kind of high-profile jobs she might actually want. The thought of that kind of existence, becoming washed-out and hard up while obsessing over fryers and two-for-one breakfast specials, was too dire to contemplate. She'd rather ossify here. Maybe.

From downstairs Laura heard a door being flung open and then the thundering sound of someone sprinting up the stairs. She barely had time to process the sounds before the door to her bedroom creaked open and a little dark-haired boy stood there, hands planted on his hips, hazel eyes wide with amazement as he looked at her.

Laura looked back, frozen in place. This was her grandson, which made her feel about a thousand years old.

"You're Mummy's mummy," he said. His voice was high and piping, and Laura managed a smile.

"Yes, that's right." She could not picture this boy calling her *Granny*. She couldn't picture him calling her anything, and yet already she was noting his silky dark hair, so like Abby's as a child. He had her hazel eyes.

"What are you doing in my bedroom?"

"Well." She cleared her throat. She'd never been good with children, and had avoided them almost entirely since her own failed attempt at motherhood. She felt no familial tug of love or longing for this little boy; despite the hair and the eyes, he was an utter stranger to her. If that made her abnormal, so be it. "I was hoping you'd let me sleep here for . . . for a while."

"Sleep here?" His face brightened at this prospect, which surprised her. "You mean, like a proper sleepover? Mummy says I'm too young for those still."

"Well, sort of like a sleepover," Laura hedged. "But you'll sleep in with your mum." The thought of sharing this tiny bed with his wriggling body and flailing limbs made her inwardly shudder. Still she kept a smile on her face, or hoped she did. She hadn't scared him off, at any rate.

"Okay." At least he seemed amenable to her suggestion. But then, rather to Laura's horror, Noah squeezed onto the bed next to her, his hot little leg pressed next to hers and wrinkling her skirt. "Do you like dinosaurs?"

"Umm . . ." Laura shook her head helplessly. She'd never been good at this. She couldn't do the singsong voice, the abnormally wide eyes, the over-the-top trill that other women seemed to take on naturally when talking to small children. "Not really."

"Oh." Noah sucked in his bottom lip as he gazed around the tiny room. "Maybe I should get you another duvet, then."

"You don't have to. I'll be fine with this one." Laura edged away from the sweaty boy; he had sand in his hair and he smelled like sunshine and peanut butter. It turned her stomach, not just the scent but the whole reality of him, a living, breathing reminder of her own failures. He looked happy and well-adjusted, secure in his place in the world, addressing her with unflinching confidence. Abby, she supposed, was a far better mother than she'd ever been. "Thank you, though," she said politely, and Noah beamed a gap-toothed grin.

"Sure." He studied her with open, unabashed curiosity; Laura kept her smile in place with effort. She couldn't remember the last time she'd been so scrutinized. "Where do you live?"

Here. "I last lived in New York City, in America. Have you heard of America?"

"'Course I have." The lofty tone made Laura blink. How on earth was she supposed to know about a five-year-old's intelligence?

"Well, then," she said, and meant it as a dismissal. Noah just kept looking at her.

"You smell funny." He took a big sniff, and Laura leaned back even more. He was saying she smelled? "Like . . . a department store."

Ah, her perfume. Alexander McQueen's Parfum for Her. Her last bottle. "Thank you," she said. "I think."

Her grandson didn't say anything else, just kept looking at her. Laura was tempted to ask if she passed, but she stayed silent, not sure if he'd take her seriously or get the joke—if she even had been joking. Coming back here had been, in part, to get to know this boy, and yet right then she had no idea how to go about it.

"Noah?" Abby called, and Laura heard the creak of the stairs as Abby came upstairs. Neither she nor Noah moved. "Noah?" Abby called again, and then poked her head in the doorway of the bedroom, surprise widening her eyes to see the two of them pressed together on the little toddler bed. "What are you doing in here, Noah?"

Noah puffed up in indignation. "It's my bedroom——"

"Not while . . . she's here," Abby said, and Laura knew she'd struggled with what to call her. No *Granny* for Laura, not that she'd expected it. "Come on. You can come help me downstairs." And pulling on her son's arm, Abby left Laura alone in the bedroom, with the dinosaurs and their cowboy hats and a faint, lingering smell of peanut butter.

3

Abby

"SO YOUR MOTHER HAS really come back?" Lucy Bagshaw's eyes were wide with both curiosity and sympathy as she looked at Abby over the scattered debris on the kitchen table: two wedding magazines, a length of gold ribbon, and the mugs of tea she'd just set down. "How's that working out?"

"I don't know." Abby took a sip of tea, unsure how to respond or even to feel. She usually loved stopping by Tarn House for a cup of tea and a chat, and she'd plunked herself down at the kitchen table, intending to luxuriate in a bit of a moan about her mother, but now that Lucy had actually asked, Abby realized she had no idea what to say. "I haven't seen her all that much, to be honest."

"Why not?"

Abby shrugged. "It's only been a couple of days, and her schedule doesn't really sync with mine." Despite Laura's offer of helping out at the café, her mother had yet to darken its door. "She sleeps in till nearly noon and then spends the rest of the day sloping about or smoking behind the café." Already Abby regretted admitting that much. But it was true; her mother had been back for three days, and save for the lingering scent of both perfume and cigarette smoke, the occasional coffee cup left in the sink, and the tense family meals, Abby would barely know she was there. She supposed she should have been relieved that this was the case, but it felt like more rejection. Even when Laura was back in Hartley-by-the-Sea, she couldn't be bothered to spend time with her, or even pretend to be interested. As if sensing her anxiety, the two greyhounds, Milly and Molly, pressed up against her. Abby stroked their narrow, bony heads, grateful for their comfort.

"She sounds depressed," Lucy remarked after a moment. "Do you think she is?"

Depressed? Laura? It was hard to imagine. Her mother always seemed so coolly confident, so impossibly remote, with that funny little half smile curving her perfectly lipsticked lips and never reaching her eyes. "I don't know," Abby said slowly. With a pang of discomfort, she realized she hadn't even asked about her mother's job, her mother's life. "Maybe."

"I suppose this is a change from New York City. I found it a bit rough coming from Boston."

And Abby had found it difficult coming from Liverpool. She sighed and took a sip of tea. "The truth is," she told Lucy, "I'm not sure I have the energy to ask her about anything, or help her if she is depressed. Is that terrible of me?"

"No, of course not," Lucy said. "It's completely understandable. You can't magic up a relationship from nothing. You both need time to adjust to each other."

"Is that what we're doing?" It felt more like they were simply tolerating each other, and barely at that. Par for the course, then, which really was a depressing thought.

"Do you want things to be different with your mum?" Lucy asked. "Genuine question."

"Yes," Abby said slowly. "I think I do. But like I said, I'm not sure how much effort I can go to."

"Hmm." Lucy's brow knitted in thought. "Why do you think she came back, really? Nowhere else to go?"

Nowhere seemed a bit much. "I doubt that. My mother has always been a highflier." The question nagged at her, though, because she had no idea why her mother had come back, no matter what she'd said about it being time. Maybe she really didn't have anywhere else to turn—wasn't that why Abby had come back? Perhaps Laura had lost her job, her money, the whole snazzy lifestyle she'd chased after for so long. Abby didn't know how she felt about that. She didn't know how she felt about anything.

"There must be some reason, though," Lucy said, taking a sip of tea. "Maybe she really wants to make amends."

"Did *your* mother want to make amends?" Abby answered, meaning to sound light and not quite managing it. Lucy, of all people, knew what it was like to have a failure for a parent. Her mother was a glamorous contemporary artist who had turned her back on both her daughters. In fact, Lucy had a lot more to complain about in the motherhood stakes than Abby did. Laura had merely been a nonentity; Lucy's mother, Fiona, had been an aggressor, making Lucy's life pretty miserable on multiple occasions, as well as her sister Juliet's, from what they'd both told Abby over the years.

"I think she sort of wanted to," Lucy answered slowly. Two years on and Lucy and Juliet seemed to have moved on, both finding love, life, happiness, the whole lot. "She just wasn't capable of it, I don't think."

"I don't know if my mum is," Abby said. "She's never seemed it before."

"But at least she's here. And she's staying, right?" As ever, Lucy was an eternal optimist. "So maybe you could make a little bit of effort. Invite her for—I don't know, a cup of coffee. Have a chat." She made a face. "Does that sound totally improbable?"

"Fairly improbable," Abby answered with a small smile. But it also didn't sound like it should be that hard. Her mother had come all the way back to Cumbria. The least Abby could do was make her a latte.

"So what do you think the deal was with your mum?" she asked. "Was she emotionally stunted or something?"

"Or something," Lucy agreed. "She had some emotional baggage, for sure."

Did Laura have emotional baggage? Didn't everyone? They were all dragging something behind them, whether it was a steamer trunk or a handbag. Abby certainly had a truckload, not just from her childhood but from her years in Liverpool, the utter up-and-down of her relationship with Ben. And while emotional baggage of any sort surely wasn't an excuse for just checking out of your child's life, the reality was Laura was here now. And Abby could choose to hold on to her resentment and anger about the past or try to forge some kind of future. When she thought about it like that, it didn't seem like much choice at all. And yet . . . just the thought of making that effort left her feeling both tired and wary. A terrible track record wasn't something simply to forget.

"But your mum," Lucy said, insistent now. "What's she really like?"

"I don't really know. She's glamorous, at least on the surface. She grew up in Hartley-by-the-Sea, but you wouldn't know it. Gran never talks about her childhood, or even my childhood before Laura left. There's a lot I don't know."

"Do you want to know it?"

"Maybe." And maybe not. What if actually asking her mother the questions she'd tried not to voice even to herself made things worse? What if her mother revealed something awful, some terrible, shameful secret? Or what if she didn't, and simply shrugged, telling Abby that she'd left because she wasn't interested in being a mother? It had been what Abby had assumed. It had seemed obvious. And often the obvious answer was the right one. She pulled one of the wedding magazines towards her. "So two months and counting until the big day." The conversation changer was like the teeth-gritting squeak of a needle scratching a record, but she couldn't help it. Talking about Laura made her feel itchy inside. She flicked blindly through the glossy pages. "How are the preparations coming?"

"Fine, I think," Lucy answered, clearly taking Abby's none-too-subtle cue in stride. "I never wanted a big do, just friends and food around, really."

Abby arched an eyebrow. "What's the gold ribbon for, then?"

Lucy grinned, slightly abashed. "We-ell, I still want everything to look nice. I was thinking of having ribbon around each table, you know, with bows on the corners? Or is that terribly naff?"

Abby fingered the gold ribbon; it was good-quality stuff. "No, it's not naff. It could look really nice." She tried to squash the slithering tendril of envy that snaked through her heart. She didn't want to feel that, not for Lucy. She'd met Lucy when she'd first moved back to Hartley-by-the-Sea; Lucy had come into the café new to the village and looking a bit lost—kind of like Abby herself. They'd struck up a friendship, bonding over quiz nights at the pub and shared moans and laughter over adjusting to village life. In the two years since then, Lucy had met and become engaged to the head teacher of the primary school as well as made a career for herself as a local artist, teaching at the school and exhibiting her watercolors, some of which were on the café's walls. They'd had a party last spring at the café, and Abby had enjoyed playing hostess while the art flew off the walls.

Lucy was happy and secure, fizzing with excitement for the future, which was sort of how Abby had felt a little while ago, full of fragile plans for the café, enjoying feeling as if she'd finally arrived, until her mother had swooped back into her life and upended everything simply by being there, smoking and silent.

"The school hall is never going to have looked so good," she told Lucy with a smile. Envy, begone.

"I know. Alex teases me about that. Says no matter how much ribbon and lace I put up, it will still smell of sweaty socks and school dinners."

Which sounded exactly like something Lucy's no-nonsense fiancé would say. "I don't know," Abby said. "Are you going to do flowers? Lilies might cover the scent."

Lucy made a face. "I can't stand lilies, ever since my mother did this revolting sculpture of a lily that was also a phallus. An optical illusion, sort of. She came into my school to talk about it at assembly, and I nearly died of embarrassment."

"Goodness, that does sound . . ."

"Horrific."

They shared a smile, Lucy rolling her eyes. Abby tossed the magazine back on the table. At least Laura had never done anything like that. She had something to be grateful for, anyway. "You must have developed a fairly thick skin, though."

"I don't think I ever did, to be honest. I just got better about acting as if I didn't care."

Which sounded uncomfortably like what Abby was doing. She really needed to get her big-girl pants on and deal with this whole mother thing. "I should go," she said, unfolding herself from the chair before scooping up their empty mugs and taking them to the sink. "It's almost time for the school run."

"Who's manning the café, then? Your mum?"

"Nope, she hasn't made it that far yet. Gran is. She still wants to keep her hand in, but I am worried about her." An admission that added to her guilt and unease. Perhaps she shouldn't have ducked out to come down here. Her grandmother had been looking particularly worn-out lately, anxious about the café, her own health, and the brewing tension between her daughter and granddaughter.

Last night, after Laura had sloped upstairs, barricading herself in Noah's old bedroom, which was starting to smell suspiciously like smoke, Mary had turned to Abby with a beseeching look.

"Give her a chance, Abby."

Abby had inwardly squirmed with guilt. Mary had done so much for her, both raising her as a child—admittedly in a hassled and harried sort of way—and then taking her and Noah in when she'd been feeling so battered by life. "I'm not sure I even know how, Gran."

Mary had sighed. "Laura's prickly. Proud too. All the Rhodes women have been like that."

"If she'd make an effort . . ."

"She made an effort, Abby, by simply being here."

So now it was time for her to step up. Abby still didn't know how to go about it. Like Lucy had said, you couldn't magic a relationship out of nothing.

"Mary's recovered from her heart attack, though, hasn't she?" Lucy asked.

"Sort of. She takes medication to manage it, but she's never going to be one hundred percent. And she is seventy-two."

"That's not that old, these days."

Yet Mary seemed far older. Perhaps it was being a single mum for most of her life, first to Laura and Simon after her husband had died when Laura was only a child, and then to Abby. "She's been huffing a lot, lately," Abby confessed. "I should fetch Noah and head back."

She was at the front door when Lucy's sister, Juliet, came downstairs with a basket of dirty sheets. "So the prodigal mother returns."

"Ha-ha," Abby answered, managing a weak smile.

Juliet eyed her over the heaped sheets, her expression stern and assessing. Juliet, eleven years older than her half sister, was the antidote to Lucy's endless optimism, but right now Abby felt like a naughty pupil being called up to the front of the class.

"Got you bothered, has she?" Juliet surmised.

"What? No—"

"You seem it." She moved past Abby with the basket, shouldering her out of the way. After that comment, Abby felt compelled to follow her.

"I'm not bothered," she said as she stood in the doorway of the utility room and watched Juliet bundle the sheets into the washer. "Not any more than usual, anyway."

"Ah."

"What's that supposed to mean?"

Juliet shrugged and straightened, one hand on the small of her back. "I know what it's like to have a crap mother, that's all. Of course you're bothered." She paused. "I met Laura, by the way. She stayed here once, about ten years ago, when I was just starting."

Abby stared, bizarrely shocked. Naturally lots of people in the village knew Laura. She'd grown up here, after all, and people didn't leave Hartley-by-the-Sea all that often. But nobody ever really talked about her to Abby. Most people acted as if she'd never existed. Abby didn't know whether they did that to spare her and Mary's feelings, or simply because once someone left Hartley-by-the-Sea, that person was really forgotten. Intentionally, because they'd turned their back on God's best bit of green earth. But Juliet was an offcomer, even if she'd been here for more than a decade.

"I hope she was a good guest," Abby said, not quite sure if she was being serious.

"She was polite and left the bathroom immaculate," Juliet returned dryly. "But she seemed sad to me."

So Juliet thought Laura was sad, and Lucy had said she might be depressed. Abby had never seen her mother as either, but perhaps that was because she'd always viewed her mother through the lens of her own bitterness. Maybe she needed to stop doing that. Another thing she wasn't sure how to go about. "She never seemed sad to me," Abby returned.

"No, she wouldn't, would she?" Juliet closed the lid of the washer with a bang. "But she's come back, so maybe she wants a second chance."

"At what? Motherhood?"

"Life, motherhood, being a grandmother. The whole lot."

"Both of you Bagshaws are rather understanding," Abby observed tartly, and Juliet smiled.

"It's easy when it's not your own. Just don't stew too long in your own juices, Abby. It doesn't make for a pleasant marinade."

True enough, but Abby still felt as if she was stewing a little bit as she headed up the high street towards the school. How could Lucy and Juliet both give her such airy advice when they'd experienced mother problems of their own? Juliet had been angry for decades, or so she'd once said. They'd both freely admitted how their mother's lack of love and attention had affected them badly for years. And yet Abby was supposed to start applauding the minute her mother walked through the door? *And yet at least she did walk through the door.*

Abby reached the school lane and stood off by herself, leaning against the stone wall, her arms folded. She didn't feel like talking to anyone, not when her thoughts were so jumbled up.

"You're scowling for England," Meghan remarked as she joined her at the wall. "What's up?"

"Nothing."

Meghan arched an eyebrow. "Like that, is it? Well, it's not exactly rocket science to figure it out."

"Oh?"

"I was walking on the beach with Nath last night and saw your mum having a fag outside the café," Meghan replied. "So I'm guessing she has something to do with it."

"I just want her to go back to where she came from," Abby burst out, not meaning it as much as she thought she would. "Leave me to my own life. She was happy to do it before."

"Has she said why she's come home?"

"Just some blather about it being time."

"Maybe you should ask for details." Meghan shrugged one bony shoulder. "There's got to be a reason, and it's probably not to play happy families with you and Noah."

Even though she knew she shouldn't be, Abby was stung. "You don't think so?"

"Do you?" Meghan challenged. "Has she been reading bedtime stories to Noah, then? Doing your nails?" Abby struggled to frame a reply, feeling weirdly compelled to defend Laura, and Meghan smirked knowingly. "I didn't think so."

Sometimes Abby forgot how snarky Meghan could be. She liked it on occasion, but not when it was so on the mark. And maybe it wasn't on the mark. Laura needed time, after all. So did Abby. In an uncharacteristic gesture of sympathy, Meghan laid a hand on Abby's arm.

"Look, it sucks, I know. Mothers are hard work. Mine's practically a vegetable lying in the front room and *she's* hard work." Abby would have thought this the height of unfeelingness, but she'd seen how Meghan had reacted to her mother's stroke over a year ago now. She used a sharp tongue and a lot of bluster to cover up her more fragile feelings.

"Well, maybe I will ask her," Abby said as the Infant doors opened and the Reception years started tumbling out. "And I'll also ask her how long she's planning to stay."

Except Laura wasn't in the flat when Abby returned, and after setting Noah up with some coloring in the corner of the café, she took over the till from Mary, who was looking a bit gray in the face. "You all right, Gran?" Abby asked even as she could tell she wasn't. "You ought to have a rest. Put your feet up."

"I'm fine," Mary replied irritably, a sure sign that she wasn't fine at all. Mary got annoyed with such advice only when it was merited. "Just been on my feet awhile, that's all. Anyone would be feeling it."

"Of course," Abby murmured placatingly. She put the kettle on to make Mary a cup of tea. When she had a moment, she'd switch on BBC for *Escape to the Country*, and Mary would eventually stagger towards the sofa and succumb to the rest she so obviously needed. "Where's Laura?" Abby asked as mildly as she could as she rang up two teas and a flapjack. "She could help out in the café instead of lounging around like Lady Godiva." Oops. She could have phrased that slightly better.

"Don't," Mary murmured, with a pointed nod towards the couple waiting for their teas.

Abby filled a tin teapot in silence, added cups and saucers and the flapjack to a tray, and handed it to the couple. "They're tourists," she said when they'd retreated to a table by the window. "Walkers. You can always tell by their gear." Knobbled, highly varnished walking sticks and high-tech all-weather parkas, despite the fact that it was, against most odds, another gorgeous, sunny day.

"Even so," Mary answered. "I don't want the village knowing our business."

"I know, but people will anyway, Gran." Abby kept her voice gentle as she dunked a tea bag in Mary's mug. "Everyone's talking about it, already. I can't blame them, really." Abby glanced around the café, the scattering of customers. A couple of secondary school students lounged back on their chair legs, skateboards and scooters at their feet. They'd ordered a single can of Coke between them. Scroungers, the lot of them, and their loud guffaws and salty talk were putting the other customers off. Every table around them was empty. She thought about going over there and telling them to leave, but the truth was she wasn't good at that sort of thing. They'd probably just stare her down or start swearing. Mary had always been the one to give rowdy customers the boot, and it was a sign of how tired she was that she was letting them stay.

"No one's saying anything nasty, anyway," Abby said as she handed Mary her cup of tea. "They're just curious. Concerned, maybe. I'm sure plenty of people remember Laura from way back when." Although besides Juliet, no one had said anything.

"They'll see her an offcomer now," Mary said glumly. "Poor lass."

"It seems that's what she wanted." Abby glanced out the huge picture window overlooking the sea, now frilled in white. Seagulls swooped and arced through the azure sky and in the distance, over the fells, Abby could see a paraglider start a descent towards the beach. "Why do you think she came back, Gran?"

"She said she wanted to see us. Make amends." Gran sounded so hopeful, Abby couldn't bear to show any skepticism.

"Well," she said at last. "That's good, I guess."

"I know you don't believe me. Her." Mary's voice wobbled along with her chin. "But when you've made a lot of mistakes in life, Abby, it takes some courage to come back and own up to them."

As far as Abby could see, Laura hadn't owned up to anything. Yet. "I know," she said, because she'd made plenty of her own mistakes.

"Give her a chance, love," Mary pleaded. It was a refrain Abby was starting to weary of.

"I will," she promised, "when she shows up to let me."

She didn't see her mother until after supper, when Noah was tucked up in bed, Mary installed in front of Channel 4, and Abby had just finished cleaning the kitchen. Laura snuck in, her head tucked low, looking like she was trying to duck the radar.

"Wait." Abby's voice came out in a bark. Laura turned, tense and guilty, and for a second Abby had the bizarre urge to laugh. Here she was, acting like the stern mother, and Laura was the stroppy teen. "Where have you been?"

Laura came to stand in the doorway of the kitchen, her arms folded, and appraised Abby coolly. "Out."

"Out where?" Abby pressed.

Her mother was dressed in skinny jeans and a flowing chiffon blouse, her hair caught up in a loose bun. She looked elegant and sophisticated but also very tired. In answer to Abby's question, she shrugged. "Walking."

Abby took a deep breath. "Look, Laura, if you're going to stay round here, you ought to . . . be around here. Talk to Gran, at least, and you could help out at the café like you said you would."

Laura arched one perfectly plucked eyebrow. "I didn't think you wanted me to."

Admittedly she hadn't wanted her to, originally. She'd just wanted her mother to go. But Laura was here now and somehow they had to make this work. "If you're staying, the help would be useful. You did run a popular nightclub, didn't you? This shouldn't be too taxing."

Laura didn't speak for a long moment. Abby couldn't tell anything from the expression on her face. "Fine," she said finally. "I'll help out."

"And Gran . . ." Abby nodded towards the sitting room, the flickering light of the television washing over Mary's face.

Laura's mouth tightened, and something almost like fear flickered in her eyes. She folded her arms, hands cupping her elbows, as if she was trying to hold herself together. For the first time Abby felt a pang of sympathy for her mother. Coming back was hard, especially when you'd walked out in a cloud. "She's really pleased you're here," Abby said quietly, and Laura threw her a slightly scornful look.

"That would make for a change."

The bitterness lacing her mother's words surprised her. Had Laura and Mary never gotten along? It made sense, of course, considering how Laura had left, and yet . . . Abby had always assumed *she* was the reason Laura had left, not Mary.

Squaring her shoulders, Laura walked into the sitting room. "Hey, Mum." She sounded both tentative and resigned. Abby watched, holding her breath. "*Garden Nightmares*, eh?" she remarked, nodding towards the TV. "Brilliant." And with a sigh, Laura sat down on the sofa and clutched a pillow to her chest as she stared glumly at the television.

4

Laura

LAURA PICKED UP THE forest green apron from the hook behind the till with a grimace. Even that hadn't changed since her days of working in the café as a teenager. How many Saturdays had been spent scooping ice cream and slinging sandwiches? She'd started at the till when she was just ten years old and her father had come down with cancer. But no, she wouldn't think of that. She never thought of her dad.

He'd been creeping into her consciousness, though, these last three days. Last night she'd dreamed of him. They'd been walking on the beach, Mel Rhodes with his hands in the pockets of his coveralls, whistling, looking like he did when Laura had been young: dark haired and eyed like Abby but always with a ready smile—even though in the dream she'd been the age she was now. Contemporaries, they'd been, in that strange dreamworld. Her father had died when he was forty-two.

She couldn't remember if he'd said anything in the dream; all she could remember was that melancholy, tuneless whistling. And the feeling that she wanted to hold on to the moment, cling to it with everything she had, even as it evaporated like sea mist and she woke up with an ache in her chest she hadn't let herself feel in years. Damned dreams.

Now she banished the memory as she tied on the apron and dutifully took her place at the till. It was ten o'clock on a Saturday morning and the café was open for business; Mary was putting her feet up
next door and Abby had taken Noah to a birthday party.

Laura and her mother had reached an uneasy, unspoken truce, or
at least that was how it felt to her. With Abby's prompting, she'd
watched a wretched episode of TV with Mary, but her mother hadn't
even spoken to her. And if she had, Laura wasn't sure what she would
have said. How did you break decades-old silence? How did you access
the guilt and regret and memories? *Sorry I left* or *Sorry I made you leave*
didn't quite cut it in this situation. Maybe the best you could hope
for was just pretending you'd always gotten along. The thought was
depressing.

Now Laura surveyed the café with its grease-spattered laminated
menus stuck between salt and pepper shakers and little vases of plastic flowers. Abby had made some nice effort with the artwork and
the fairy lights, the notice board with all its community posters, but
underneath these touches the bare bones of the café, the ancient
grimness of it, remained. Or perhaps that was just the way Laura
looked at it.

She wandered over to the notice board and read the flyers and the
posters with a detached kind of interest. A toddler group met at the
café on Tuesday mornings. An art evening had happened last spring.
Considering it was the only place to get a cup of coffee in the whole
village, Laura supposed it did do a fairly good business, and the ice
cream trade during the summer kept it going when some days in winter, when the weather didn't cooperate, they didn't have a single customer come through the door. But maybe that had changed. Abby
seemed to be doing her best to revitalize the café, even if the place
needed a lot more than a few cozy touches.

Today would most likely be busy, though. It was sunny enough,
with a few scattered clouds being blown away by a brisk sea breeze,

and Laura knew the weekend routine when the sun was shining. First would come the dog walkers for their morning coffees and teas, then the early-bird families who had brought their kids to the beach for the whole day and ended up cashing out after a couple of hours, appeasing their little darlings with ice-cream cones and apologetic smiles. Then the out-of-town walkers would come in with an affected air of puzzled disappointment, clearly expecting something more in the gastropub line, before accepting that the only food the café did was cold sandwiches and microwaved jacket potatoes. There would be a slight lull then, as everyone headed back out into the sunshine, and then a second run of families for ice cream, which would last until six, when she closed up.

Just thinking about it made her tired. And she felt even more tired when she acknowledged that a good number of those people might know her, would probably recognize her. She'd managed to avoid cringe-inducing conversations in her three days back, mainly because she'd kept to her bedroom, the back of the café, and the coastal footpath that ran behind the café all the way to the next inlet. She'd spent the last three days smoking far too many cigarettes and staring at the sea, trying not to remember and flirting with memories at the same time. Her dad. Abby as a child. The hope and then the darkness, the decision to leave, which hadn't felt like a decision at all.

She wasn't ready to face the village. She couldn't stand the curious smiles, the dawning of recognition, the speculative looks, and no doubt the off-color remarks. *You've finally come back home, Laura? You're not up the duff again, are you?* Honestly, she wouldn't put it past some of the people here, although perhaps she was being unfair. It was the thoughtless—and, worse, the deliberately cruel—comments that you remembered. Not the quiet kindnesses, the understanding smiles, and Laura knew there had been some of those. People here cared even if they didn't always show it in obvious ways.

The door to the café swung open, and a woman with a halo of

frizzy red hair, being led by a large and excitable golden retriever, blew in.

"Hallo," she called before Laura could give her a tight-lipped professional smile. "I don't recognize you."

"Good morning," Laura said pleasantly. "Dogs need to stay outside, I'm afraid."

"Oh, sorry, sorry." The woman sounded cheerfully unrepentant. "It's just she howls if I leave her outside. Abby always said it was all right." She tilted her head, her bright, inquisitive gaze like a searchlight. "You must be Abby's mother."

So the inquisition had begun. "Yes." She could hardly insist the huge beast stay outside, so Laura did what she'd learned to do in twenty years in the hospitality industry. She gave in gracefully. "Let me get your dog some water."

"We actually went to school together," the woman said when Laura had returned from the kitchen with a bowl for the dog, who lapped it up with greedy enthusiasm. "I'm Diana—Diana Hope, back then."

The name didn't ring a single bell, but then Laura had left Cumberland Academy before the end of Year Ten. "Sorry. I'm afraid my school years are a bit of a blur." She kept her voice polite but a little distant. "Did we share any lessons?"

"Oh, no." Now Diana looked slightly abashed. "No, you wouldn't have had any reason to know me, really."

"Ah." She propped her elbows on the counter. "But you'd heard of me, I suppose."

Diana looked as if she was going to prevaricate, and then, with a gap-toothed grin, she owned up. "Yes, you were a bit of a legend, swanning off before you'd even taken your GCSEs."

"I don't know how much swanning I did when I was eight months pregnant."

"Still you seemed cool to us. Like you knew exactly what you wanted

43

in life and went and got it, and screw everyone else." Laura let out a disbelieving laugh and Diana raised her eyebrows. "Was that the fifteen-year-old's view of things?"

What on earth could she say to that? Laura managed a dry laugh. "Pretty much."

"It must have been tough," Diana agreed quietly. "But Abby's turned out all right."

With no thanks to me. Laura pushed off the counter. "What can I get you? Coffee? Tea? Cappuccino?" The espresso machine had wheezed a bit when Laura had turned it on, but hopefully it could make some decent milk froth.

Diana took the rather abrupt change in conversation with rueful grace. "A pot of tea, please."

Several hours later Laura was tired, her feet aching, and she'd been recognized by half a dozen different people but had managed, by maintaining a cool demeanor that was only just on the right side of friendly, to keep any prying questions at bay. She'd even enjoyed herself, a little.

In a quiet moment she'd wiped the grease from the menus and the built-up grime from the fake flowers. She'd rewritten the drinks menu on the chalkboard, adding some color and curlicues. Twenty years in the hospitality industry had reinforced the realization that success was found in paying attention to detail. Not that it mattered all that much. No matter how much spit and polish you put into the café, and Abby had certainly done her fair share, it was still a ramshackle afterthought of a building with its cinder block exterior and faded inside. Still, it looked a little better, and for that she was surprisingly pleased.

Three, now nearly four days back, and she still felt adrift in a place that had once been her home. Making a life in Hartley-by-the-Sea seemed impossible; leaving, even more so. Laura didn't think she'd be allowed to remain in this numb stasis for much longer, anyway. Every time she saw Abby, her daughter looked more and more wound up. Darkly Laura wondered how long it would take before Abby truly lit into her. She'd been working herself up to it last night, when Laura had returned. Abby had been pursed-lipped and bossy, her whole body radiating disapproval. It had almost made Laura want to laugh. Who was the mother in that scenario? And yet she knew what Abby would say to that. *You never acted like a mother to me.*

Maybe I did, Laura imagined responding. *Maybe I did and you don't remember.* But even that much wasn't true, not really. She'd tried. Sort of, at the beginning. But when you were sixteen and you'd practically been torn in half giving birth to a nine-pound baby you weren't entirely sure you wanted, it was hard to act like a mother. It was hard to know how to act when your own mother hadn't been much of one to you, besides the occasional bellow or clip round the ear.

As if somehow tuned into her thoughts, Mary came shuffling into the café from the flat, wearing her dressing gown and ratty old slippers.

"How's it going, love?" Mary asked. She held one hand to her side as if she'd been running a marathon rather than walking from one room to another.

"Fine." Laura had been refilling the ice cream tubs before Sophie, the girl who manned the counter, came for the afternoon shift of sticky schoolchildren and surly teens. "Are you sure you should be on your feet?"

Mary drew herself up impressively. "I'm not an invalid. Not yet, anyway."

Almost, Laura wanted to say, but kept herself from it. She wished she could think of something more pleasant to say, something encouraging or funny or wise. She settled for a murmured "Just don't want you to tire yourself out."

Mary deflated, softening, that cringing look of apology in her eyes that Laura didn't know what to do with. "It's kind of you to think of me, love."

Laura had no idea what to say to that. She and Mary had never gotten along, not since Laura had been a little kid, her father's favorite. When Mel had died, her relationship with her mother had soured further, almost as if Mary resented Laura for having been loved. Almost as if she blamed her for her husband's death.

"I was thinking," Mary said as she sagged against the counter. "We ought to have a proper Sunday dinner tomorrow. Pork roast and Yorkshire puds, the works. We could invite Simon." This last was said tentatively, an entreaty, because even Mary couldn't be so hopefully sentimental as to forget how awful things had been between Laura and Simon towards the end.

"I'm not sure that's a good idea," Laura said with as much tact as she could muster. *No effing way* would have been a more appropriate response.

"Don't you think," Mary said quietly, "after all these years . . . you and your brother . . . I'm not a well woman, Laura."

"I thought you just said you weren't an invalid." Laura closed the lid of the ice cream freezer. "I haven't seen Simon in over twenty years, Mum."

"Then perhaps it's time."

"For what?" Laura snapped, and then took a deep breath. This was why she'd come back. For these types of awful reconciliations. Because when she'd lain alone in her king-sized bed in her loft apartment in Soho, staring up at the ceiling and counting her true friends on one hand, if that, she'd wanted to go home. She'd wanted to make things right, or at least see if she could. She'd wanted to stop running and pretending that she wasn't.

Right now, though, she just felt like hightailing it back to Soho. Too bad that life didn't exist anymore.

"Okay," she managed, and turned to her mother with a rictus of a smile. "Let's invite Simon. Is he still living in Whitehaven?" Selling cheap mobile phones and thinking he was far more important than he was.

"Yes, he bought an apartment right on the harborside. Lovely, it is."

"Wonderful," Laura said.

Several hours later, the last of the sticky day-trippers gone, clutching their ice-cream cones, Sophie had left and Laura was emptying the ice cream containers and tidying up for closing time when Abby came in with Noah.

"Well." There was a surprised note in Abby's voice as she stood in the doorway and surveyed the café. She sounded like a parent who felt the punishment she'd meted out had worked just as she'd hoped. And maybe Abby did enjoy seeing her wear this wretched apron, her hair falling out of the neat ponytail she'd had it in this morning, her clothes wrinkled and stained. At that moment she felt too tired to care. "Busy day?"

"Yes, as it would be on a sunny Saturday in June." Laura kept her voice mild. "How was the birthday party?"

"Great." Noah moved towards her, an enthusiastic skip-jump that had Laura backing away instinctively. The boy had so much *energy*. "We went bowling afterwards, and had lunch in Whitehaven. Plus ice cream." His chest swelled with the import of all this information and he started kicking a chair, for no reason that Laura could fathom.

"Sounds like quite a day out."

"I can't even remember the last time we had a day out together," Abby interjected, and Laura thought she sounded defensive, or possibly accusing. Maybe both. "I work almost every Saturday, while poor Noah—"

Laura held up one hand to stop the tirade she hadn't meant to invite and had no desire whatsoever to listen to. "I was just making a comment, Abby." Abby bit her lip, and Laura regarded her for a moment, this near stranger that she'd actually given birth to. How *odd.* Remembering herself as a sixteen-year-old girl, scared and defiant, giving birth alone, was like looking at someone else's home movies. In her own mind she could hear the explanations: *Oh, that was the hospital where I delivered, all by myself in a room like a prison cell. And that was the horrid nurse who told me pain relief was for proper mothers. And that was the pink dress and bonnet I bought with my own money to bring her home in, but she was so big I couldn't even get her in it.* It was as if she was talking to herself, two strangers chatting inside her head. All of it felt unfamiliar, as if it had happened to someone else. Maybe it had. She certainly felt like a different person now. She'd felt like a different person for a long time.

"How long have you been back in Hartley-by-the-Sea?" she asked, and Abby looked surprised by the question.

"Two years next month."

Laura nodded slowly. "Why did you come back?"

Abby stared and blinked. "Why?" she repeated.

"Yes, why? Why did you come back here? Did you want to?" The questions seemed to bounce off the concrete walls of the café, echo in the emptiness of the room, the early-evening sunshine slanting through the picture windows. Six o'clock and it was still bright out. The sun wouldn't set until nearly midnight this time of year. Laura had watched it sink to the horizon, night after sleepless night, trying to enjoy the stunning beauty of it all, feeling leaden inside.

Abby pursed her lips even further, so they were a thin, puckered line, like a scar. "Noah, why don't you go check on Gran?" Noah, seemingly oblivious to the tension tautening between them like an invisible wire, glanced at his mother before doing his skip-jump move towards the flat. When he'd gone, the door swinging closed behind him, Abby said carefully, "I suppose it depends what you mean by 'want.'" Before Laura could clarify, she added, a slightly querulous note entering her voice, "Anyway, shouldn't I be asking you the questions? Such as: how long are you going to stay?"

"Do you want me gone that badly?" Laura managed to hold on to the light, wry tone she'd practiced over the years. Her armor. Nothing could hurt her then. Nothing could affect her, as long as she acted as if it didn't.

"It's not that, exactly," Abby said. She looked as if she was torn whether she wanted to shake Laura by the shoulders or give her a hug. Or was that merely wishful thinking? "It would simply be good to know. I don't know what to expect from you." The admission made Abby sound vulnerable, and made Laura feel guilty. Her daughter had never known what to expect from her, and with good reason.

"I wish I knew more myself," Laura said with an attempt at a laugh. "I came back because it felt like the right thing to do, with Mum being so poorly and never having even met my own grandson." Abby looked disbelieving and Laura couldn't blame her. She'd barely said boo to Noah since she'd arrived. "But it all feels a lot harder than I expected," she admitted, and to her complete horror she felt the thick gathering of tears in her throat. Good Lord. She absolutely could not cry right now. She hadn't cried in years. Twenty-two years, to be precise. Quickly she cleared her throat, angry with herself for being that soft. That weak. "Anyway. I'm at a bit of a loose end, to tell you the truth." Which was a massive understatement.

"Loose end?" Abby frowned. "Do you mean with work? What happened to the fancy nightclub in New York?"

Laura couldn't miss the slight sneering note in her daughter's voice. Maybe she deserved it. "It's gone. What happened to Noah's father?" she threw back, because two could play at this game. Maybe. And yes, she had wondered what had happened to the man in question. He was so clearly not part of the landscape, and as far as Laura could tell, he never had been.

"He died," Abby said shortly, and Laura blinked. Of course he'd *died*. Of course he hadn't scarpered off or drifted away, as if her daughter couldn't hang on to a man. And now she felt wretched.

"I'm sorry."

Abby let out a short, hard laugh. "Thanks."

"I really am." Abby just shook her head, disbelieving, and Laura wondered when she'd lost absolutely all of her credibility. When she'd left twenty-three years ago, in one sharp blow, or had it been chipped away gradually, over years of infrequent visits and maternal disinterest? "Was it a long time ago?"

"Before Noah was born." Abby's voice sounded tight. "He never even knew him," she added, and Laura wondered how much to ask. How much to care. Did she even have any right to care about her daughter's life?

"So what did you mean, your job's gone?" Abby asked.

"I quit." Laura wouldn't give Abby the satisfaction of knowing she'd been sacked. Publicly, shamefully shown the door, her phone and laptop unceremoniously stripped from her in front of a skeleton crew of cleaners. That's how it all went down in the entertainment industry. When you were suddenly out, you were really out. And Laura hadn't possessed nearly enough of the energy and determination to claw her way back in.

"Why?" Abby pressed. "Last time you were here, it was all la-di-da, swanning around, bragging about life in the big city."

Now, that was unfair. Abby made her sound like an idiot and Laura knew she'd been a class act. She'd worked hard at her image, honed it to a polished and glossy sheen. She might be a bit tarnished at the edges now, but she'd never swanned or bragged. At least she didn't think she had. "Well," she answered, keeping her voice as light and even as she could, "that was six years ago. And the bright-lights, big-city thing got a bit old, I suppose."

"You got fired, didn't you?" Abby said, her hands on her hips. "Why else would you show up here?"

Her daughter was officially a bitch. Even so, Laura supposed she deserved it. She supposed, in Abby World, she'd never stop paying for her sins. She'd just keep doling out, time and time again. "Got it in one," she said tiredly, and turned to cash out the till.

5

Abby

THE ROAST POTATOES WERE burning. Abby swore under her breath as she yanked the roasting tin out of the oven and banged it into the sink. A few potatoes, their edges blackened, rolled into the soap-scummy water at the bottom as oily smoke poured out of the oven. Her grandmother's dream of a Sunday roast dinner was fast turning into a disaster—no surprise there, considering Abby was in charge. She could do the toasties and jacket potatoes for the café, and occasionally she went all out and made a *Bake Off*–worthy cake, but a full roast dinner was sadly beyond her capabilities.

"Everything all right in there?" Mary called from the sitting room, where she was watching *Storage Wars*, the TV on close to ear-bleed level. Noah was watching it too, even though Abby didn't really like him watching those tawdry reality shows.

"Yes, fine," Abby called. She fished the less blackened potatoes out of the sink and dumped them in the bowl. Out of the corner of her eye she could see the table Laura had set, her contribution to the Sunday dinner. It was beautifully laid with the best china, which usually came out only at Christmas, and the nice napkins that Laura had twisted into intricate, elegant shapes. Not exactly the top of Abby's priorities when it came to the meal, but after she'd done the napkins, Laura had disappeared upstairs to get ready, and left Abby sweating in the kitchen.

"I don't cook," she'd said simply when Abby had hinted that she could use a little help. "Never have. But I'll hoover, if you like."

She had hoovered, thankfully, as the sitting room carpet had certainly needed it. And in truth the kitchen wasn't big enough for two cooks. If Laura had elbowed her way in, Abby knew she would have been annoyed. Yet here she was, being annoyed anyway, because that seemed to be her default setting with her mother, and she didn't know how to turn it off. No matter what kindly advice her friends or grandmother gave, sitting down and having a nice cuppa with Laura didn't feel like an option. First, they had to call some kind of truce, and Abby didn't know how to go about it. Neither did Laura, judging from the tension that had thrummed in every conversation they'd managed to have so far.

Abby had gone over their exchange in the café yesterday, wondering how Laura admitting she'd lost her job and Abby her fiancé had led them both to snip at each other. Where had been the sympathy, the commiseration, the bonding over shared loss and grief? Maybe it had been her fault, because she'd been so on her guard. But how did you let something down that had been up for a lifetime? There were no directions, no easy conversation openers.

And now, to top it all off, she had to make a big old-fashioned roast dinner with all the trimmings, something she'd never actually done before. She'd managed a decent curry for her and Ben, back in their student days, and she could make the full array of child-friendly meals for Noah: chicken nuggets, chips, fish fingers, the occasional sliced vegetable to make it all look healthier than it was.

Her grandmother had, predictably, intended to make the whole meal. She'd bustled about the kitchen for a quarter of an hour, huffing as she yanked out bowls and sacks of flour, only to subside into a breathless heap on the sofa.

"Sorry, love," she'd said, looking so abject Abby couldn't be annoyed with her. "But if I tell you how, you can do it, can't you? Making

Yorkshire puds is a doddle, really." She'd called out random instructions for a little while—give the potatoes a good shake before you put them in the pan; make sure the oil is piping hot—but then *Storage Wars* had come on and Mary had fallen silent. And as for the rest of the meal . . . Abby had no idea how to make Yorkshire puddings; she usually bought them frozen and heated them for three minutes. So did Mary, but for some reason she wanted to pull out all the stops for lunch today, everything made from scratch, as if Simon was the prodigal son when he'd actually never lived farther than Whitehaven— not that you'd know by how often he visited, which was basically never. He'd left home when Abby was six and she'd more or less forgotten about him, except when he turned up, reeking of cheap aftershave and sporting too much hair gel, usually to brag or else to ask for money.

With a heavy sigh she flipped through the pages of the cookbook she'd dug out from the bottom drawer, an ancient copy of *Delia's Complete Cookery Course*. The pudding recipe seemed simple enough, just flour, milk, and eggs. Abby checked on the shoulder of pork sizzling in the oven and then started dumping ingredients into a mixing bowl. Over the din of *Storage Wars* she could hear her mother moving around upstairs, and she suppressed a sour stab of resentment.

Half an hour later Abby managed to have a meal, more or less, on the table. The potatoes were a bit blackened, yes, and the Yorkshire puddings clearly weren't as simple as she'd hoped, because they were flat and dense, like Scotch pancakes, instead of light, airy puffballs of golden dough, the way her grandmother used to make them at Christmas.

"Was the fat sizzling when you poured the batter?" Mary asked with a frown. "It needs to be sizzling."

"Sorry," Abby said, blowing a strand of hair from her eyes as her mother, dressed immaculately in a sleeveless silk blouse in silvery gray and a matching narrow skirt, came downstairs. Abby hadn't been able to change—she was wearing jeans and a grease-spattered top. The fat had been sizzling enough to spatter all over her, at least. Uncle Simon, whom all these preparations were for, had yet to arrive despite it being fifteen minutes past his expected arrival time.

"We should make a start," Abby said as she pulled a chair out for Noah. "Before it gets cold."

"Oh, not before Simon arrives . . . ," Mary protested, and Abby saw Laura's expression tighten.

"Who knows when he'll arrive? And Noah is hungry." Resolutely Abby sat down and yanked the twisted napkin onto her lap, smoothing out the shape her mother had spent about an hour creating. It was pettily satisfying.

"Oh, but the table looks so pretty . . . ," Mary murmured as she sat down. "What a lovely job you've done with it, Laura. It looks like something out of a magazine."

Abby started spooning potatoes onto Noah's plate. He pushed them away with one hand, his lower lip jutting out. "Mummy, they're burned. I don't like burned potatoes."

"Does anyone?" Laura murmured, and Abby gritted her teeth.

"You'll eat them," she said shortly. She looked up with a beady, fixed expression aimed at Laura and Mary, sitting across from her. Damn it, she'd made this dinner when it hadn't even been her idea. "Everyone will eat them."

The door to the flat opened, and with an overpowering waft of cheap cologne, her uncle Simon ambled into the room. "Hey, everybody. Sorry I'm late." He sounded completely unrepentant, which was no surprise. In the two years since Abby had returned to Hartley-by-the-Sea, she'd seen her uncle no more than a handful of times. He was uncomfortable with his mother's health problems and impatient with Noah and children in general. Abby didn't relish his infrequent visits.

Now he glanced at Laura, and Abby could see the surprising gleam of malice in his eyes, and she felt a tremor of apprehension. "Well, well," he said, rocking back on his heels. "Big sis has finally come home with her tail between her legs. City life too much for you?" He didn't wait for her reply as he continued, not even hiding his gloating. "I heard you got the sack."

Laura's nostrils flared and she put her napkin on her own lap. "You heard right. Not that Cumbrian crack is to be relied upon, usually."

"Listen to you," Simon mocked as he pulled out a chair. With five around the little kitchen table, not to mention all the china and dishes on it, it was a most uncomfortable squash. "Sounding very la-di-da."

Laura's cool gaze flicked to Abby and back again. "Funny, I've heard that before."

Weirdly, Abby felt more than a prickle of guilt at this. She hated the idea that she and Simon were at all similar, but yes, she knew some of her gibes at her mother had been cheap shots. Simon seemed on particularly top form today, though. Usually he hid his irritation behind a thin veneer of false joviality; Laura's presence, it seemed, had taken off that micro-layer of gloss.

"It's good to see you, Simon," Mary said with a wan smile, and Simon gave her a sideways glance before murmuring something dutiful back.

"Well, dig in," Abby said brightly, and she put some more food on Noah's plate. Her son was glancing between the adults warily, clearly sensing the undercurrents pulsing in the air but not understanding them. Abby wasn't sure she understood them, either. Why did Simon hate her mother so much?

Why shouldn't he? You do.

Except she didn't actually *hate* her mother. Abby put a flattened Yorkshire pudding on her plate as she considered the matter. "Hate" was such a strong and vile word. A child's word, with face screwed up and fists clenched. Or a terribly adult word—a word belonging to bigots and terrorists. Real hate, anyway. You could hate brussels sprouts or traffic jams or paper cuts, but that was something else entirely.

"Abby? Hello? Do you want the potatoes or not?" Abby looked up to see Simon holding the bowl of overroasted potatoes. "I wouldn't blame you if you didn't."

Why are you such a pillock? Abby wanted to ask but of course didn't. She took the potatoes in silence and put two on her plate. She didn't want them, but she would eat them as a matter of principle. Laura, she saw with a flare of gratitude, had taken three.

The next hour was more or less excruciating. Simon went on and on about his job as a mobile phone sales rep, his chest swelling importantly as he shot triumphant glances at Laura, who made a point of ignoring them. Abby found she was actually amused by her mother's cool self-possession in the face of Simon's dull pontificating. Did he really think anyone was interested in the future of smartphone technology, or how many Androids he'd sold in the last week? Apparently he did.

By the time Abby had served dessert—a chocolate cake she'd made last night when it had been far too late—she was nearly swaying on her feet with fatigue. Noah, having been held hostage at the dinner table for over an hour, had escaped to the park with Meghan and Nathan, who had stopped by in a much-needed rescue bid. All she had left was coffee and clearing up, which she'd no doubt do on her own. Simon would scarper, Mary would need to rest, and Laura would most likely slip out back for a cig.

She was surprised when, Simon having made a half-mumbled excuse about needing to tidy up his flat—as if—and Mary having heaved herself upstairs for a rest, Laura joined her in the kitchen with a stack of gravy-smeared plates.

"Still no dishwasher," she said on a sigh. "I remember begging Mum for one." And then, to Abby's shock, her mother started to fill the sink.

"Well, this is a first," she said, and then wished she hadn't sounded so snippy. She hadn't meant to, honestly. The comments just kept slipping out. She needed a stapler.

Laura sighed. "I'm sorry for not being more helpful these last few days." She seemed willing to leave it at that, and Abby did for a few minutes, while they stacked plates and filled the sink, working in surprising, stilted harmony.

"So what's the deal between you and Uncle Simon?" she asked as Laura pulled on a pair of yellow rubber gloves and took her place at the sink. Abby reached for a dish towel to dry.

"I assume you mean the lack of brotherly affection he feels for me?"

"Yes. I mean, I know Simon isn't the cuddliest person around. Ever since Gran had her heart attack, he's basically been MIA."

"Not a surprise," Laura muttered, and Abby just kept herself from replying that her mother was hardly one to talk about being MIA. Now was not the time.

"But he seems to really have it in for you," Abby remarked. "Why is that?"

Laura didn't answer for a long moment, just kept wiping the same now-clean plate with a sponge. "We've never really gotten along all that well," she said slowly. "For a lot of reasons. But when I got pregnant . . . well, he took it as a personal offense, I think. Seemed like it, anyway."

Abby boggled a bit at this. "Why?"

Laura shrugged. "Because everyone was gossiping about me."

"Everyone gossips about everyone in Hartley-by-the-Sea. And you can't have been the first teenager in the village to become pregnant. Not by a long shot."

Laura pressed her lips together and said nothing. It occurred to Abby, far too belatedly, how little she knew about her own birth, or, for that matter, her own conception. She'd asked Mary once who her father was, and her grandmother had said she didn't know. Abby had believed her, and she wouldn't have pressed anyway because by that point her mother had been long gone and she'd just wanted to draw a line across her whole sorry parentage, pretend she'd emerged fully formed from a cabbage patch.

Now she wondered. "So why was he so angry about it?" she asked in a low voice. She kept her eyes on the plate Laura had silently handed her, wiping the streaks away. "Was it because you were dating one of his mates or something?" It was the closest she dared come to asking about her father.

"Dating one of Simon's mates?" Laura let out a genuine laugh. "Please, don't you know me better than that? Simon's mates were all graceless yobs like he was. And still is."

Abby smiled reluctantly. Yes, actually, she *did* know her mother that well, at least. "Then . . ."

"Because he wanted me to get a termination," Laura said wearily. "Just like everybody else did. 'Why muck up your life, Laura?'" she mimicked. "'You've got everything ahead of you. Why bring shame on the family?'"

She slammed a plate onto the dish drainer, nearly cracking it. Abby stood frozen in place, shocked by this revelation. Had her *grandmother* pressured Laura to have an abortion? She felt both hurt and confused. And yet . . . "So why didn't you have a termination?" she asked.

Laura turned to stare at her, her expression unreadable. "You really want to ask me that?"

"Well, not really, considering we're talking about *me*. But you did leave a few years later, and you were only sixteen. So it stands to reason. If you didn't have moral objections, you must have considered it." There. That sounded logical and not snippy. She hoped.

Laura rested her elbows on the sink and stared out the kitchen window at the promenade, which was bustling with families and walkers, several of them shooting semidisconsolate glances at the shuttered front of the café. A shaft of sunlight caught the gray at the roots of her hair. "Actually, I didn't consider it, not really," she said. "Not that you'd necessarily believe me."

A thousand questions were on the tip of Abby's tongue, from who her father actually was to why Laura had left. She wasn't brave enough to ask any of them, and she didn't even know if she wanted to hear the answers. Did she really want to hear that her father was some feckless sixteen-year-old who had done a runner the second he'd discovered his girlfriend was knocked up, or that Laura had driven to the clinic for an abortion and then backed out at the last minute? None of it was welcome knowledge. None of it would make her feel better or more wanted. Basically, it all sucked, which was the reason why she'd never pressed for answers before, from either Mary or Laura.

"Simon just didn't like having his life disturbed in any way," Laura said on a sigh. "When you came along, I was given the big bedroom and he had to be put in the small one. He didn't like that, and he didn't like being kept up by your crying. You were a fussy baby." She said this matter-of-factly, without any hint of maternal affection, so Abby felt as if she should apologize.

It was so strange to think of her mother nursing or rocking her, *caring* for her. Abby couldn't remember her ever doing it. The earliest memory she had of her mother was from when she was about four, when Laura had come for her birthday. She'd stayed for only a couple of hours, and all Abby could remember was the smell of perfume and the click of heels, the generous gift certificate that Mary had explained would be like money in a shop, when all Abby had seen was a piece of paper instead of something to unwrap and play with.

"So Simon is still angry about that?" she asked. "What happened when I was a baby?"

"No, he's angry that I got a decent job that made decent money and then got the hell out of here." Laura laughed again, the sound weary. "I can't even blame him for gloating now that I've come slinking back. It's like his birthday and Christmas wrapped up into one."

"Well, he's pretty much a tosser," Abby said as she started to put the plates away. "Even if he is a relative."

"Simon has his own issues. I don't blame him for being who he is, not anymore."

Now, what was that supposed to mean? Once again Abby realized how little she knew about her mother, her family. Everything. And now that Laura was back, she could start finding the answers . . . if she wanted to.

"I'm going to go check on Gran," she said as she hung up the dish towel. "I think today tired her out."

"It tired you out, more like," Laura answered. "I should have helped more."

"The kitchen's pretty small for two cooks."

"I thought maybe you wanted to manage it on your own, but maybe I was wrong. And Mum seemed like she wanted to be involved. Did she actually do any cooking?"

"No, but having everyone here . . . Simon . . ." Abby shrugged. Laura nodded and reached for the scrub brush to tackle the blackened roasting pan.

"That would exhaust anyone," she said, and started to scrub.

Upstairs the house was quiet, almost peaceful. Abby knocked once on her grandmother's door before poking her head round. "Gran, are you all right . . . ?" The words bottled in her throat as she caught sight of her grandmother, her face in a rictus of pain as her breath came out in shattered gasps, one hand clutching her chest.

6

Laura

THE SCREAM THAT SPLIT the still air had Laura spinning around from the sink and sprinting up the stairs.

"Abby—"

Her daughter met her at the top of the stairs, her face pale and shocked. "It's Gran. She's having another heart attack. A bad one, I think." Her voice was high and thin, and she was trembling.

"I'll call 999." Laura's voice was calm, authoritative, as if it were coming from outside herself. She felt numb and yet also in control, strangely powerful. Here was a crisis, a crisis she could handle, a way she could actually help. "Stay with your gran, Abby." With one hand on Abby's shoulder she steered her back into the room. Mary's face was gray, beads of sweat visible on her forehead. Her breath came out in awful, tearing gasps that made Laura both wince and tremble. "It's going to be all right, Mum," she said, her voice surprisingly steady. "I'm calling 999 right now."

With Abby seated next to Mary, holding her hand, Laura hurried downstairs and called 999, giving all the details she could. Then she went back upstairs; Abby threw her a frightened glance, for Mary's gasps of breath were spaced farther apart, her eyes were glazed, and she didn't respond when Laura spoke to her.

Panic clutched at Laura's chest, digging in its claws. She hadn't had much of a relationship with her mother basically ever, but she didn't want to *lose* her. She couldn't lose her, not yet, when so much hadn't been said—and yet what would she say, even now, with Mary's life trembling in the balance? *I'm sorry you didn't love me? I wish I hadn't let you let me leave?* She'd never found the right opening.

The wail of sirens broke the taut, still air, and both Laura and Abby let out their breath in a rush of relief. The next few minutes were taken up with the paramedics who invaded the tiny flat with their neon jackets and efficient manner, suddenly making everything seem more serious. Laura's heart felt like a stone suspended in her chest as she watched Mary hauled onto a stretcher and then taken downstairs.

"Would someone like to go in the ambulance with her?" one of the paramedics asked, and Laura exchanged an uncertain glance with Abby.

"You should go," Laura said. Abby nodded, not debating the point. She was closer to Mary than Laura was. They both knew it.

After they'd gone, the flat felt alarmingly empty, the silence ringing. Laura finished cleaning the kitchen, although she knew she really should have been jumping in her rental car—which she needed to return tomorrow anyway—and driving to the hospital, bursting through the automatic doors of A&E, demanding to know where her mother was and if she would be okay.

She could picture it, like something out of a film, the end when everything seemed like it was going to go pear-shaped but then it miraculously didn't. The only trouble was, Laura didn't believe in miracles. She hadn't had many in her life. And she was afraid if she stepped outside the flat, if she drove to the hospital, it wouldn't turn out like that stupid film at all.

Fifteen minutes passed before she finally grabbed her keys and headed out, driving in tense silence to the hospital in Whitehaven where she'd given birth to Abby. The place was still a mishmash of squat, 1960s ugliness, all concrete blocks and boxy windows. Parking was a nightmare, and it was another fifteen minutes before Laura finally managed to find a spot in the far corner of the rambling lot. Finally she made it to A&E, striding through the doors, taking in the dozen patients who waited in plastic chairs in various states of distress.

She averted her eyes from a woman who was moaning and then had to look away from a girl who couldn't have been older than five or six, cradling an obviously broken arm. Laura suppressed a shudder. Who on earth would want to work in a place like this? Give her a nightclub any day. Not that anyone was.

After checking in at the front desk, she was asked to wait, and then ten agonizing minutes later Abby came through the doors to the examining rooms; her hair and eyes seemed extraordinarily dark against her pale skin, so she looked like a silhouette of herself.

"What is it?" Laura asked. Her voice sounded harsh. "What's happened?"

"I don't know. It's not good." Abby bit her lip, looking near tears. Laura watched her, feeling strangely unemotional, even for her, as if everything were happening at a great distance, unrolling like film.

"How not good?"

"I mean . . . they're trying to stabilize her now. They've got her hooked up to all sorts of machines, and they said they might have to do emergency surgery, but they have to wait. . . ."

"*Wait?* For emergency surgery? Bloody NHS."

"It's better in America, I suppose?" Abby surmised with a sniff.

"You pay an arm and a leg, but you get *seen,* at least." Laura sank onto a plastic chair; her legs suddenly felt weak and trembly. Maybe she wasn't as unemotional as she'd thought. "So what now?"

"I need to call Meghan. She took Noah out. He doesn't even know. . . ."

"Don't tell him," Laura said quickly. A memory flashed through her mind like a slide slotted into a microscope, the details suddenly, excruciatingly vivid. Her mother's rouged cheeks, her lipstick nearly orange. She'd put on the full slap to go to the hospital and hear the news. Her voice was a rough husk from both cigarette smoke and grief. *Your dad's sick. Really sick.* Laura had been ten years old. She'd blinked, wondering why her mother's lips were orange, and what she meant by really sick. Her only frame of reference was six-year-old Simon's bouts of asthma and when she'd had chicken pox. The next year had completely altered the landscape of her childhood. She didn't want the same for Noah, or for anyone.

"I have to tell him something," Abby said as she sank into the seat next to her. "He'll wonder. He'll *ask*."

"There will be time later," Laura insisted. "When we know more. The uncertainty is terrible, especially for a child."

Abby cocked her head, curious even in the midst of her fear and sadness. "You sound like you speak from experience."

"I do," Laura said, and pressed her lips together. She wouldn't say anything more. She wouldn't even say the word *Dad*, because if she did . . . "Look, why don't you just call Meghan and ask her to watch Noah for a little longer? I'm sure she wouldn't mind." Not that she even knew who Meghan was. All she'd heard when Meghan had come to the door was a rather raucous laugh and the snap of gum.

Abby looked undecided and Laura placed a hand on her shoulder, which felt thin and bony and somehow *young*. It was the second time she'd touched her daughter that day. "Abby, call her. But don't bring Noah into this situation, please. It will only scare or even scar him."

After an endless second Abby nodded. "Okay," she said, and nodded again. "Okay. Thanks."

Laura watched as Abby walked out of the hospital, her slight shoulders set resolutely. Laura felt a weird churn of emotion, feelings she couldn't identify mixed with fragments of memory. She leaned her head back against the chair and closed her eyes.

Her mother might be dying.

She sifted the words through her mind, taking each one and

examining it and then putting it down again, like objects whose value she needed to determine. And the truth was, she couldn't. She felt nothing and too much at the same time, a howl of rage and grief starting inside her, down in her stomach, working its way up. A grief she feared was older than she wanted to admit, for too many people and things she'd lost.

She took a deep breath and clamped her lips together. She wasn't going to give in to the emotion. Not here, and maybe not ever. Losing one parent had been hard enough. She didn't want to drag herself through that pain again, and even though she'd insisted all these years that she didn't even care about Mary anymore, she knew from the churning inside her that she did. Damn it, she did.

"Meghan's going to take Noah back to hers. He can stay the night if he wants, although he never has before."

Laura opened her eyes to see Abby standing in front of her, her phone clenched in one hand. "He'll be fine."

"How would you know?" Abby snapped, and then sat next to her with a sigh. "Sorry. I'm on edge."

"I know."

"Should I ask for news?"

"I assume they'll tell us when there is news. Hopefully she's in surgery now." Emergency heart surgery.

"You should call Simon."

Simon. Ugh. He might not have cared, but he still deserved to know. Laura rose from her seat. "Okay. I'll go outside. Can I use your phone?"

Wordlessly Abby handed it to her and Laura walked outside. She realized she didn't even know Simon's number—why would she, after all?—but fortunately Abby had it in her contacts. Laura had to call three times before Simon finally arsed himself to pick it up.

"Abby? What is it?" He sounded tetchy, and she could hear the tinny sound of football on the TV in the background, a commentator's voice rising in excitement, and then a cheer.

"It's Laura, actually. Mum's in the hospital."

Simon exhaled through his nose. "What, again?"

"Yes, Simon, again. And this time it's serious."

"It was serious before."

"Really serious, then. She's having emergency heart surgery. I think there's a question if . . ." She couldn't make herself put it into words.

Simon was silent for a few seconds. "Call me tomorrow when you know if it's serious or not."

"Really? That's your response?" Laura was nearly speechless with a sudden, shocking rage.

"Like you can talk, Laura. Last time you didn't even visit."

"I . . . I sent flowers," Laura protested, knowing it was paltry.

"Oh, *okay*, then," Simon snapped. "Last time I was the one who took her to the hospital. Who took up the slack, okay? Abby was in Liverpool and you were off in effing America. So don't act like the dutiful daughter now. It's a little too late, even if you always acted like you were better than me. The *favorite*."

Each word had been spit out with such vitriol that Laura could not even frame a reply before she heard the *beep beep beep* and realized Simon had hung up on her. He was still angry about that? She slid the phone into her pocket. Of course he was. He'd always been angry that Dad had favored her. But Mary had always treated Simon, jackass that he could be, like a little prince, even more so after their father had died. Spoiled Simon and screwup Laura. That had played out for years before Laura had had enough. She really needed a cigarette.

Thankfully she had a crumpled packet in her purse, and studiously avoiding the NO SMOKING signs plastered all over the place, Laura took a few more steps away from the doors, half-hiding behind a pillar, and lit up. The first drag was the best, sucking the smoke deep into her lungs, waiting for the hit.

She'd smoked only e-cigarettes until two weeks ago, more because smoking was bad for her skin than for her health. But when Tyler Lawton had smarmily informed her that she was past it in looks, Laura had decided she'd had enough of preserving her beauty. Forget the Botox injections every three months, the judicious selection of minor surgical procedures. Forget the hours at the gym and eschewing wine and chocolate in order to avoid that awful bloat. What did it matter anymore? What did *anything* matter anymore? She took another deep drag on her cigarette and avoided the disapproving look of a mother walking into A&E, holding a child by the hand.

"Laura? Laura Rhodes?"

Damn it. Laura stiffened, lowering her hand so the cigarette was half-hidden behind her back, and turned to face the woman who had addressed her. She looked vaguely familiar. She was wearing a funky-looking embroidered smock top and skinny jeans, and her dark hair, which was liberally streaked with gray, was pulled back into a messy bun. She was holding the hand of a boy who was about five or six. "It's Isobel," she said with a little laugh. "Isobel Starr—well, Hartford, as was. Izzy."

Izzy. Laura forced her mouth into a smile of remembrance as she dropped the still-lit cigarette and crushed it under her heel. "Of course I remember you."

How could she not? Izzy had been her best friend, or the closest thing she'd had to one, until she'd gotten pregnant and dropped out. In secondary school Izzy had been a lazy rule breaker, hippieish and pretending to be all arty and cool, while Laura had been trying to figure out what she was. Not sporty or one of the in crowd, and not quite geeky or smart enough to hang out with that group. She'd been nothing, a vacuum inside, all the interesting parts of her sucked out by grief and tiredness. She'd been waiting to be filled up, and she had been. Too bad that hadn't worked out all that well.

"What are you doing back in Cumbria?" Izzy asked. "Last time I heard, you were in Manchester, living some kind of high life."

Izzy sounded as if she was genuinely curious, rather than secretly delighting in the fact that someone who had dared to venture out into the wide, waiting world had been forced to come creeping back.

"Actually, I was in New York City," Laura said. She took a deep breath, about to go into her I-wanted-a-change spiel that no one really bought, and then she wondered why she bothered. Everyone guessed the truth, anyway. Maybe she needed to own it. "Unfortunately I got fired and I'm too old to start again. Forty-two-year-olds are past it when it comes to the nightclub industry." She shrugged. "So I'm living at home and trying to figure out my next step."

"Oh. Wow." Izzy's eyes were as wide as her son's. "I'm sorry, I guess?"

"Thanks. It's good to be back, in a weird way." A very weird way. If she hadn't been feeling so raw from Mary's condition, she wouldn't have said any of it. "What are you doing here?"

Izzy gestured to the little boy at her side. "Rufus has an ear infection. Couldn't wait until Monday for the antibiotics—it was really killing him, poor love." Concern softened her features. "What about you?"

"My mother." The two words were hard to get out, the next two even more so. "Heart attack."

Izzy's mouth dropped open. "Oh no, I'm so sorry. Is it—is it serious?"

Weren't heart attacks always serious? "Yes," Laura said. "It really is."

"Oh no. Really . . . if there's anything I can do . . ." Izzy seemed to realize the vagueness of such an offer. "We should get together. I mean, when things have settled down. Come by for a cup of tea and fill me in on all your news."

I just did, Laura thought, but she smiled and nodded. "That would be lovely. Thank you." And actually, she wouldn't mind catching up with Izzy. They'd had a few good laughs, before Laura had had to leave school. She had a memory of Izzy singing under her breath as she'd drawn a fake tattoo on Laura's arm with a permanent marker. It had lasted for months, and it had actually looked quite cool. Some violets entwined with ivy, and a bird rising above it, wings outstretched, soaring.

"Okay. Well, then." Izzy nodded a few times, smiling, and Laura performed the same ritual back as they awkwardly lurched into good-byes. "Wait. You don't have my number," she said, and Laura duly pro-grammed her number into Abby's phone. "Text me so I have yours."

"Will do," Laura answered, and watched as Izzy led her son across the car park. He was clutching his ear.

She needed to go back inside, but she didn't feel like she could face it and she'd only smoked half her cigarette. She was reaching for the packet of cigarettes again when she saw Abby at the doors, her face as pale as a moon, eyes dark and shocked.

"What is it?" Laura asked as she hurried towards her. Abby just shook her head, and fear clutched at her. "She's not out of surgery yet, is she?"

"She's not having the surgery."

"What? Why not?" Abby shook her head again, and Laura was about to launch into another diatribe about the NHS when a tear spilled down Abby's cheek, shocking her into silence. "Abby . . . ," she began, and then trailed off, genuine fear—the horrible, metallic kind that coated your mouth and curdled your stomach—settling inside her. *"Abby."*

Another tear fell unchecked. "She's . . . she's gone," Abby said, and put her hands up to her face, her shoulders shaking.

7

Abby

IT WAS SO STRANGE, the way a person could just be *gone*. One minute someone was living and breathing, annoying or amusing you, and the next it was all over, the petty concerns that had consumed you for so long made utterly, awfully irrelevant. Abby had felt this way after Ben had died, although his parents had bustled in and demanded to manage everything, precious only child that he'd been. It hadn't been for Abby to sort his clothes or mementos; they hadn't even wanted her in his flat. They'd been furious with her, because they blamed her for his death. Just like she'd blamed herself, even though she knew it wasn't fair. Fair didn't matter to how you felt.

Now she kept thinking about those stupid Yorkshire puddings, and how only yesterday she'd been annoyed with Mary for watching *Storage Wars*. She was standing in the middle of Mary's bedroom, which felt strange in itself because her grandmother's bedroom had always been off-limits to her as a child, and even as an adult Mary hadn't liked anyone to come in there. Even at her most ill, she'd insisted on lumbering down to the sitting room. "Staying in bed makes me feel like a bloody invalid," she'd grumbled, and Abby had wanted to protest, *But you are an invalid.* She'd admired Mary's stubbornness, but it had aggravated her too, and that was the emotion she'd given in to all too often. Why hadn't she laughed more at Mary's bloody-mindedness,

71

given her a hug, for heaven's sake, and told her that she wouldn't be an invalid even when she was a bedridden old bat? Mary would have laughed at that. She would have smiled and been secretly pleased.

Abby looked at the bed, still rumpled from where Mary had been lying on it. She smoothed the quilt, a faded patchwork one that Mary's mother had made. Her great-grandmother, whom Abby had never known. Abby knew she'd died from breast cancer when Mary was a teenager; it seemed like the Rhodes women didn't get to grow old gracefully.

The last twenty-four hours of navigating the aftermath of Mary's death had been both exhausting and surreal. The doctor had ushered them into the A&E cubicle, no more than a curtained-off corner, to say good-bye to Mary before they took her body to the morgue. The first thing that Abby had thought was how on earth anyone could think a dead person was merely sleeping. Mary didn't look like she was sleeping. She looked *dead*. Her skin had turned a mottled yellowish gray, her cheeks already hollowing out, her body as stiff as a waxwork, and yet only minutes ago she'd been alive. Abby had been silently horrified by the change. She didn't think she'd ever get the image of her grandmother's lifeless body out of her mind; it transposed itself on every memory she'd ever had of Mary.

Next to her, Laura had gone still, silent, her gaze trained on the wasted bulk of Mary's body. Then she'd looked away quickly, saying nothing. For once, Abby thought she could see beneath Laura's cool exterior, note the bright eyes and the bitten lip. It made her want to give her mother a hug. She didn't, though, although perhaps she should have. Laura was giving off definite don't-touch-me signals, and Abby suspected she was, as well.

With a screech of the curtain rings, the nurse had left them alone, and they'd stood there, the two of them, in appalled silence. Were you actually supposed to say good-bye? What was the point? Mary was so obviously long gone, her body no more than a shell. Abby had never given much thought to the whole question of a soul, but if people possessed one, Mary's had definitely left the building.

Then Laura had straightened, turning with a brisk nod, that brief flicker of vulnerability vanished. "Right, we're done here, don't you think?" Abby nodded, wanting only to leave, and then she had followed her out and they'd taken Mary's body away.

She and Laura had gone back to the flat, which still had the lingering smell of burned potatoes in the air. It had been only a couple of hours ago that they'd all been sitting there, the tension palpable, Simon lounging in his chair, Mary heaving herself to her feet.

"You finished cleaning the kitchen," Abby had observed, and Laura merely shrugged. Abby didn't say anything more; she didn't know what to say, to feel. They both drifted around for a few minutes, at a loss. When Ben had died, Abby had only heard about it after the fact; the police had notified his parents first, because they were his emergency contact. And his parents hadn't thought to inform her. Had chosen not to, most likely, because they'd always thought she brought Ben down. She'd discovered what had happened when she'd broken down and called them, half-crying with panic because Ben had been missing for over twenty-four hours. They'd told her the barest of details before hanging up the phone. Abby had found out when the funeral was only by reading his obituary in the newspaper.

So it was different this time round, the awfulness of the immediate aftermath, when the house felt emptier than it should have and there was nothing to do. Abby had a bizarre desire to stay busy, clean the oven or strip a bed, but getting down to housework felt inappropriate, an insult to Mary's memory. In the end Abby had gone to get Noah, even though Meghan had offered to have him for the night. She didn't know if it was better or worse to have Noah bouncing around the house with his manic boy-energy, oblivious. He hadn't even asked where his gran was; Abby supposed he thought she was sleeping.

She'd taken him to school without anyone asking anything; she'd told Meghan last night and thankfully the crack hadn't gotten round yet. Abby didn't think she could cope with all the stammered condolences, the well-meaning hand squeezes. She didn't think she could cope with anything. What was she supposed to do with all of Mary's clothes? Bundle them in bin bags? It felt wrong to simply get rid of stuff, but what could you do? Each minute of this postdeath existence felt like an unholy slog. How did you get through a whole day? A month? The rest of your life?

Downstairs Abby heard the creak of floorboards. Her mother had disappeared sometime late morning, and was only now returning four hours later. Abby had no idea where she'd gone, but she supposed everyone dealt with grief in their own way. She didn't know how she was dealing with hers, staring into space and trying to stave off the tidal wave of loneliness she could feel looming.

Mary had been ornery, stubborn, razor-tongued, but she'd also been loving and larger-than-life, and Abby missed her. A lot. She had a sudden, sharp memory of Mary enveloping her in a big, bosomy hug when she'd arrived back with Noah. She'd barely been able to sit up in her hospital bed, but her arms had been open wide. It had been exactly what Abby had needed.

Now she knew she needed to get Noah soon, needed to tell him about his gran, needed to tell the vicar and then arrange the funeral. . . . The list felt endless, impossible. She wanted Laura's help, but they'd barely spoken since Mary's death. Tragedy was supposed to bring people closer, but Abby wasn't feeling it yet.

On the bedside table she saw Mary's little enamel pillbox, which Abby had gotten her for Christmas last year, as well as her reading glasses, and a tattered Mills & Boon paperback, lurid pink cover on proud display. Mary had always loved her romances. Just the sight of those everyday objects was enough to make Abby let out a strangled sob. She clapped a hand to her mouth; she hadn't cried since they'd left the hospital and she didn't want to cry now. She wasn't ready for all the tears, to feel all the grief. She just wasn't. It was too mixed-up, tangled with leftover grief from Ben's death and sorrow that Mary had had to act like her mother for so long. She'd done her best, God knew, but in childhood at times it had felt mediocre. Was it wrong to think that way now?

"What is it?" Laura stood in the doorway, looking less than her immaculate self. Her hair was loose about her face and she wore a pair of yoga pants and a faded T-shirt. Her face was drawn, her eyes and hair dull. Her gaze moved from Abby to the table. "Oh."

"The glasses . . . ," Abby managed to choke out, and Laura nodded.

"I know. It's the little things that hurt the most." She spoke dispassionately, but Abby saw how she folded her arms, pressed them against her body. Her mother was hurting just as she was.

"It's just she won't need them anymore," Abby explained. "For years she was always going on about losing her glasses, and she never wanted the stupid chain that goes around your neck because she said that made her feel old." Abby drew a shuddering breath. "And now they're just *useless*."

"I know." Laura's face looked different, without the makeup and the hauteur, drawn now into lines of sadness. She looked old. "I remember finding my father's passport after he'd died. I don't know why he even had one. He'd never been farther than Blackpool for a holiday." She laughed, the sound tired. "But it was so strange to hold his passport, this important document you're never meant to lose, and it wouldn't matter if I ripped it up. I couldn't stand that, somehow."

"Yes." Abby sniffed, holding back her tears with an effort that hurt her chest. "Exactly."

Laura leaned against the doorway. "There's always so much to do after a person dies."

Abby sniffed again. "Yes, I was thinking that too." It felt strange to be in such solidarity with her mother, and it made her yearn for more.

"And people always tell you it's best to keep busy, and maybe it is, at least for some people, but what about when you just want to curl up in a ball and act as if you don't exist?"

"Is that how you felt after . . . after your dad died?" Strange, how she'd never even asked about Mel Rhodes, the grandfather she'd never met. Never even cared to ask, which was shaming.

"Yes. But I was only ten."

"Ten? I didn't realize you were so young." Although she should have, if she'd ever bothered to do the math. She'd gone with Mary enough times to the headstone in the churchyard to lay a wreath or a wilted bouquet of flowers.

Laura shrugged. "It was a long time ago."

"Were you close to him?"

Her lips tightened and she looked away. "Yes. Yes, I was."

There was a lifetime of restrained sorrow in those simple words, and Abby wanted to acknowledge it somehow. She wanted her mother to know that she got it, that she sympathized, but she had no idea how and so the silence stretched on. She'd learned more about her mother today than she had in all twenty-five years previous.

"But I don't want to curl up in a ball now," Laura said, her voice turning bright and artificial. "I want to get legless. How does that sound to you?"

"At three in the afternoon?" Actually, it was tempting. A little bit of oblivion sounded glorious. "I have to fetch Noah from school."

"Fine. You get Noah and I'll get the alcohol. There's got to be some perk to life being such crap sometimes."

Abby didn't know if getting drunk counted as a perk, but she was fully on board with the idea. They both needed a little anesthesia.

She took Noah to the park after school, and they walked slowly home as the sun shimmered on the placid sea. She'd closed the café for the whole day, even though they couldn't afford the loss of business, not on a sunny day in June. Although actually, Abby reflected, she had no idea what they could or couldn't afford any longer. She'd had access to the café's business account with its paltry amount of petty cash, but she had no idea what Mary's personal finances looked like.

When she'd first arrived, she'd arranged for all the bills to be put on direct debit, but beyond that . . . Did Mary have life insurance? Savings? Was there a will? It seemed wrong to be thinking about those sorts of things now. Mercenary, although Abby doubted there was much to be mercenary about. The café had always struggled to break even. Since her arrival there had been a bit of an uptick, with the toddler mornings and the art showings, but not that much of one. Hartley-by-the-Sea was a small place, and not everyone treated themselves to a cuppa on a regular basis.

Anyway, before she dealt with all that, she had to tell Noah. How did you explain death to a five-year-old? How did he understand? Abby unlocked the door to the café rather than going around the back to the flat's private entrance. She wanted some privacy, although perhaps Laura had more experience with this kind of thing than she did. Abby had never had a father, but Laura had known and lost hers. She'd know a lot more about what Noah might be feeling than Abby. And yet . . . this was something she needed to do herself.

"Why are we in here?" Noah asked as Abby flicked on the lights and pulled two chairs out from a table. The café stretched around them, silent and dim, the only sound the labored hum of the ancient refrigerator.

"I wanted to talk to you for a bit."

"In the café?" Already Noah looked wary.

"Just so we can have some privacy." Abby sat down and patted the chair next to her. "Come here, Noah, please."

Slowly, dragging his feet, he came. He plopped himself down in the chair and looked up at her from under his fringe, his expression more apprehensive than ever. "What?"

"It's about Gran, Noah." Abby brushed his fringe out of his eyes, his silky hair sliding through her fingers. If she could have spared her son this pain, she would have. She wanted to spare him everything—from scraped knees to sudden deaths. The fact that she couldn't was enough to make her heart lurch and her breath quicken. How much pain would his little body and tender heart absorb over the coming years? And there was nothing she could do about it.

"What about Gran?" Noah asked, a petulant, impatient note entering his voice. His first line of defense. Abby thought she saw a flicker of knowledge in his dark eyes, a hazy understanding.

She took a deep breath. "You know she had trouble with her heart."

"Yes, but the pills made it better. She said. So did you." His lower lip jutted out, the image of determined obstinance.

"Yes, they did. For a while. But last night, Noah . . ." Abby stopped, her chest so tight, it hurt. Noah was searching her face, trying to make sense of what she was saying while at the same time trying not to. Abby could tell; she felt the same. "Last night, Noah," she tried again, "Gran had another heart attack. A big one. And this time . . . this time she didn't survive."

Noah stared at her blankly. "What do you mean?" His voice rose, strident, angry. "What do you *mean*?"

"She died, Noah." Abby's voice shook. She wanted to gather her baby up in her arms and rock him like a newborn, but he was quivering with anger, vibrating with emotion. He flinched away from her when she reached for him, and Abby let her hand fall. "She died, sweetheart. She's gone. I'm sorry."

Noah rose from his seat, his fists clenched. "No," he said. "No, you're wrong."

Abby took another gulping breath. This was so *hard*. "I'm sorry. I wish I was."

"She can't just be gone. It doesn't happen like that."

It shouldn't, Abby agreed silently. There should be neon warnings and flashing lights, an obvious way for someone to prepare for the sudden swoop and then the ensuing, endless emptiness. But there wasn't. Even when someone was old and ill, someone like Mary, death came as a huge shock. "Sometimes, Noah," Abby said softly, "it does."

He kicked the chair away and strode, his fists still clenched, to the door to the flat. Wrenching it open, he stalked inside, going from room to room, looking for his grandmother.

Abby followed him, fighting back tears, staying silent as Noah kept looking. Maybe he needed to do this, to see the proof for himself. Laura stood in the kitchen doorway, watching them, her expression tight and pinched, her arms cupped round her elbows. No one spoke. Finally Noah returned to the sitting room. He didn't say a word, just turned on the TV, sat on the sofa, and started watching CBeebies as if *Justin Time* were the most fascinating thing he'd ever seen. Abby glanced at Laura, her eyes full of tears and misery. *Help me,* she wanted to say, but the words were stuck in her throat, filling her chest. Laura pressed a finger to her lips and shook her head.

"What . . . ?" Abby whispered.

"Let him be," Laura said in a low voice. "Just let him be."

Noah didn't speak for the rest of the evening. Dinner felt endless, sausages and mash that Abby could barely choke down. Noah toyed with the food on his plate and no one said anything. Abby offered ice cream for dessert, straight from the café, but Noah just shook his head.

He went to bed shortly after, and Abby sat on the edge of the bed, waiting for him to fall asleep, holding his hand and clinging to the look of gradual relaxation softening his features, telling herself that meant he was going to be okay. Sunlight was slanting through the window; it was half past seven but as bright as an afternoon. Plenty of people were out on the beach, walking dogs and flying kites; a couple of people had dragged out disposable barbecues and the smell of frying meat drifted through the open window.

All of it gave Abby such an overwhelming feeling of loneliness, of otherness. She could not imagine ever feeling that carefree and happy again. She only hoped Noah could.

Noah lay on his side, his knees tucked up to his chest, one hand under his chin. "Do you think Gran is in heaven?" he asked in a quiet voice.

She wasn't ready for theological questions. Did she believe in heaven? It certainly seemed like an attractive idea at the moment. "I hope she is, Noah."

"You *hope*?" His eyes narrowed. Clearly he didn't think much of her wavering agnosticism. "You don't know?"

"I'm not sure anyone can know, not absolutely."

He shook his head, disgusted, and Abby knew she needed to give him some real reassurance. She could use some herself. "This is something I know. Gran isn't hurting anymore, Noah. She isn't puffing and panting for breath."

"Is she happy?"

Sod the cautious truth telling. "Yes," Abby said firmly. "I'm sure she is."

It took another twenty minutes for him to fall asleep, and then Abby tiptoed downstairs, nearly crying in relief when she saw her mother pouring two large gin and tonics.

"I raided the post office shop and bought their only bottle of gin and all their tonic water," Laura said briskly. "We'll have to do without lime."

"Dan Trenton must have given you the death stare."

"The big bloke at the till? Yes, he didn't seem too impressed with me." Laura sounded unconcerned. "I suppose a middle-aged woman buying a lot of alcohol on a Monday evening is a bit suspect. Or maybe just sad." She handed Abby one of the drinks. "Cheers."

"Cheers." Abby took a sip, nearly gasping as the alcohol hit the back of her throat. She'd never been much of a drinker; a glass of wine on a Thursday night at the pub quiz was about all she managed.

"Let's go outside," Laura said. "I feel like I'm suffocating in here."

Abby thought of the rickety picnic tables set up on the café concrete terrace. "People will see us. Talk to us. You know how it is."

"I certainly do. And I have no intention of kicking back in full view of the village. Round the back." She motioned to the side door that led to the drive, and Abby hesitated.

"Noah . . ."

"I'll check on him every so often if you like. He'll be fine, Abby." There was the slightest edge to Laura's voice, and Abby stiffened. Maybe she was slightly a bit of a helicopter mum, but it made up for Laura's utter lack of parenting. And she didn't feel like any criticism of her parenting skills just now, when her baby was hurting as much as she was.

"He's five. . . ."

"And he's asleep. But if you want to stay in the lounge, by all means." Laura gestured to the sagging sofa, where Mary had spent most evenings in front of the telly. Abby glanced at it and knew she couldn't sit there. Not now, and maybe not ever. Maybe they'd get a new sofa.

"Okay," she said. "For a few minutes." She followed Laura outside and then around to the back of the café. The only thing back there was the bins, overflowing because Abby had forgotten to take them out front last night for the weekly rubbish pickup.

"Great atmosphere," she said, and Laura looked back at her, rolling her eyes.

"Up here." Laura started climbing up the steep hill that led to the coastal path on the cliff top. It was beautiful up there, but Abby rarely went. When Noah had been little, she'd been worried about the dangerous drop-off to the beach and then later she'd been too busy.

Abby watched Laura scramble up the hill, and then, still unsure, she flung one hand out to balance herself as she followed, clambering up the side and then emerging amidst the gorse bushes, now awash in bright yellow flowers, at the top of the cliff. The sea stretched out on one side, sparkling and blue, and the sheep fields rolled away towards the village on the other. Everything was bathed in sunlight, golden and perfect.

"It feels wrong," Abby said quietly, "for things to be beautiful, when someone has died."

Laura positioned herself on a rock overlooking the sea. "Yes, I know what you mean. The sun was shining when my father died. I wanted it to rain."

Abby perched next to her on the rock and gazed out at the sea, shimmering in evening sunlight, perfectly placid. The sight was so gorgeous and peaceful that she felt a little of it imbue her, giving her the courage or perhaps the recklessness to ask, "Were you close to her, as a child?"

"Your grandmother?" Laura took another sip of her drink, frowning slightly. "Truthfully? Not really. Not at all, towards the end. Not this end," she clarified, even though Abby had known what she'd meant. "The other one. Before I left. Things went pretty far south then."

It was the perfect opportunity to ask why she'd left all those years ago, but as usual Abby couldn't quite form the words. She didn't think she could handle more knowledge, more grief.

"But I still miss her," Laura continued quietly. "Which is kind of a bitch."

"Yeah." Abby laughed sadly. "I took her for granted, I think, growing up. I resented her a lot of the time for not—well, for not being my mother."

Laura's expression remained neutral as she murmured, "Understandable."

"She did her best. I know that. Sometimes it was great. She found things funny just at the right moment." Even now Abby could imagine Mary's great, big belly laugh, how she'd hold her sides as if to keep the laughter in. "She could always make me smile, even when I didn't want to."

"Yeah." Laura's eyes were looking a little bright. "She had a sense of humor, did Mum. Especially before . . ." She trailed off, looking away, and Abby filled it in.

"Before your dad died?" Laura nodded, her face still averted. "Do you still miss him?" Abby didn't know where the question came from—somewhere deep inside, surfacing unexpectedly.

"I try not to think of him, to be honest," Laura answered. "Easier that way."

"Yes, I suppose I know what you mean."

"Noah's dad?" Laura guessed, and Abby nodded.

"Yes, although . . ." She didn't talk about Ben for a whole lot of reasons. "It wasn't as simple a relationship as . . . well, as it might have seemed." A simple tragedy, a golden, gleaming life cut abruptly short. No, not quite like that.

"It's never simple, is it?" Laura returned on a sigh. She rested her chin in her hand, her half-empty glass dangling from her fingertips. "I didn't think I'd miss Mum so much, to be honest." Abby didn't answer, because she sensed her mother had more to say. "I also thought I'd have more time," she added quietly. "Although I'm not sure I would have used it. What I would have said. So much time had passed. . . ." Her breath came out in a weary gust. "I wasn't so unrealistic as to expect some sort of sappy reunion, but . . ."

"Gran was expecting it, maybe," Abby said. "She was so pleased you'd come back. That's something, at least."

"Maybe." Laura didn't look convinced.

"I mean it," Abby said, wanting to comfort her mother now, to see her forehead smooth, her eyes lose that clouded look. "She really was."

Laura gave her a brief, unhappy smile. "I'll take your word for it."

"You should." Abby took a sip of her G&T. Two sips and she was already starting to feel a little tipsy. "It's so beautiful here. Makes me wonder why I didn't want to come back."

"I know what you mean. People come here for holiday, after all. And while the villagers can gossip like it's a professional sport, they're also some of the kindest people I've ever known. Most of them," she qualified, making Abby wonder. "It's just the damn memories that are so hard." Laura slid her a sideways glance. "I'm guessing it can't have been easy for you, growing up on your own, with only your gran for company."

Abby shifted on the rock, uncomfortable with this moment of honest perception. "It had its challenges."

"That's very diplomatic of you." Laura stared straight out at the sea. "Look, I know you're angry with me. You've a right to be angry with me. And I know my mother was more of a mum to you than I ever was. More of a mum to you than she was to me, as well, not that I'm bitter about that. Not really."

It was too much to absorb all at once. "Why wasn't she a mum to you?" Abby asked.

"I was always my father's favorite. I think she resented that. And when he got ill, it consumed her, and then his death . . ." She shrugged. "Death sucks, basically. It throws you for a loop for . . . well, forever. I don't think my mother ever recovered. I'm not sure I did." She let out a ragged laugh. "But let's not talk about that, please. I don't think I can handle it, not on top of everything else."

"Noah asked me if she was in heaven. I didn't know what to say."

"She used to go to church, you know. Every Sunday until my father died." Laura pursed her lips. "Then she decided she didn't have much use for God. Can't say I blamed her."

"I hope He has some use for her now," Abby said in an awful attempt at a joke.

"Who knows? I can't think about the hereafter. The here is hard enough."

They both lapsed into silence; in the distance Abby could hear a child's laughter, making her think guiltily of Noah. How long had they been out here? What if he'd woken up alone? She rose from their perch on the rock. "I should go check on Noah."

"Yes, you probably should."

"Are you coming . . . ?"

Laura hefted her glass, still half-full. "I think I'll stay out here for a while. Have a sneaky cigarette." She smiled, but it didn't reach her eyes. Abby noticed now; her mother's smiles had changed a little, over the last week. Some *had* reached her eyes.

"If you're sure," she said, not really wanting to leave her alone, and Laura nodded.

"I'm sure." She paused, the glass halfway to her lips. "Thanks, though, Abby."

Startled, Abby paused. "For what?"

Laura just smiled, shaking her head, and drained her glass.

8

Laura

SHE HATED FUNERALS. SHE hated everything about them, from the sickly-sweet smell of the funeral flowers and the cloying odor of incense to the muted hush of people gathered to grieve who didn't know what to say. And the clothes—would you ever wear something you'd worn to a funeral again, except to another funeral? Death polluted everything, a stink in your nostrils, a stone in your gut.

For her father's funeral, she'd worn a black dress of imitation crepe de chine that had felt scratchy and stiff. Her shoes had been too small and her mother had insisted on putting her hair into ringlets, so she looked like an oversized Shirley Temple with an attitude. It had been awful, every bit of it, and when she'd resisted, Mary, wiping tears from her eyes with one hand, had slapped her with the other.

This felt no better, even though Laura had control of her clothes and hair. It had been a week since Mary's death, an endless week to wade through, each moment a mire. The stifling silence of the house, the awkward conversation with the vicar, a kindly enough man in his thirties who had four parishes in addition to Hartley-by-the-Sea's and had never actually met Mary.

"She used to go to church," Laura had said, rather lamely. "A long time ago."

Abby had suggested they have the funeral service at the crematorium rather than at the church, but Laura had been adamant. Mary had been a churchgoer, once upon a time, and funerals at the crem were awful. For heaven's sake, you could *see* the smokestack towering above the place. At the end of the service they pushed a button and the casket went down a conveyor belt and through a curtain. You could practically hear the flames crackling.

But having the funeral at the church meant talking to the vicar, and choosing hymns, and sharing memories of Mary that he could reference in the eulogy. Laura had struggled to come up with anything she wanted the man to mention in front of a crowd of villagers. It had been Noah and, more surprisingly, Simon who had come to the rescue. Noah had told of the boiled sweets she'd kept in a tin on a high shelf in the linen cupboard for when he'd been "really, really good" and Simon, his voice toneless, had said how Mary had been respected by everyone in the village "for her honesty and plain speaking." Well, that much was certainly true. Mary had never shied away from speaking her mind.

You're sixteen with your whole life ahead of you, and you want to tie yourself down with some tosser's baby?

Yep. Pretty much.

Abby had volunteered a few bits too, memories of when Mary had come to school and yelled at her teacher for calling her fussy because she didn't like bananas for her fruit snack. Another time she'd waited by the gate and clipped a boy round the ear who had been giving Abby grief. Those memories made Laura both smile and wince; Mary hadn't done those things for her, and Laura was the one who should have been doing them for Abby. A double dose of regret.

They'd gotten there in the end with the funeral arrangements, and the news had filtered out through the village, so the casseroles and cards started coming in, some merely dropped off at the door and others brought inside, with hugs and sad smiles and murmured words. Gossipy though they might be, the people of Hartley-by-the-Sea had good hearts. Laura couldn't fault them. Her unwillingness to return home hadn't been about the people there, not really. It had been about her. Her sadness. Her stupid choices. And maybe one true tosser.

Since Mary was a lifelong Cumbrian, even if her parents had moved to the village from Liverpool, she had a traditional Cumbrian funeral. No filing in behind the vicar and sitting sedately in rows. No, they did it properly, from the lych-gate, the church bell tolling dolefully as they walked in a silent procession all the way down the church lane. As if in obedience to Auden, the sun had packed up behind a thick bank of clouds, and the air was as chilly as a February morning.

They made an uncertain assembly, the four of them, Simon in a shiny suit and a ridiculously narrow tie, Abby holding Noah's hand, looking pale and shapeless in a baggy black dress, and Laura trying to appear cool and remote in black crepe Prada, sheer tights, and high heels. She felt overdressed, which was ridiculous, but she half wished she'd chosen something a little less stylish. A couple of cousins she vaguely remembered meeting as a child had come from Liverpool; they shuffled in beside them after a round of awkward I-don't-know-you-but-I'm-related-to-you type greetings.

Quite a lot of villagers had come, offering hugs and cheeks pressed alarmingly firmly to Laura's as they murmured how much they'd liked Mary, how much they'd miss her. That was an odd thing about someone dying; you learned everyone else's perception of the person. Since Mary had died, Laura had discovered she'd done the church flowers every Sunday, up until she'd had her first heart attack, even though she'd stopped attending church thirty years earlier.

"Did you know that?" Laura had asked Abby, and her daughter had shaken her head.

But why should either of them know that much about Mary? They'd both busted out of Hartley-by-the-Sea in their teens, coming back only when Mary was ill and in need of help, a shadow of her former self. For the first time Laura wished—almost—that she'd stayed around longer. Gotten to know her mother, and maybe even her daughter, a bit more. But that had been impossible then and half of it was impossible now.

In a slow, shuffling procession they followed the casket with its six professional pallbearers into the church, and Laura sank into the first row with a tiny sigh of relief. At least now she wouldn't feel so much on show. Glancing discreetly behind her, she watched as the rows of the church filled up with mourners. It seemed like at least half the village had come out for Mary's funeral.

The service passed in a haze of numbness—prayers, hymns, and then a stilted eulogy by the vicar, who mentioned Mary's flower arranging and how the beach café was a "hub of the community." It hadn't been when Laura had been a child, but Abby was doing her best to make it so now. She'd decided not to cancel the toddler morning on Tuesday, something Laura was rather keen to avoid.

She glanced at Abby, who was holding Noah's hand, her eyes bright, her lips trembling. Even Simon was looking a little suspiciously bright-eyed, Laura noticed. Why was she such a hard-hearted shrew? Why did she just want to get out of here, breathe some fresh air, yank off this stifling dress, and try to *forget*? That's what had worked before. That was the only thing she'd found that worked. Forget the grief. Ignore the pain. Move on.

The vicar wound up his eulogy, and then with a creak of joints and pews, they were all standing again. Four verses of "Amazing Grace" and finally, thankfully, they were processing out again. The pallbearers whisked the casket away, and Laura watched the hearse steal down the church drive with a weird pang. So that was that. Mary wanted to be cremated and so it would be done back at the crematorium; next week they'd pick up her ashes in a tasteful little urn. Death was a strange business.

The ladies of the church had organized a lunch of sandwiches and lemonade in the church hall, on account of Mary's flower arranging, and Laura stiffly circulated amidst the crowd of people, most of whom she semirecognized, and managed a few awkward and stilted conversations. Someone handed her a plate of sandwiches of wilted cucumber and cream cheese and a glass of lukewarm lemonade; she murmured her thanks even though she had no appetite.

The hall smelled like old coffee and sweaty feet, no doubt from the decades of coffee mornings and Cub Scout meetings that had been held there. Laura had briefly been a Brownie, enjoying the crisp brown uniform and yellow sash, the myriad of possibilities in the badge book—looking at all those badges, she'd felt as if the world was a shining and wonderful place that could be explored through Girl Guiding; one term in, her mother had sputtered in outrage at the subscription fees—fifteen pounds—and taken Laura out. She could hardly begrudge her mother that small act now; fifteen pounds had been a substantial sum back then, and in any case, it was her funeral. She couldn't begrudge her mother anything right then. She didn't want to.

"Hello, Laura."

She turned, stiffening instinctively at the sound of sympathy in the woman's voice. Gingery blond hair, freckles, a stern expression. It all rang a faint bell, but Laura couldn't come up with a name. The woman supplied one.

"Juliet. Juliet Bagshaw. You probably don't remember, but you stayed at my bed-and-breakfast a few years ago now. Tarn House, on the high street."

"Oh. Right." Yes, she remembered. A trip back to Hartley-by-the-Sea for Abby's sixteenth birthday. Because, for a little while, she'd felt tearfully maternal, remembering how she'd been at sixteen and wanting something different for her daughter. Something better.

Laura didn't know what she'd been expecting that weekend—a mother-daughter heart-to-heart, really?—but she hadn't gotten it. She'd come bearing gifts and good intentions, a little tearful in the hopes of having some reconciliation, and Abby had barely spoken to her.

The evening of her birthday Abby had informed her she was going out with friends, and Laura had ended up watching *Strictly Come Dancing* with Mary, both of them silent and morose. The next day had been even more stilted, with Abby opening Laura's gift of a diamond-encrusted heart pendant stony-faced. Laura had left soon after.

"You did a good fry-up, as I recall," she told Juliet, and a smile flickered across the other woman's face. She was eyeing Laura with a tad too much compassion and understanding. Laura didn't like it.

"Thank you. I am known for my fry-ups."

"Well, then." Laura tried for a smile. "Did you know Mary?"

"Everyone knew Mary, I think. The café's been an institution of the village, don't you think?"

"I suppose it has."

"Abby's done a good job of it," Juliet continued quietly. "Brought it up a bit. The art showing last spring was a fun do. She exhibited my sister Lucy's paintings. Sold a few, as well."

Laura just nodded, too tired to drum up the enthusiasm that seemed required. Juliet gave her a small smile of sympathy in return, and Laura looked away. She just wanted this all to be over, so she could go back home and examine her feelings the way a dog licked its wounds. And preferably have a cigarette and a large gin and tonic.

"I know how hard it must be," Juliet said after a moment, and for a second Laura thought she must have spoken out loud, for Juliet to say such a thing. Thankfully she didn't think she had. "Actually," Juliet continued, "I don't know. But I can imagine. I think."

Laura, caught between wanting to dismiss the moment and feeling flayed by it, could not think of a suitable reply. Fortunately Juliet didn't seem to expect one. "I know it sounds trite, but I truly am sorry for your loss. I'll miss Mary."

But would she? Did she miss her mother? On one hand, yes, with a terrible ache. But that ache felt like emptiness—missing something she'd never had rather than something she'd lost. A different feeling entirely.

After murmuring a polite good-bye to Juliet, Laura had started moving towards the door, away from the milling crowds, when a woman stepped in front of her. Laura's mind stuttered to a halt, because the woman looked familiar, but she was too young to be a schoolmate. She was looking at Laura like she knew who she was, but then Laura supposed everyone here knew who she was. That was the unfortunate nature of the occasion.

"You don't know me," the woman said. "But I'm a friend of Abby's. I just wanted to say I'm sorry for your loss." She grimaced. "Which I'm sure is what everyone is saying."

Laura found a polite smile and pasted it on. "It doesn't make it any less sincere."

"I knew Mary. Not well, but . . ." The woman ducked her head, her smile vague, and something clicked inside Laura's head. She recognized that smile, the slide of dark hair as the woman ducked her head.

"Thank you for your kind words. What's your name?"

"Oh, sorry. I should have introduced myself. It's Claire. Claire West."

Laura didn't think her expression changed. Inwardly she was rapidly trying to reassemble her armor. Cool, remote hauteur. She'd been far too raw these last few days. "Claire," she said, simply to stall for time.

"Yes . . ." Claire was frowning. "You almost sound like you knew me."

"I knew your family, of course. I grew up here, after all." Her smile stretched thin. "But they moved a long time ago, didn't they?"

"Yes, about twelve years ago."

"Right." Laura eyed the door, longing for escape. She had a sudden image of the casket being bundled into the hearse, away, away, while they all milled about aimlessly, spouting pleasantries and picking bits of cucumber from their teeth, bumping into people she hoped never to see again. "I'm sorry," she said to Claire. "I just need a breath of fresh air."

Outside the air was cool and damp, the wind starting to gust from the sea. Big gray clouds billowed up on the horizon, and sunlight filtered through the spaces with the weird, hazy purplish light that promised rain in the not-too-distant future. Laura leaned against the doorway and breathed in great lungfuls of the cold, fresh air, wondering when she could leave. Was it like a wedding, when the bride and groom left first as everyone watched? Should she and Abby and Simon all quietly shuffle away, and then everyone would follow? Laura didn't know the protocol. The only other funeral she'd been to was her father's, and that, thankfully, was a blur.

Although not a complete blur. It was strange, the little things she remembered—the scratchy dress, the dusty smell of the church mixed with her mother's cheap and cloying perfume. She'd been fidgeting and Simon had been scuffing the floor with his shoes, but she'd been the one to get the cuff round the ear. She'd burned with indignation over that, all through the service—she hadn't even paid attention to what the vicar was saying, or her mother's tears.

The door creaked open behind her and Laura saw Simon come out, reaching for a crumpled packet of cigarettes from the inside pocket of his jacket. His suit was the same cheap, shiny material of his other suits, only in black; he wore a white button-down shirt with no undershirt and a skinny black tie. He looked, Laura thought dispassionately, exactly like what he was: a mobile phone salesman who liked to call himself a "sales executive" and tried to act far more important than he was or ever would be.

Feeling mean for the thought, Laura decided to be the first to wave the olive branch. "It was a nice service, wasn't it?"

Simon shrugged and blew out smoke. "It was okay."

His eyes, Laura noticed, were red. Poor spoiled mama's boy. Why hadn't he come round more when Mary had gotten ill? *Why hadn't she?*

"At least it's over. Funerals feel like something to be got through, to me."

Simon arched an eyebrow. "And now you're going to move on? Where to next, sis?"

Laura hesitated. "I'm not necessarily going anywhere." Although she still couldn't imagine staying.

"So you're going to stick around here? Hoping for a nice little packet of cash from Mum's inheritance?"

Laura hadn't even considered her mother's inheritance. "I doubt she had much, Simon. We were always skint growing up, and look at the café." She gestured vaguely towards the sheep pastures that rolled out to the sea.

"That's a bit harsh to our Abby and all the work she's done."

"It's nothing to do with her. She's worked hard, but the café needs a complete refurb." Laura sighed, tired of feeling as if she was offending everyone. "I should think that was obvious."

Simon's eyes narrowed. "Why did you come back, anyway? Run out of dosh?"

Laura thought of her little nest egg patiently waiting for her next move. "I'm not broke."

"Then why?"

Why indeed? At times like this, she wasn't sure she could answer. She certainly wasn't about to tell Simon how her life had fallen apart and she hadn't been able to stand the thought of papering over the emptiness once more. How, in the loneliness of her New York life, she'd hoped to strengthen the family ties she'd severed in one snip twenty years ago. "It just felt like it was time to come home, Simon," she said tiredly. "We should go back inside. Say our good-byes."

"Fine." Simon dropped his cigarette butt and crushed it under his heel. "I'm Mum's executor, you know. She had a will on file at the solicitor's in Whitehaven. I made an appointment for Tuesday."

Laura blinked, startled. She'd never even thought about a will. Mary had been more organized than she would have expected. "Do you know what it says?"

"No, but I imagine we'll split the café three ways: you, me, and Abby. Sell it up and we'll all get a tidy profit. Prime property right by the sea—it should go for half a million at least."

Laura winced, disgusted by his undisguised greed, and shocked at the thought of selling the café. They'd only just buried their mother, for heaven's sake. Or rather, cremated her. "I can't think about that yet."

"Can't you?" Simon smiled. "I think you could do with a cool hundred and fifty grand."

"I think you're forgetting about inheritance tax. And in any case Abby might not want to sell the café."

"Then she'll have to buy us out."

"There's no way she could do that—"

"Only fair."

Laura shook her head. She couldn't think about this. Not yet, anyway. She was too tired. "Leave it, Simon. At least until Tuesday."

Back inside, the good ladies of the church were wrapping up the soggy sandwiches, kindly meant for them to take home for their dinner, and Laura took them obediently, because to refuse them seemed churlish. Noah was leaning against Abby, half-asleep, and people were thankfully filing out with more hugs and murmured condolences.

Half an hour later it was all over, and they were back in the flat, the plastic-wrapped pile of soggy sandwiches on the kitchen table, Noah asleep on the sofa.

"I'll have to open the café tomorrow," Abby said as she kicked off her heels and stretched. She looked faded, as if the life had been leached out of her. Laura suspected she looked the same. "It's been closed for nearly a week. I can't afford any more loss of business."

Silently Laura noted the "I." "Okay," she said, and unwrapped the sandwiches. "You're not going to eat these, are you?"

Abby glanced at the pile of sandwiches, the bread damp, the cucumbers wilted, and grimaced. "No."

"Good," Laura said, and lobbed them into the bin. She paused, unsure how to move on from here. "I can help tomorrow, if you like. With the café."

Laura watched as a host of emotions chased across Abby's face. Finally she nodded. "Thanks."

Later, with the house quiet and everyone settling into sleep, Laura lay in bed, her knees bent, her feet jammed up against the bottom, and stared at the fluorescent star stickers that were starting to peel off the ceiling. It was silly to stay in this bed, but she couldn't make herself take her mother's room. Or maybe Abby should take it, since it was the biggest room, and Noah could have Abby's old room to himself. And she'd stay here, as some sort of penance for being a bad mother. A bad daughter. That seemed like the least she could do. The very least.

Tired of the poisonous mix of guilt and self-pity and knowing she wouldn't be able to sleep, Laura rose from bed and headed downstairs. She thought of stealing outside for a cigarette, but that was something else she was starting to feel guilty about. Her father had died of lung cancer, after all. She should switch back to e-cigarettes or maybe even that nicotine gum. Or nothing at all.

Downstairs she was just about to flick on the sitting room lights when she saw the small figure hunched on the sofa, knees drawn up to his chest.

"Noah?" He turned his head slightly but didn't say anything. Laura walked cautiously towards him. "What are you doing here?" He shrugged and she came to sit down beside him. She could see the traces of tears on his cheeks, and something tugged hard inside her. "Couldn't sleep?" she asked softly. "Me neither." Still nothing back, but then what was there really to say? Death sucked. Grieving was hard. Silently Laura put an arm around his thin shoulders. His body felt as fragile as a bird's and his back was sweaty. Her arm was at an awkward angle and nothing about the gesture felt natural, but even so, she stayed where she was. She had a feeling they both needed a hug.

9

Abby

OPENING THE CAFÉ FELT like pulling a plaster off a barely formed scab. The screech of the metal grills that covered the windows as they rolled up made Abby wince, as did the sunlight that came streaking through and showing the thin patina of dust that had settled everything; she'd barely been in the café for a week and it showed. At least she'd gotten rid of the old milk. The day's fresh milk was already outside the door, and the ice cream would be there shortly; a local supplier brought the baked goods that Abby kept under glass domes on the counter. She'd need to do a shop to get the fillings for the sandwiches and jacket potatoes on the menu; maybe she could ask Laura to do it. Her mother's offer of help had yet to materialize into anything concrete. As far as Abby knew, she was still asleep.

Twenty minutes later the café was mostly clean, the coffee brewing, and Abby felt a much-needed, albeit fragile sense of peace settle over her. Everything looked good, or as good as the café could look. A bit on the shabby side, yes, but Abby thought it was lovably shabby. The villagers were protective of their café, she knew. She'd heard more than one person snap back at a tourist who had been expecting fancy Frappuccinos and an evening menu worthy of a Michelin star or two.

Abby had just installed herself behind the till as two dog walkers came in for a cuppa. She slapped a smile on her face, glad that she didn't recognize them. She didn't think she could deal with too many conversations that centered on the offering and accepting of condolences. She wanted life to move on, even if she acknowledged it didn't happen that fast. It shouldn't, anyway, even if you wanted it to.

A little after ten Laura strolled in, looking casual and elegant in a pair of navy capris and a cream cashmere sweater that slid off one tanned shoulder. "How's it going?" she asked as she glanced around the mostly empty café. The dog walkers had tapered off and the pensioners who came in for their elevenses hadn't started yet.

"Fine," Abby answered briskly. "But if you want to be helpful, you could go into Whitehaven and do some shopping. I haven't got anything for the lunch rush."

Laura arched an eyebrow. "Is there much of a rush?"

"Yes, actually, there is. Especially on a sunny day like today."

"All right. Do you want to make a list?"

Abby nodded, surprised that her mother had accepted so quickly. For a reason she couldn't quite articulate, it made her uneasy. "We should probably talk about the future sometime," she said in a low voice, although the one customer in the café, Felicity Carmichael, was at least partially deaf. Every week she shouted her order a little bit louder. Abby reached for a pencil and a scrap of paper and started making a list.

"Yes, I suppose we should. Simon mentioned to me at the funeral that there's going to be a meeting at the solicitor's to discuss the will."

Abby looked up, shocked. "The will?"

"You didn't know, either? Apparently Mary made one. No one knows what it says, though." Laura paused. "Simon seems to think we'll sell the café and split the proceeds three ways."

"Sell it? But . . ." *We can't.* The words remained unformed. They could, if Simon had anything to do with it. He'd want the money. And yet the thought was awful. She'd poured everything she'd had into the café. What on earth would she do without it?

"It might be for the best," Laura said in a gentler tone. "We'd all get a decent bit of dosh, be able to move on."

"You think I want to move on?" A lightning streak of anger blazed through Abby. "You think I want to unsettle Noah again, start over *again*? He's happy here. *We're* happy here. Just because you scarper at the first sign of trouble—"

Laura sighed. "Don't, Abby. Not again."

"Fine, but I still want to stay. I'm happy here. I've done a lot of work on the café, you know, even if it might not seem like it to you—"

"I know you have."

"And," Abby continued, unable to let go of her righteous indignation, "I actually like living in Hartley-by-the-Sea. I know I left once, but I came back for a reason. I have friends here, and so does Noah." Even if sometimes living in a crowded flat by the beach, away from everyone else in the village, felt a little lonely. Even if at times she wondered if there was anything more to look forward to. Didn't everybody?

The point was, she'd built something here in Hartley-by-the-Sea. Something small and fragile, yes, but still *something*. "I don't want to sell it," she said flatly, and handed her mother the list.

Laura glanced down at it, silently reading the items. Ham. Roast beef. Cheddar. Mayo. Tomatoes. Prawn salad. "We'll discuss it Tuesday, I suppose," she said, and turned to go.

The possibility was like a stitch in Abby's side for the rest of the day, making it hard to breathe. *Sell the café*. How much would it go for? Where would she live? She could stay in Hartley-by-the-Sea, she supposed, and get some sort of other job . . . but what? What on earth was she qualified for, having dropped out before she'd gotten her BA? Waitressing? But she didn't want to waitress. She wanted to run her own business, like she'd been doing, more or less, since she'd come back here two years ago. Except it never had actually been her business to run.

The thought of losing everything she'd been starting to build made her feel sick with fear. *Why is everything taken away from me?* It was the cry of a child, but Abby still felt like screaming it. She couldn't lose the café. *It wasn't fair.* Another child's cry.

Right before lunchtime Laura came back with armfuls of groceries, which she dumped in the tiny kitchen in back of the café. Abby hurried to help her, but Laura was already unloading the food, seeming to know where everything went. Abby stood there uncertainly, a bit discomfited by her mother's air of calm efficiency.

"I can stay," Laura said as she put away several packs of sliced ham in the laboring fridge. It would need to be replaced one of these days, probably soon. All the electrics were dodgy and had been for a while. The money to fix it all simply wasn't there. "Help out with that lunch rush."

"You don't need to." The refusal came instinctively, before Abby had thought it through. "It's not that busy, really."

"But it might be, when it gets closer to lunchtime. How are you going to manage on your own? Mum manned the till while you made the food, didn't she?"

"Yes, but . . ." There didn't seem to be anything Abby could say. *I don't want you in the kitchen, taking over.* "All right," she finally said, a tad ungraciously, and left the kitchen while Laura continued to unpack.

Actually, she did need the help. Even though it had turned cloudy and cool, it was June and not raining and so people came to the beach in droves. Laura was kept busy making jacket potatoes and toasties, which, Abby noticed, were perfectly turned out, golden and crisp. It was silly to feel threatened, she knew, but she felt it all the same. She didn't think there was room for both her and Laura in the café, not in the long term. Would her mother start trying to take over? She'd turned her nose up at the café already, which stung more than a little. Abby had spent a lot of time and effort brightening the place up.

As the lunch rush died down, Claire came in, smiling in her shy way. "I thought I'd see how you were doing. Dan's manning the shop."

Claire worked at the post office shop and was dating its owner, Dan Trenton. Like Abby, she'd left the village for university, coming back only a year ago. She and Abby had become friends through the pub quiz on Thursday evenings, a staple of both of their social lives.

"I'm okay," Abby said, and began to mindlessly wipe at the countertop, chasing crumbs.

"It's got to be hard," Claire said quietly.

"Yes."

"Sorry. Do you not want to talk about it? I can understand that." Claire hesitated and Abby kept wiping even though there were no more crumbs. "Do you want to go for a walk? The sun's out."

"I can't leave. . . ."

"Yes, you can." Laura had appeared behind Abby, as silent as a cat. She was drying her hands on a dish towel. "Sounds like a great idea to me. You need to pick up Noah soon, anyway. I can manage here."

Everything in Abby resisted. She didn't want Laura taking over the café, nudging her out. Not even a little.

"Great," Claire said, smiling. Clueless.

Abby knew to refuse now would have been the height of pointless ingratitude. And she probably could do with some fresh air. She certainly felt out of sorts, at any rate. "Thanks," she muttered, and grabbed her coat.

They didn't talk until they were walking along the promenade, the waves crashing against the breakers and sending spray flying up, the sunlight streaming from between the clouds and catching the drops, making them sparkle.

"Okay, so I know I'm not the most emotionally attuned person out there," Claire began, "but I sensed some tension back there."

"Yeah." Abby dug her hands into the pockets of her coat, the sea breeze whipping her hair about her face. "I suppose there is."

"Is it over your grandmother? Or . . . ?"

"Just everything. We never had a relationship, you know." She glanced at Claire, who was looking at her with far too much sympathy. "I'm not even sure why she's back. She talks about it being time and making amends, but honestly she's not making much effort." And neither was she. "Maybe you just can't mend some relationships," she said on a sigh. "They're too broken."

"Maybe," Claire agreed after a moment. "But it's worth trying, surely?"

Was it? It was a question Abby hadn't really asked herself, mainly because she couldn't even imagine what a mended relationship with her mother would look like. They were never going to go all girlie and giggle and paint each other's nails. What was she hoping for?

"I don't know what I feel," she confessed to Claire. "About anything. Or maybe it's just I feel too much. I'm sad about Gran dying, but I'm angry with her too, for dying in the first place. She was only seventy-two. If she'd taken better care of herself . . ."

"I think we're always angry with people for dying. It just doesn't feel fair."

"No, I suppose it doesn't." Abby slumped onto a bench overlooking the sea and Claire joined her. "And I don't know if I want my mother here. I was fine without her." Mostly. "And she's so smug and interfering—you don't know her, but she always acts condescending towards me. She has since I was a child. I need to get over it—I know I'm being a bit petty about it—but it's hard."

"I think we always have a tendency to act childishly with our parents. I know I do." Claire's mother, Abby knew, was snobby and overbearing. She had yet to darken the door of the café, preferring to eat out in ritzier places like Keswick or Cockermouth.

"I feel like she brings out the worst in me," Abby admitted. "But that's my fault, not hers. I just go into this prickly self-defense mode, like a hedgehog." She laughed, the sound carried away on the wind.

"Also understandable. You don't want to get hurt again."

Abby blinked, startled and more than a little discomfited by her friend's perception. Appalled, really. Was that what was going on? She was afraid to open up to Laura, to let her close, because she thought she might leave once more, hurt her all over again? Maybe you never stopped being a child. Never stopped longing for your mum.

"Maybe" was all she could manage. Her irritation with Laura had left her like a gust of wind, blowing in and out, the door slamming behind it. "Maybe I don't."

A little while later she walked up the high street to fetch Noah from school, her mind still swirling with the possibilities Claire's irritating perception had opened up inside her, making her feel edgy. She walked fast, as if she could outrun herself, or at least the angry maelstrom of her thoughts. She'd just started sorting herself out, making her way in this village, and Laura's presence was upsetting everything. The last thing she wanted was to start depending on her mother, actually caring about her, only to have her scarper once more. And what about the café? Perhaps they'd both have to scarper, if Simon had his way. Everything was uncertain.

"Abby? You all right?" The question, posed by Andrea, a kindly mum who was also heading up to school, had Abby remembering the last time she'd been asked that Cumbrian question, two weeks ago, right before she'd come back to find Laura in the café.

Abby gave her a quick, unconvincing smile. "Yes, I'm okay. Just took the beach road a bit too fast." She smiled, tensing inwardly at the look of naked compassion on Andrea's face.

"Sorry about your gran. I would have come to the funeral, but I had Eva with me. . . ."

"It's okay. There was a good crowd there. We certainly felt the whole village's support." The sentences came quickly, meaningless and yet sincere at the same time. Abby started walking and Andrea fell in step beside her.

"Grief is hard," Andrea said quietly. "That's how I felt after Anthony left, even though he didn't die." She grimaced wryly. "Though sometimes I wish he had."

"I'm sure." Abby knew Andrea had been married and had a child, and then her husband had done a runner. She didn't know much more; Eva was three years older than Noah, a worldly-wise Year Three to his wide-eyed Reception year.

"Are you looking forward to the school fete next month?" Andrea asked brightly. "Eva loves it. She's going as Elsa for the costume parade. What else?" She rolled her eyes in supposed solidarity, but Abby came up blank.

"Elsa?"

"You know, *Frozen*?" Andrea laughed. "How have you missed it?"

"I have a boy," Abby answered with a wry smile. "We're more into Transformers and Pokémon."

"Ah. Right. What's Noah going as, then? For the costume parade?"

Abby hadn't even thought about the costume parade or the school fete. They'd watched the costume parade in years past, standing by the railings, enjoying the show of elaborate homemade costumes. Last year someone had been the TARDIS, walking in mincing steps in a huge cardboard contraption painted like a police box. Noah had been enchanted. And now he was meant to take part in it? Abby had a feeling buying a costume from the shop would win her the Bad Mother Award. "I'm not sure yet," she hedged. "What with everything going on, I haven't thought . . ."

"Of course, I'm sorry." Andrea slapped her hand to her forehead. "Sorry. Silly question."

"No, I need to think about it." Or go to a shop. Normally she'd have gotten excited about a project like that; Noah would have been buzzing with ideas and she'd do her best, armed with craft scissors and fabric glue, to make his dream a reality. The fact that he hadn't even mentioned it gave her a little pang. Her poor boy. Even though he'd skipped happily enough to school today, Abby knew he was still hurting. They all were.

They'd reached the school yard and Abby took up her usual position against the wall, away from the knot of Reception mothers who were talking loudly about the Pilates class it looked like they'd all gone to, judging by the amount of spandex and Lycra they were wearing. From day one of school that year, when all their precious four-year-olds had trotted off to class, a knot of "cool" mums had formed: the twenty- and thirtysomething version of the in girls back in secondary school.

Abby had never been an in girl, never even close. She'd had one best friend in primary school, Chrissa, who had been her partner in PE, her Saturday playdate, her comrade navigating the heaving crowd of the lunchroom. She and Chrissa had depended on each other utterly; whenever Chrissa had been off ill, Abby had drifted around, anchorless and alone, sitting by herself at lunch, left over at games time, unpicked, watching everyone else. She and Chrissa would have faced secondary school together and emerged triumphant if Chrissa's family hadn't decided to emigrate to Australia the summer before Year Seven had started.

The utter desolation Abby had felt walking alone into a school of nearly two thousand pupils could not be underestimated. Everyone from primary had already paired up with a bestie, and Abby had done her best to attach herself to a twosome, but girls at that age—well, she was glad she had a son. Third wheel would have been putting it mildly.

She'd spent the next seven years trying to make herself invisible to the threatening masses of cool kids. There had been a handful of them, the detritus of Year Seven that drifted through the entirety of their secondary schooling, clinging together as best as they could and hopefully ignored by everyone else. Abby's best friend, the girl she had counted on to sit with at lunch and partner with at PE, was named Li Deng, a Korean girl who had only a handful of English words. And so Abby had survived, and gone off to uni at Liverpool, determined to do better.

Standing here, watching the cool mums, Abby felt a little bit like she did in Year Seven. She supposed she'd always felt that way, sometimes more, sometimes less, throughout university and adulthood: always on the outside, watching other people navigate life with seamless ease while she stood still or stumbled around. Part of it came from growing up with only a tetchy grandmother for company, and knowing that neither of her parents had wanted her. Coming back to Hartley-by-the-Sea had made her confront it all over again, and just when she thought she'd put it to rest, Laura came back and stirred it all up once more. She could never get away from her childhood hang-ups. Maybe no one could.

"Hey." Meghan approached her, a paper bag with a bottle sticking out of it in one hand. "This is for you. Everyone will be making you casseroles, but I reckoned this is what you really need."

Abby took the bag and glanced at the bottle of Absolut with a laugh. "Thanks. I could down a few shots right now." And she was going to look like a right lush, walking down the high street with her five-year-old son, a bottle of vodka in one hand.

"That bad, huh?" Meghan nodded soberly. "Well, let me know when you want to have a moan or a drink. Or two. Or three." She grinned. "I'm always up for it."

"I'm sure you are." Meghan had always liked her nights out at the pub, and Abby couldn't blame her. She had a hard home life, with a dad who had been out of the picture since she'd been in primary school and a mum who was a complete invalid. "Maybe in a bit. I need to focus on the café and Noah now."

"And what about the mum?"

"Her too, I suppose. I don't know how long she'll be staying, though." It felt like an addendum she had to add, a reminder to herself not to get invested. If they sold the café and all ended up with a decent bit of money, Laura would most likely swan off again. The thought brought a weird mix of relief and disappointment.

The doors to the Infants opened and the children swarmed out; Noah looked pale, but at least he was smiling as he came towards Abby, and her heart pulsed with both love and fear. She wanted so badly to shield him from the hurts of life, the kind of pain and loneliness that no one had shielded her from. But you couldn't. No matter how hard you tried, you couldn't, and that hurt most of all.

"Hey, sweetheart." She settled for ruffling his hair even though she wanted to pull him in for a hug, feel his bony elbows and knobbly knees press against her. "How was school?"

"Okay. Did you know cows have four stomachs?"

"I'm not sure. Are you learning that in science?"

"Yes, and sheep and giraffes have four stomachs too. It helps with their digestion."

"So it would."

He chatted away to her all the way back to the café and Abby walked next to him, glad for the steady stream of cheerful babble, his enthusiasm a much-needed balm. She'd much rather think about the digestion of a giraffe than all the uncertainties she faced back at the café.

"Mummy, look!" Noah grabbed her arm, nearly making her drop the bottle of vodka tucked self-consciously under her arm.

"What is it, Noah——"

"They look like birds!"

Abby tilted her head to the sky, the sun warm on her face, and watched as several paragliders drifted across the hazy blue sky, graceful and free. She couldn't imagine wanting to take your life in your hands that way; she'd never been a thrill seeker. How did you even land? She pictured concussions and broken bones and inwardly shuddered.

Yet for a moment, watching the gliders head towards the horizon, Noah standing enthralled next to her, both their faces tipped to the sun and sky, Abby wondered what it would feel like to be that free, soaring through the air. What it would feel like to rise above all the petty concerns and fly.

10

Laura

LAURA STOOD AT THE start of the rutted dirt road that led to Bega Farm, the evening sunlight glinting off the alarmingly deep mud puddles. Juliet had told her she could walk, and Laura had assumed that meant real roads. She was wearing suede heels, which in retrospect had been an idiotic wardrobe choice, but she'd wanted to look nice. More important, she'd wanted to look like herself. A pair of linen trousers, a silk blouse, proper jewelry, and heels. As she'd put each item on, she'd felt a little bit of her dented confidence restored.

Yesterday afternoon, when she'd been minding the café, Juliet Bagshaw had come in and invited her to dinner at her boyfriend Peter Lanford's house. Laura had been about to refuse out of instinct when something had made her pause. She remembered Peter Lanford from school. He'd been one of the farming lads, those big, burly boys who had had to cram their bodies under the desks and scarpered from school as soon as they'd finished their O levels.

Peter had been the silent type, but Laura had always thought he'd seemed gentle. He'd defended a tearful Year Seven from the teasing of several hapless Year Ten goons, and it had taken only one terse statement for them all to fall guiltily silent.

And so, to her own shock and discomfort, she'd said yes. And now she was here, having to walk what looked like a mile of muddy, rutted road in her heels, clutching the best bottle of wine that the post office shop had to offer, which wasn't saying all that much.

That had been another shock—seeing Claire West at the post office. Laura had stopped in the doorway, tempted to bolt. "You work here?" she'd said, surprise in every syllable, and Claire had nodded happily.

"Yes, I've been working here for the last year. I just passed my postal assistant training." She'd shared a complicit and rather tender look with the man behind the till, a man nearly as wide as he was tall, with tattooed arms and a fierce scowl. As unlikely as it seemed, something was clearly going on there.

Laura still couldn't fathom any of it. Claire West, rich, privileged, born of the aristocracy of Hartley-by-the-Sea, was working in the post office shop and dating its owner? What would her parents have to say about that? But no, she couldn't think that way. Wouldn't. And so she'd bought her bottle of decent-ish plonk and left without chatting much to Claire at all.

She started down the road, edging past the puddles, swearing when a bit of mud splashed onto her heels. Now she was going to look ridiculous. Except she'd already look ridiculous to Peter and Juliet, who would probably be wearing jumpers and jeans while Laura swanned in with her designer gear. What had she been thinking? She'd just wanted a little bit of herself back, something small to steady herself, remind herself of who she was. Who she'd been able to make herself be.

The sound of a car's motor had Laura practically leaping to the side of the road. An extremely battered Land Rover emerged from around the curve, Peter at the wheel, a large sheepdog sticking his head out the passenger window. He barked crazily when he saw Laura, and she pressed back against the fence, nettles brushing her leg and stinging her even through her trousers. She sucked in a hard breath.

"I thought you might want a lift," Peter said as he stopped the car.

"Juliet said you'd walk, but it's a fair bit." He glanced at her shoes and a tiny smile quirked the corner of his mouth.

"This road should come with a warning."

"I was just going to say the same about your shoes."

"Fair point." Gingerly Laura walked around to the passenger door. "What about the dog?"

"Jake? He can go in the back. Unless you want him in your lap?" Humor glinted in his eyes and Laura felt herself grinning; it was like exercising a muscle that had started to atrophy, a painful but necessary stretch.

"Maybe next time, when we know each other better."

"I'll hold you to that." Peter opened the driver's door and whistled, and the dog obediently leaped out and jumped in the back of the Rover.

Laura slid into the car, half-wondering if she would have fared better on the road. The ripped seat was covered with an old plaid blanket that was awash in dog fur, and the footwell was a sea of rubbish—paper cups, crumpled packets of crisps and biscuits, and a map that looked like it had been half-folded before the driver lost patience with lining up the endless creases and squashed it instead.

"Sorry," Peter said. "I suppose I should have tidied up."

"It's no bother," Laura assured him, and nudged a browning banana peel away with her toe.

The drive to Bega Farm was bumpy enough to have her grabbing onto the car door handle, but it was beautiful, the road snaking along the bottom of a steep hill before rising to a vantage point that had the sparkling sea on one side and the cluster of cottages and terraced houses of the village on the other. A few sheep milled about in the field closest to the house, bleating plaintively.

"They'll really be putting up a racket in a couple of weeks," Peter remarked as he parked in front of the farmhouse, a low, rambling whitewashed stone house that looked battered by both wind and age. "When their lambs are taken."

"You take their lambs?"

Peter eyed her askance. "Aren't you Cumbrian? Don't you know the male lambs go to the slaughterhouse?" He sounded both amused and incredulous.

"I suppose I did." She'd grown up with sheep farming all around her, but she hadn't thought about it much. "Still seems kind of sad, though." She glanced at a frisky little black lamb that was gamboling merrily through the pasture. "They're so cute."

"Tasty too," Peter replied, and she couldn't help but laugh.

He opened the door to the house, stepping out of the way so she could go in first, and Laura ducked her head to avoid hitting the low stone lintel before stepping straight into a cozy kitchen, complete with a large Aga range cooker built into the old fireplace and a worn sofa with stuffing coming out of its cushions pushed up against one wall. The room was messy and cluttered in a comfortable way, with houseplants on the windowsill and an assortment of muddy Welly boots kicked off by the door. It was cozy and homely and very real, with no pretension at all. Laura wished again that she'd chosen something else to wear.

"You made it," Juliet said as she came into the room, predictably wearing the jeans and jumper Laura had expected. She eyed Laura's outfit for one beady moment but said nothing. Laura held out the wine.

"Thank you for inviting me."

"No trouble." Juliet took the wine without comment and Laura felt slightly chastised.

"Thank you for the wine," Peter said, and she felt a little better. Juliet took getting used to, she supposed, but Laura thought she'd like her. Mostly.

"Something smells delicious," she remarked. There was a deep Le Creuset pot, ancient and well used, bubbling away on the top of the Aga.

"Coq au vin," Juliet said. "But I can't take any credit. Peter's as much of a cook as I am, if not more."

Laura watched, trying not to feel envious, as they exchanged loved-up glances. Juliet found a corkscrew from a drawer and handed it to Peter.

"So how long have you two been a couple?" Laura asked, sitting on a stool at the kitchen island, a huge block of scarred oak. Peter fetched a couple of glasses from a cupboard and began to pour the wine.

"A year and a half, or thereabouts," Juliet answered.

"Only a year and a half? You seem like an old married couple."

"Nope, just old," Juliet said a little tightly, and Laura had the distinct feeling she'd just put her foot in it. Was Juliet waiting for a ring? She didn't seem the type.

Peter handed her a glass of wine. "With many more years ahead of us, I hope," he said, smiling, and Laura liked him for it. Of course, Peter Lanford was completely not her type. She'd always favored younger men for relationships, if she could even call the transactions she had with the opposite sex relationships. She wasn't looking for a father figure, or someone she would yearn to love or trust. Nope, all she'd ever wanted was a little companionship, a little fun, a little sex. And that's all she'd ever gotten. A *little*.

"Hear, hear," she murmured, and took a sip of wine. It was quite pleasant, sitting in the cozy kitchen, drinking wine and chatting more or less easily—Peter was easy, Juliet not so much. Half a glass in, Laura started to loosen up.

"So what's your story, Juliet?" she asked, even though the last thing she wanted was anyone turning that question back on her. "How did you end up in Hartley-by-the-Sea?"

Juliet looked trapped by the question for a few seconds, but then she shrugged. "I was in the hospitality industry and then I cashed out and decided to start up my own business. I bought Tarn House and did it up as a bed-and-breakfast." She paused. "That's the short version." Her tone suggested the long one was not up for discussion. "What about you?" she asked, flipping the question back at Laura just as she'd feared. "What's your story?"

Laura gestured to the bottle on the counter. She needed a refill for this. "I imagine my story is known by most of Hartley-by-the-Sea."

"Only the short version."

"And that's the only version you're getting." Laura nodded her thanks at Peter for the top-up. "But humor me. What *is* the short version, in your opinion?"

"Well." Juliet eyed her over the rim of her glass, and Laura saw Peter start to look a little wary. "I'd say it's this. You grew up in the village, worked at the café, were a nice enough girl, if rather quiet, and then you got pregnant."

"That's the beginning, anyway," Laura agreed. Even having Juliet say that much made her feel tense and exposed, and yet she wanted to hear more. Needed to know what people were saying about her, at least the gist.

"And the rest is that you saw it through for a couple of years, wheeling Abby around in a pram, staying tight-lipped about who the father was, and then one day you scarpered." She paused, and the silence that descended on the room felt taut. "And only came back a handful of times since then."

"Juliet," Peter said quietly, an entreaty, or perhaps a warning. Juliet was looking levelly at Laura, and Laura made herself look back.

"And what about now?" she asked. "What is everyone saying now?"

"That you must be down on your luck and you've come back to Hartley-by-the-Sea because you have nowhere else to go, because that's the only reason you'd ever come back." Juliet paused. "Are they right?"

Laura broke Juliet's gaze, unable to take any more. She stared into her wine instead; she was well into her second glass. "Not quite," she said, although she didn't know how truthful she was being. "I got fired, it's true, but I could have gone somewhere else, if I really wanted to."

"So why didn't you?"

"Because at some point you've got to go home," Laura answered.

"Not necessarily."

"Or keep running," she finished. "I decided to go home."

Juliet cocked her head in acknowledgment, and Laura thought she saw, amazingly, a glint of admiration in the other woman's eyes. Well. That was something, at least.

A short while later Juliet brought the food into the dining room, with its dark mahogany furniture and fusty velvet drapes, and Peter regaled them with a story about lambing that involved inserting a greased arm up a sheep's backside and had Laura shuddering and laughing in turns, even as Juliet's words echoed inside her.

Down on your luck with nowhere else to go. So the whole village was either pitying her or holding her in contempt, maybe both. She couldn't say she was that surprised, but it didn't make the knowledge any easier to bear.

"So what are you going to do?" Juliet asked when the plates were cleared and the dessert had been served, a chocolate mousse pie that she was unabashed in admitting had come from Tesco's refrigerated section. "Are you going to stay in the village? Run the café with Abby?"

Laura guffawed at this. She'd had a third glass of wine by that point, and vowed not to have any more. "I don't think Abby would like that very much. She didn't even like me doing the toasties, as far as I could tell."

"She's probably just wondering what you're doing here, and how long you're going to stay."

"Maybe I don't know that yet."

"Maybe you should find out."

"You're a bossy old broad, aren't you?" Laura said, and then hiccuped. She really had had too much to drink. "Sorry," she added, and she sounded unrepentant. To her surprise and relief, Juliet just laughed.

"Yes," she said. "I am. And I don't like seeing people waste their lives. God knows I wasted enough of mine."

"How?" Laura asked, curious, and Juliet waved a hand in dismissal. "We're not talking about me."

"Maybe we should."

"Juliet didn't get together with me for ten years," Peter chipped in. He'd had a fair few glasses himself. "I call that a waste."

Juliet smiled, her face going soft with love, and with another pang of envy Laura thought what a wonderful pair they made. Although if she was honest, she didn't know quite what Peter saw in Juliet. Something warm and cuddly beneath the stern exterior, apparently.

"Anyway," Juliet said, pouring them all more wine that Laura vowed not to touch, "why shouldn't you run the café with Abby? She could use the help, now Mary's gone. And the café could use the help, as well, I think."

"I suppose it could."

"So? Why don't you?"

"It's not that simple." She didn't feel like going into the whole will thing, and Simon's determination to sell the place, which to strangers could sound soulless and selfish. She had a little family loyalty left and in any case, with three glasses of wine in her, she could get maudlin and talk about how some people didn't get second chances, how sometimes it might be better to just draw a line across and move on. No, better simply to call it at a night.

"I should go," she said, lurching from the table. "It's quite a walk back."

"I'd drive you, but I think I've had too much wine," Peter said.

"We'll lend you a pair of Wellies," Juliet declared in a tone that said the matter was settled. "Those shoes are ridiculous."

A few minutes later Laura was half-stumbling down the road, her linen trousers now crumpled and stuffed into a pair of overlarge, mud-spattered Welly boots. Peter had also given her a torch so she could actually see where she was going, and the cool night air cleared her head a little, so hopefully she wouldn't end up facedown in the mud and sheep poo.

It was a beautiful night, cool and clear, the stars twinkling high above, the sheep bleating occasionally from the darkness. Picking her way through the puddles, Laura started to embroider a fantasy in which somehow, Simon's share pushed to the side, she and Abby were running the café together. She pictured a goofy montage of them laughing and doing the place up, bonding over paint samples. God knew she'd never been much of a mother and it was probably too late now, but perhaps she and Abby could at least be friends. Find some common ground and build on it.

Halfway down the road, Laura came round a curve, so the lights of Bega Farm were no longer visible and the houses of the village were hidden by the trees. She stopped, the daydream melting into the darkness. It was ridiculous to think that could happen, that Abby would even want that to happen, which was what hurt the most.

Standing there alone in the dark, Laura felt, quite suddenly, like the last and loneliest person on earth, half-drunk and hopeless, tears rising in her eyes, a lump forming in her throat, the attack of emotion so swift and brutal she didn't have time to assemble her defenses, give herself a little distance from her own feelings.

For a second she thought about sitting right down in the road, mud and all, and having a good cry. When had she last let herself really cry? The answer to that question was about twenty-three years ago, when she'd left her two-year-old to pursue a cheap dream in the city. She'd been lying alone and afraid in a tatty hotel room in Manchester, feeling cheaper and dirtier than she ever had in all of her nineteen years. It had been the lowest moment of her life and she had no intention of repeating it, or the tears.

A sheep bleated nearby, the sound mournful and alarmingly loud, making Laura jump a little. Fortunately it kept her from giving in to that maudlin desire, and after taking a deep breath, she straightened her shoulders and clumped on down the road.

11

Abby

THE SOLICITOR'S OFFICE WAS in a Georgian town house in Whitehaven that had had its heyday about a hundred years ago. Laura and Abby drove into town together, meeting Simon on the steps of the building; they'd all dressed up for this meeting with Mr. George Westing, although Abby didn't know whom they were trying to impress. The will was going to be read, not changed. The solicitor didn't have the power to do anything but enforce her grandmother's intentions, whatever they had been.

Abby had felt increasingly anxious waiting for this appointment and her whole future to be decided. Laura had kept busy in the café, and while she'd been quietly helpful, Abby had still felt the need to step around her, to watch her back. She definitely didn't want to start depending on her mother, imagining that she might actually stick around. In any case, there might not be anything to stick around for.

She'd lain in bed at night, Noah snuggled up next to her, enjoying the feel of his warm little body and trying to imagine them somewhere else. She tried to see the positives. Maybe she could go back to school. They'd find a little house or flat somewhere, a good school, make a few friends. . . .

She felt as if she might as well be spinning fairy tales. Starting over somewhere strange made her insides shrink with terror, and the thought of uprooting Noah when he was so young and fragile was even more panic-inducing. She *couldn't* start over. She needed to stay in Hartley-by-the-Sea, where she belonged, even if she hadn't always felt like she did.

"The will is fairly straightforward," Mr. Westing said after he'd introduced himself and they were all seated around his desk. Abby could see her grandmother's will on top of it, a thin sheaf of stapled papers emblazoned with the words *The Last Will and Testament of Mary Catherine Rhodes*. She felt as if she were in a Dickens novel. George Westing certainly fit the caricature of a solicitor: lantern-jawed and lugubrious, he placed his hands flat on his desk as he looked at each of them in turn. "I don't think there will be any surprises. Besides the property, your grandmother's assets were modest."

Which was probably a massive understatement.

"So?" Simon asked when the solicitor didn't seem inclined to say anything else. "She left us the café, yeah?"

Abby winced at her uncle's blatant greed. Mr. Westing looked distinctly nonplussed. "She left the café to the three of you, yes," he said. "In equal parts." He cleared his throat. "It was her wish that the café not be sold."

"Her wish?" Simon repeated. "But she can't stipulate that in her will, can she?"

"No," Westing said after a pause. "It would simply be up to her family to undertake the honoring of her intentions."

Simon sat back, satisfied and completely oblivious to the note of censure in the solicitor's voice. "So it's not binding."

"No."

"And that land must be worth half a million at least," Simon mused, and Abby didn't know whether he was talking to himself, them, or the solicitor.

"Actually," Westing interjected, "Mrs. Rhodes had the property valued six months ago. It was assessed at two hundred and fifty thousand pounds." He sat back, seeming almost pleased to have delivered that bit of information to Smug Simon.

"What!" Simon's eyes narrowed. "But it's prime beach property. Right on the seafront . . ."

"The plot is actually quite small and not zoned for residential building," Westing answered. "And the current building is . . ." He trailed off diplomatically, and Abby imagined how he might have filled it in. *In need of complete renovation.*

Simon drummed his fingers on the arm of his chair. "Well, a third of two fifty isn't that bad."

Abby saw Laura wince. "Really, Simon," she murmured, and he gave her a sharp glance.

"Don't tell me you're not in it for the money, Laura. You haven't been back here in years."

Laura pursed her lips and said nothing.

"So if one or two of us wants to sell," Abby ventured, her hands clenched together in her lap, "and the other doesn't . . . ?"

"Then you would have to buy the other party or parties out. The property can be valued again, of course, and if, for example, you wished to keep the café, Miss Rhodes, you could pay the others each one-third of the assessed value."

"Eighty-three thousand pounds each," Simon supplied. "Although I still think it's worth more than that. I think we ought to get another surveyor. Who did you use?" he asked Westing, whose mouth turned downwards at the blatant questioning.

"I will have to look in the file, Mr. Rhodes."

"It doesn't matter," Abby said. She felt a hollow feeling opening up in her stomach; she wasn't surprised it had come to this, but it still hurt. "I can't afford to buy anyone out."

"There are business loans," Westing suggested, but he sounded dubious. Abby shook her head. She felt as if she might cry, which would have been devastating. She couldn't stand to face her mother's, her uncle's, or even the damn solicitor's reaction to her tears. Laura would look away, Simon would exhale impatiently, and in true Dickensian fashion the solicitor would probably silently hand her a pressed handkerchief. She blinked rapidly and thankfully the threat receded.

"I don't think any bank would be willing to loan that kind of amount to me," she said, when she trusted her voice to sound relatively normal. She deliberately didn't look at her uncle, who shifted in his seat. Did he feel remotely guilty for insisting on selling? Probably not, and if she was going to be a reasonable adult about the whole thing, Abby knew he shouldn't. One-third of the café was his inheritance. He didn't have to hand it to her on a plate.

"I propose an alternative solution," Laura said, her voice low and well modulated, the voice of Laura Rhodes, Businesswoman.

Westing raised his eyebrows. "Yes?"

"I'll buy Simon out." Laura didn't look at either Abby or Simon as she spoke, seeming to address the solicitor only. "Abby and I can have joint ownership of the café."

Westing brightened at this. "You have the funds . . . ?"

Laura didn't hesitate for a second. "Yes."

"I thought you were broke," Simon snapped. He sounded distinctly put out that Laura might actually have some money.

Laura flicked her brother a dismissive glance. "I never said I was broke, Simon."

"The details will need to be worked out, of course," Westing said. "And first the property will need to be assessed again. But it sounds as if we have reached a satisfactory conclusion."

Abby opened her mouth to protest, and then realized she had no idea what she'd say, or even what she felt. *Laura* run the café with her? Stay in Hartley-by-the-Sea? Own two-thirds of the café? She didn't know whether to cheer or scream. She felt both relieved and panicky. Here was a solution, and it was complicated.

It seemed she wasn't required to say anything, because somehow they were all rising from their seats and shaking George Westing's hand in turn before heading out of the office, and she hadn't said a word.

"I'll arrange for the valuation," Simon said, his chest swelling with self-importance. "I know a bloke. . . ."

"Why don't we go with a disinterested party?" Laura interjected mildly. "Rather than a friend?"

"Are you accusing me of—"

"Let's keep this aboveboard and friendly, Simon, all right? For Mum's sake." Without waiting for a reply, Laura headed down the street, her heels clicking on the pavement, pulling Abby along with her.

"You haven't said anything," she remarked when they'd reached the car.

"I'm not sure what to say," Abby replied. She got in the car and Laura pulled into the street, her lips pursed.

"Well, you could tell me what you thought of the idea."

"It's not like I have any choice, though, is it?"

"For goodness' sake, Abby." Laura sounded genuinely annoyed, and Abby couldn't blame her. Her mother had just offered to cough up the better part of a hundred grand and she was whining about it. "Of course you have a choice. You can choose to sell up. I can't afford to buy out two of you."

Abby was silent for a moment, watching the houses and shops of Whitehaven slide by. "I'm sorry," she said stiffly. "It's just all a surprise. Why didn't you say anything to me before the meeting?"

"Because I didn't even know if it would be relevant. My mother could have left you the café free and clear, for all I knew. She certainly had reason to. Or just to Simon, for that matter. He always was her favorite."

"Why was he her favorite?" Abby asked, even though they were getting seriously off topic with that question.

"Because I was my dad's." Laura sighed. "Well? Can you stomach doing business with me?"

Could she? "I didn't think you even wanted to stay in Hartley-by-the-Sea. You never did before."

Laura sighed again, and Abby wondered how on earth they could possibly run a business together. She hadn't meant it as a cheap shot, but her mother had obviously taken it as one. "I admit, I don't have a lot of options," she said after a moment, her eyes on the road. "I'm getting a bit old to continue on in what I was doing."

"But you were a manager, not a . . ." Abby struggled to find the right word. "Hostess."

Laura laughed hollowly. "I started as a hostess, but never mind about that. Even managers, female managers, show their age. The owner of the club decided I had a few too many wrinkles to be effective in my job, greeting high-profile guests, that sort of thing."

"Isn't that illegal?"

"Maybe it should be, but the reality is it happens all the time. Corporate restructuring, blah, blah, blah. It's just as well. I couldn't have gone on like that forever, and I didn't feel like negotiating some god-awful sideways move into PR or whatever."

"So you're thinking of staying in the village because you have nowhere else to go?"

"Maybe a little bit, but . . ." Laura hesitated, and Abby thought she saw a surprising vulnerability in her features. "I wonder if this can't be a second chance of sorts. For the café," she clarified, just in case Abby thought she was getting soppily maternal on her.

"You think the café needs a second chance?" Abby said, getting prickly again. She just couldn't help herself.

"It's looking a bit worn, isn't it? We could work together, do it up properly. . . ."

"I don't think Hartley-by-the-Sea is looking for a Michelin star,"

Abby said, but already she was imagining the two of them working together, giving the café the time and attention it deserved. What if they could make a proper go of it? Offer more of the community events Abby had been struggling to get going? What if they could actually get along? And then what if her mother left again?

"I don't know," Abby said. "We'd go from never seeing each other to living in each other's pockets. It seems a bit . . . unlikely."

"Unlikely? But it's completely possible, Abby." Laura's voice was calm. They were driving into Hartley-by-the-Sea, fields flashing by, the river snaking through sheep pasture below them on its way to the sea, sunlight sparkling over it all. On the horizon Abby could see the flat roof of the café, the bit of bluff above it where she and Laura had sat and drunk gin and tonics. "All you have to do is agree."

"And what about the flat?" Abby pressed. "How's that going to work?"

"One of us can take my mother's bedroom."

"But living together—"

"Not permanently," Laura interjected. "I'm thinking of buying or at least renting a property in the village eventually."

For some stupid reason this stung. "It sounds like you have it all planned out."

"No." Laura let out a little laugh as she turned into the beach car park. "Not at all. I'm thinking off the cuff, as it were. Who knows? Maybe Simon will rustle up some property guy who puts the café at the half a million he wanted. In that case, we're sunk."

The *we* caught Abby on the raw. When had there ever been a *we* of any description? Never in her memory . . . and yet maybe there could be now. She was nervous and unsure and scared of trusting her mother an inch. "I don't know," she said. She got out of the car and went directly to the café entrance, flipping the sign from CLOSED to OPEN. "I need to think about it."

"Fine," Laura said. Without asking, she went back to the kitchen and slipped an apron on over her smart outfit. "But don't take too long. Simon will want his money."

That evening after Noah was tucked up in bed, Abby presumed on Laura's surprising goodwill and asked her to babysit so she could go for a walk.

"Of course," Laura said, waving a hand. She was sitting on the sofa, her stocking feet propped up on the coffee table, reading a glossy magazine, the kind that Abby never bought and cost five or six pounds. "Take all the time you need."

"That means you don't go outside for a cigarette," Abby clarified, and Laura's smile became a little fixed. Abby felt mean for saying it, but she was worried about Noah. He'd been in tears at bedtime, asking about Gran. Abby had fought back tears while she'd answered him as best as she could, trying to be calm and sensible when he asked what happened to the ashes, and did they cremate bodies in fireplaces? Little-boy questions that she understood but still hadn't been easy to answer.

"I won't go out," Laura said with a sigh. "I've stopped smoking, anyway."

Abby headed for the coastal path, wanting the height and the air, the space. It was another beautiful evening, the clouds from the afternoon having scattered to clear blue sky, the sun still high above, setting the surface of the sea to shimmering. On a day like today there was nowhere you'd rather be. It was what Laura had said, and Abby had to agree with her. Even if Hartley-by-the-Sea was small and gossipy and on the edge of nowhere. Even if she'd come back only because she'd had nowhere else to go.

Could she choose to stay? To make a go not just of the café but of her relationship, or lack of it, with her mother? Of her life? She pictured herself in the café with Laura, sharing a laugh behind the counter, orchestrating more community events. She'd wanted to start a knitting circle, something Eleanor Carwell had been interested in. She'd even offered to teach Abby to knit, but Abby hadn't had time to take her up on the offer. And after-school clubs . . . Noah had been thrilled about the idea of a fossiling club, with tea in the café after. The café had so much potential, but Abby hadn't been able to do more than make a start on her own. But with her mother's help . . .

Abby kept walking, navigating the tussocky ground as she headed for the far inlet at the bottom of Sea Cove Lane. Baby rabbits were hopping about the gorse, looking cute until Abby saw how many there were. Good grief, it was practically an infestation of bunnies. No one else was out despite the glittering sunshine, so it was just her and the rabbits and the deep blue sea.

What should she do? What was she afraid of?

She'd spent so much of her life being afraid. It hadn't been a numbing terror, the kind that could fog over your brain and leave no room for anything else. No, it had been a low-level kind, a DEFCON 5 on the scale of fears, always present, always presenting the possibility of becoming something more sinister and serious. Fear of someone leaving her. Of losing yet another person—and she had, hadn't she? Her mother. Her best friend. Her boyfriend. And now her gran.

Tears pricked Abby's eyes and she wiped them away, impatient with herself. There was no point in tears. There never had been, even if lately she'd felt like a leaky faucet. In any case, she was afraid of someone coming into her life now, not leaving it.

Except that wasn't the truth. Laura was already in her life, and offering the possibility to be even more in it. Take it over, practically, and Abby was tempted. She could do with a mum right about now, and yet—Laura wasn't the coziest person around. She could very well get bored after a few weeks or months or years. And then what?

Then Abby was left holding the bag and hurting. Again. Something she'd really rather avoid.

Her thoughts were circling like the gulls overhead, wheeling and wheeling without going anywhere, and so Abby headed back to the flat, leaving the bunnies and the gulls and the fading sunlight for a boxy bedroom and her son's knees in her kidneys all night long. They really should use Mary's bedroom. It was ridiculous that they weren't, and yet the thought of sleeping in there, clearing it out . . .

Starting over, without having actually to move anywhere.

Abby lay in bed, listening to her mother moving quietly about, as that thought circled and circled, looking for a place to land.

12

Laura

EIGHTY-FIVE THOUSAND POUNDS WAS a lot of money. In fact, it was *all* of her money, right down to the change in her purse. Laura lay in bed the day after the meeting with the solicitor and wondered just what she'd committed herself to—and why. Not, of course, that Abby had agreed to her proposal to buy Simon's share in the café. No, in fact her difficult daughter had seemed distinctly put out by Laura's rather generous offer. Perhaps she'd wanted Laura simply to give her the café, free and clear. Simon too. Hand her the whole thing because she'd been toughing it out in Hartley-by-the-Sea for the last two years.

The surge of bitterness that came with this thought surprised her. She wasn't angry with Abby—no, more just exasperated with her. The chip on her shoulder practically went down to her belly button. And all right, yes, she was more than exasperated with Abby's intransigence. She was hurt. Stupidly she'd expected something from Abby when she'd offered to buy out Simon. She'd expected a little gratitude, or even a lot. A shy smile, a sudden hug, a realization that Laura was actually, finally stepping up, offering her life savings, for goodness' sake, to keep Abby's job and life afloat.

And yes, of course there was some self-interest involved. Over the last few days Laura had toyed with the idea of staying on at the café, really doing the place up, putting down her own roots. Making something of both herself and the café. The idea held a surprising appeal, for someone who had left Hartley-by-the-Sea intending never to look back.

But if Abby was going to be difficult and drag her heels over the whole thing . . .

Sighing, Laura rolled off the bed, wincing at the crick in her lower back from sleeping in a toddler bed for two weeks. She showered and dressed and was downstairs by eight o'clock, a record for her. Her club days had made her something of a night owl, and despite the sunlight pouring through the kitchen window, it felt like the crack of dawn.

Noah was in his school uniform, seated at the kitchen table with a bowl of soggy-looking Shreddies. He looked up in surprise when Laura came in.

"Hey. You're not usually up now."

"Well, I know it." Abby was moving manically around the tiny kitchen, wiping counters and taking hurried slurps from a mug of tea. Laura edged out of her way and switched on the kettle.

"What's the rush?" she asked mildly.

Abby threw her a hassled glance. So it was going to be like that. "I have to get Noah to school."

"Oh." Right. *Something she'd never had to do* felt like the unspoken subtext. "When do you open the café?"

"Mary used to open it at eight and I'd take over after the school run, but there's no point opening it for fifteen minutes and then closing it again. I'll just open it afterwards."

"But then you'll miss an hour of business." Abby wasn't the only one who was irritated. Was she trying to make things difficult for both of them? "Why not open it at eight? I can stay—"

"No—" The refusal was instant, unthinking.

"Why not?" Laura challenged. "What are you afraid of, Abby?"

This seemed to annoy her daughter further. "I'm not *afraid*."

"How about I take Noah to school, then?" The suggestion surprised her. She'd avoided her grandson, not to be mean, but simply because she didn't know how to act around him. Besides that one half hug in the middle of the night after Mary had died, she'd barely interacted with him at all. The realization made her feel guilty. She was as lousy a grandmother as she was a mother.

Abby eyed her uncertainly. "You'd do that?"

Laura spread her hands. "I'm offering, aren't I? Do I have time for a cup of tea first?"

"Yes . . ." Abby still sounded like she didn't know whether to trust Laura's offer. "You have to leave at half past."

"That's all right, then." It was barely past eight. "And after that, we can talk about the café." She kept her tone mild, but she still saw Abby tense. Good grief, what was the problem here? Why was she being treated like the wicked stepmother when she was acting like the fairy godmother?

"I'll just finish getting dressed," Abby half mumbled, and brushed past Laura on her way out of the kitchen.

Laura made a cup of tea, glancing out the window at the seafront. The tide was half-out, the sand dark and wet, a few dogs frolicking gleefully across it. Their obvious, exuberant joy couldn't help but make her smile. She'd never thought of herself as a dog person, but it seemed a shame not to own some big, goofy dog when you lived right by the beach. Maybe she'd get a puppy. Maybe she'd get Noah a puppy. Would Abby object to that? She took a sip of tea and then turned around to see Noah staring at her openly.

"Well, hello," she said, trying for a smile.

"What should I call you?"

"Call me?" Laura took another sip of tea to stall for time. "What would you like to call me?"

"'Cause you're really my gran, aren't you? Not Gran-who's-gone."

Gran-who's-gone. The stark simplicity of that statement broke a chip off Laura's heart. "Yes, I am your grandmother," she said rather briskly. "But I don't know about being called Gran. That name's already taken, I think."

"How about Granny?"

Please, no. She was only forty-two. She wasn't remotely ready to take on any kind of grandmotherly title or role, and yet she knew she needed something, for Noah's sake and maybe for her own. "You could just call me Laura."

"That's boring. You ought to have a special name."

"What do you suggest, then?" Laura asked. Noah frowned, thinking.

"How about Nana? My friend Thomas has a nana."

Nana. Laura rolled it around in her mind. It didn't sound so bad. "All right," she said. "You can call me Nana."

"Good." Noah's face split in a grin that had Laura smiling back in spite of herself.

Abby appeared in the kitchen doorway, still looking hassled. "You should get going."

It was eight twenty-six. "All right," Laura said lightly. She smiled again at Noah, but it didn't come as easily this time. Everything felt fragile. "Ready to go?"

"Yes," Noah replied, and added, with happy emphasis, "Nana."

"Wait. What?" Abby's surprised glance swiveled between the two of them. "Nana?" she repeated, a question.

"She said I could," Noah said. "She's my real gran, anyway."

"Gran was your gran," Abby answered automatically. "More than—" She stopped, thankfully, although Laura knew it was for Noah's sake rather than hers.

"Let's get you to school, Noah," Laura said, her voice ringing with that false jolliness that adults uncomfortable with children always took.

"Don't forget this," Abby said, and handed Laura a navy blue school satchel.

Noah kept up a steady stream of chatter all the way to school, skipping along to match Laura's brisk stride. At first she tried to keep up with what he was saying, but the sudden leaps in topic and thought were too fast for her, and she ended up merely murmuring vague noises of approval or interest.

"Do you think Gran's in heaven, Nana?" he asked. "I mean my great-gran."

"You can just call her Gran, Noah, since I'm Nana." Amazing how quickly he'd gotten accustomed to calling her Nana. Each time it jolted her. "I think your gran's in a better place, Noah." Which was basically a nonanswer.

"That's what Mum said. But nobody really knows, do they? Unless you're a vicar, maybe."

"Maybe," Laura agreed, and left it at that. They'd reached the school lane, and it gave Laura another jolt because she hadn't been up the narrow little lane since she was a child, dragging her feet, pulling Simon along with her. She hadn't been a particularly bright pupil, academically. After her father had gotten ill, her grades had gone right down, and while the teachers had pitied her at first, they'd eventually lost patience with her stubborn lack of communication or interest. As for Laura . . . she'd just felt empty inside. Days had been to get through, people to be managed or ignored.

She wasn't much older than some of the mums hurrying up the lane, smartphones in hand, heels clicking as they hurried to and fro, to and fro. A shaft of envy sliced through her and her hand curved around a nonexistent phone. She'd had the latest iPhone, filled with apps and contacts, practically glued to her fingers. It had always been pinging or ringing or beeping, because so many people had been trying to get in contact with her. Agents who wanted their celebrity clients to be seen at Density but not overwhelmed or hassled, PR people hoping to plan a party there, wannabe employees and hopefuls and starlets.

She'd been so *important*, once. And when it had been taken away, she'd realized how pointless it all was. She hadn't wanted to chase after another shallow dream, try to reignite contacts with people who had dropped her. And the worst thing about it, the *funniest* thing, was that she didn't even care. Not about the people, anyway. But right now she missed her phone.

"You must be Noah's grandmother."

Laura blinked, startled to realize she'd walked with Noah all the way up the lane and right to the door for the Infants. Noah was tugging on her hand and a teacher was standing in front of her.

"She's my nana," he explained.

"Ah, well, then." From the way the woman smiled at her, Laura had a feeling she knew who she was. Was mentally accessing everything she'd ever heard about her.

"Have a good day, Noah," Laura said, and handed him his satchel. She gave him a lopsided smile and a shoulder squeeze and he grinned back, rather beatifically, before skipping into the classroom. Laura watched him go with a little lurch of her heart, surprised by the affection that had grabbed hold of her so suddenly. This, she supposed, was what they called putting down roots.

She walked away quickly, mingling with the herd of mothers heading down the lane, on their way to jobs or, by the looks of some of their outfits, the gym. For a second Laura pretended that she was going somewhere, with people to see, things to do, feeling busy and important.

But she was going somewhere, she reminded herself as she turned onto the beach road. She was going home. And she was going to try her best to make Abby agree to her plan.

The café was almost empty when Laura let herself in, the sunlight catching the dust motes in the air and the streaks from a quick wipe of the cloth on the tables. A single woman in full walking gear was blowing on her latte in the corner. Abby appeared in the kitchen doorway, her hands on her hips.

"I was just checking on our stock."

"Do you want me to go shopping?"

She shook her head, watching her warily, and Laura wondered who was going to break first and say something. Something either one of them might regret, unless Abby had an unprecedented change of heart and was now going to thank her.

"So. What's this about being Nana, then?"

Laura could tell Abby was trying to sound light and inquiring and failed. "It was Noah's idea," Laura answered mildly. "Do you have a problem with it?"

Abby folded her arms, shooting a glance at the woman in the corner. "I don't know," she said quietly. "I don't want Noah becoming close to you only for you to decide you want something else and high-tail it out of here."

Laura would have been offended if Abby hadn't spoken with such honesty. No snipe, no rancor, just a genuine concern. "I've been suggesting doing the opposite," she said as evenly as she could. "It's you who doesn't seem interested in keeping the café."

"But I wouldn't be keeping it, would I?" Abby returned. "You would."

Ah, precious control. "Is that what this is about? You resent the fact that I'd be using my own money?"

"No, it's not that." Suddenly Abby looked very young, making Laura remember how she'd been as a toddler, with round cheeks and chubby limbs, snuggling next to her in bed. It was telling, she supposed, that the moments she'd most enjoyed with Abby had been when she'd been asleep. "I know I should be grateful that you're willing to put the money in."

"Should be," Laura repeated. "I see."

"I am grateful," Abby said quickly. "Sort of. But it's just . . . I don't trust you. I don't trust that you'll stick around, that you won't get bored and decide to try something else, and demand that we sell up.

That you won't have Noah caring about you and me depending on you and then you just sashay away, no backward glances."

The truth stung sometimes. It stung *hard*. Laura struggled to keep her expression neutral. "Fair point," she said after a moment. "I realize there is a precedent here."

"What if you got your old job back? What if some other club comes calling?"

"They won't," Laura said shortly. "But if they did . . ." She paused. Could she say she wouldn't leave Hartley-by-the-Sea if she got a decent job offer? If she heard the old siren song of a life of importance and glamour? She didn't feel like going back now, but ever? She wanted to be honest. And the truth was, she didn't always trust herself. Abby must have seen the indecision in her face, because she let out a short laugh and nodded.

"I thought so."

"I'm trying to be fair, Abby. And yes, if I got a really good job offer, I might consider it. Might. Wouldn't you?"

"I can't even imagine what that would look or feel like."

Which was a rather bleak statement, and made Laura realize how little she knew Abby the adult. "What did you study at university, anyway?"

"Animal science. I was going to be a vet."

"Going to be?"

Abby hunched one shoulder. "I got pregnant in my second-to-last year. It's a demanding program and I couldn't manage it with a baby."

Laura wanted to ask several questions at once—whether Abby had tried to go part-time, or if she'd ever thought of going back. Or even, if she dared, why Abby kept the baby in the first place. And what about the father? He'd died, but had Abby loved him? Had they been think-ing about staying together, getting married? She'd said "fiancé," hadn't she, but how close had the wedding been?

The shuttered expression on her daughter's face made Laura swallow all the questions. "I'm sorry," she said simply, and after a second Abby nodded her thanks. Laura could see a pair of walkers, complete with designer sticks, coming up the path towards the café. "Look," she said hurriedly. "What if I agree to sign the café over to you if I decide to leave? You get it free and clear if I end up moving away. No strings."

Abby's eyes widened. "Just like that?"

"Just like that."

The walkers were nearly at the door, exclaiming in loud voices over the view of the sea while one of them attempted to fold an enormous ordnance map. They looked the type to chat.

"What if you need the money?" Abby asked.

"Doesn't matter, I won't get it. I'm not planning on leaving, Abby, but I'm just trying to give you some security." She didn't know what else she could do, but Abby still looked uncertain, and suddenly Laura hated that. She wanted Abby to trust her. She wanted to be the one to make it okay. For once.

The bells on the door jangled as the walkers came in. Laura stared at her, waiting for an answer, hoping . . . for what? Some absurd reconciliation by the coffee machine? Yes, okay. *Maybe.*

"Okay," Abby said at last, and it felt like an enormous admission. The smile she gave Laura was wobbly. "Okay," she said again, and with her eyes suspiciously bright she turned around and went back into the kitchen, leaving Laura to deal with the two walkers, who still hadn't managed to fold the map.

Okay. It felt, at that moment, like a wonderful word. It wasn't a contract signed in blood or even in Biro, but it was something. Abby— her daughter—had agreed to her plan. The realization made Laura feel ridiculously ebullient. Her mind buzzed with plans all afternoon as she served customers their tea and coffees and lumpy scones and Abby stayed in the kitchen. They'd definitely need to repaint the place, maybe something cheery but tasteful, primrose yellow, perhaps, or a soothing sage green? And the furniture needed a complete overhaul. The tables and chairs were probably good for nothing but the tip; Laura didn't think even a charity shop would take them.

For a few blissful seconds Laura let herself imagine it all . . . nice wooden tables and chairs, the old, peeling linoleum pried up and wooden laminate placed down, maybe with a few colorful throw rugs to brighten things up. They could even bump out the windows that overlooked the sea, put in a few sofas and easy chairs to make a cozy nook.

And why not offer proper meals instead of just tired sandwiches and jacket potatoes? They could hire a cook for the evenings, offer an expanded menu, nothing too ambitious, perhaps just a few evenings a week to start . . . two mains, a couple of starters and desserts. They'd need to get an alcohol license, or they could do the old bring-your-own-bottle thing and charge a corking fee, nothing too exorbitant, maybe two pounds a pop? Excitement fizzed in her, like soda running through her veins. Why not? Why not dream big? It wasn't even that big, anyway. When she thought of what she'd had at Density: a plush office on the balcony overlooking the main floor, a huge budget, the power to turn away an A-lister if she felt like it . . .

But never mind about that. She needed to focus on the café. And the café had heaps of potential. Abby had started to see it, but Laura could see so much more. Get the place *really* buzzing. She dunked two tea bags in a tin pot and put it on a tray for a waiting customer. Heaps and heaps. They could get a new espresso machine, something that made proper lattes rather than a bit of halfhearted foamy milk. Better pastries too, and fresh cakes—all ways to attract the high-end tourists, the luxury walkers with their special sticks and neon neoprene gear. They could even get reviewed in *Cumbria Life*, a mother-daughter team reworking a tired café, giving it a whole new start. . . .

"Oi. *Oi.* Are you going to take my fiver, or what?"

Laura blinked at the five-pound note a woman was waving in front of her nose. "Sorry."

The woman let out a raucous laugh as she took the tray of teas. "Most people can't wait to take a fiver off you," she said. She shook her head, clearly despairing of Laura's retail skills. Abby poked her head around the kitchen door, eyebrows raised in query, obviously having overheard the exchange.

Laura managed a laugh. "Sorry. I was miles away," she said as she handed the woman her change.

The woman took herself off to a table in the corner, still laughing. They definitely needed to attract a better kind of clientele.

At three Abby went to fetch Noah, and as the café was quiet, save for a queue of children at the ice cream counter, Sophie having them well in hand, Laura took the opportunity to jot some notes down. *Ideas for Improvement*, she wrote at the top, feeling a little giddy. Underlined it twice. The ideas came thick and fast, filling her with the kind of excitement she hadn't felt in a long while.

Of course once she paid Simon off, she wouldn't have ten pence to her name, she realized as she looked down at the list. Everything on it cost money, and some of the items cost quite a lot. They could get a business loan perhaps, but in today's economic climate it wouldn't be easy. Still, they could manage it, maybe. She could call on her expertise, her business history. . . .

She was nibbling on the end of her pen, lost in thought, when Abby and Noah came through the door.

"Hey, Nana!" Noah called out joyfully, and Laura gave him a cautious smile. She knew she hadn't done anything to deserve Noah's unrestrained affection, and she could tell Abby knew it too. She didn't want to reject it, but responding in kind, accepting it as her due, didn't seem either right or fair. Not yet, anyway, but she did love his smile.

"Hi. How was your day?" she asked, and Noah launched into a lengthy explanation of the game he'd played at recess. Laura managed to glean that there were two teams and Noah had been on one and then he'd switched to the other, and it involved collecting pebbles and keeping them safe, so the big, bad Year Ones didn't steal them.

"They've been at it all year," Abby said when she caught Laura's bewildered look. "The Pebble Wars, apparently, of Hartley-by-the-Sea."

"I vaguely remember similar things when I was at school." Very vaguely. "It gave me a strange feeling to go up there again, actually."

"Did it?" Abby reached for her apron as Noah made himself comfortable at one of the tables with a coloring book and some felt-tip pens. A host of walkers was heading for the front doors, looking ready for a round of cappuccinos. Hopefully the espresso machine wasn't acting up. "Do you know," Abby mused, "sometimes I forget that you grew up here?"

Laura couldn't help but be a little nonplussed by that. "How could you forget such a thing?"

"Because you don't seem like you're from around here. And no one ever talked about you much, at least while I was growing up. It was like there was a big silence around it all."

"I suppose that's better than being gossiped about." Laura tried for light. It would have been very like a West Cumbrian to act like you didn't exist once you chose to leave the county. She'd turned her back on Hartley-by-the-Sea; there were a lot of people here who couldn't forgive that, her daughter perhaps included. At least she hadn't encountered outright hostility from anyone but Abby.

"I can handle the café till closing." Abby nodded towards the door to the flat. "If you want to go in and make a start on our own tea?"

Laura clocked the glint of both challenge and question in her daughter's eye. So she wanted to call the shots in this strange new life of theirs? Fine. Laura had been around long enough to know what battles to fight and when to accede gracefully. It was the war that mattered, anyway, although comparing her relationship with her daughter to warfare probably wasn't helpful. She needed to convince them both that they were on the same side.

"Okay," she said, and went around the till. "Shall I take Noah across, as well?" she added, satisfied to see Abby look thrown. "We can make tea together."

Noah looked up, eyes alight. "*Can* we?"

Laura instantly regretted her rash suggestion; what did she know about entertaining, much less cooking with, five-year-olds, or actually cooking at all? Would ordering a takeaway be a cop-out? Out of the corner of her eye she saw Abby looking at her speculatively, waiting for her reply, and it suddenly felt like much more hung in the balance than their dinner. This was a mother moment, a grandmother moment, and she wanted to prove herself adequate at both.

"Of course we can," she said, and reached for Noah's hand.

13

Abby

THE NEXT MORNING ABBY came downstairs, still blinking sleep out of her eyes, to find Laura seated at the kitchen table, showered and dressed, a cup of black coffee at her elbow as she wrote on a pad of paper.

It was some sort of list, and from one quick, bleary-eyed glance, Abby saw it was about the café. *Property Valuation. Business loan. Paint. Building estimates.*

Abby's stomach churned with anxiety and, yes, a little excitement as she reached for the kettle. There were some pretty big things on that list. "You're up early," she remarked. "It's not even gone seven yet."

"No need to be a night owl anymore," Laura said lightly.

"Is that what you were in your clubbing days?" She tried to sound merely interested; she'd wanted to call a cease-fire on the snark a while ago, but somehow it always seemed to sneak back in.

"My clubbing days," Laura repeated on a sigh. "Yes. I worked most nights until three or four in the morning. It was part of the job." She leaned back in her seat and took a sip of coffee. She was wearing a cashmere sweater that looked ridiculously expensive and skinny jeans, her hair piled messily on top of her head, and yet somehow she managed to look more elegant and sophisticated than Abby ever could, even if she'd had a complete makeover and wardrobe overhaul. It was a little hard when your mother outdid you in elegance every time.

"Did you like it?" Abby asked. "The nightclub? Do you miss it?"

Laura pursed her lips. "I miss being busy." A pause, and then she added wryly, "And feeling important." She glanced down at her list, and Abby wondered whether she regretted revealing that much. "Now. I've just been writing down all the things we need to do."

"Oh, yes?"

"First, of course, we need to have the property valued. I don't want Simon to use someone he knows, although he'll probably insist. He'll just try to get the value inflated."

"Has he always been like that?" Abby asked curiously, and Laura sighed.

"More or less. Mum spoiled him and Dad . . . well." She shook her head. "He didn't have an easy time of it."

"Neither did you, though." Abby leaned against the counter. "What was your dad like?"

Laura's face clouded and Abby almost wished she hadn't asked the question. Her mother looked so sad.

"He was a bit of a feckless layabout, if I'm honest," she said after a moment. "Mum really kept everyone going. But he was fun and spontaneous and he always had time for me." She took a deep breath and looked back down at her list. "Now enough of that. I'll call a real estate agent today."

"Okay." That brief moment of sharing was evaporating into brisk business mode.

"Once we get the valuation, we can figure out how much we'll owe Simon."

"You mean you'll owe Simon," Abby pointed out. Laura's gaze narrowed and Abby knew she'd taken it as a snipe. She'd meant it kindly—this was her mother's money, not hers—but as the silence stretched on, Abby knew there had been something ugly underneath the remark. There always was.

"My money," Laura agreed tautly. Abby looked away. She heard the sound of her mother putting down her pen, the deep exhalation. "Just what is the problem, Abby? Because I'm sinking eighty-five thousand pounds into this and considering that fact, you seem to have a lot of attitude."

"*That* is my problem. That attitude of yours, right there." The kettle switched off and Abby busied herself making tea. She didn't think she could face her mother's superiority at that moment, the exasperated lift of her eyebrows.

"My attitude?" Laura repeated. "I'm not seeing it."

"You wouldn't." The words were popping out of her mouth, unable to be restrained. Laura's eyes flashed with anger.

"Can you just tell me, then?" she demanded. "Instead of muttering under your breath like some surly teenager?"

"How would you know what a teenager acts like?" Abby threw back, half-amazed that everything had escalated so quickly. The veneer of politeness between them was thin indeed. "You were never around when I was a teenager."

Laura sat back in her chair with a tired sigh. "It always comes back to this."

"Of course it does," Abby cried, her voice vibrating with hurt. The ugliness underneath was finally revealed. "How can it not? You know, you've never ever explained why you left. How you could leave, when I was two. *Two!*" Her voice was shaking; her body was shaking. She wanted to stop talking, stop *emoting*, but the words kept pouring out, a torrent she couldn't control. She needed to say this, even though she didn't want to. "That was something that always got to me. I think I could have accepted it better if you'd left when I was a newborn. I would have just been this squalling little thing, red-faced and scrawny, and you wouldn't have really known me. I know what newborns are like. Half the time you fantasize about handing them off to somebody because you're so sleep-deprived. But two years old!" She stared at her mother, knowing the agony was evident in her face, even after all these years, the pain as raw and deep as ever, even though she tried to act like it wasn't. "I remember Noah at two," she continued, her voice ragged now. "He was so cute and cuddly, I just wanted to eat him up. Or tickle or hug him to pieces." Abby sniffed. "I couldn't imagine leaving Noah at that age. Just walking away, no looking back. It would have broken my heart. It would have broken *me*." She stopped, her chest heaving, her throat tight, waiting for her mother to say something. Something that made sense of it all, that would make her, even now, smile and nod in understanding and relief. *Oh, I get it. That's why. I get why you left. It makes sense to me now.*

But Laura was closing up like a fan, her mouth pursed, her eyes blank. "I don't want to talk about this."

Abby had just ripped out her soul and handed it to her mother in bloody tatters, and *that's* what she got back? "You don't *want* to?"

"I don't think it's helpful," Laura clarified coolly. "The past is the past, Abby."

"Yes, the past is the past. At least, that's what I always thought until you decided to swan back into my life. For good, apparently. And now the past is very much in the present, *Mum*." The word slipped out of Abby's mouth like a sneer, an insult. She flung her wet tea bag into the sink and, cradling her mug, stalked out of the kitchen.

Unfortunately there wasn't anywhere to go. Noah was asleep upstairs in her bedroom and the only other room downstairs was the sitting room. So she sat on the sofa, not more than ten feet from Laura in the kitchen, and wished she could have made a slightly grander exit.

She sipped her tea and stared moodily into space, trying to force the emotion back into its little box while she listened to her mother in the kitchen. She could hear the scratch of pen and paper, the clink of her cup as she drank her coffee. She could hear Laura *breathe*. And from all those normal sounds, Abby didn't think her mother had been affected by her outpouring at all. It had bounced off her perfect Teflon-coated exterior right back at Abby.

But had she really expected Laura finally to crack? This was the woman who had left her two-year-old to work as a hostess at a nightclub. Who had come back no more than once or twice a year since then, and then hardly at all after Abby had turned sixteen. The woman who had had no interest in meeting her grandchild, or in helping out when her mother had had a heart attack. What on earth had Abby expected? Tears and recrimination? An explanation that made sense? She'd gotten nothing. Of course.

Abby was just finishing her lukewarm tea, trying to gear herself up to wake Noah up and start the whole morning routine, when Laura came into the room. "I'll contact someone to value the property today, if it's all right with you," she said, her tone as brisk as ever, her expression completely neutral and unfazed.

Abby almost felt like laughing. So they'd just sail past that moment, keep floating down the River of Denial. "Fine."

"And we should clear out Mary's room. There's no point having us all squeezing into two small rooms when the largest one is going spare."

She sounded so *cold*. "What about her things?"

"We can take what sentimental items we want to keep and give the rest to charity. I don't think she had anything that was worth much."

It was true, but Abby still resented it, disliked Laura's casual dismissal of all of Mary's possessions. And she hated the thought of clearing Mary's things out like so much rubbish, throwing her clothes and mementos into bin bags and tossing the lot. But what else did you do when someone died? Turn her room into a shrine? The flat wasn't big enough for that, anyway. "All right," she said tonelessly.

"You can have the largest room," Laura offered. "If you want it. And Noah can have yours."

Abby turned to look at her. "You want to sleep in that tiny room, in a toddler bed?"

A smile flickered across Laura's face and then vanished. "Well, no," she said. "I definitely want a proper-sized bed. But the room is fine for me." Without waiting for a reply, she turned and headed upstairs.

A surveyor came that afternoon, and he gave a value for the property by the next morning. "Two hundred and forty thousand pounds," Laura told Abby, a note of triumph in her voice. "Simon should have gone with last year's valuation."

"He'll insist on getting another one," Abby said tiredly. She'd spent the entire afternoon on her feet, dishing out ice creams because Sophie had called in sick. Laura had cooked in the kitchen, and between the two of them they'd managed a very full day. They'd even managed not to fight. But she was exhausted now, and wanted only a bath and a large glass of wine.

"We'll get three valuations," Laura decided. "And take the middle one. He can't argue with that." She was already on the phone, calling another Realtor, and Abby, frying sausages for dinner, didn't have the strength to protest. Let her mother take over. She was bound to do so no matter what, and at least Abby could save some energy for the bigger battles, whenever they came. Whatever they were.

By Friday afternoon Laura had all three valuations; the middle one came in at 250,000. By that evening she and Simon had an agreement, with an appointment at the solicitor's on Monday morning.

"And then the café will be ours," Laura said in triumph, and Abby resisted replying, *Yours. It will be yours.*

"I feel like I'm being so petty," she told Meghan when she'd managed to slip away on Saturday evening for a drink at the Hangman's Noose. Laura had offered to babysit, and Abby had guiltily accepted. It felt wrong to take advantage of her mother's generosity when she was feeling so fed up and resentful, but she needed to get out. She needed to talk to someone who could hopefully see her side of the story.

Meghan lounged back in her chair, tipping most of her glass of wine into her mouth. "Eighty-odd thousand pounds is quite a lot of dosh."

"I know. And I do realize I should be grateful." Abby swirled the wine in her glass. "But I feel like Laura thinks she can sweep everything under the rug, and act like none of it ever happened. She's here now, and so that's all that is supposed to matter. Even worse, the fact that she's putting this money up is supposed to even out the score somehow. Everything I've felt, all the years of her totally ignoring me, ignoring my son, and it's like I'm not even allowed to mind."

Meghan nodded in understanding. "Have you had it out with her? You know, proper why-did-you-completely-cock-up-my-life kind of thing?"

"I tried," Abby said, remembering her outpouring the other morning with an inward wince. "But when you yell at Laura, she just closes down. Goes all frosty and remote, like you're wasting her time."

"Defense mechanism, maybe?"

"Maybe," Abby allowed. "But I wish she'd just explain something, except maybe there's nothing to explain. She left because she didn't care." She shook her head and glugged down some more wine. "I don't even know what I'm looking for."

"You could insist she buys you out," Meghan suggested. "Take your own eighty-odd thousand pounds and run."

It had crossed her mind more than once in the last week, but Abby still resisted it instinctively. Utterly. "I don't want to run anymore. I've done enough running."

Meghan's face softened in sympathy. "I know."

Abby hadn't even told her the whole story. Just a few of the basics: an unexpected baby, a less-than-thrilled boyfriend. The rawness of it all she'd kept hidden, the endless fights and angry words, the guilt and regret, the way Ben's family had cut her off so completely.

"Anyway, I like it here," she said. "It hasn't always been easy, but Noah is settled and people are friendly and I actually like working in the café. I could even get excited about the possibilities for the future if Laura wasn't . . . well, Laura."

"Shame, because you're stuck with her," Meghan answered with a grin. "But cheers."

"Cheers," Abby returned, and finished her wine. She roused herself to ask Meghan, "How are things with you? How's the childminding business?" Meghan had set up as a childminder in her own home, and now had four under-fives to take care of several days a week. With her acerbic tongue and cynical attitude, Meghan seemed like an unlikely choice as babysitter, but she was surprisingly good with kids, fun but firm.

"It's fine," she answered with a shrug. "It pays a few of the bills, and allows me to be home with Mum."

"How is your mum?"

"The same." Meghan grimaced. "She's always going to be the same. The rehab's done as much as it's ever going to do."

Abby had seen Janice Campbell on occasion, when she'd dropped Noah off at Meghan's; Janice usually stayed in her bedroom, but sometimes she lumbered around with the aid of a walker. She was mostly paralyzed on her right side and her speech was garbled, although it didn't stop her from trying to chat up anyone who came through the door. Abby had done her best to respond, but she'd been quietly horrified by Janice's condition; it seemed so utterly despairing and miserable to be trapped the way she was, both in her body and in her house.

"It must be hard," Abby said, knowing the sentiment was terribly inadequate.

Meghan's smile was ready and brittle. "How about another glass?"

Sunday morning Laura came downstairs, alert and purposeful, while Noah was picking at his toast and Abby was reading yesterday's newspaper, slightly hungover from the second glass of wine she'd had with Meghan last night. She'd never been a big drinker.

"Right," Laura said, slapping her thighs. Abby looked up, startled. "I think we should make a start."

Noah was instantly alert. "A start?"

"We're cleaning out your gran's things, Noah," Laura said in her brisk way. "If there's something you'd like to keep, you must let us know."

"Cleaning them out?" Noah's lip wobbled and Abby closed her eyes briefly. It wasn't even eight thirty on her one day off a week. Did they really have to start this now? "You're getting *rid* of them?"

Laura threw a slightly panicky glance at Abby, who dutifully jumped into the breach. "No, of course we're not getting rid of them, Noah. We're keeping anything that is special, like Laura said—"

"Nana," Noah corrected. "She's Nana."

"Right." That still stuck a bit in her throat. "The things we don't feel we need to keep we can give away to people who need them. There are some people, you know, who could really use clothes and blankets and things." She smiled at her son, encouraging him to get on board with the idea. Ever since Mary's death, Noah had been excited one minute, desolate the next, veering between joy and sadness. Abby knew it was normal, but it hurt to see it and it was hard to deal with. Especially early on a Sunday morning.

"But they're Gran's things," Noah said in a low voice. His lower lip was jutting out now, tears giving way, as was often the case, to stubbornness.

Abby sighed. It would have been so much easier to have done this when Noah was at school, but then they would have had the café to manage, so she supposed she could see Laura's point in waiting until Sunday. But it wasn't how she wanted to spend her day off, and she didn't have the emotional energy for shepherding Noah and dealing with her own sadness while they cleared the bedroom. "Gran wouldn't want us to waste anything, would she?" she asked, pitching her tone somewhere between philosophical and cajoling. "You know how thrifty she was. Always clipping coupons and reusing tea bags."

"I used to hate that," Laura chimed in with a soft laugh. "There's nothing worse than a cup of tea that tastes like milky water."

"Absolutely," Abby agreed without thinking, and their eyes met in a glance of unsettling complicity.

Noah was sifting through all their statements in his mind, and then he pushed his toast away, the crusts still left. "Can I help?"

"Of course you can," Abby said, filled with relief. She shared another smile with Laura, unsettling her even more.

They went upstairs all together, coming into Mary's room quietly, as if it was a sacred place. And perhaps there was something shrinelike about the quilt pulled tight across the bed, the glasses and the book on the bedside table, the page still marked.

Abby let out the breath she hadn't realized she'd been holding. The room felt quieter than the rest of the flat, hushed and expectant. A spill of pill bottles lay scattered across the bureau top, along with a prescription that hadn't been filled, none of it needed anymore. It was so strange how everything that had once been necessary and even crucial became redundant and unimportant in the matter of a moment. It felt wrong.

"Where should we start?" Abby asked, and realized she was whispering.

"The clothes might be easiest," Laura suggested. She spoke normally, but Abby saw that her mother's face looked a little pale, a bit drawn. Laura snapped open one of the bin bags she'd brought upstairs. "Why don't you open a drawer, Abby?"

Slowly Abby opened a drawer; it was Mary's underwear. She looked at the enormous pants and bulletproof brassieres of beige nylon and felt the most ridiculous and inappropriate urge to laugh.

Laura took a step towards the bureau and glanced into the drawer. "Goodness," she murmured, and a snort escaped Abby. She put her hand over her mouth, appalled at herself.

"I'm sure someone will be very appreciative of these," Laura said, and reached for one of the bras. Noah looked at it, goggle-eyed.

"Wow," he said in a tone of quiet respectfulness. "That's really big."

"Yes," Laura agreed solemnly. "It is." She was just about to put it in the bag when Noah piped up.

"Wait—can I have it?"

Laura's eyebrows rose towards her hairline and Abby nearly let out another snort. "Noah, what on earth are you going to do with—with that?" she asked.

"I can use it as a slingshot," Noah said, as if it were the most obvious thing in the world.

Abby met Laura's gaze over the top of Noah's head and this time she couldn't keep it in. She let out a hiccupy sort of laugh, and then Laura did too, and suddenly they were both laughing, tears starting in their eyes, shoulders shaking. Noah stared at them both, mystified.

"What's going on?" he kept asking, but neither Abby nor Laura could respond, because they were laughing too hard. Abby's stomach hurt and she clutched her sides, tears starting to stream down her face. She couldn't remember the last time she'd laughed that hard, silently, her stomach hurting.

Finally Laura managed to gasp out, "You'd need an awfully big rock for that slingshot, Noah. More like a boulder." And they collapsed into laughter again. Noah, annoyed now, stomped over to the bed and sat down on it, his arms folded, his lower lip stuck out dramatically.

Even her son's annoyance didn't dent her good humor. Although laughter was an awful lot like crying: tears, emotion, overwhelming. Finally, after about five minutes, Abby let out a long sigh and wiped her eyes. "Wow, that felt good. I haven't laughed like that in ages."

"Me neither." Laura dabbed at her own eyes and Abby sank onto the bed next to Noah, putting her arm around his skinny shoulders.

"Sorry, sweetheart. Grown-ups act strangely sometimes. Silly."

"Yes," Noah agreed sternly. "That was very silly."

"Sorry, Noah," Laura murmured, her eyes downcast, the picture of contrition.

Their laughter subsided now, Abby felt a weird tug of affection for this woman who had given birth to her, this woman she still barely knew. "Look," she said suddenly, "I usually go to the quiz at the Hangman's Noose on a Thursday night. Why don't you come with me this week?" Laura looked up, clearly flummoxed by the invitation, and her silence made Abby want to backpedal. "I mean, if you want to. It can be kind of a laugh and I go with a group. . . ." She trailed off, wishing she hadn't said anything. She couldn't bear it if Laura gave her that chilly silence, the arched eyebrow. *Thank you, but that's not quite my thing, is it?* "It's no big deal," she muttered, looking away.

"Abby," Laura said quietly. "I'd love to come."

14

Laura

WHAT DID YOU WEAR to a pub quiz? Or, more important, what did she wear? For the first time since she could remember, Laura didn't want to go with her usual chic separates. She didn't want to stand out. She'd spent a lifetime apart from everyone, in one way or another, and now, at age forty-two, she finally wanted to fit in.

The last few days, since Abby had asked her to the quiz, had felt a bit like balancing on a tightrope. She'd signed her life savings over to Simon on Monday, and even though she'd been sure, she still felt as if her stomach were lined with concrete when her brother took her check with a smug smile, going so far as to hold it up to the light to ensure that it wasn't counterfeit.

"Really, Simon?" Laura had asked, exasperated. "It's a *check.*"

"You never know," he'd muttered, and, folding the check, put it in his breast pocket. Laura's only consolation was George Westing's look of silent distaste. Abby hadn't said anything; if Laura had been expecting a thank-you, she'd been disappointed. And it was more than a little irritating that her daughter didn't seem to realize she was doing this, at least in part, for her. Yes, she now owned two-thirds of the café. But eighty-five thousand pounds, the entirety of her nest egg, could have seen her set up somewhere, starting over.

As what? The daytime manager of a Little Chef on the M6?

She was deceiving herself if she thought she was doing this for Abby's sake. She was doing it for her own. The realization made Laura feel guilty and weirdly resentful of herself. Could no act be altruistic? Maybe not.

Since then, she and Abby had rubbed along, more or less, at the café; Laura was eager to get started with a business plan, ripping up the linoleum, painting walls, making plans. Abby, however, was entirely focused on the day-to-day running and left Laura no time even to discuss the café's future. Sophie, the girl who scooped ice cream and spent most of her time plugged into her iPod or on her phone, had quit suddenly to move in with her boyfriend in Carlisle, leaving both Laura and Abby busier than ever. They'd gotten into a routine of sorts; Abby did the shopping and the kitchen while Laura stayed at the counter; Laura closed up while Abby went to make dinner at the flat with Noah.

Evenings had been odd too; Laura had made a point of eating with Noah and Abby, which felt weirdly domesticated and family-like and yet so not. Noah was the only somewhat sticky glue that was holding them together, as he chatted about his day, asking questions about everything. Without him sitting there between them, spooning in mashed potatoes or playing with his food, it would have felt like the ninth circle of Dante's *Inferno*, all of them encased in ice and isolation for their treachery. Or something like that—the only reason Laura knew about Dante at all was that there had been a themed evening at Density once, based on the circles of hell. Very popular.

But she wasn't going to think about the café now, or the nonrelationship she was navigating with her daughter. She was going out; she was going to have fun; she was going to make an effort in this new life of hers. And so she needed to put something on.

"Laura?" Abby knocked on the door of Noah's bedroom. They had yet to change rooms; on Sunday they'd cleared out Mary's clothes, but the rest of her belongings still remained in her room, some in sad-looking piles, and neither Abby nor Laura had talked about it again.

That moment of shared laughter had brought them together, but it seemed they'd quickly sprung apart again. "We need to be at Meghan's in ten minutes, and it's a long walk from the beach."

"I'll be right out." Laura grabbed a pair of jeans and a billowy top with lace inserts and yanked them both on. Maybe if she made less of an effort, she'd fit in, and it wouldn't matter what she wore. She couldn't keep from sliding her feet into a pair of low heels rather than the hiking boots or trainers that nearly everyone else seemed to wear. Seemed making at least a little bit of an effort was ingrained.

Abby was waiting with Noah downstairs, looking smarter than usual in a sundress and a cute cardigan. She'd pulled her hair back into a ponytail and Laura thought she detected lip gloss and eyeliner. Maybe everyone made a little bit of an effort for the pub quiz.

"You look nice," she said, and Abby let out something that sounded like a snort.

"As nice as I can manage. I don't have your way with makeup and hair stuff."

"Still, you look nice," Laura said firmly, willing her daughter to just take the compliment.

After a second's pause Abby nodded. "Thanks," she said quietly, and Laura felt like it was a win.

Laura reached for her jacket—even in late June the evenings were chilly—and they headed outside. Clouds were piling up on the horizon, and the breeze from the sea was colder than Laura expected, so she zipped up her jacket and ducked her head, the wind tearing her hair into tangles after just a few seconds. So much for her "hair stuff."

They walked in silence up the beach road, Noah half-walking, half-dancing between them. He'd talked nonstop over dinner about spending the evening at Nathan's house, which apparently involved eating crisps and sweets and playing on Nathan's DS for hours at a time. Abby grimaced slightly over the top of his head.

"The rules are a little more relaxed at Nathan's house."

As if she would know about rules. She looked at Abby and some-times she felt a flicker of that maternal pull between angst and love, and sometimes she felt as if she were looking at someone who wasn't related to her, a near-stranger with whom she happened to share a living space, a life. And when Abby, in an unguarded or perhaps merely unthinking moment, talked to her about parenting, about setting rules and enforcing bedtimes and no snacking as if she under-stood and could empathize, Laura felt the gaping abyss of her own ignorance and inexperience.

And yet she knew about parenting. She knew about giving birth alone, her body gasping and tearing. She knew about trying to breast-feed and wincing as a greedy mouth attached to your flesh. She knew about pushing a pram against the onslaught of rain and wind, trying to escape the hissing voice behind you. *Get out of here. I'm warning you, Laura. I can make your life so miserable.* She knew about sleepless nights, about standing and swaying, more than half-asleep, as you cradled this precious infant that you weren't even sure you liked and willed her to just sleep for one godforsaken minute. She knew about walking away, feeling equal parts relief and regret, overlaid by terror and hope.

But when it came to this? To the mundane details of raising a child, of feeling both the exasperation and the joy? Nope. She didn't know any of it. And sometimes it made her more than a little sad.

They reached Meghan's house and Laura stood silently by the door while Abby explained all the necessary information: an hour of telly, crisps but no sweets or soda, bedtime by eight thirty at the latest.

"Yeah, yeah," Meghan said, rolling her eyes in a way that made Laura think she wasn't going follow any of Abby's earnest directives. "Go on, or you'll miss the start of the quiz. We'll be fine."

They left the house and headed up to the pub; ridiculously, Laura was actually starting to feel nervous. She, who had rubbed elbows with more celebrities and socialites than Abby had even heard of, was experiencing jitters over walking into a West Cumbrian pub, drinking a glass of mediocre plonk, and taking part in a pub quiz.

Because there might be people there she knew, or who knew her. People who remembered. People she really wasn't sure she wanted to see, much less make small talk with. But she'd chosen to live in Hartley-by-the-Sea, and that meant facing her past, or at least some of it.

Taking a deep breath, Laura straightened her spine and followed Abby into the pub. The interior was dim and overly warm; even though it was June, there was a fire in the grate, squashy sofas and armchairs pulled up to it. Every chair in the place had a person on it, and the noise was a din of excited chatter, raucous peals of laughter, and the clink of pint glasses.

Laura caught the eye of the bartender, a rumple-haired man about the same age as Abby, maybe a little older. He gave her a slow smile that had Laura reacting in both annoyance and pleasure. It was nice to be noticed, even if it was absurd. She looked away, following Abby, who was weaving her way through the maze of crowded tables to one in the back that had three people sitting at it—Juliet Bagshaw and Peter Lanford, and another woman that had to be Juliet's sister, judging by the frizzy hair and the freckles.

They exchanged hellos while Laura hung back. She could feel a chilly little smile curving her lips, a remoteness coming over her face. She felt like a spare part, and even more so when Abby stepped aside to introduce her.

"You know Juliet and Peter. . . ."

"And I'm Lucy," the third person said with a wide, engaging smile. "Nice to finally meet you." Which implied she'd heard of her from Abby, but Laura did not want to imagine what she'd heard.

"Nice to meet you," she said politely. There were only four stools around the table, and so sitting down would mean Abby had to stand. She stayed where she was. "I'm looking forward to this quiz." She sounded like a little girl attending a birthday party, all best manners, stiff and shiny. "Shall I get another stool . . . ?"

Juliet, Peter, and Lucy all exchanged looks that had Laura tensing. What had she said? What was wrong?

"I won't play," Lucy said quickly, and Laura caught Abby biting her lip, the classic sign, even as a toddler, that she'd done something wrong.

"No, I won't play," Abby said. "Sorry. I didn't think. . . ." She looked miserable, and Laura realized why. Every table held four people, not five. There must have been a rule, four members per team. Of course.

"No, no," Laura said. She actually felt bad for Abby, as well as for herself. She could feel the evening sliding away from her, spooling out of control and turning into yet another unfortunate episode in the mother-daughter melodrama of her and Abby, and she really didn't want that to happen. They needed to have some fun, score an easy win. A pub quiz should have been it. "I don't mind not playing. Not at all. You all are a team, aren't you? You play every week?" Telling silence greeted this statement. Laura could see Juliet watching her, looking slightly amused by the whole situation. "I'll just listen in," she said as brightly as she could. "I'm terrible when it comes to trivia anyway. Honestly." She let out a tinkling little laugh that made her inwardly cringe.

"I don't mind staying out . . . ," Lucy began.

"No, no—"

"I should," Abby insisted, and Laura shook her head again. She really didn't want to take part now; it would feel awful.

"If you're sure . . . ," Lucy began.

"She's sure," Juliet cut in dryly. "Can I pour you a glass, Laura?"

There were only four glasses. "Actually, I think I'll have something a little stiffer," Laura said. "I'll be right back." She made her way to the bar, her head held high, as she tried not to feel ridiculously hurt, like the last kid in PE who wasn't picked for a team. Stupid, stupid, stupid.

It was an easy mistake for Abby to have made. It didn't have to mean anything.

She reached the bar, placing her hands flat on the scarred wooden top, desperately in need of a drink. The rumple-haired bartender turned his sleepy smile on her. Laura ignored it.

"What can I get you?"

"A large gin and tonic please, heavy on the gin." She gave him her most glittering smile and his smile widened.

"You want lime with that?"

"Of course," Laura answered haughtily, and now he was practically grinning, damn it. She amused him. Laura slid onto the stool while she waited for him to make her drink. She was in no rush to hurry back to the cozy table of four. In fact, she might just stay here for the whole evening, smarmy bartender aside.

"You're Abby Rhodes's mum," he remarked as he popped the tab on a mini can of tonic water. "Aren't you?"

"Got it in one." She cocked her head. "Did you go to school with Abby?"

The smile he gave her was knowing, as if he understood exactly how she was trying to put him in his place. "No. I'm five years older than Abby."

Thirty, then. A child. "So you would have been at the primary at the same time."

"Yeah, I think she was in Reception when I was in Year Six. Not exactly on my radar." He handed her the drink. "That will be five fifty. Unless you want to start a tab?"

"Why not?" Laura answered, and took a much-needed sip. The tonic water was fizzy and the gin hit the back of her throat, the lime tart on her tongue. Perfect. She put the glass down on the bar and looked away. The bartender had propped his elbows on the bar and was watching her. Unfortunately no one else needed a drink. They'd already gotten them and were waiting for the quiz to start.

"I'm Rob Telford, by the way."

The Telfords were an old Cumbrian family. Laura had a vague memory from her own childhood of Donna Telford weaving her way down the street at about two in the afternoon, either already drunk or still hungover. Was that Rob's mother? An aunt or a cousin? She had no idea. "I'm Laura," she said, wanting to keep the introductions brief if they couldn't be nonexistent. "But you probably already knew that."

"Oi, Rob," someone called. "Away with you. Are you gan to start the quiz now or keep flirting with that mott?"

Rob made a face and Laura almost laughed. She hadn't heard a Cumbrian accent that thick in a long time, or the use of the old dialect. At least the guy hadn't called her something offensive. "Mott," as she remembered, just meant woman.

"Keep your grotts on," Rob called back with a smile. "I'll start when I'm ready." He turned back to Laura. "Are you going to take part?"

"No, I'm good here with my drink." She swiveled on the stool so she was facing outwards; Juliet, Lucy, Peter, and Abby were all huddled around the table, heads close together as they chatted.

"All right, lads and lasses," Rob called. "Time for the quiz. Remember the rules. No cheating—no talking too loud or someone might chaff your answer. Twenty questions, winning team gets a decent bottle of plonk for a prize."

A few people called back good-natured insults about everything Rob had said—how difficult questions were, how decent the wine. Laura glanced round the tables and saw how everyone was ruddy-faced and smiling, most a few drinks in at least. It was a happy, if slightly rambunctious, crowd, and she felt utterly separate from it. Abby glanced up as if she could sense Laura's stare and mouthed "Sorry." Laura nodded back, managing a small smile. She might have felt left out, but she didn't want it to set her back with Abby. That mattered more now than anything else.

Besides, she could happily sit here on a stool all night and drink herself into oblivion. That felt like a fine plan. Rob started the quiz and Laura let the questions and the following banter wash over her as she drank her way steadily through two G&Ts. After ten questions Rob called for an intermission, and everyone swarmed the bar.

Laura slid off her stool and made her way only slightly tipsily to Abby's table. "How's the quiz going?" she asked brightly. "Easy questions?"

"The usual mix," Juliet replied. "We've won a couple of times, though, in the past, haven't we?"

"Have you?" Laura sat down in Peter's place; he'd gone to the bar. "How marvelous." She couldn't tell if she sounded sarcastic or not, or even if she felt it. She was definitely a little drunk. "It's very quaint here, isn't it?" she remarked. "When I was younger, it was a bit of a dump."

"Yes, it was, rather, wasn't it?" Juliet replied. "Not that I remember back that far. I've only been here twelve years. But Rob Telford bought it about seven or so years ago, turned the place around."

"Good for him." Laura nodded a little too much. "Oops, Peter's back. Better give him his seat." She stood up, managing not to stumble.

"Why don't you pull up a stool, Laura?" Lucy suggested. "I don't think Rob will mind."

"Yes, pull a stool up," Abby said hurriedly. "We should have asked Rob before. Who cares whether it's four or five?" She sounded so desperate, Laura felt sorry for her. And she really had wanted this evening to go better.

"All right," she said, and Peter gallantly brought over another stool. "As long as I don't get in trouble," she added, and plonked herself down on a stool. Abby met her eyes and smiled.

15

Abby

"HERE'S WHAT WE NEED to do first."

It was nine o'clock on a Monday morning and Abby had just taken Noah to school. Laura stood in front of the till, a piece of paper in her hand, her expression bright and determined. After the disaster when Abby realized she had very stupidly not arranged for Laura to be included in the pub quiz, they'd managed to bounce back a little. The evening had ended well, although her mother had seemed a bit drunk. It had actually been kind of amusing to see Laura loosen up a little. She'd warbled the lyrics to some terrible eighties pop songs as they'd stumbled back down the beach road to home. By the end they'd both been laughing, which was something.

Of course the morning had reverted back to the semitense truce they always seemed to find themselves in, and which Abby did not know how to morph into something else. Something better.

"What do we need to do first?" she asked. The café was empty, summer rain steadily drumming down outside, obscuring the sea. Abby doubted they'd get many customers that morning, or perhaps even all day. A handful of hardy walkers, perhaps, and a couple of mums with babies who were desperate for a morning out. It was the kind of day that she usually enjoyed in the café, at least once in a while. She'd take the opportunity to give everything a good clean or

make a big pot of soup for the determined customers who had ventured out. She didn't think she'd have time to do either today, judging
by her mother's steely look.

"Why don't we sit down and discuss it?" Laura suggested, gesturing
Abby towards one of the empty tables.

"Okay." Abby came out from behind the till and sat down.

"So." Laura sat across from her, slipping her spectacles onto
her nose. She looked older with them on, the gray visible at her
roots. How often had she visited a salon in New York? She'd been in
Hartley-by-the-Sea for three weeks and hadn't, as far as Abby knew,
had any treatments or touch-ups. Perhaps she'd decided to go natural
for a while. "The first thing we need to do is apply for a business loan."

"A business loan?" Abby didn't know whether that prospect made
her feel excited or alarmed. "Why?"

"Because we need to finance the improvements to the café."

"Improvements." Of course she'd been expecting something like
this, judging from the number of lists Laura had made. Still she resisted, out of both fear and hurt. "Why do we need to make improvements?"

"Abby, are you serious?" Elegant eyebrows rose in eloquent skepticism.
"This place is . . ."

"*Don't* say it." Abby held up a hand. "Don't sit here and tell me how
awful everything is, because I know it's all a bit shabby, but I've been
working my bloody behind off, trying to make a go of this place, and
I don't need you to *rescue* it." She broke off, her chest heaving, wishing
she hadn't flared up quite so much—but damn it, she *had* worked
hard. And yes, the café could do with a lick of paint, a few new appliances. But the customers came and people liked it and she was fine
with how it all was. *Fine.* Well, mostly.

"This isn't a criticism of you or how hard you've worked," Laura
said quietly, her hands folded on the tabletop. "If anything, it's a compliment. You've done amazing things, and I want to build on them.

The art showing, the toddler mornings—I think it would be great to do more of that. You source local scones and cakes—why not source more, fruit and veg and the like? I want to build on your foundation, Abby, not tear it all down. And the simple fact is this place needs some decoration and updating. Even you can't deny that."

A small smile tugged at Abby's mouth. The sincere praise her mother had given her, so unthinkingly, had made a warm glow start in her chest, a hum of pleasure at receiving such approval. "Yes, even I can admit that," she said with a good-natured roll of her eyes. Laura grinned.

"Also, I was thinking about opening in the evenings, for supper. Just a few nights a week. Offer maybe just two main courses, but really high—"

"Quality." That nice glow was starting to fade. Abby got where this was going. Her mother wanted to turn the little café by the sea into some tony gastro-café. "I don't see this place getting a Michelin star anytime soon."

"No, I don't mean that kind of thing." Laura leaned back in her chair. "What? Do you think I'm being snooty? Too New York?" Her lips twitched and Abby felt a pulse of relief that they were avoiding another argument.

"Maybe a little."

"We could do a nightclub on weekends," Laura continued, her smile widening. "Have Rob Telford DJ."

Abby let out a snort of laughter. "I can almost picture it."

"So can I. He's quite the flirt, isn't he?"

Rob Telford? And her mother? Abby tried to school the expression on her face into something safely neutral. "Um. I guess. Maybe."

"Anyway." She waved that aside. "Back to the café. I promise, I'm not going to try to turn it into some pompous place. But I want more for it, Abby, and for us. A proper project, something to really work for and get behind."

"It's been that, for me," Abby protested, although that wasn't quite the truth. She'd been too harried, taking care of Noah and Mary, balancing budgets and busing tables, to get really excited about much of anything.

"You're in a rut," Laura stated. "So am I, for that matter. We both need to dig ourselves out."

"You can say I'm in a rut when you've been here all of three weeks? And haven't seen me for six years before that?"

"You're not denying it."

Abby pressed her lips together to keep from retorting a dozen different things that she knew would not be helpful. Just when it felt like they were getting along, everything turned into a battle. She wanted to stop, but she wasn't sure she knew how to lay her weapons down, take off her armor. "Maybe not," she said at last. "But if it's a rut, it's a very small one. I admit, this wasn't what I wanted with my life originally. But I've been here for nearly two years, and Noah and I . . . we're happy. We're safe."

"Safe?" Laura frowned. "Were you not safe in Liverpool?"

"We weren't in danger," Abby clarified. "Not like you're clearly thinking. But everything felt . . . precarious. I was living in a council flat with no money, eking out a life on benefits and part-time jobs, and it was miserable. I wanted more from my life, and trust me, this is more. A lot more."

Laura was silent for a long moment. Abby had no idea what she was thinking. "I didn't know you were on benefits," she said at last.

"Why would you?" Abby responded with a shrug.

"I thought . . ." Laura was silent again. "I didn't realize it was as bad as all that."

"Well, it was. Really bad, if I'm honest, and I felt too proud to go home even though I wanted to. Because Hartley-by-the-Sea has always been my home, even if I dreamed of getting out when I was younger." Abby sighed. Stirring up those old memories didn't feel all that good. "I wish I'd come back sooner, rather than wait until Gran was poorly. If I had . . ." Maybe Mary wouldn't have had a heart attack. Abby could have taken over more of the business, given Mary a proper rest. Some things were too painful to be said out loud.

"Hindsight is twenty-twenty and all that," Laura said with a sad smile. "I wish I'd come back sooner too."

"Do you?" She meant it honestly, and Laura gave her a wry smile.

"Yes, actually, I do. But I also know I wouldn't have, because I was clinging to my city life, my city self, with my French-tipped fingernails. Ah, well. Look at me now. I haven't had my highlights done in eight weeks."

"Horrors," Abby said dryly, and Laura laughed.

"For me, yes, it actually is. How much of my gray can you see? Tell me the truth." She lowered her head so Abby could have a good look.

"Half an inch tops," Abby said, and Laura shuddered.

"There must be a decent hair place between here and Manchester. Anyway." Laura slapped her hand down on the table. "We always seem to be getting off track. Back to the café. Why not try for a business loan, Abby? What's the downside?" She paused, her eyes narrowing thoughtfully. "What are you afraid of?"

Afraid? Abby swallowed uneasily. Yes, she was afraid. She didn't like admitting it, but fear had dogged her in one form or another for far too long. Fear of failing. Fear of losing someone else. Fear of life not going according to plan, which of course it never did. So much fear.

A pair of pensioners came into the café then, shaking out their umbrellas and exclaiming over the weather, as if rain in Cumbria were an oddity. Laura rose from the table and went to serve them, while Abby sat there, still reacting. When was she going to stop feeling afraid?

There was a steady trickle of customers from then through lunch, so she and Laura didn't have a chance to discuss the café or the business loan for several hours. But as she kept busy in the kitchen, Abby started to notice things. The microwave was on its last legs, and they really could use an oven rather than just a stove top. And the paint was peeling and faded, a hospital green color that she'd always hated. As for the café itself . . . when she'd first started back two years ago, she'd just been trying to keep body and soul together. Noah had only just turned three and the change had unsettled him. Mary had been seriously ill, in hospital for weeks while Abby had raced between, trying to keep Mary's spirits up and Noah from melting down. After a few months things had evened out and she'd started to dream a little. She'd had Lucy exhibit her paintings on the walls and she'd begun the toddler mornings, mainly for Noah's sake. She'd imagined holding events, craft fairs or gallery exhibitions, poetry readings even. She'd even gotten as far as doing up some flyers, but time was always slipping through her hands, and she'd hated the thought of failing at something yet again.

That was what was really holding her back, she acknowledged as she slid a ham and cheese toastie onto a plate. Fear. Always the fear.

At half past two the café was empty again and although she really should have been restocking the ice cream, Abby confronted Laura instead.

"Maybe we can compromise."

"I don't usually like that word, but I'm willing to listen." Laura smiled faintly.

"I don't want the café to be all chichi," Abby said slowly. "That's never been the spirit of the place, and frankly I think we'd have to tear it down and start over completely if we wanted to go for that look."

"Maybe," Laura agreed cautiously. "But a few basic improvements . . ."

"Yes, a few basic improvements are needed. I can certainly acknowledge that. We could paint and replace the tables and chairs—"

"And this dreadful lino—"

Abby was about to object and then she glanced down at the floor with its warped and peeling pea green linoleum. "Yes," she agreed. "Definitely the lino."

"I was thinking wooden laminate," Laura offered cautiously. "And I thought we could create a nook overlooking the sea, with sofas and chairs—"

"A nook?" Abby glanced at the rain-smeared picture window. On a clear day it provided a lovely view, but that was all.

"We'd have to bump it out a bit, but it's possible."

"There's nothing on the other side," Abby objected. "It drops right away."

"So we build it on stilts. It would feel fantastic, sitting there, curled up on a sofa with a cappuccino. Like you were almost in a sailboat."

And for a moment Abby could see it. For a few seconds she could picture the café transformed, everything freshly painted and new-smelling, with sofas and chairs, a new and improved espresso machine burbling away. . . .

"Yes," she said slowly. "Maybe. But . . ."

Laura, so nearly buoyant, deflated a little. "But what?"

"I don't want to change what the café *is*. I don't want to turn it into the kind of place you'd find in Keswick or Windermere, the kind of place where everyone wears Barbour or Burberry. The kind of place where the Wests go, if you know them. Not to disparage the Wests, of course. At least not much."

Laura had gone still, saying nothing. Had Abby offended her? "Do you know what I mean?" she continued uncertainly. "I just don't want it to become something hoity-toity and fake. . . ."

"Yes," Laura said after a tiny pause. "I know exactly what you mean."

"I need to get Noah," Abby said. She added, as a peace offering, genuinely meaning it, "But we can talk about this later . . . ?"

"Yes, of course. We'll need to think carefully before we submit a business plan, anyway." Laura was busying herself at the till, moving the napkin dispenser and the army of salt and pepper shakers with unnecessary precision. Abby wished she could see into her mother's head for a few seconds. She had no idea what was going on in there.

"Okay," she said at last. "Well." When Laura, still busy with the salt and pepper shakers, didn't respond, she turned to go get Noah.

Thoughts of the café kept her occupied all the drizzly way up to school. She didn't want to turn the place into a gastropub, but Laura's ideas, so much grander than anything she'd been able to dream up, sparked an excitement inside her she hadn't felt in a long time. Why shouldn't the café be more of a community hub? Hartley-by-the-Sea had a small and shabby village hall, a church that was so cold inside people wore their winter coats in summer, and a pub that had sometimes hosted the school's PTA meetings. That was the extent of its social spaces, besides Raymond's, the tiny bistro by the train station, and the café.

She started walking faster, fizzing inside with ideas she'd had all along but allowed to be buried under the avalanche of everyday needs. More art showings, classes even, book signings for local authors, an after-school baking club . . . The possibilities were endless. They also didn't generate much income. But *still*. She liked the idea of the café being more than a café, of being somewhere people gravitated to, where they wanted to be. She'd made a start, as Laura had said, but together they could do so much more. Together. A word she'd hardly ever associated with her and her mother.

"Hey, slow down." Abby turned to see Lucy coming out of Tarn House. "You looked like you were speed-walking to school. We're not late, are we?"

Abby checked her watch; it was still ten minutes until pickup. "No. How come you're not at school?"

"I don't work Mondays, but I'm picking Poppy up. She needs to have her flower girl's dress fitted."

Poppy was Alex Kincaid's eight-year-old daughter. Abby had seen her on occasion, with her big eyes and ringlets. She was almost annoyingly adorable. "She's going to make an amazing flower girl."

"Isn't she?" Lucy let out a small sigh of satisfaction. "I have to say, I've been really lucky in the stepchildren department."

"Didn't Bella give you some trouble?" Abby asked as Lucy fell in step next to her. Bella was fourteen going on thirty, as far as Abby could tell. She'd seen her hanging outside the post office, all scarlet lipstick and attitude, but still a little too scrawny to pull it off convincingly.

"Yes, a bit at first. And she is a teenager. But I know underneath the surliness and sulks there beats a good heart." Lucy gave Abby a wry smile. "Or so I keep reminding myself. She's a good girl, really. It's been hard on her, losing her mum the way she did."

Alex's first wife had died in a horse riding accident a couple of years before Abby had come back to the village. Abby had heard the murmurs of an unhappy marriage, the sudden accident, but since Alex was new to the village and the head teacher at the primary school to boot, the gossip had been kept to a minimum. He certainly seemed happy these days.

"Well, not long now," she said with a smile. She couldn't imagine meeting someone in Hartley-by-the-Sea. The only single guy she knew was Rob Telford, and he'd been flirting with her mother.

"No, only eight weeks," Lucy agreed. "And there's still so much to do. I was wondering, actually, should I send an invitation to your mother? I don't want her to feel left out. . . ."

"Umm . . ." It didn't seem fair, asking Lucy to invite Laura when she barely knew her, but the gesture might be appreciated. "Maybe . . . if you've got one going spare. Although I don't know if Laura would even go."

"Why don't you call her Mum?" Lucy interjected. "I'm just wondering, because my mother insisted I call her Fiona. She was always saying how she wasn't mumsy."

"I don't know," Abby admitted, a little startled by the question. "I never knew her well enough to call her Mum, I suppose. She was just this glamorous person who drifted in and out of my life and gave me presents."

"Nice presents?" Lucy asked with a smile.

"Expensive ones." The diamond pendant on her sixteenth must have cost a couple of hundred pounds at least. The memory still made Abby want to grit her teeth in frustration and bitterness. Her mother could afford to splash out on a necklace Abby would never wear, but she didn't have the time to visit? Money, she'd thought then, was the cheap way out. Was it the same now?

"I can't see Laura wanting me to call her Mum now," she said, trying to put an end to that line of conversation. "But I'm sure she'd appreciate an invitation to the wedding."

It wasn't until later that evening, when Noah was tucked in bed, that Abby was able to talk to Laura again. *Mum.* She tried the word out in her head. Besides the one time she'd hurled it at her mother like an insult, she'd never called her that. Had she as a two-year-old? She pictured herself as a little girl, chubby and smiling, hands stretched out, toddling towards Laura. *Mama.* The image made her eyes sting and she quickly banished it. No point thinking that way now. No point at all.

"I've been thinking about your improvements," she said when she found Laura at the kitchen table, squinting down at one of her lists.

"Our improvements," she corrected. "Yes?"

"Our improvements," Abby agreed. "I was thinking I like what you said about the café being more of a hub. That's what I was trying for before, and I know I didn't manage much—"

"You've managed a lot, Abby," Laura interjected quietly. "More than I ever did."

"Well." Abby didn't know what to do with her mother's compliments, especially when they sounded so sincere. "Thank you. I was also thinking that Hartley-by-the-Sea doesn't have many nice community spaces. The church is freezing and the village hall smells like stale beer and wee. . . ."

"And sweaty socks," Laura agreed with a faint smile. "Do the Scouts still hold their meetings there?"

"Yes . . ."

"I used to take Simon to Scouts. About a million years ago." She glanced down at her list and again Abby felt that weird, tumbling sensation, like missing the last step on a staircase, falling down a rabbit hole. Her mother had *grown up* here. Her mother knew Hartley-by-the-Sea just as well as she did. Her mother had no doubt helped out at the café on Saturdays as a teenager, just as she had. Had gone to the primary and then Cumberland Academy, just as she had.

It was so *strange*. Her mother had always been an exotic stranger, like a scarlet hibiscus stuck into the thick, miry clay of Cumbrian soil, but she'd grown up here all along. Her roots were just as deep as Abby's.

"So?" Laura prompted. "A community center?"

"Well, like we talked about before. Art showings, book signings, and maybe even after-school clubs, for baking or crafts or something like that. And I'll keep on with the toddler mornings. . . ." She trailed off, because Laura had pursed her lips, her usual sign that she didn't like something. Then she started nodding slowly.

"If we're offering community events, we could try for a grant from the council. And it would be nice to host things like that. Friendlier. Make it a social center, a home away from home." She nodded again, smiling at her in a way that Abby had never experienced before. "I really like it," she said, a definitive statement, an unequivocal acceptance that Abby had never felt from Laura before. And so she nodded and smiled too.

16

Laura

BUSINESS LOANS WERE A bitch. Twenty pages of small type and legalese, personal and professional references, a business plan that had taken her and Abby the better part of two weeks and several bottles of wine to draw up, and then you sent it all in and had to wait for a simple yes or no, no appeals, no second chances. But she wasn't used to those anyway.

"What if they say no?" Abby asked. She and Laura were sitting in the small waiting area in one of the big banks in Whitehaven, waiting to be called in and given their verdict. It was early July and baking hot, the kind of day that had every Cumbrian out in vests and T-shirts, spritzing on the tanning accelerator and soaking up the rays as if they were in Tenerife. "If they say no," Abby persisted when Laura hadn't responded, "it's over. We won't be able to do any of the improvements. We'll just have to go on as is." Which was what Abby had wanted originally, but after two weeks of designing their business plan, her daughter had started to get excited about the possibility of change. Laura had liked seeing it, the sparkle in her eyes, the sudden smiles. *She'd* had something to do with that. She felt proud in a way she never had before.

"We can paint, in any case," Laura said, shifting in her seat. Her bum was sticking to the plastic; it was that hot. She'd probably have a damp patch on her skirt. Really classy. "A couple tins of paint won't cost that much." Although considering she didn't have more than a few wrinkled tenners to her name, even paint was beyond her budget. She and Abby had had a look at the bank accounts while going over the business plan, and the news had been fairly grim. Mary hadn't had savings besides a few hundred pounds in personal checking, and the business account covered the café's running expenses and only a little more. Abby had been living off the child benefit she received for Noah—a mere eighty pounds a month—and a tiny wage she paid herself out of the café's profits.

"You do know you're making less than half of the minimum wage, even with your child benefit?" Laura had said one evening when they'd been sitting in front of the accounts, and Abby had shrugged.

"I felt guilty, taking money from Gran."

"She was taking money from you, in a sense, letting you work for practically nothing."

"She raised me," Abby said quietly. "I owed her."

God help her, but that had stung, more so because Abby hadn't flung it at her as an accusation as she'd done in the past, merely quietly stated it as a fact. And it *was* a fact. But it was just one of many, and there were plenty that Abby didn't know, wouldn't understand. Even so, Laura wasn't about to tell her any of them. It wasn't fair to bring all that up now, so many years later, no matter how Abby had asked for answers. If she knew the answers, she might wish she hadn't asked. And Laura didn't want to invite pity or worse.

In the end Laura had insisted on having them both paid a minimum wage, as part of the business plan. "It's not sustainable, otherwise," she said.

"It might not be sustainable, full stop," Abby answered grimly. "The café doesn't make that much money. The summer tides us over in the winter, and it has had an uptick in the last year or so, but it's still a struggling proposition. It always has been."

"It's doing a lot better now than it was when I was a child," Laura said, although she didn't really want to bring all that up. She'd rather banish the memory of being skint for her whole childhood, never having enough money for holidays or treats or sometimes even the basics. When her father had died, it had been even worse. His on-again, off-again work as a car mechanic hadn't paid much, but it had helped, and when he'd gone, Mary's attitude towards the café had been grudging at best.

"Miss Rhodes?" The bank manager stood in front of them, a small, paunchy man dressed in a gray suit with a lavender shirt and a deeper purple tie. It reminded Laura of something Simon would have worn, and it made her spirit wilt just a little. She didn't want to be subject to a small man with small ideas. She wanted someone who would dream big, who could picture life beyond dreary making do and columns that only just added up. "Or should I say the Misses Rhodes?" he said with a small smile and a sparkle in his eye that made Laura like him a little better.

"We are the Misses Rhodes," she confirmed with a touch of grandeur, and followed him into a small office crammed with furniture made of fake wood and several dull-looking certificates in cheap frames on the walls.

"So, your business plan for a small loan." The man, Adam Barston, slipped on a pair of glasses to look down at the application on his desk that Laura and Abby had sweated blood, or at least a lot of cheap wine, over. "You're applying for a loan of twenty-five thousand pounds to renovate the existing café at the Hartley-by-the-Sea beach promenade."

From his tone Laura couldn't tell if it was a question. "Yes, that's right."

"Your business plan is quite thorough."

"Thank you," she said after a tiny pause where she wondered about the right response. Next to her Abby sat tensely, hands clenched in her lap, teeth sunk into her lower lip.

Adam Barston perused the plan for a few more excruciating moments before he looked up, taking off his glasses and rubbing the bridge of his nose where two red indents remained. "You must know, in the current economy, most banks are very wary of approving all but the most watertight of business plans."

"We are aware, yes," Laura said. She was already bracing herself for the bad news, could feel the first ripples of the tidal wave of disappointment that was coming her and Abby's way.

"And you might also know, Miss Rhodes"—he turned to face Laura, smiling slightly—"with your experience in the industry, that most start-up restaurants close within the first year."

"Ninety percent," Laura confirmed coolly. "Yes, I do know that." She made herself smile as pleasantly as she could. "But we're not a start-up."

"No," the banker agreed—he wasn't the manager, just an associate—with a shake of his head. "But with the current profit the café is making, it's clear you need to appeal to a far wider customer base."

"We intend to achieve that with our renovations," Laura replied swiftly. "As you can see from our business plan."

"Yes, I did see that. I also saw that you are applying to the council for a grant?"

"Yes . . ." She'd gotten as far as looking it up on the council Web site. Abby's laptop was ancient and they didn't have a printer.

"Have you had any interest from the council?"

"We're in the process of submitting our application."

"I see." Laura was afraid he saw too well. *Look*, she wanted to say as she leaned forward and grabbed him by his violently purple tie. *We're not amateurs. We're not afraid of hard work. We can do this. Give us a chance to prove it to you, to the village, to each other.* She bit her tongue instead. Hard.

"Well." Barston folded his hands on his desk. "I'm pleased to say we are in a position to grant you a loan of twenty thousand pounds, with the café property used as collateral."

Twenty thousand rather than twenty-five, and if it went pear-shaped, they could lose it all, but . . . they had a loan. Laura felt a smile spreading across her face like butter on toast. They'd actually succeeded at something. Together. For once.

"Thank you," she said when she managed to find her voice. Abby was staring dumbly at Barston, as if she hadn't understood a word he'd said. "Abby?" she prompted.

"Thank you," Abby managed, her voice coming out a bit choked. "Thank you very much."

He spent the next ten minutes going over all the details of the loan, and then they signed a bunch of paperwork, and Laura knew she really should pay attention to it all because it was clearly very important, but she couldn't. Her brain was fizzing like a firework, and mentally she was doing a celebratory chicken dance. *They'd done it.* They'd actually done it.

Eventually they stumbled out to the street, turned to each other, both of them no doubt looking slightly stunned. And then they started laughing.

"We must look like a pair of lunatics," Laura gasped out as she clutched at her sides. This was the second time she'd laughed like this with Abby. It really felt good, buzzier than the biggest G&T she'd ever had. "Laughing our heads off in the middle of the street."

"I don't care," Abby answered as she wiped at her streaming eyes. "We actually got the money. Do you think he knocked five thousand pounds off just to be cheap?"

"Probably," Laura said. "But who cares? I'll take twenty."

"So will I," Abby agreed fervently. "So will I."

On the drive back home in Abby's banger of a car—Laura had returned her rental weeks ago—Abby swung into the car park of Tesco's. "We should celebrate."

"With what?"

"Champagne, cake, and pizza for Noah."

"Sounds good to me."

Noah was elated when he came home that afternoon to a party atmosphere, pizza in the oven, and a fancy shop-bought cake with *Congratulations* swirled in blue on top. Laura didn't think she'd ever seen Abby so animated, humming as she cooked, her eyes bright, her mind clearly racing. She felt as if her daughter had woken up from a stupor, a mental Sleeping Beauty. And she'd been the one, at least in part, to give her the kiss.

"What do you think we should do first?" she asked Laura when Noah was tucked up in bed, although judging by the squeaks and creaks coming from upstairs, not to mention all the sugar he'd had, he wasn't going to sleep anytime soon.

"First we need to deal with the home side of things," Laura said. "Clear out Mary's room properly and get ourselves situated."

"But the money . . ."

"We also need to buy a decent computer and printer. Any small business should have one. And then, when we're set up as we mean to go on, we can turn to the café."

"Okay," Abby said after a moment. "Then what?"

Laura opened her mouth to launch into what she thought they should do with the café, starting with the paint and the floor, and then she closed it. Abby stared at her, forehead wrinkled.

"Well . . . ?"

"What do you think we should do?" Laura asked.

"Me?" Abby looked startled. "I don't know. You're the one with the business expertise. . . ."

"Not that much expertise," Laura dismissed. "You're the one who has been working here for the last two years. So what do you think we should do first? What do you *want* to do first?"

"I'd like to extend the kitchen first," Abby said, sounding shy, a tentative smile lighting up her face. "I've realized how awful it is. Tiny and cramped and the paint's peeling. We need a proper cooker, and the wiring needs redoing, I think. . . ." She trailed off, looking uncertain, and Laura realized the expression on her face was less than enthusiastic.

The trouble was, the kitchen was the last thing she wanted to do. Yes, they needed a newer and bigger kitchen, but it would be expensive and no doubt swallow up far too much of their money. Better to do the interior decorating first, spruce the place up to attract the wider customer base Adam Barston said they needed, than to spend half their loan at least on a part of the café no one else saw.

"What do you think?" Abby asked, and Laura injected a bright note into her voice as she answered, "Sounds like a good idea to me. We can start offering a more extensive menu then."

"Yes, although . . . can you cook?"

"I'm sure between the two of us we can manage something." Hiring a cook was definitely outside the budget for now. "You do a mean bangers and mash."

Abby laughed. "Hardly gourmet, though."

"If people want gourmet, they can go to Raymond's. The important thing is to start." Because she had a feeling Abby wasn't so good at the starting.

"Then we should do some interior decorating too," Abby said. "If we're going to offer proper meals, we need better chairs and tables."

Laura sat back, nodding. "I think that's a terrific idea."

The next week was a flurry of activity. First they cleared out Mary's room, boxing up the few photographs and bits of cheap jewelry they decided to keep, and putting the rest in bin bags for the charity shop. As both of them had expected, there hadn't been much to save.

At the bottom of a cupboard Abby came across a stack of photo albums, the old-fashioned kind, with the pictures pasted in. "I've never seen this," she exclaimed, and Laura, in the middle of bundling up some very old sheets, looked over and tensed.

"I haven't seen those since I was little," she said quietly. She could feel her heart beating hard because she wasn't sure she wanted to see them now. Abby looked up at her with a question in her eyes, as if she sensed her mood.

"Can I..."

Laura took a deep breath. "Go on, then."

Abby brought the albums over to the stripped bed, and they sat together, the first album on their laps. The pasteboard cover creaked as Abby turned it; the pictures were old and faded, their corners peeling up, the glue yellowed beneath.

"Goodness," Laura murmured. She felt faint as she caught sight of the first snap: her and her dad building sand castles on the beach. She was about three.

"Is this you?" Abby brought the book closer to her face, peering at the blurry, sepia-tinted seventies photo in amazement. "You're actually blond!"

"I was, as a child," Laura said dryly. "It's only as an adult I've had to have a little chemical help." She glanced back at the book and then away again; part of her wanted to stare and stare and part of her wanted to push the album away.

"And this is your dad," Abby said softly. "My grandfather."

"Yes." Mel Rhodes was sporting seventies-style sideburns and a droopy handlebar mustache. Laura had forgotten about that mustache. He'd shaved it off when she'd been about five, after her mother had complained it made him look like a bank robber.

"He looks like someone who laughed a lot," Abby said, and Laura felt her throat go tight. This hadn't been a good idea.

"Yes, he was," she said, and reached over to flip the page. Two full pages of Simon squeezed into a high chair with a sour look on his face. She could handle looking at those.

"Charming as ever," she said lightly, and Abby smiled and flipped the page. Damn.

"Your fourth-birthday party . . ." Complete with party hat and streamers, and a pink gooey cake. "Did Gran make that? I didn't think she liked baking."

"My dad made it. He always baked the birthday cakes." And they'd always looked awful, with lopsided layers and runny icing, but tasted absolutely delicious. "It was a family tradition, at least for a while."

Abby touched the photo lightly with her fingers. "He sounds like someone I would have liked to have known."

For a moment Laura let herself imagine it, if her father hadn't died. Her mother wouldn't have withdrawn; they wouldn't have fought, or at least not as much. Her father would have *been* there. And she wouldn't have had Abby. It was too much to think about.

"So, what about a lick of paint?" Laura suggested, closing the photo album and standing up. "Brighten the room up?" The walls were the same faded and stained magnolia that they'd been when she was a child.

"Maybe," Abby agreed slowly. "Do you mind if I look through these?" she asked, gesturing to the albums. Laura nodded, not quite trusting herself to speak.

"And the paint?" she prompted after a moment, when Abby didn't seem inclined to say anything else. She was resting her hands lightly on top of the albums, as if she didn't want to let them go.

"I don't know. It would take up so much time. . . ."

"Not that much. Why not pick something bright and cheerful?"

Abby, Laura reflected later, was not a doer. She hemmed and hawed and dragged her feet, and yet when Laura got her going—steering her towards the DIY superstore in Workington and picking out a raft of paint samples—she became excited and animated, waking slowly from her state of inertia.

"I love this rose color," she said, waving a paint sample as they sat at an outside table at Costa Coffee, sipping iced cappuccinos through straws and enjoying the watery sunshine. "What do you think?"

Laura thought it looked like the inside of someone's stomach, but she smiled and nodded. "Lovely. It will really brighten the place up."

They painted the next day, with Noah helping after school, and tracking footprints the color of raspberry puke all over the upstairs. "Never mind. The hall needs painting too," Laura said brightly. She was determined to be positive, nearly manic, needing to keep everyone sailing along, sucking the enjoyment out of every moment of this new start. She liked being busy, feeling needed, but it also exhausted her. It seemed sometimes that Abby would start to flag or wilt at the smallest setback; when the luridly pink paint wasn't able to be ready-bought but had to be mixed at the shop, she'd almost gone for another color. Laura had had to buoy her along, insisting they could wait for it to be mixed, that it would be worth it. Even if she wasn't crazy about the color, Abby was.

She arranged for several local companies to come and give estimates for a new floor; she and Abby spent over an hour dabbing paint samples on various spots on the walls of the café, trying to determine whether the primrose yellow looked too much like wee, or if the soothing sage green reminded them of a hospital. They ended up settling on a pale spring sky blue that made the interior of the café feel light and airy.

One Friday morning she and Abby drove to a furniture warehouse near Carlisle and picked out a dozen oak tables. They weren't cheap, and Laura sucked in a hard breath at the price of a single chair. Forty-eight of those suckers were going to put a serious dent in their already depleted twenty grand.

"Why don't we get a whole bunch of different chairs?" Abby suggested. "From charity shops, in all different styles? We could paint them bright colors, emphasize their differences rather than make everything look samey-samey."

Laura thought it would make the café look like a nursery classroom, but new chairs were going to cost over three thousand pounds. Cheap and cheerful it was. She could live with it, and Abby's idea of painting them was actually a pretty good one.

The workmen started the next week, bringing in their hammers and drills and generating a ton of noise and dirt. They closed the café for three days, covering everything in tarps, and visited nearly every charity shop between Whitehaven and Carlisle in search of chairs, rickety, wobbly, unique.

Abby picked out paint in a variety of bright colors and pastels, and Laura picked out a couple of more soothing shades herself. "Just to round it out," she told Abby. The café wasn't going to be quite the elegant space she had once envisioned, but what was emerging was just as good, if not better. It was a joint project, a shared venture, which was better than any vision Laura could have conjured on her own.

All the change and activity swirling around had hyped Noah up, and he tended to bounce around the flat like a rubber ball. A noisy rubber ball. Laura had forgotten, if she'd ever known, how loud children were. How *much*. When they were around, there was never a break. Noah was constantly getting in the way, standing in front of the fridge while she held the milk, asking questions while she was reading the paper, pushing his elbow into her stomach when he sat next to her on the sofa. At first she didn't mind it; she liked the way he flopped next to her, instantly making himself comfortable. But after several weeks of constant motion and noise, she started wanting to scream.

"It's just because of the school fete next weekend," Abby explained when Laura must have been looking particularly disgruntled. Noah had done a running jump onto the sofa where she'd been sitting, causing her to spill hot tea all over her lap. Abby had dragged him off and handed Laura a dish towel to blot herself dry. "And the summer holidays coming up," she added.

Summer holidays. Laura tried to arrange her face in a pleasant expression at this news. "What do you do with Noah during the summer?" she asked, amazed that she hadn't thought of this before. Six of the café's busiest weeks with Noah constantly underfoot. Lovely as he could be, it didn't bear thinking about.

"We manage," Abby said, which didn't sound good at all. "He goes to Meghan some days—she's a registered childminder. Other days he just bops about here or I take him to the beach if it's not too busy, and Gran was up for managing on her own."

Bops about? Laura nodded slowly. "I see."

"You could take him out sometime," Abby said unexpectedly.

"Me?" Laura realized how surprised she sounded. "I mean, yes. That would be . . ." Terrifying. Noah may have latched onto her a little bit in Mary's absence, but Laura still wasn't sure how she felt about it. The thought of actually being in charge of him filled her with alarm. But telling her daughter she wasn't good with children hardly seemed tactful. "Lovely," she finished. "That would be lovely."

A smile twitched Abby's mouth. Laura knew she didn't believe her. "It would be good for you to have some quality time with your grandson."

Quality time. That was a concept Laura didn't think she bought into. She certainly hadn't had any quality time as a kid. "Great," she said. "Super. We'll definitely have to do that."

17

◦

Abby

"WHAT DO YOU THINK?"

Abby emerged from the dressing room of the wedding boutique in Cockermouth and looked doubtfully down at the bell-shaped pink tulle skirt that ended above the knee and the white lace top that her bridesmaid outfit comprised. She looked like a cross between a sugar-plum fairy and a piece of bubble gum.

"I love it," Lucy enthused. "It's so fun."

Abby looked at her friend's bright smile and knew there was only one answer. "I love it too."

"Do you, really?" Lucy asked, her enthusiasm morphing into concern. "Are you sure? I know it's not . . . Well, I suppose it's not *elegant*. . . ."

"No," Abby agreed. "Not elegant, exactly." It wasn't something she could see, for example, her mother wearing.

"But I don't want an elegant wedding. I hate the whole concept of elegance." Lucy gave a theatrical shudder.

"The concept of elegance?"

"My mother," Lucy explained with another deliberate shudder. "Elegance personified."

Which was kind of like Abby's mother, although in the last few weeks, as they'd been doing up the café, Laura had started to let herself go. It was still a bit of a shock to see Laura without a professionally made-up face, a sleek hairdo, the designer clothes. Actually, it was kind of nice. Abby felt less inferior, and less pressure to match her mother's panache—not that she had ever really tried. But Laura in a fleece and worn jeans, her gray roots showing, and not a lick of makeup on her face—that was someone Abby was starting to think she could actually like.

"This dress is definitely you," Abby said, because even if she looked like a piece of gum, it was a dress that looked lighthearted, promised fun. And, she dutifully reminded herself, it was Lucy's day, after all. "How does Juliet feel about the dress?" she asked.

"I haven't shown it to her yet," Lucy admitted. "I have a feeling she's going to resist."

"A feeling?" Abby couldn't keep from letting out a laugh. "I'd say that's a massive understatement, Luce. But you've always been an optimist."

"True." Lucy grinned. "I'm putting off having her try it on so we won't have time to find something else. Is that awful of me?"

"Strategic," Abby answered. "What about your American friend? Chloe?"

"She's bought it online and is fine with it," Lucy said with a wave of her hand. "Really, it's only Juliet that might botch things up."

"I'll just go change." It might be Lucy's wedding day, but Abby intended to wear the dress for as little time as possible. A pink bell-shaped skirt did not do her legs any favors. "What about your dress?" she called from behind the curtain as she slipped off the pink tulle. "Have you had your final fitting?"

"Not yet, but . . . do you want me to try it on?" Lucy's voice bubbled with suppressed excitement and longing.

"Is it here? Sure." Abby emerged from the dressing room in her usual wear of jeans and a fleece to see Lucy disappearing into a different one with a huge plastic-wrapped bundle. The Dress.

She sat on a cream divan, trying not to get anything dirty, while she waited for Lucy to emerge, a bridal butterfly from the chrysalis of the dressing room. "Where's Noah today?" Lucy called over the rustle and slide of her dress.

"He's at Nathan's. And Laura's minding the café." She felt guilty, leaving Laura managing on her own for half of a sunny Saturday, but her mother hadn't seemed to mind. The café had new floors, painted walls, oak tables, and colorful chairs. Phase One of their redevelopment plan was complete, and it gave Abby a little ping of pride every time she came into the room and saw how nice it looked.

Laura, though, barely seemed to stop long enough to notice. She was already on to new plans—a bigger and better espresso machine, hiring someone to do the ice cream, finding estimates for the expanded kitchen. Abby's resistance had melted in the face of her mother's indefatigable determination, and realistically she knew she never could have done this stuff on her own. Amazingly too, Laura had deferred to her opinion more than once. They were actually getting along. Sort of. As long as they didn't talk about the past or do any emoting. They'd keep focused on the café and they'd be fine. -Ish. Because the past still loomed there, like something dark and prehistoric beneath the surface of still water. Something that came with creepy music and shadowy camera angles in a horror movie.

"Well. Here it is." Lucy emerged from the dressing room, swathed in slim-fitting ivory satin with intricate beadwork down the sides and a mermaid's tail of lace pooling around her feet.

Did anyone not get teary when presented with the sight of a friend in all her wedding glory? "Oh, Lucy," Abby said, sniffing, "you look gorgeous."

"Thank you." Lucy swished around in front of the three-way mirror. "I have to ask. Does my butt look big in this?"

"Definitely not."

"You probably wouldn't tell me anyway, would you?"

"Are you kidding? Of course I wouldn't."

Lucy laughed. "Juliet would. She told me she was the only person who would tell me the truth about whether I looked like a meringue."

"That's Juliet. And there is nothing meringuey about you or this dress. You look exactly like you should look. A radiant bride."

Lucy turned back to Abby. "Did you ever pick out a wedding dress? When you were engaged?"

"What?" The abrupt turn in conversation startled Abby, although it was typical of Lucy to think about other people that way. "No, never got that far." Never actually got to the engaged part, not really, although Abby had told people she and Ben were engaged. Because they had talked about it. She still thought he would have come round if he hadn't crashed his motorcycle into a concrete bollard. At least, she hoped he would have.

"That must have been so hard, though," Lucy said quietly. "Going from planning a wedding to planning a funeral."

She hadn't actually planned either. "Yeah, well, it wasn't the best time of my life."

Lucy finally got the hint that Abby didn't want to talk about it. "Let me get this thing off and we can grab some lunch. You don't have to be back yet, do you?"

Abby gave the clock a guiltily cursory glance. "No, not yet." Soon, though.

They bought sandwiches at one of Cockermouth's upscale delis and took them to Harris Park, along the River Cocker. It was wonderfully pleasant to sit on a park bench watching the river flow by and have nowhere to go, nowhere to be.

"So things seem better with Laura?" Lucy asked as she bit into her ham and cheese baguette. "The café looks amazing."

"Yes, it does look pretty good, doesn't it? And things are better between us, for the most part. We're not arguing or ignoring each other, anyway, which is something."

"She ought to come to another pub night," Lucy said. "I feel badly she wasn't included before—"

"That wasn't your fault. It was mine. I stupidly didn't think about telling everyone and making space."

"Easy enough to do."

"Yes, but..." Abby sighed. Her olive branch had been an epic fail, which somehow seemed typical. And although they'd spent plenty of time debating paint samples and pricing espresso machines, they hadn't actually talked about anything personal or important. What was going to happen when they ran out of improvements, and they had to face all the things they hadn't said? All the questions Abby hadn't dared to ask, which she knew Laura didn't want to answer?

"At least we're getting along right now," she told Lucy. "More or less. She's even taking Noah to the school fete next weekend while I man the café."

"Turning into a proper grandma?"

"Nana, actually. And yes. Sort of." Laura wasn't a particularly cuddly grandmother, and sometimes a look of panic crossed her face when Noah came at her full throttle. But Abby thought she was trying, and it made her veer between a kind of cautious joy and a trembling panic. What if Noah started to depend on Laura? What if she did? Hell, they already were, both of them, and if Laura went—when she went—it was going to hurt. Stupidly.

Later, driving down into Hartley-by-the-Sea, the houses and shops nestled between the sea and the fells, Abby felt a sudden pang of affection for the place, for her life. For most of her childhood and teen years, she'd wanted only to get away, start over somewhere new, be someone new. Someone who wasn't a misfit in school, a lonely orphan at home. Coming back had felt like failure at first, and then, for the two years since, she'd felt as if she were huddling against the world, hoarding what happiness she'd managed to eke out for her and Noah. She'd told herself it was enough, and in a way it had been.

And yet it seemed as if it was taking Laura coming back into her life—or, really, into her life for the first time—to make Abby dare to dream a little bigger, or even at all.

"How have things been?" she asked as she came into the café. Laura was at the ice cream counter, dishing out double scoops, with a queue snaking around to the bathrooms.

"Busy." Her mother, for once, looked a little hassled, her hair coming out of its usual neat ponytail, her face red and a little shiny with both heat and effort.

"Let me help." Abby shoved her bag behind the till and took up residence behind the counter. The café was pleasingly busy, and it gave her a lift to see the room full of people, to hear the sounds of laughter and chatter.

After an hour the ice cream rush dropped off and only a couple of tables were filled as late-afternoon sunlight slanted through the windows. Laura came from behind the counter, taking off her scoop-stained apron with a grimace. "I forgot how sticky ice cream is."

"Did you dish it out as a teenager?"

"Every Saturday and most school day afternoons. Your grandmother didn't believe in employing paid help." Laura spoke lightly enough, but Abby sensed a hidden rancor beneath the words.

"That must have been tough. I only did the occasional Saturday when I was in secondary." It felt like an apology. "She said I needed the time to study."

"Perhaps she learned a lesson there, then. I think I would have barely scraped five Cs if I'd stayed on."

"Five Cs? You mean, GCSEs?"

"Yes, my year group was one of the first to do GCSEs instead of the old O levels."

"But . . . you didn't even get your GCSEs?" Somehow this had escaped Abby. "I thought you were in sixth form when . . . when you had me."

"I would have been in sixth form, but as it was, I dropped out when I was just a few months pregnant. I had terrible morning sickness. Couldn't keep a thing down." Laura was using that light, almost disinterested tone that Abby was starting to realize masked much deeper emotions. Emotions she had assumed her mother hadn't had.

"I didn't realize that."

Laura raised eyebrows that were a little shaggier than usual. "Does it really matter?"

"I don't know." Somehow it did matter. Her mother hadn't even gotten her Grade 11 exams—there was no way she could have ever gotten a job that required any kind of qualifications, or tried for a university degree. Had she wanted those things? Had she had dreams beyond Hartley-by-the-Sea? *Of course she had. She left you to follow them.* And yet Abby still couldn't reconcile the image of a struggling teenage dropout with her glamorous, worldly mother.

"A few GCSEs wouldn't have made much difference," Laura dismissed with a shrug. "Now, I wanted to talk to you about this idea I had—"

"I just don't understand why you had me," Abby blurted. The words fell into the stillness of the room like rocks chucked into a pool, each one creating a loud, awkward splash. The family in the corner, who had been quietly nibbling scones, fell entirely silent.

Laura fell silent too, staring at Abby, her lips slightly parted. "I mean, really, why?" Abby asked, trying to moderate her voice and not quite being able to. "You've never said. My—my father wanted a termination, right? Why didn't you? You screwed up your whole life by having me."

Laura closed her mouth and pursed her lips. "That's not a great way to see yourself, Abby."

"But seriously. You were only fifteen when you fell pregnant—"

"Almost sixteen."

"So *young*," Abby said in a low voice. "Did you like school? Would you have wanted to stay on?"

Laura shrugged. "I was never that academic. Like I said, I would have scraped a couple of GCSEs, that's all."

"Even so . . ."

"I made the choice I did for a reason, Abby. You're right. I could have had a termination. It was a choice not to, and one I accepted." She paused, her lips pursing again. "Even if I didn't realize all of the consequences."

"All of them? What do you—"

"Now how about my idea?" Laura said, raising her voice to talk over Abby. Now clearly wasn't the best time for the heart-to-heart Abby had been trying for. "Lunch boxes." She gestured to a dozen fold-up boxes that they used to make children's lunches. "You sell them in the café for kids, which is a brilliant idea, but what about adult ones, offering a sandwich, a drink, some crisps? Sell it for less than all the parts separately."

"And this will make us money?" Abby said. She'd drop the questioning about the past for now. She needed time to think through what her mother had said, as well as what she seemed reluctant to say. She felt as if her assumptions had been put in a kaleidoscope and twirled, everything she'd thought she believed falling into a new and confusing pattern.

"Yes, they will make us money, because we'll go out and flog them on the beach and the caravan site." A note of triumph had entered Laura's voice and she picked up one of the boxes with a flourish. "I've made up about a dozen for you to try today."

"What?" Abby took an instinctive step back. "You want me to try to sell those on the beach *now*?"

"What's so unreasonable about that? Think of the people who come to the beach but don't bring any food. They can't be bothered to go the café, but when it's there in front of them, offered at a discounted price . . . how can they resist?"

"I'm not really good with the hard sell. . . ."

"Have you ever actually tried?" Laura's lips twitched as if she was suppressing a laugh. She knew she was pushing Abby out of her comfort zone. She was doing it intentionally.

"No, I haven't tried," Abby said tartly, "because I already know I'm not."

"Abby." Laura skewered her with a look as she held out the lunch box. "Try it."

Standing there, receiving that maternal just-do-it glare, Abby felt more like a daughter than she had in a long time, maybe ever. It was a weird feeling, annoying and gladdening at the same time. It made her want to both smile and stamp her foot. She felt like a child, and that was actually no bad thing.

"Fine," she said, and took the lunch box.

"Take all of them. There's twelve. I thought we could retail them for a fiver each."

"Five pounds seems a lot—"

"There's a sandwich, a soda, a packet of crisps, and a millionaire shortbread. I think it's a deal."

Abby glanced dubiously at the pile of lunch boxes. "I need to get Noah soon—"

"Then you're motivated to sell them quickly, aren't you?" Laura turned back to the till; a couple of sandy, barefoot children had come in, wanting ice cream, pound coins clutched in grubby hands.

"I suppose I'll forgo the shirt-and-shoes policy in this instance," Laura murmured before greeting them with a smile.

Abby loaded herself up with the lunch boxes and headed outside. What, exactly, was she supposed to do? Walk up to random strangers and ask them if they were hungry? She'd never been good at the retail side of things; she'd always preferred staying in the kitchen while Mary, in her loud and comfortable way, handled the till. Abby had always felt too shy, too unsure, to manage the banter that had come naturally to her grandmother. It came naturally to her mother, as well; despite her seeming aversion to children, she'd been calmly in control, dishing out ice cream to those two towheaded tots.

Laura, Abby mused as she walked reluctantly towards the beach, was in her element anywhere in the café. As they'd progressed with the renovations and envisioned a new future for the place, Laura had become more and more vibrant and energetic. Abby had too, in her own way; she'd been having fun these last few weeks, doing the café up. Starting to dream.

But this?

Taking a deep breath, she squared her shoulders and headed out onto the sand. The tide had been out for a while and the sand was nearly dry. Day-trippers were making the most of it, spread out with towels and sunshades, buckets and spades and butterfly nets. Abby watched two small children intently studying a crab scuttling towards a rock pool, and smiled. Noah would have been the same. The beach and all its offerings had saved her sanity more than once in the last two years.

Burdened down by her tray of boxes, as well as a genuine need to fetch Noah from Nathan's soon, she decided to head for the nearest family spread out on a blanket with a spill of discarded Welly boots and jumpers.

"Hello," she called, her voice already sounding a false note. "Anyone hungry?" The family turned to regard her with narrowed eyes. "I work at the beach café," she explained, nodding towards the building above them on the end of the promenade. "I've got some ready-made lunch boxes for people enjoying themselves down here." She thought she saw the mother's interest perk up and she continued quickly. "A soda, sandwich, crisps, and a homemade biscuit for four pounds." Sod five pounds. It was too much.

"Four pounds?" The father and the mother exchanged glances while the children clambered forward to see what was on offer.

"I'm hungry," the girl said plaintively, and the mother got up to peer in one of the boxes.

"Is it organic?"

"Umm . . . no. Just . . . your usual."

The woman pursed her lips. "Sorry. We eat all organic." She pulled the girl away. "Come along, Daisy. We'll have something at home."

The girl continued to whinge while Abby walked away, trying to keep her chin up. Rejection was part of the sales pitch. She knew what her mother would say. *So try again. They're only one family on the beach.* Funny, how she could imagine what Laura would have said. For years she'd had no idea.

Abby walked up to a pair of women in their twenties sunbathing in string bikinis and almost immediately regretted it. They were stick-thin and unlikely to want a calorific picnic lunch. But to her amazement they did, exclaiming at the convenience, and within a few minutes Abby was walking away two lunches lighter, with a tenner in her pocket.

She walked away as the women cracked open the cans of soda, and saw several people looking her way in curiosity and hope. A smile spreading across her face, she headed to the next group of people, ready to sell some more lunches.

18

Laura

ABBY HADN'T SAID ANYTHING about a parade.

"I thought you knew," Abby exclaimed when Laura mentioned this fact the morning of the school fete. Noah stood between them, resplendent in a shop-bought luridly yellow costume. "Didn't you go to the fete when you were a child?"

Had she? It felt like looking through the wrong end of a telescope, trying to recall those aspects of her childhood. "I never dressed up," she said at last. "I might have watched once or twice." Curiosity compelled her to ask, "What about you? Did you dress up?"

Abby looked almost guilty as she admitted, "A couple of times. Gran made me a Tweenies costume once. I was Bella. Yarn hair and everything."

"Were you?" Laura tried to sift through the feelings this admission caused her. Envy, that Abby had had the kind of maternal interest from Mary she hadn't had. Gratitude, that her mother had done the things she should have for her own daughter. Sadness, for having both feelings. She turned to Noah with as bright a smile as she could manage. "Well, you make a very good . . ." For the life of her she couldn't remember what he was.

"Minion," Abby filled in. Her tone was almost gentle. "I would have sewn something, but . . ." She grimaced guiltily.

198

"Why sew when you can buy?" Laura answered with a shrug. "Right." She clapped her hands even though she really wasn't a clappy-hands kind of person. "Well. I suppose we'd better get on. Where does the parade start?"

"Top of the high street, at the turning circle to the Phillips estate."

"Ah, that wasn't there when I was growing up."

"Even Hartley-by-the-Sea changes a little." They shared a smile of understanding that felt both good and strange at the same time. They'd been so busy with the café for the last few weeks that Laura didn't know where she and Abby actually stood, as friends, as well as mother and daughter, if they stood anywhere in regard to that fraught relationship.

Noah was practically dancing beside her as they started walking up the beach road towards the village. A few other children and parents were walking along, and some of them greeted Noah and gave Laura an appraising look, a cautious smile. She did the same. It felt like some sort of truce between her and the village, a step in the right direction.

The crowd of parents and children swelled as they turned up the high street, so it seemed like a parade in reverse. People were coming out of their houses with deck chairs, cups of tea, and the odd pint to watch the show stream by their house. Laura had forgotten what an event something like this could be in Hartley-by-the-Sea. Everyone got involved. Colored bunting decorated the whole of the high street, waving in the breeze, and the post office was decked out with flags and streamers. Claire West stood in the doorway, smiling and waving.

"Hello, Noah! What a fantastic Minion you make!" Her smile turned slightly unsure as she caught sight of Laura. "Hello . . ."

"Hello." Laura knew she should thaw towards poor Claire West. She couldn't help being from a family that was rich, entitled, and smug. She couldn't help it and had no idea that they'd made Laura's life a misery a long time ago. Claire had nothing to do with it; she'd been two years old at the time. "I like the decorations," she said, nodding towards the shopwindow. She was pretty sure Claire and not Dan Trenton was responsible for the bright display of fete-related products—sweets, bunting, and some character-themed decorations.

Claire's smile was wide and surprised. "Thanks!"

At the top of the street, children milled around in various costumes; plenty of them were shop-bought like Noah's, but others were masterpieces of cardboard and felt, including the elaborate costume of a little girl who was walking around as a full English fry-up; someone had manufactured an enormous plate made of cardboard that she was somehow managing to wear, with a couple of fried eggs and rashers of bacon glued onto it. Her friend was dressed up as a huge bottle of ketchup. First prize right there. Parents were snapping pictures with their phones and digital cameras, and slightly harassed-looking teachers were trying to shepherd the children into year group formations.

"You're in . . . ?" Laura asked Noah, ashamed to realize she didn't actually know what year he was in. Reception? Year One?

"I'm in Reception, Nana," Noah told her kindly, and Laura gave him a grateful smile. At times like this she really didn't deserve the Nana moniker.

They found the Reception group and Noah got into place next to a ginger-haired boy who was industriously picking his nose and inspecting the result before flicking it away. Laura stepped back, grateful to be away from the press of anxious mums tweaking costumes and snapping pictures, a lot of them around the same age as she was. She didn't belong here. Not like this. And yet . . .

"Nana," Noah called plaintively, holding out one hand from underneath the bright polyester swathe of his costume. "Aren't you going to walk with me?"

"What . . . ?" It took Laura a moment to realize that many of the parents were lining up next to their children, clearly intending to accompany them down the length of the high street. It made sense at

Noah's age. He was only five years old. And yet the thought of parading down the high street, past all those prying eyes, all those people who remembered and perhaps judged . . .

"Nana?" Noah's eyes were big and dark, like Abby's. Laura had a sudden, piercing memory of lying on the bed with Abby next to her, a couple of months old, all chubby limbs and dark eyes like Noah, gurgling up at her, her toothless smile wide and drooly. It had been one of the few moments when she'd actually felt like a mother.

"Um, yes, of course, Noah." How could she say no? Maybe the good people of Hartley-by-the-Sea wouldn't judge her. At least, not as much as she'd judged herself. Offering him a reassuring smile, Laura took her place next to her grandson. Noah slid his sweaty little hand in hers.

She hadn't brought a camera or a phone to take pictures; she didn't own either anymore, but right then, with Noah beaming, looking around at everything with wide-eyed interest, she wished she could take a snap. In truth Laura felt like a fraud. At any moment she half expected someone to point at her and tell her to leave, that she wasn't a proper grandmother, hadn't been a proper mother, not by a long shot. She didn't deserve to be part of this celebration.

No one did. No one talked to her at all, beyond a few cheerful pleasantries accompanied by weary smiles and good-natured eye rolls. Then Laura spotted Nathan's mother, Meghan, half-dragging him up the high street, and when he caught sight of Noah, he broke free and ran towards him.

Meghan gave Laura an appraising look before heading towards them. She looked as unlikely a mother as Laura felt, wearing ripped jeans and a rock festival T-shirt, her dirty blond hair piled up messily on top of her head. She had the ropy, sinewy look of someone who had too much nervous energy and probably subsisted on coffee and crisps.

"Now he's happy," she said with an exaggerated sigh as she came to stand next to Laura. "He threw a complete strop about his bloody costume." Nathan, Laura saw, was wearing a shop-bought costume that looked to be some sort of alien, judging by the goggly eyes and the gold glitter. She tried to think of some light remark to make and came up empty.

"So Abby's foisted Noah on you?" Meghan said. The boys were giggling together and didn't overhear. Laura smiled tightly.

"She's working in the café. And I wanted to come. I haven't been to a fete since I was a child."

Meghan gave a mock shudder. "I'd be happy to skip the whole thing. But hey, at least there's a beer tent."

Laura thought briefly of Rob Telford, putting on a little bit of the flirt at the pub quiz a few weeks ago. "That's something," she said. She felt utterly unequipped to handle the chitchat that had once come so easily to her—as a club manager she'd had to turn on the sparkle all the time, and she'd relished it even if she'd found it exhausting. At the café, with a counter safely between her and a customer, she could do it easily. Now, in this basic social situation, she found she couldn't manage it at all.

"So you're back here for good?" Meghan asked. "How does that feel?"

"Strange." Laura looked around at the milling crowds, longing now for someone to start the parade properly. She had no idea how much Meghan knew about her, or what Abby had told her. She wasn't sure she wanted to know.

"At least you got out for a while," Meghan remarked. "I got knocked up at twenty-one and never left. Never had the chance, or maybe just the guts. But it's an all-right place, in the end." She arched an eyebrow. "Don't you think?"

Laura managed a jokey kind of smile. "I came back, didn't I?"

"Maybe you didn't have the chance or the guts, either."

Laura inclined her head. "Touché."

"Is that French?" Meghan let out a raucous laugh and folded her arms across her skinny body. "It's bloody freezing out here."

The breeze at the top of the high street *was* brisk, and Laura was glad she'd put a fleece on over her top. Glancing at Meghan, Laura realized rather uncomfortably just how much she had in common with her. Pregnant at a young age, feeling trapped and a little bitter, covering it in one way or another—cool remoteness or brittle jokes, what did it really matter?

"Have you ever thought of leaving?" she asked, against her better judgment since she wasn't sure she actually wanted to continue this conversation. But she was curious.

"Me?" Meghan shrugged. "Once in a while. Doesn't everybody?"

"I suppose, although most people here would never admit it."

"Maybe not."

"Sometimes I think people see me as some sort of traitor." As soon as she said the words, she wished she hadn't. She'd meant to sound light and wry and instead she'd come across as . . . fearful.

"You would have been a traitor," Meghan answered, "if you hadn't come back."

"Ah, so all's forgiven?"

"Between you and the village? Of course. As for you and certain individuals and even yourself . . ." Meghan shrugged. "That's up to you, isn't it?"

"I'm not sure it is," Laura murmured. This conversation was getting far too deep. "So what's keeping you here now?" she asked Meghan.

"Well, this tiddler, for one," Meghan said with a nod towards Nathan, whose thumb was snaking towards his mouth. "Oi, Nathan. You're too big for that." Meghan batted his hand away. "He's happy here. And of course my mum."

"Your mum?"

Meghan staggered back, one hand pressed to her chest, her eyes wide in mock amazement. "You mean one person in Hartley-by-the-Sea doesn't know about my mum?"

"I haven't really been back here in twenty-four years," Laura returned lightly. "I think it passed me by."

"She broke her back when I was little," Meghan explained, dropping the astonished act. "About eighteen years ago, so you'd been gone for a while then, I guess."

"I'm sorry. . . ."

"Oh, that's old news. We're all over that." Meghan waved a hand. "That's not why I have to stay. Last spring my mother had a stroke. She's paralyzed on one side." For a second Meghan faltered in her airy explanation. "I help care for her at home. I couldn't leave Rachel to deal with that alone. Not again."

"Again?"

"That's another story. Not worth telling now."

The music had started up, and someone important with a megaphone had begun to call out year groups. Laura watched the preschool shuffle forward. Meghan's story had resonated with her—the feeling of being trapped, of having to stay. And yet unlike Meghan, she hadn't. She'd left not only her mother but her daughter. And she wasn't sure anyone could forgive that kind of abandonment.

"Reception class, please move forward!" the voice boomed from the megaphone, and obediently children and parents began to inch down the high street, some hampered by their elaborate costumes.

Watery sunshine bathed the street in an almost ethereal glow, the pavement still wet and gleaming from a recent shower. A brass band had started up at the front of the parade, lending a jolly feeling to the proceedings, which was essentially less of a parade and more just a troop of children trudging down the high street, trailing glitter and bits of cardboard, giggling excitedly.

Laura smiled down at Noah, her heart softening with a strange kind of affection, a squeeze or tug that caught her by surprise and felt both painful and sweet. She'd liked Noah well enough, for a five-year-old, but she hadn't felt *related* to him before. Hadn't felt protective and proud and scared all at once.

"Hey, Nathan! Noah!"

Laura turned to see a tall redheaded woman waving at both Noah and Nathan. A large woman in a wheelchair was next to her, no doubt Meghan's mother. Laura felt a twinge of pity mixed with guilt. Who was she to complain about her lot in life? Other people had it so much harder.

Noah was waving to everyone, his grin splitting his face, and many people were waving back. Laura vaguely recognized a lot of the faces, whether from the café or her past, she couldn't be sure. She felt stuck in a time warp, and even more so when the parade ended up on the playing field above the school. The sun had gone back in and the wind had picked up, so children dressed in costumes of polyester and nylon with a dash of cardboard were now shivering. The judge, an officious-looking woman who, Meghan had told her, was a local GP, quickly made her choices, the plaques were handed out, and then the fete truly began.

Noah, his enthusiasm undented from lack of a prize, clutched at Laura's sleeve as he asked for the five pounds Abby had given her for spending money.

"What do you want to do first?" Laura asked, a little reluctant to hand a fiver over to a boy who had only recently left preschool.

"Bouncy castle!" Noah and Nathan chorused, and so Laura led them over, with Meghan waving them on. She took off their shoes and helped them onto the inflatable before paying the money—fifty pence each. Then she stood back and watched, enjoying the obvious delight Noah took in being thrown around on top of what was essentially a huge air-filled mattress. Laughter bubbled up inside him, coming out in chortles and screams that made Laura smile even as she felt a sudden, surprising swoop of sorrow.

She'd missed all of this with Abby. She'd missed *everything*. Lost teeth, first period, birthdays and Christmases, first dates, school exams . . . there was a lifetime of memories she'd chosen simply to walk away from. She'd thought she'd dealt with that long ago, had told herself she'd had no choice, that it was best for Abby. But right now all she was conscious of was what was missing, the emptiness whistling through her, the utter lack of memories.

To her horror she felt her eyes sting, and she blinked rapidly, glancing around the school field, the yard below, all of it assailing her with sudden, unexpected memories. She'd huddled against that low stone wall during recess after her father had died. She'd had some friends in primary, but they'd kept their distance after her father's death, and she couldn't really blame them. She'd been angry, striking out at whoever came near, and eventually no one did. She'd told herself she preferred it that way, and as she'd gotten older, there had been little time for friends, what with working most afternoons and weekends. At secondary school her only real friend had been Izzy—she thought of her friend's offer of coffee and wondered if she would ever take her up on it, or even be able to. She hadn't seen Izzy since that awful night in the hospital.

It was too hard, remembering her own childhood as well as her absence in Abby's. Too much sorrow and regret and loss. Right then Laura wished she hadn't come to the fete; for a moment she wished she hadn't come to Hartley-by-the-Sea at all.

"I remember you. Laura, isn't it?"

Laura turned to see a tall, dark-haired man with a slightly geeky look smiling at her. She tensed, because while he looked vaguely familiar, she had no idea who he was and he couldn't have been much more than thirty. Too young for her to have gone to school with, so . . . ?

"Andrew," he supplied. "Andrew West. You used to babysit us, didn't you? Claire and me, I mean."

"Yes." Of course he would remember. Claire had been only two, but Andrew had been six. She remembered him now, a serious, dark-haired little boy who studied his children's encyclopedias with an air of endearing intensity. "I remember you. You're just a bit bigger now."

She smiled, or tried to, glancing back at Noah to see him still bouncing away.

"Rachel mentioned you've only just returned to Hartley-by-the-Sea?"

"Rachel?" Laura repeated, because the name didn't ring any bells.

"Rachel Campbell. Nathan's aunt?" He nodded towards the bouncy castle. "Meghan's sister. Do you know her?"

"No, sorry. I don't really know Meghan, either, actually." She could hear herself starting to sound frosty, and wished she could stop it. The self-defense mechanism was innate. "I haven't been back here in a long time."

"So what you brought back?"

Laura took a deep breath. She needed to get over this deep-seated resistance to personal questions. She was going to face a lot of them if she intended to stay here. "I lost my job and decided to head home for a bit," she said, wishing there was a more appealing version of the story. "I'm helping Abby run the café."

"That's great." Andrew's smile seemed genuine. "I'm sure she appreciates the help."

"Hopefully." She thought Abby did now, but that certainly hadn't been the case from the start.

"It seems like it's been hard for her, these last few years. I'm sure she does." He sounded like he knew Abby, like he was a friend. Laura glanced at him, curious but not wanting to ask, or admit she didn't know.

"You should stop by the café," she said instead. "We've really done it up."

"I'll do that."

Noah and Nathan clambered off the bouncy castle then, and Laura left to fetch their shoes and then attempt to jam their chubby little feet into them as they wriggled like fish on a line, eager to find the next entertainment.

"I'll take them to the coconut shy if you like," Meghan offered, and Laura thanked her, grateful for the opportunity to have a little space. She stood by herself, breathing in the damp air, the wind buffeting her, trying to enjoy the moment. Then she caught sight of the beer tent and decided that would help.

Rob Telford was pulling pints with alacrity as Laura queued up for her own. His eyes crinkled at the corners as he handed her a plastic cup, the beer foaming over the top and onto her hand.

"For you, it's on the house."

"I insist," Laura replied shortly, and handed him a fiver.

"What's got your knickers into a twist?" Rob asked as Laura moved to the side so the next person could be served. She hesitated, torn between striding off in a strop or staying and having someone to talk to. She suspected Rob was the kind of careless charmer who flirted with everyone; in fact, he was the type of guy she'd gone for in her former life, minus the money and style. "Well?" he prompted when she didn't move.

"I think that's a revolting expression." She sounded so prissy. Laura took a sip of beer and moved to lean against one of the tent's supports. She didn't miss Rob's little smile of satisfaction that she was clearly staying. Smug bastard.

"Sorry. I'll use another one. What's got you into such a gammy fettle?"

She laughed in spite of herself. "Putting on the Cumbrian slang a bit, aren't you?"

"Born and bred here, same as you."

Her eyes narrowed. "What do you know about me?"

"Just what everyone knows." Rob shrugged. "You've come back after a long time away." A pause as he handed over another foaming pint. "You wouldn't be the first."

Laura felt a little calmer at this. "That's all?"

"Not quite."

"What . . ."

"I know that you grew up here, working all hours at the café, and that your father died when you were young. Your mother was a fixture of the village, loud and lovable, but maybe not the greatest mum?" A questioning lilt entered his voice along with a lift of his eyebrows. Laura thought she saw pity in his face, and suddenly she felt furious.

"I didn't think everyone knew all that," she said, her voice sounding suffocated. She felt raw, as if he'd peeled back a layer of her skin. Of her *soul*. She took another sip of beer, wishing she'd never started this conversation yet even now not quite willing to walk away.

"Perhaps not," Rob agreed. "But I knew it."

"How could you? You must be fifteen years younger than me at least."

His eyes crinkled again. "I'm thirty."

"And I'm forty-two." She straightened, giving him her best mumsy glare, not that she'd had a lot of practice. "You were five years old when I left this village."

"Mmm." Rob pulled another pint.

"Or are you speaking from experience?" Laura snapped, and Rob glanced at her, confused.

"Pardon?"

"Never mind," Laura muttered.

"No, seriously." Rob stopped pulling pints, propping one muscular arm on the counter as he leveled Laura with a serious look. The crowd of thirsty fete-goers anxious for their pints stirred restlessly. "What did you mean, I was speaking from experience?"

Laura felt herself start to blush, something she hadn't done in decades. Faces swiveled towards her, the scent of gossip in the air. She swallowed, her mind racing with ways she could back down gracefully. She should not have started this line of conversation.

"Well?" Rob demanded. He clearly wasn't going to pull another pint until she'd given him an answer. Fine, she would.

"Only that I remember Donna Telford parked in the pub when she should have been picking you up from school." As soon as she said the words, she wished she could take them back. For a split second Rob looked like he'd been slapped. And she barely knew what she was talking about. Yes, she remembered Donna Telford as a bit of a drunk, but she didn't know the full story. She hadn't been a hundred percent sure that she was even his mother. And who was she to bring up bad memories?

"Fair enough," he said, his voice mild as he went back to pulling pints. "You're right. I suppose my mum was a bit of a town fixture, as well."

"And not very mumsy," Laura said quietly, struck by sudden pity.

"No," he agreed. A small smile quirked his mouth, but he kept his eyes on the taps in front of him. "No, she wasn't. Seems we have something in common."

"Oi, Laura!"

Laura turned to see Meghan striding towards her and she wondered if she was going to get a bollocking for leaving her in charge of Noah for too long. She regretted the half-empty pint of beer in her hand; she semiregretted the whole conversation with Rob.

"Did Noah come back to you?"

"Noah?" Alarm had her nearly dropping the plastic cup. "No— what? I mean, what do you mean? Where is he?"

"I sent him back here because he didn't want to do the hook-a-duck with me and Nath. Isn't he here?" He obviously wasn't.

Laura's mouth felt dry and she licked her lips. "No. No, I didn't see him." She hadn't looked for him, either. Had basically forgotten that she was in charge of a little person for the last fifteen minutes.

"Well, he's bound to be around here somewhere," Meghan said with an unconcerned shrug. "Let's have a look."

Meghan could be laid-back about it, but Laura knew Abby would have a fit if she heard about this. And what if Noah was really lost? She already knew her mothering skills were virtually nil. What had possessed her to think she could take care of a five-year-old boy, even for an afternoon?

Panic was curdling Laura's stomach as she tossed her cup into the bin and started hurrying around the field, looking for a little boy in a lurid yellow costume. A distant part of her recognized that she *might* be overreacting, that Noah had to be here somewhere. This was Hartley-by-the-Sea, for goodness' sake. Kids as young as six years old walked to school on their own. And yet if something happened to Noah on her watch . . . It didn't bear thinking about. Abby would never speak to her again. And as for Noah . . . Laura pictured his dark, liquid eyes, remembered his bubbling-up laughter; panic seized her again, making it hard to breathe.

She hurried from stall to stall, the crowd a blur of faces, and was barely aware of the people who were starting to murmur, to feel her fear. Some joined her in looking; after ten minutes of fruitless searching, the organizer of the fete, a Yummy Mummy type with sunglasses pushed on top of her highlighted hair despite the rain clouds and on-again, off-again drizzle, used the PA system to make an announcement.

"If anyone sees Noah Rhodes, five years old and in Reception, please bring him to the front of the stage. Noah Rhodes . . . he's wearing a yellow Minion costume. . . ."

Another agonizing five minutes ticked slowly past. Plenty of people were looking now, calling out his name, searching the inside of the school, the classrooms and the toilets. *Where was he?* Laura felt as if she'd forgotten how to breathe.

And then suddenly, miraculously, there he was in front of her, tearstained and wobbly-lipped, holding Meghan's hand.

"I was playing hide-and-go-seek," he explained in answer to Laura's wordless question. A note of truculence entered his voice. "I didn't know everyone was looking for me."

"Oh, Noah." Laura dropped to her knees in front of him and gathered his small, skinny body into her arms. She buried her face in his neck; he smelled like cotton candy and sunshine and little-boy sweat. "Oh, Noah," she said again, and then she started to cry.

Awkwardly Noah patted her back. "It's okay. Don't cry. I'm okay, Nana."

Nana. Laura didn't think she'd ever heard a sweeter word.

19

Abby

WHEN MEGHAN TOLD HER what had happened at the fete, Abby's initial reaction was a streak of ice-cold panic, that something might have happened to Noah, followed by a blaze of fury. Laura hadn't even mentioned the incident when she'd returned from the fete, all sunshine and smiles.

"Honestly, your mother was that panicked," Meghan said, clearly relishing the details of the story as they stood in the school yard, the two boys having already rushed in. "I've never seen her look so rattled. Like she was about to have a heart attack." She made an *oops* kind of face. "Sorry. That was tactless, even for me."

"It's okay." Abby was still trying to process what Meghan had told her. Laura had actually *lost* Noah at the school fete. If she allowed herself, Abby knew she could get into a proper, towering rage about the whole thing. She could picture herself confronting her mother, all self-righteous indignation touched with an awful smugness, because at least a small part of her had been waiting for her mother to mess up and now she'd have the chance to call her on it. She could be a right cow sometimes.

"It was kind of sweet," Meghan continued. "When she finally saw Noah. I'd found him hiding in the bushes by the swings—he'd been playing hide-and-go-seek with a couple of Year Ones."

"Right . . ."

"Anyway, your mum actually started crying when she saw him. Dropped to her knees and gave him a bone-crunching hug before she started blubbing away. I didn't think she had it in her."

"I didn't, either," Abby murmured, and then immediately felt disloyal. She couldn't picture it: her mother on her knees, Noah in her arms, the tears. It was like imagining a scene from a movie. And yet . . . it had happened. A sign that her mother cared.

"All's well that ends well, any road," Meghan said as they started walking down the school lane, joining the trickle of mums heading off to work or Pilates or the more mundane housework. "She found him again and they had a nice time at the fete."

"Yes . . ." Except Laura hadn't mentioned anything about the incident when she'd brought Noah back in the late afternoon. Abby had spent the day at the café, bored and lonely with a lack of customers due to the gray weather as well as the fete attracting most of the locals. Noah had seemed tired but happy when he'd returned, his mouth pink and sticky from eating too much candy. Laura had looked exhausted but cheerful. Abby had made some joke about Noah tiring her out, and she'd just smiled. She hadn't said anything about losing him for a good fifteen minutes.

The flicker of rage she'd felt when Meghan had first told her started to catch fire. Really, Laura should have told her Noah had gone missing. What if something had happened? What if Noah had been hurt or abducted? The thought was enough to make her insides freeze with terror. Sometimes it felt as if something bad was always about to happen.

And yet . . . the same thing could have happened to her. Hadn't she lost Noah in a Tesco when he was only three? He'd been missing for at least ten minutes, hiding behind a display of Valentine's Day chocolates. She'd been so terrified and then relieved that she'd nearly passed out. Could she really blame Laura? And more important, considering where their relationship was, did she *want* to blame Laura?

Back at the café, Laura was behind the till and Abby took a moment to survey the peacefulness of the scene. The café looked great, but on this gray morning it was also mostly empty. They hadn't, as far as Abby could tell, drummed up much more business with their costly refurb. She pushed that niggling worry aside as she walked up to the till. Laura looked up, eyebrows raised expectantly.

"School run okay?"

"Yes . . ." She hesitated, knowing she needed to mention it for both their sakes, but reluctant to cause an argument. "I heard something from Meghan."

"Oh?" Laura's expression was calm, but Abby could tell she was wary.

"Yes, Meghan told me that Noah went missing at the fete," Abby said, her voice ringing out louder than she'd meant it to. Two customers in the corner looked up. "Why didn't you tell me what had happened?"

Laura took a deep breath and then let it out slowly. "I should have told you," she said. "I'm sorry."

Any indignation she might have fired up went out with a puff of smoke and a hiss of steam. She hadn't expected such an unvarnished apology from her mother. She couldn't remember ever having received one before.

"I didn't want to tell you because I was afraid you wouldn't let me take Noah out again," Laura continued.

"You want to take him out again?"

"Of course I do." Laura let out a shaky laugh and brushed at her eyes with one hand. "I know it might not seem obvious, and I haven't been . . . well, you know all that I haven't been. But Noah is my grandson and I . . . I like him. I like spending time with him." She turned away, fussing with the displays of cakes and scones, her head bent so Abby couldn't see her expression.

She was totally flummoxed. Touched too, and yet sad because it all felt like it was too late. Too late for her, anyway, but not too late for Noah. "It could happen to anyone," Abby said at last. "It happened to me, once, in Tesco's. I had an absolutely heart-stopping ten minutes." She let out a breath. "I understand these things happen. I just wish you'd told me."

"I'm sorry." Laura's head remained bent. "I should have. I know I should have."

"It's okay."

Laura looked up, shocked. Those two simple, little words felt weirdly momentous. "You mean . . . you're not angry?"

"No." Abby let out a self-conscious laugh. "I was thinking about it, though."

Laura laughed, as well. "I bet you were."

"I was working myself up into a proper hissy fit," Abby admitted. "I had every intention of coming in here and letting it fly."

Laura busied herself with the cake display again. "Why didn't you?"

"I didn't feel like it, really." Abby hesitated as she sifted through her feelings. "It didn't feel right. I feel like I've wasted too much time being angry or resentful or just . . . I don't know. Ticked off about something, with you."

"It's easy to feel bitter."

"Do you?"

"Sometimes." Laura looked up at her; standing there in her green apron, her hair pulled carelessly back, she looked every one of her nearly forty-three years. "Sometimes I just feel sad."

"I feel like there are a lot of things you aren't telling me," Abby blurted. "About . . . about everything."

Laura stilled. "Maybe," she allowed. "But anything I'm not telling you, Abby, is because it's not worth knowing."

"Maybe I should be the one to decide that."

"How? You can't unknow something." Laura smiled faintly. "I wish you could."

"Still . . ." Abby debated how hard to push. How much she actually wanted to know. There was a reason, after all, why Laura hadn't told her any of this. A reason she really might not like. "I'm twenty-six. Shouldn't I get to decide?"

"Decide what?"

"Whether I want to know . . . something."

"And what," Laura asked, "is this something exactly?" She straightened, staring hard at Abby, making it difficult to look away.

Damn it, she didn't have enough courage to ask about her father. Or even ask anything. In the face of her mother's unflinching look, Abby backed down. "Just . . . things."

The door to the café creaked open and several old ladies shuffled in, faces creased in expectant smiles. "You are open for teas and coffees . . . ?"

"Yes, of course." Laura moved from behind the till, every inch the gracious hostess. "Why don't you sit down? You might notice the tables and chairs are new."

One of the women blinked at the café with its cozy scattering of oak tables and painted chairs. "Oh," she said. "Is something new?" Laura exchanged a wry look with Abby, and she smiled back. Even if no one ever noticed, renovating the café together would still have been worth it.

The old ladies started the morning rush, and Abby didn't get a chance to talk to her mother again about anything more than the shopping they needed to do and how many toasties a party of six wanted. Slinging sandwiches on the grease-spattered grill, she struggled with a growing sense of annoyance aimed mainly at herself. Why had she chickened out? She should have demanded her mother tell her something, like who her father was for starters. She'd never let the question bother her before, but now it was like an insect buzzing in her brain, refusing to be silenced. What if it was someone from Hartley-by-the-Sea? Someone she knew? The possibility made a tremor of appalled outrage ripple through her. What if she was looking in her father's face every day?

The possibility was unlikely, Abby suspected, but it was still *there*. And she ought to know. But even more than the issue of her own parentage, she wanted to know other things, things about Laura herself. Like why she actually left. What her childhood was like. Whether she'd been happy in Manchester or New York City. She wanted, Abby realized, to know her mother.

"Right." Laura came into the kitchen, swiping a strand of hair away from her face. "Things are quieting down a little. Why don't you go out with some lunch boxes?"

"Again?" She'd done the lunch box experiment several times in the last week and on each occasion it had been successful, but it still made her a little nervous. It was so outside her comfort zone.

"Why not? It's a sunny day, and there are a lot of people out there." Laura gestured to the beach. "This is the last week of school, isn't it? We should get into a good routine, for when it really gets busy."

"If it gets busy." The words slipped out before she could think better of them.

Laura frowned. "What do you mean?"

"Only . . . we haven't exactly had much of an uptick, have we?" Laura's lips pursed and Abby rushed to explain, "I'm not pointing fingers, honestly, and I'm not trying to complain. But it's like no one even knows what we've done."

"It's been a little busier," Laura said, and Abby could tell she was trying not to sound defensive. "Maybe."

"Maybe," Abby agreed. "But we're not attracting that wider customer base the bloke at the bank said we should."

Laura's shoulders slumped and Abby had the bizarre urge to comfort her or, God forbid, even hug her. Crazy. "No," she said. "I suppose not."

"But it's not that much of a surprise," Abby continued, trying to inject a bolstering note into her voice. "Considering we haven't actually told anyone what we've done, beyond a few friends."

"This is Hartley-by-the-Sea," Laura pointed out dryly. "I think word gets around."

"Yes, but I mean something splashy. Like a party. A grand opening."

Laura brightened at this. "A grand opening . . ."

"We could do something in the evening," Abby continued, thinking off the cuff. "And maybe something during the day, for families. Free ice-cream cones . . . although perhaps that isn't such a good idea, considering."

"You've got to spend money to make money."

Abby almost smiled at the authoritative note that had entered Laura's voice. Her gaze was distant, her mind clearly racing. And something that would have gotten up her nose a few weeks ago now made her smile. Made her happy. She was looking forward to watching her mother go to work. How bizarre.

"I like it," Laura said in the definitive way that suggested she was passing judgment. "I like it a lot. A whole weekend of events." She shook her head, laughing. "Why didn't I think of this?"

"I don't know—maybe I'm the one with the business genes?" Abby dared to joke.

"Hey, you got them from somewhere, sweetie." Laura waved her away, smiling. "Now go sell some lunch boxes."

Still smiling, Abby did just that. It was lovely out, sunny and warm, the breeze from the sea benevolent rather than punishing. Dogs raced across the beach and a few families skiving off the last week of school for an early holiday were camped out on the sand. Abby sold half her stock right on the beach, and then, feeling adventurous, she headed towards the caravan park on the far side of the fetch, hidden by a sweep of pasture.

She didn't go to the caravan park much, if at all. The caravans stretched in uniform lines all the way into the hazy distance, permanent camper vans, some with flower beds and little wooden fences built around them. The residents were a strange mix of happy families, bustling pensioners, drunken layabouts, and temporary construction workers.

Abby faltered, not sure whether she'd made a smart choice. The caravans had kitchens, after all. And the two oldies sprawled in deck chairs in front of their caravan were looking at her with decided suspicion.

She was just about to turn around and slink away when she heard someone calling to her.

"Hey, are you selling lunch?" A guy with curly blond hair and a wide white smile came striding towards her. He had a lean, ropy build and was decked out in a lot of expensive-looking spandex. Abby hesitated.

"Yes . . ."

"Great. I'm starving." His grin widened impossibly and he unzipped a money belt around his waist. "How much?"

"Five pounds." She put down her tray of boxes to select one. "Comes with a sandwich, crisps, soda, and a biscuit." Perhaps they should add a piece of fruit.

"Excellent." He handed her a wrinkled tenner. "Like I said, I'm starving."

"Are you staying in one of the caravans?" Abby asked as she fumbled in her pockets to make change.

"For the summer. I'm giving paragliding lessons up there." He pointed to a hill above the caravan park.

"Oh, you're one of the paragliders?" Abby heard the enthusiasm in her voice and obviously the guy did, as well.

"Yeah, do you paraglide?"

"Me?" She laughed, a snorting sound that had her mentally cringing. "No way. I am definitely not a thrill seeker."

"You sounded keen, though."

"It's just that they look nice, up in the sky." She handed him back a five-pound note. "So free." Another inward cringe, but the guy was unfazed by her pontificating.

"Yeah, you definitely feel free up there. It's like nothing else in the world. You really should try it." His gaze turned appraising, making Abby fight a blush. "I'm running a taster one-day course the third weekend in August. Why don't you give it a go?"

For a microsecond Abby was tempted. When had she last done something fun and free and actually exciting? But even as that thought was flitting through her mind, she shook her head. Paragliding? Seriously? That so wasn't her. "Sorry. I don't think so."

"Well, come back with your lunch boxes, anyway," the guy said, his enthusiasm and cheer undented by her refusal. "I don't usually have time to leg it up to the café for lunch, so this is much appreciated." He hoisted the bag. "Cheers."

"No problem," Abby murmured, and started to turn away.

"Hey, what's your name? So I know who to ask for if I need to?"

"Abby." She paused and then rushed ahead. "What's yours?"

"Chris." His teeth really were almost blindingly white. "Thanks again, Abby."

"No problem," she said yet again. She wasn't coming up with the most stellar remarks. Chris nodded once more in farewell and slowly, reluctantly, Abby turned away. She'd enjoyed that meaningless little exchange. Made her realize how little she talked to someone of the opposite sex, someone who was attractive and interesting. She needed to either get out more or simply get a grip.

She walked with a spring in her step all the way back to the café, and it was only when she came through the doors that she realized she'd forgotten to sell the other nine lunch boxes. Oops.

"What are you back here for already?" Laura asked, and Abby shrugged.

"Um, I needed change." With a small secret smile curving her mouth, she scooped a bunch of change from the till and headed outside again.

20

Laura

"I ENVY YOU, I really do."

Sitting in Izzy's enormous kitchen, sipping an espresso from the gleaming high-end machine perched on the counter, Laura had to suppress a snort of incredulity. Izzy, with the perfect family, the gorgeous husband, the amazing house, envied *her*?

"You shouldn't," she said, keeping her voice light so she didn't sound bitter. So what if the espresso machine was one Laura had decided they couldn't afford for the café? So what if Izzy's life reeked of wealth and privilege and *Country Life* glamour, from the cashmere throws discarded carelessly on the sofas to the artfully wild garden Laura could see through the French doors, with huge, unruly rose-bushes dripping with blowsy blossoms and a chicken coop that even looked expensive? It didn't mean she had to feel envious.

The invitation had come suddenly, when Izzy had appeared in the café a few days ago with two of her children, both towheaded boys, and done a dramatic double take at the sight of Laura.

"Laura," she exclaimed. "I've been hoping to run into you. You must come over for a coffee. This week, before we head off to France." They'd arranged a date then and there, and that Wednesday Laura had duly shown up at Izzy's rambling stone farmhouse, perched on its own large plot of rolling hills a few miles outside Hartley-by-the-Sea.

"Close your eyes," Izzy had cried as Laura entered the vaulted stone-flagged entrance hall. "Everything is a tip. I haven't had time to tidy—I've been so busy packing. . . ."

Laura stepped over a single pair of Hunter boots left on the floor with a small smile. "It's fine," she assured Izzy. "Where are you going in France?"

"The Dordogne," Izzy replied with a roll of her eyes. "The same every year. So boring, but there's a pool and the kids seem to like it. We always rent the same villa."

"Of course," Laura murmured.

Izzy led her through to the kitchen, which was twice as big as the entire downstairs of the café's flat, with a huge granite island and a living area with sofas and chairs. There were funky, arty touches, like the bright aquamarine Aga range cooker and the framed pop art on the walls, that reminded Laura of her friend's hippie days, but everything was top-of-the-line in both money and taste. And Izzy, apparently, envied *her*.

"But you're so free," Izzy said emphatically, waving her coffee cup around, so a few drops spilled onto her cream-colored linen trousers. "Remember our school days, Laura? Sneaking cigarettes behind the games sheds and dreaming about when we'd finally get *out* of this village?"

"And here we both are, back," Laura replied. "I'm not sure what you need to feel envious about, Iz. Hartley-by-the-Sea is a beautiful village, and a great place to bring up kids." Or so it seemed.

"Yes, but . . . I don't know." Izzy flopped into a large armchair, hooking one leg around the arm and flashing a perfect and very pink pedicure. "It's just . . . you're free from the whole rat race, aren't you? The endless drudgery of housework and cooking and ferrying children to football and Brownies and piano lessons . . ." She made a face.

"Maybe a little," Laura allowed. She certainly could not put herself in Izzy's shoes as a busy mother of two. She could not imagine herself bustling around a kitchen, even a beautiful, big one like this, making meals and wiping noses. And yet . . . she'd been taking Noah to school several times a week, and she and Abby had agreed on a schedule for making dinner. So maybe she was more domesticated than either she or Izzy realized. "But it's not as if I can swan off to Paris or Rome whenever I feel like it," she said. Not anymore. For a second she let herself remember a holiday to a high-end spa in Palm Desert a few years ago. She'd gone by herself; she'd never been interested in vacationing with someone. She craved only peace and solitude, a release of the constant pressure. But the Indian head massage, the seemingly endless supply of cosmopolitans (although the spa attendants had advocated some nasty spinach juice beverage instead), and the gorgeous toiletries in her room had all been lovely perks. And yet over it all, she could see now, had been a patina of loneliness.

Her life now was so far from that glamour, and yet she didn't think she'd trade places with her former self. No, she definitely wouldn't. Not in a million years. The realization made her smile.

"And, anyway," she added for good measure, since this whole exercise seemed to be about making Izzy feel good, "I don't have a husband."

"Oh, that," Izzy said with a groan. "Sometimes I think I could take or leave *him*."

Of course. "How come?"

Izzy shrugged, her gaze sliding away. "Well, you know . . . a marriage is so much work."

"Actually, I don't know, having never been married."

"But a relationship, even . . ."

"Haven't really had many of those, either," Laura interjected breezily. And then, simply for the shock value, she added, "I've been more into one-night stands."

Izzy's eyes goggled for a few seconds. "See what I mean?" she said on a sigh. "I really do envy you."

"Trust me, Iz, it sounds better than it feels. And in any case I haven't had anything like that in a long time." Years, actually. And they'd always made her feel emptier afterwards, an annoying side effect of meaningless sex.

"Well, the grass is definitely not greener on this side. Dominic is away Monday to Friday in London, and when he is home, he just wants to relax, preferably by himself." Izzy pouted a bit. "I might as well not be married at all."

Except for the lifestyle her venture capitalist husband was funding for her. Laura decided not to mention that. "It must be lonely sometimes."

"It is. Sometimes I think it's lonelier to be married and yet be solitary than to be single."

"Maybe." Loneliness was tough, whether you were with someone or not. Despite the huge house and the holidays in France, Laura didn't envy her.

"So do you think you really will stay in Hartley-by-the-Sea for good?" Izzy stretched languorously. "What were you doing before? I never seem to catch the local crack. . . ."

"That's not a bad thing." Izzy, with her farmhouse in the hills and her children all in private school, was removed from the hustle—if she could even use that word—of Hartley-by-the-Sea. It made for a nice change, someone not knowing something about her.

"I was in the entertainment industry. I managed a nightclub."

"A nightclub!" Izzy looked gratifyingly impressed. "That sounds fabulously glamorous."

"It was, for a time." It was hard not to feel the tiniest pang of longing for those heady days, the prestige, the power, even just the manicures. When had she last treated herself to a spa day? Laura glanced down at her ragged and dirty fingernails. If her former self could see her now . . . "That life is over," Laura told Izzy. "I can't go back. As for staying here . . . I'm taking it day by day right now." And each day held a surprising amount of enjoyment and even excitement.

For the last week she and Abby had been working on plans for their grand opening events for the first weekend in August. They'd decided on several events: a grown-up cocktail party on the Friday night, and then a bunch of children's activities on the Saturday, plus free ice-cream cones for the first hundred customers on Sunday afternoon. All of it would create a significant dent in their bank account, but they both felt it would be worth it. At least, they hoped it would be worth it. And Laura had been enjoying the planning with Abby—at first she'd wanted to kick herself for not thinking of the idea herself, but in retrospect she decided it was better that Abby had thought of it. Her daughter was more excited and confident knowing that this was her idea. And it gave Laura an unexpected inner glow to see Abby start to shine.

"I'm sorry," Izzy said abruptly, and Laura stared.

"For what?"

"Before, in school. I should have . . ." Izzy shook her head. "I should have stood by you, Laura. I know I wasn't a very good friend back then, basically dumping you the minute you . . ." She trailed off with a grimace.

"I don't think it was the precise minute," Laura returned. Amazingly she felt a smile tugging at her lips. Could she actually be amused by something that had once caused her no end of heartache and pain? "It was a long time ago." Even if she could still remember how hard it had felt, how lonely and isolating, to be pregnant at fifteen-almost-sixteen and realizing you weren't even going to take your exams, that your future had narrowed rather than expanded. She couldn't blame Izzy for not keeping up the friendship. When Laura had dropped out of school to have a baby, she'd entered another universe, one of hospital appointments and dirty nappies and endless sleep deprivation. It would have taken Izzy a lot of courage to brave the trip even for a visit.

"How are things with . . . ?" Izzy asked tentatively.

"With Abby. They're okay." Laura managed a smile. "Obviously I haven't been the best mother over the years, but I'm trying now." Sort of. This was trying, wasn't it? Sometimes she felt more like Abby's friend and work partner than her actual mother. Although on occasion she *had* felt something distinctly maternal stir in the area of her breastbone. At least, she thought that's what it was. Perhaps it was just heartburn.

"It must have been so, so hard back then," Izzy said in a tragic-sounding voice. "Raising a baby on your own. We were so *young* . . ."

"It was hard," Laura replied briskly. She didn't want to give in to Izzy's desire for melodrama; she remembered now, from school, how Izzy tended towards theatrical. "But it wasn't impossible, and plenty of young women have coped with the same."

"You should give yourself a break, Laura—"

"I've been giving myself a break for twenty years," Laura answered, her bluntness surprising her because she knew she meant it. "Perhaps it's time I stopped."

Izzy raised her eyebrows. "How are you going to do that?"

"I don't know." Taking the smallest bedroom, letting Abby make decisions she was itching and aching to make, forcing a smile every time she met someone's speculative look . . . was it all just penance? Would any of it ever be enough to make up for her abandoning her daughter? Laura doubted it. So why bother at all?

That had been her attitude for the last twenty years, the reason why she'd stayed away, hadn't tried. She'd told herself there was no point, that she could never make up for her earlier failures. She wanted to be different now—at least she thought she did. God knew she was tired of the status quo, but could she really go on like this, her life an apology, cramming herself in a single bed, trying to avoid or at least brazen out the awkward questions? It didn't feel like a life, but then Laura wasn't sure anymore what a real life felt like. Her existence in New York and Manchester had been endless, elaborate pretending.

"I don't know," she said again. "I'm still figuring that one out."

Laura mused on the conversation all the way back into town. Maybe penance wasn't the way to go, at least not forever. The whole self-sacrificing thing only went so far, really, didn't it? Eventually it got boring for everyone involved, Laura especially. Besides, penance meant always looking back, always atoning, and Laura wanted to look forward. She wanted to make up for the past and then move on, better and stronger than before, with her daughter.

"I was thinking," she said as she came into the café later that afternoon, the place mostly empty, save for a few couples lingering over their coffees and teas, and Abby wiping down tables, "we should treat ourselves to a day at the spa."

Abby looked both wary and surprised. "The spa?"

"Yes, why not? Get dolled up for the opening parties. And we could both do with a full mani and pedi." Laura held her hands out. "My nails haven't looked this bad since I was in primary school."

"I think the manicurist would run away from my hands, screaming," Abby returned wryly. She held out her hands for inspection and Laura noted the eczema between the fingers, the clearly chewed nails and ragged cuticles. Poor girl.

"I don't think she'd run away screaming, but she might shudder a little. But why not? Don't we deserve a treat?"

"Do we?" Abby sounded doubtful. "Spa days are expensive. . . ."

"Sod expense. We've put every penny into this place and I think we can spare a hundred quid for ourselves. They might even have mother-daughter packages." As soon as Laura said the words, she wished she could snatch them back. *Mother-daughter packages.* As if. Cue Abby's surly look and snarky remark.

But her daughter didn't rise to the bait Laura had inadvertently dangled. She just smiled and turned back to wiping down the tables. "Maybe," she said. "It could be fun."

Laura spent the evening on the new laptop they'd bought as part of their business expenses, looking up spas in the Lake District. Anything decent was at least an hour away, but they could make a day of it. She was already picturing herself swathed in sumptuous towels, her skin tender and moist from various treatments, a cocktail—or two—to hand. The image nearly made her salivate with longing. She *needed* this. And she wanted to experience it with Abby.

"What will I do about Noah?" Abby asked as she came to stand behind Laura, peering over her shoulder to look at the specs on a day package at a place near Windermere. "If we're gone all day . . ."

"Couldn't Meghan have him?"

Abby grimaced. "It's a lot to ask. The childminding really kicks in over the summer. . . ."

Laura sighed and leaned back in her chair. "What about Lucy? She's a teacher, isn't she, so she has the time off?"

"Her wedding is in four weeks. . . ."

"True, but it's only one day. You could ask." Or *she'd* ask. Or maybe she'd just go to the spa by herself, and sod everyone else. The thought was tempting, but at the same time Laura knew she wanted a bonding experience with her daughter.

"Okay," Abby said, surprising her yet again. "I'll ask."

The next morning, as Noah thundered down the stairs a little after six and Laura rolled over, her pillow over her head to drown out the overjolly voices of the CBeebies presenters that rang up through the floor, she thought of the spa again. A whole day without Noah. He'd been off school for a week, and as precious as he could be, he was also driving her a little bit mad. She'd never realized how much noise a small person could make. Abby hadn't made as much noise as Noah even when she'd been a colicky newborn. And he *moved* so much, constantly jumping on and off furniture, getting in your face, speaking in a loud voice as he hopped around, arms and legs endlessly windmilling.

He'd spent most days in the café with them, asking for ice-cream cones or if he could help, which usually meant Laura biting her tongue as Noah fiddled with the cash register or insisted he could carry a tray of toasted sandwiches (he could not). Abby, back in the kitchen, seemed oblivious, although Laura wondered if her daughter was administering a little payback, and was enjoying watching her mother struggle to manage Noah. Maybe she deserved it. If she'd been Abby, she probably would have done the same.

She'd asked once, tentatively, if there were some summer camps Noah could attend, but Abby had insisted everything was too expensive. Laura would have been willing to pay quite a bit to have someone take Noah off their hands for a few hours, but she didn't press the matter. She tried to remind herself of the positives—Noah was a bright, inquisitive little boy and she was really getting to know her grandson, which she did actually appreciate, for the most part—but she finished every day with a headache and a strong desire for a gin and tonic.

If she'd been a really good grandmother, or a half-decent mother for that matter, she'd give Abby a break and get up with Noah some mornings. Take him outside, even, onto the beach, for an early-morning run around. Abby could certainly use a lie-in. As it was, Laura could barely stir herself to slouch downstairs at half past seven and put the kettle on. She'd never been a morning person, but it didn't make her feel less guilty for trying to ignore the noise at what felt like the crack of dawn.

"I asked Lucy about watching Noah," Abby said as she came in two mornings later, looking surprisingly fresh-faced. Noah was skipping inside behind her, holding a pail of rocks he'd collected on the beach. It was barely seven and they both looked like they'd been up and active for hours. "She said she'd be happy to. It'll have to be a Sunday, of course. We can't lose a day of business."

"No, definitely not," Laura agreed. Noah was now swinging the bucket of rocks back and forth, and with each alarming arc Laura tensed for the inevitable spray of smooth stones to hit her. "I'll arrange it for this Sunday. Then we'll still look good for the party on Friday."

By mutual agreement she and Abby had split the planning for the opening activities; Abby was in charge of the children's activities on Saturday and Sunday, and Laura was taking care of the evening do. She'd ordered decent champagne and had arranged for local caterers to do the canapés, hiding both bills from Abby, who would no doubt want to make do with normal plonk and a couple of appetizer trays from Tesco. She'd also put posters up in the church and the post office, limiting the number of guests to the first 150, as anything over that was apparently a fire hazard. Juliet and Peter had promised to come, as well as Lucy and Alex, Meghan and her sister, Rachel, with her boyfriend, Laura had learned, Andrew West. Claire would be coming too with Dan Trenton, and Laura tried not to think about either of the Wests; hopefully they wouldn't want to relive old times. They barely remembered any of it, anyway.

In any case, she fully intended to look fabulous for the party.

21

Abby

THIS WAS HER MOTHER'S world. Abby eyed the loungers in the "tranquillity room" slightly askance, because while Laura had sailed in, every inch the confident and assured customer, Abby felt utterly out of her depth. She didn't look like she belonged here, with her hair that hadn't been cut in six months, her raggedy nails, her complexion that barely saw makeup or even daily cleansing. And her clothes, a pair of her best jeans with a cotton smock top that had some nice embroidery around the neckline, didn't feel right. She'd thought about wearing a summery skirt, but the weather had turned and the breeze was chilly, plus it looked like rain, so sandals were out.

"Sit down, Abby." Laura had stretched out elegantly on one of the loungers, her eyebrows raised in expectation. "Relax. That's what we're here for."

"Right." Abby sat on the edge of the lounger next to Laura's. An attendant fluttered around them, adjusting the volume of the sounds that were being piped into the room—a *shoosh*ing like the sea interspersed with crickets chirping.

"Please feel free to handle the stones of serendipity," the attendant said, and Laura nodded, as if this were a language she already spoke. Abby didn't dare ask what the stones of serendipity were. She could see

233

a huge bowl of glazed pottery placed on a low table, filled with rocks that looked like gray eggs. *Handle* them? Seriously?

"And would you like a drink? I can recommend the spinach, mango, and carrot juice."

Abby couldn't keep from making a "gross" face, but Laura merely smiled. "Actually, I'd like a mimosa, please."

The attendant's expression didn't flicker. "Very good, ma'am."

Laura turned to Abby. "What would you like?"

"Um . . . I'll just have water," Abby murmured. She didn't belong in a place like this.

"Relax, Abby." Laura leaned her head back against the lounger and closed her eyes. "I know it takes a while to get into the groove, but this is meant to be an enjoyable experience. We could both use some destressing, don't you think?"

"I know. It's just not something I've done before."

"Not ever?" Laura opened her eyes. "Not even as a carefree single-ton in Liverpool?"

Abby thought of her student days, struggling on a pittance and burdened with loans, determined to prove herself and then falling in love instead. "Nope."

"What was it like, anyway?" Laura asked. "As a student? I never even dared to dream about uni."

"I think I probably should have tried to relax and enjoy myself a bit more." Abby settled back against the lounger. The ocean and cricket sounds provided a soothing, if slightly disconcerting, backdrop to their conversation. "I was so stressed-out all the time."

"About what?"

"Studying. Surviving. I had to take loans out for everything—the fees, my accommodation, spending money. And I worked two part-time jobs to keep afloat."

Laura was silent for a moment. "You could have asked me for money."

"Really?" Abby couldn't keep the surprise from her voice. "Because you never gave me the impression that you'd have welcomed that."

Laura's mouth tightened. "I know I wasn't around, but I did send money regularly. I didn't want Mum having to struggle alone. There should have been enough. . . ." She trailed off, no doubt taking in Abby's expression of shock.

"Gran never said you sent money."

"Didn't she?" Laura leaned back against the lounger and closed her eyes. "She cashed the checks."

"Why didn't she tell me?"

"I don't know. Maybe because she didn't want to admit I was capable of some kindness."

Laura spoke without rancor, but Abby still heard the hurt. "Were things that bad between you?" she asked. A shrug was all the answer she got.

"In any case, struggling so much doesn't sound like it made university much fun," Laura said after a moment.

"It was, actually," Abby said quietly. For a second she pictured herself in a lecture room or a lab, following her passion, daring to dream. "I loved the course. It was worth all the financial worry and struggle."

"And you wanted to be a vet."

"Yep."

Laura cracked one eye open. "Have you always loved animals or something? Because you didn't get that from me."

Abby laughed. "I don't know. I wasn't bandaging every bird's broken wing as a kid, if that's what you mean. But I liked helping to make something better, and if it was a cuddly kitten or a cute dog, so much the better."

"And now?" Laura asked after a moment. "Is it something you'd still want to do now?"

"I haven't even thought about it. There hasn't been any point."

"There could be."

"How?" Abby didn't want to deal in those kinds of dreams. "We're barely making a go of the café. Now all this talk is stressing me out. Maybe I need to handle one of those serendipity rocks." Laura guffawed, which made Abby smile. "What are those things, anyway? And how are you supposed to handle them?"

"They're like stress balls but not squeezy?" Laura guessed. "Go on and touch one."

Tentatively Abby reached out to take one of the rocks. She yelped and jerked her hand back. "They're *hot*."

"There is steam rising from the bowl."

"True. I didn't notice that." She sucked her fingers, bemused by this whole surreal experience. "So, what, is this like do-it-yourself hot rock massage?"

"Must be."

Abby sat back on the lounger. "I'll give it a miss."

The attendant returned then with their drinks, but before Abby could take the tall glass of water, Laura threw out one imperious hand. "We won't be needing that. My daughter decided she'd like a mimosa, as well."

The attendant was certainly a professional. "Very good, ma'am," she murmured, and put Laura's mimosa down on the table next to her lounger before withdrawing again.

Abby was still tingling slightly from the way Laura had said *my daughter*. She didn't think she'd ever heard her mother say those words. "It is a bit early for me," she said with a little laugh.

Laura was unfazed. "That's why there's orange juice in it." She plucked the menu of spa treatments from the table. "Now, what do you fancy? Indian head or deep-tissue massage? Antiaging facial? We definitely both need the luxury mani- and pedicures."

"It all sounds pretty good." And rather scary. Abby didn't relish the thought of some polished beautician examining her body with all its flaws. At least she'd shaved her legs that morning.

The attendant brought back another mimosa, and after she'd left, Laura raised her glass in a toast. "To us," she said grandly. "Cheers."

"Cheers," Abby murmured, and they clinked glasses. She took a sip, the champagne in the drink fizzing pleasantly through her. "Thank you for this," she said awkwardly. "All of this, I mean. The whole idea. It's great."

"I'm glad you think so." Laura paused before continuing as awkwardly as Abby had spoken. "I'm glad we can do something together. I know it's not much," she added hurriedly. "Considering, well, everything. But at least it's something, right?" She made a little face. "That wasn't the most coherent thing I've ever said."

"No, but I got the gist," Abby said with a smile. Her trepidation at being here was starting to ease. She wanted to enjoy the day, especially since she was sharing it with Laura. Her mother.

Several hours later Abby had been rubbed and pummeled with an hour of deep-tissue massage, her finger- and toenails were gleaming pale pink, and her face tingled from the facial she'd had. She and Laura had had huge, fancy salads for lunch while their faces had been covered in slimy gunk, and now they were led back to the tranquillity room, swathed in thick terry cloth robes. Laura ordered them both cosmopolitans while Abby relaxed into the lounger.

"I feel all new and shiny," she said.

"You look good," Laura remarked in approval. "A haircut and highlight and you'll be like a new person."

Abby felt too relaxed to take offense at the implied criticism. "Makeover courtesy of Laura Rhodes?"

"Something like that. You're an attractive woman, Abby, if you'd just make the most of what you have."

Okay, maybe she did feel a little stung. "It's hard to have the time for an extended beauty regimen," she returned lightly. Abby leaned her head back against the lounger. "Were you always glamorous? Even in Hartley-by-the-Sea?"

Laura snorted. "No, definitely not."

"Then what happened?" Abby asked. She really wanted to know. "Why did you suddenly change?"

Laura was silent for a long moment. Abby braced herself for the usual rebuff. "Because I wanted to become someone else," she said at last. "I didn't much like being myself anymore."

The honest response startled her, and made her sad. "Why didn't you like being yourself?"

Laura's lips twisted and she shrugged, the movement impatient. "Because I'd made a lot of mistakes, Abby. Obviously."

"You mean"—did she dare ask? *Assume?*—"leaving me?" Laura didn't reply and Abby held her breath, waiting, hoping . . . even if it wouldn't make any difference now.

"Yes, that," Laura said at last. "Among other things."

The old Abby, the one who always bristled and flinched, would have made some retort about how abandoning your daughter was just one item on the laundry list of regrets. This time Abby held her tongue. She was starting to get glimpses of her mother's old life, the sadness and limitations that had led her to act the way she had. She still didn't understand, couldn't see the whole picture, but more and more, she wanted to, even if it hurt. And of course it was going to hurt. Abby just didn't know in what way or how much.

"So you moved to Manchester and started hostessing. Turned into a glamour queen."

"It wasn't quite as quick as that," Laura answered. The words seemed drawn from her reluctantly, but she was still speaking them. "Yes, I started hostessing, but I realized pretty quickly that I wanted to be doing something else."

"Why?" Laura pursed her lips and shook her head. Abby decided to press. "Was it dull or something?"

"Dull? Not exactly." Laura sighed and leaned her head back. "Abby, what do you think a nightclub hostess does?"

She'd never even considered the question before, which was odd, since it was the reason her mother had left her, after all. "Show people to their tables?"

Laura nodded slowly. "Among other things."

"What other things?"

"What do you think?" Laura sighed again. "Look, it was a long time ago. I was nineteen and stupidly naive. I changed myself because I didn't want to be a Northern tart with a thick accent who wouldn't ever get anywhere. Eventually, with a lot of hard work and determination, I became the assistant manager and then moved my way up."

A sour sensation was starting in the pit of Abby's stomach. "What do you mean, 'among other things'?"

"It doesn't matter."

"I think it does."

"And maybe, Abby," Laura said, an edge to her voice, "I don't want to tell you. Maybe I want to forget rather than dredge it all up, and make you think even worse of me than you already do."

The door to the tranquillity room opened and the attendant entered with a tray bearing two pink cocktails. Abby watched her come closer, observed as if from a great distance as she placed them on the table and asked if she could get them anything else.

"No, thank you," Laura said, all gracious condescension, and Abby wondered if she'd imagined the last exchange they'd had. Her mother was certainly acting as if it hadn't happened. The attendant left and Laura plucked her cocktail from the table and took a large sip.

"If it was so awful," Abby asked, because she couldn't drop it now, no matter how much Laura wanted her to or how much her courage was wavering, "why didn't you come back to Hartley-by-the-Sea?" *Why*, she wanted to ask, *didn't you come back to me?*

Laura took another large sip of her cocktail, nearly draining the glass. Abby didn't think she was going to answer, and she wasn't sure if she possessed the stamina to ask again. To insist. "Sometimes you go too far away to ever come back," she finally said, her voice low. Abby didn't think she was talking about miles.

She reached blindly for her own drink, her mind spinning. "I wish you'd told me," she said after she'd had a sip, the alcohol burning the back of her throat. "It would have made a difference."

"Don't turn me into a complete victim," Laura answered. She was speaking in her usual light tone. "I wanted to get out of Hartley-by-the-Sea, Abby. I *needed* to get out." She paused for a moment, reflecting. "I knew what the cost was to you, and I decided it was worth it." She met Abby's gaze, unflinching. "That's still the same, and always will be."

Yes, it was, but somehow it didn't hurt quite as much as it used to. Her mother wasn't completely the coldhearted bitch Abby had decided she was a long time ago. There was still so much to discover, to learn, but she was that much closer.

"I don't think badly of you, you know," she said after a moment when the only sound was the soothing noises of a waterfall and birds chirping. At some point they'd changed the sound track of the tranquillity room.

Laura shrugged, not meeting Abby's eyes. "I wouldn't blame you if you did."

"I did—you know that. I did, a lot. But I don't anymore. At least, not as much."

"Well." Laura let out a soft laugh. "That's something, I guess."

"Sorry if it doesn't seem like enough—"

"No, no, I didn't mean it like that. I'm grateful, Abby. Truly." Laura turned to her with a small, tired smile. "You've given me more than I deserve. I'm really glad we've . . . we've been able to reconnect. *So* glad. But enough of this emotional stuff, please. I can only take so much."

Abby nodded, unable to hide her relief. This was all getting pretty intense, and she needed time to sort through her own feelings, process what her mother had—and hadn't—said. "Yeah, cue the swell of music and let's get another drink."

That evening, after Noah had gone to bed, Abby headed outside. She hadn't told Laura where she was going, just that she'd be out for a few minutes. Less, if she lost her nerve.

She didn't have anything to lose, she reminded herself. This was no biggie. Just a casual invitation to a group event. No problem. But she was glad she was looking her best, the best she'd ever looked, with her nails pretty and pink, her toes on display in a pair of flip-flops. Her skin was glowing from the facial, and while her hair was still ragged, she had, at Laura's prompting, booked herself in for a trim and color. Crazy times.

Now she headed towards the caravan park, aware with each step that she didn't actually know where Chris lived or even if he'd still be there. She'd seen him twice more after that first meeting; both exchanges had been quick, only slightly flirty, and ended with her selling him a lunch box. Each time he'd asked her about the paragliding, and each time Abby had put him off. But she was tempted, even if the taster day cost over a hundred pounds. But she wasn't going to talk to him about paragliding tonight.

The smell of frying sausages wafted through the air as Abby made her way through the maze of caravans, holidaymakers lounging in beach chairs or busy at their barbecues. She couldn't see Chris anywhere. She'd already rehearsed her opening line: *Hey, I was hoping I might bump into you.* Imply that she hadn't come out simply to see him, but had been busy doing something else. Keep it all offhand, easy and light. The way Laura spoke.

Except she needed to actually find Chris for any of this to happen. Nerves gave way to frustration and finally defeat. It was coming on eight o'clock and she couldn't hang around the caravan park much longer. People were starting to give her suspicious or, worse, pitying looks. Perhaps she wasn't the first girl to hang around, waiting for Chris.

And then, amazingly, he appeared, coming up the hill in his usual Lycra gear, a helmet in his hand. He didn't see Abby at first, which meant she waited, an expectant look on her face, for several awkward seconds. Then Chris caught sight of her and she got an eyeful of that white smile.

"Hey . . ."

"Hey." She was smiling back, goofily. "I was hoping I'd run into you." That sounded light enough, she hoped. Not as if she'd been wandering around the caravan park, searching for him.

"Oh, yeah?" Chris adjusted his stance, brought the helmet closer to his body. "What's up?"

"We're having a party on Friday night," Abby said. "For our grand opening—or reopening, really. We've done some work inside, on the café. . . ." She trailed off, wishing she'd rehearsed this bit. "So we're celebrating it all with a party, and I thought you might want to come. It's open to everybody, I mean. It's just a thing . . ." She trailed off again, embarrassed. When was the last time she'd asked someone out? Not that she was doing that, of course. This wasn't a date.

For a second, a poignant memory slotted into place, like putting a reel into one of those kid View-Masters. Quite vividly she could see Ben, his hair rumpled, his expression sheepish and a little pained, fumbling through an invitation to the pub. It had been more rehearsed than her own spiel just now, every word precise and emotionless because he'd practiced so much, until she'd asked him a question and then he hadn't known what to say, because he no longer had a script. They'd laughed about it, later. A little bit, anyway.

They'd met at the library; Ben was on a law course, while Abby was doing animal science. Both of them studying all the time, anxious to do well, forgoing the normal university pleasures of partying, drinking, living life like the world was one gigantic playground. At the time it had seemed important; looking back, Abby wished she'd relaxed more. Wished Ben had relaxed more too, had been willing to let life unfold differently.

"Friday night . . ." Chris was musing, and Abby refocused on the man in front of her. He was tall and lanky, while Ben had been short and stocky, a rugby player's build. He'd never been sporty, only academic. "Yeah, that sounds fun. I'll try to make it."

Which definitely meant it wasn't a date. "Okay, well, good." Abby tried for nonchalant, but it felt like wearing her mother's designer clothes. "That's great. So . . ." Cue utter blankness. Small talk was so exhausting. "See you around," she finally managed, and Chris just nodded. Somehow the whole exchange wasn't giving her the sense of elation, of victory, that she'd hoped for.

Abby headed back towards the café. Eight o'clock at night and the beach was still full of people and dogs, the smoky, slightly charred smell of barbecues in the air, the sound of laughter and various excited shouts carrying. Maybe it didn't actually matter what Chris's response was. Maybe it hadn't been about that at all. It had been about her reaching out, daring to sneak a toe out of her comfort zone. And she had. So, victory after all.

Doing a self-conscious little fist pump, smiling now, Abby walked into the café.

22

Laura

LAURA SURVEYED HER REFLECTION in the mirror, squinting to catch sight of any and every flaw. She would be forty-three in a little over a week. Forty-*three*. That was more mid-forties than early forties. The next big birthday would be the awful one with a five in front. Once, it had given her a sick feeling in the pit of her stomach, because she'd known, even if she'd been doing her damnedest to keep time at bay, that she had a limited shelf life. But now she didn't need to worry about every sag or wrinkle or gray hair.

She'd dreamed of her father again last night. She'd been a child in the dream—at least she thought she'd been a child, although the dream had been from her point of view, so she hadn't actually seen herself. But she'd *felt* like a child.

She'd been with her dad and he'd been taking her somewhere, somewhere she needed to go, although in the exasperating way of dreams she couldn't remember where or why. But it had been important; there had been an urgency about the dream, a sense of time slipping away. Her father had been his usual careless self; as a child, Laura had loved his easy way of being, the cigarette dangling from his lips, the slouchy walk, the way nothing had fazed or concerned him. The grown-up Laura recognized that if she'd met Mel Rhodes as an adult, she would have written him off as a feckless tosser.

But in the dream she'd been clinging to his hand, happy and yet worried at the same time. And now, hours later, she still had that same sour mix in the pit of her stomach.

She'd spent a long time debating what to wear; she had several suitcases full of designer clothes that had been pretty much irrelevant since she'd moved to Hartley-by-the-Sea, and she'd been relishing the chance of wearing something expensive and glamorous. She'd gone back and forth but had finally settled on a Catherine Walker cocktail dress that was so deep a blue it was almost, but not quite, black. It had lace panels on the side and some exquisite detailing on the hem and the neckline, and it fit her perfectly. Most important, it didn't make her look like cringe-worthy mutton dressed as lamb.

She'd realized, soon after she'd moved to New York, that the understated sexy look no longer worked for her. She'd been thirty-seven, and despite the best beauty treatments and Botox injections, she didn't look twenty-two anymore. Not even close. And a thirty-seven-year-old in leather jeans or a slinky top looked, in Laura's opinion, sad. So she'd changed her look, shedding the tough, sexy, hard-nosed businesswoman-with-attitude look that had worked for over ten years in Manchester. She'd developed a classier look, understated, re-strained glamour, making sure everything looked expensive and to-gether without being at all grannyish. Except stupid Tyler hadn't agreed.

Catherine Walker worked, though. Nothing sexy about the dress, but nothing matronly, either. She wasn't showing too much cleavage, which was a good thing, because she'd just noticed that her breasts were starting to get that wrinkly crepe-paper texture that old ladies had. Her mother had certainly had it, the skin of her pendulous breasts reminding Laura of a newspaper someone had scrunched up and then tried to smooth out again, to no avail. What she had to look forward to. Grimacing, Laura reached for her lipstick.

Downstairs she could hear Noah flying around the kitchen, making loud motorboat noises, interspersed with high-pitched shrieks. Abby had promised he'd be asleep by the time the party started at half seven, but Laura had her doubts.

It was now two weeks since he'd left school, and every day had felt like an exercise in patience and self-control. A couple of days ago Laura had, on impulse, booked a viewing of Thimble Cottage, a rental just off the high street. She'd felt a bit traitorous walking around and exclaiming over the varnished oak floorboards, the granite counter-tops, the sunken marble tub in the bathroom, but goodness, that place had felt like a few rooms of heaven compared with the café flat.

It had once been a toll office for the bridge that crossed Pow Beck, about two hundred years ago. Then an investor from London had bought it, done it up properly. Besides the kitchen, the sitting room with French doors and a tiny, adorable balcony of wrought iron, there were two bedrooms, a spacious bathroom, and a lovely wedge of garden with high stone walls covered in wisteria. It was gorgeous. Laura had put a deposit down on the spot, because she couldn't countenance letting it slip away from her. And the rent was semifeasible—four hundred pounds a month. She deserved this, she'd told herself, even though recently she'd been telling herself she didn't deserve anything.

She hadn't told Abby yet, hadn't dared. Surely Abby would appre-ciate the space, though. They were working and living together, after more than twenty years apart. Surely Laura's leaving would be a relief. She'd tell Abby later, maybe after the party. With one last nod for her reflection, Laura headed downstairs.

"Nana, you look a stunner!" Noah exclaimed, stopping midjump to stand still for a few blessed seconds, his mouth agape.

Laura choked back her laugh. Abby rolled her eyes. "Noah. Where on earth did you hear that word?"

"What?" Noah blinked, all wide-eyed innocence. "I heard it on telly. At Nathan's house."

"Of course you did," Abby muttered.

Laura clocked that Abby was still dressed in the T-shirt and jeans she'd worn all day while working in the café kitchen. "Why don't you go get ready?" she suggested. "I'll keep Noah company here."

"Would you?" Abby gave her a heart-meltingly grateful smile. "Thanks." She was upstairs before Laura could reply.

"Well, Noah." Laura smiled at her grandson. "Shall we go over and have a look at the party preparations?"

"Yes!" Noah's voice came out in an earsplitting screech. He started hopping up and down, his hands outstretched towards Laura, and she saw they were smeared with jam. She backed away. The last thing she needed was jammy handprints on her front.

"Let's get you washed up first and then we'll go over."

"Wow." Noah's voice dropped to a breathy whisper of wonder when a few minutes later Laura opened the door to the café and they stepped through. It *did* look pretty good. Abby had strung fairy lights along the windows, and Laura had bought bouquets of agapanthus and roses that lent both splashes of color and a lovely scent. Several tables had been pushed to one side to create a bar as well as more space, and the catering team had dropped off the trays of appetizers that afternoon. Now they needed only guests.

"It looks dead posh," Noah said. Laura laughed softly.

"Is that another expression from the Campbell household?" she asked, and Noah grinned.

Laura moved around the space, twitching a curtain here, moving a vase there. She felt incredibly nervous, more nervous even than when Density had had one of its big parties with a raft of A-listers coming and every expectation on Laura to have it be perfect. And those parties *had* been perfect, because she'd dealt with all the details, from what the bouncers wore to the cocktail napkins on the bar. She'd had a reputation that she'd carefully cultivated of being a professional, sophisticated and gracious, but also someone who wouldn't take any crap. Being known that way had felt so validating. When she was

Laura Rhodes, nightclub manager, she wasn't the teenage girl who had drifted around fatherless, or the poor slag who'd gotten herself pregnant. She wasn't a tarty hostess dressed in a cheap and too-tight cocktail dress and tottering heels, needing to be "friendly" to the male customers.

Her stomach twisted sourly at the memory of sharing that tidbit of her life with Abby when they'd been at the spa. Why on earth had she? She'd buried that girl, along with all her other incarnations, a long time ago. And yet some perverse part of her had wanted Abby to know. Had wanted some understanding and compassion, but that only came with the look of confused pity she'd seen on Abby's face since, which made her want to scream. The last thing she needed was her daughter's pity.

"I think you need to get your jammies on," she told Noah, who sulked predictably. "It's seven o'clock," she reminded him in her best mumsy voice. "Your bedtime."

"Can't I stay up to see everybody come in?" Noah wheedled, and Laura shook her head.

"Absolutely not."

Half an hour later Noah was tucked up in bed if not asleep, and Abby was the one twitching and tweaking, flitting around the café, clearly nervous.

"Relax," Laura said. She'd entered that state of preternatural calm that came over her immediately before an event. "You look lovely," she added, because Abby did. She was wearing a floaty pink dress that Laura wouldn't have chosen for her but somehow worked, and she'd left her hair loose and dark about her shoulders. Her open-toed sandals made the most of her pedicure.

"What if people don't come?"

"Of course they'll come. Who can resist free booze?" Abby smiled weakly. "Besides," Laura continued, "we already know a load of people who have said they're coming. Juliet and Peter, Lucy and Alex . . ."

"Rachel and Andrew, Claire and Dan." Abby nodded slowly. "Yes, okay. It should be all right. It just feels like so much is on the line."

"I'd be more worried about the toddler craft time tomorrow morning," Laura replied. "That whole concept gives me nightmares. But I suppose you're used to it, with the toddler mornings you do." The ones she'd deliberately avoided.

Abby smiled. "Yes, but tomorrow I'm letting them have glue."

A few minutes later the first guests started trickling in, many of them exclaiming over the café, the decorations, the new flooring, the tables and chairs. Even those who had seen it before seemed inclined to enthuse, making Laura swell with pride. Even Simon, who had come with a blowsy blonde on his arm, looked reluctantly impressed by what they'd accomplished. Laura hadn't wanted to invite him, but Abby had insisted, saying it would be a bit of sweet revenge. Now, noting her brother's speculative and slightly envious look, Laura decided her daughter had been right.

Abby was glowing, laughing and moving around the café as it started to fill up, and that made Laura feel even more proud. *My daughter,* she thought. *I helped put that spring in her step, that lift of her chin. Me.*

Was it arrogant to take at least partial responsibility? Laura didn't care. It felt good to know she'd helped Abby, that she might have made a difference. It felt like a tick in the "Good Mother" column of her life, which had been empty forever. Just one tiny tick, but still, something.

She noticed Abby's step get even springier when a tousle-haired surfer type entered the café. He looked about Abby's age, with dirty blond hair and a blindingly white smile. He wore loose, baggy jeans and a T-shirt with some sports logo on it, and Laura thought he looked a little bit like he was trying too hard to be a certain type. Still she noted the way Abby looked at him and then looked away, and thought, *Aha.*

Then she caught sight of Rob Telford coming in behind the surfer guy and she felt herself doing the same thing as Abby. Look in his direction, look away. Being coy, or maybe just pretending to be coy, all of it stupid because she wasn't interested in Rob. He was thirty, for goodness' sake. A child.

He found her the moment she was by herself, restocking the bar. The booze was flowing freely and people were taking happy advantage, her brother most of all, it seemed, judging by the number of whiskey sours she'd seen him knock back. She hoped his date was driving.

"This place looks amazing," Rob said. "You're going to give me a run for my money." He angled himself sideways to her so his body felt closer, one hip braced against the table.

"I don't think so," Laura returned lightly. "We don't have a liquor license."

"Even so." His gaze rested on her, assessing, approving. "You've done wonders with the place, Laura."

There was something about the way he caressed the syllables of her name that made Laura want to shiver even as she prickled with annoyance. "Abby's done a lot of the work."

"Of course, but you kick-started it. You have that kind of natural ability." He smiled at her, his eyes dark, his expression a little teasing, annoying her further.

"Do you flirt with everyone?"

Rob's eyebrows rose. "You call this flirting?"

"I don't know." She was, uncharacteristically, discomfited. She'd been calling the shots with men since she was twenty, when she'd decided she wouldn't let herself be used anymore. She'd made a conscious decision to change, to be in control. Part of that had been about not caring. Another part had been about not letting people close. Rob was challenging her on both fronts.

She didn't like feeling wrong-footed, unsure. Not at her age, and not about anyone. "You seem to be putting on the flirt," she said dismissively. "But maybe I'm being paranoid."

"It's hard not to flirt with a beautiful woman."

Laura rolled her eyes. "I could have predicted that one. It was so cheesy it's practically fondue."

"Fondue? Ouch. Okay, I'll stop." His smile was slow and easy, making her unsure whether he was still flirting. *What are your intentions, young man?*

"Can I get you a drink?"

"Please."

"What's your preferred poison?"

"A bottle of Windermere Pale will do me."

She pried the top off the bottle and handed it to him. "I'm sorry," she said abruptly, and Rob waited, the bottle raised to his lips. "For what I insinuated the other day, at the fete. About . . . about your mother." Rob's expression froze and Laura wished she hadn't started this ill-timed apology. Why on earth had she? She should have sent Rob on his way with his beer.

"I shouldn't have said as much as I did," Rob replied before taking a long swallow of his beer. "Everyone's got crap they want to forget."

"Or pretend never happened."

"Same difference."

"Maybe." She sighed. "Anyway, I know I'm touchy about my own past. I shouldn't have delved into yours."

"Consider it forgotten."

"Okay." And she would also consider this conversation over. They'd already gotten way too personal, and she'd been the one to go there first. "Well." Her voice took that upward lilt, friendly but slightly cool, and she didn't have to say anything else for Rob to get the message.

"Right. You need to go circulate."

"Exactly. So." She smiled, and realized she was doing her old trick of not letting it meet her eyes, tongue to the back of her teeth. Now it felt a little strange, like putting on someone else's clothes. "Enjoy your beer."

She spent the rest of the party mingling and chatting, keeping her cool, professional persona in place, from the practiced smiles to the sparkling laugh to the way she tilted her head just so. It occurred to her that she'd once considered this whole ritualized act as being in her element, but now at least part of her just felt like a fake. A part of her, a surprisingly large part, wanted to peel off the dress, kick off the Louboutins, and relax on the sofa with Abby and Noah. She must have been going mad.

"It went well, didn't it?" Abby asked when it was well past midnight and the last guests had gone. The café was a tip of empty bottles and paper plates smeared with the remnants of appetizers. The fairy lights had come down and were trailing on the floor.

"It did. But I think we made an error of judgment, thinking we could clean this place up and have it ready for toddlers by ten a.m."

"Oh, Rachel and Claire said they'd help with that. They run a cleaning business together, you know. They offered to come by at eight and do a couple of hours for free."

"They did?" Laura was touched. That, at least to her, went well beyond the call of friendship's duty. "Claire West, you mean? She cleans houses as well as minds the post office shop?"

"Yes." Abby looked at her curiously. "Why do you sound so disbelieving?"

"Because her family is so rich," Laura said after a tiny pause. "And her parents have some serious attitude about their position in this village, their exalted social status."

Abby leaned against the counter, crossing her arms. "You sound like you have personal experience with them."

Her voice was too mild, too level. Alarm bells started clanging internally, an unholy sound. She shouldn't have said anything about the Wests. Abby was obviously suspicious. "Oh, you know," she said, sighing and stretching her arms above her head, lacing her fingers together. "We were skint growing up and they had so bloody much and loved to remind everyone. It annoyed me, as a kid." Abby didn't look convinced and so Laura continued, dropping her arms. "I used to babysit Claire and Andrew. Marie West would always go on about how I *had* to take my shoes off before I came in, and *please* don't help myself to anything but the stuff kept in the cupboard for sitters. All budget stuff, of course. Cheap digestives and orange squash." She laughed, genuinely, because the memory actually amused her now. "Marie West was the pettiest woman I've ever met."

"Claire used to be terrified of her," Abby said. Laura nearly sagged in relief that the conversation was, more or less, moving on. "I think she's gotten past that a bit, though."

"Well, good for her," Laura answered, determinedly indifferent. "Now maybe we should leave this mess for Rachel and Claire and go to bed."

"Sounds good to me."

"But first, a toast." Laura was seized by a sudden impulse, an actual need to make this moment special. Important. She found a bottle of champagne with the flat dregs left and poured them both sips. "To the beach café," she said in her grandest voice. "*Our* beach café."

Abby, she saw, looked rather misty-eyed. Maybe it was just the alcohol, but maybe it was real emotion. Happiness. She hefted her glass in a toast before swigging the single sip. "To our beach café."

23

Abby

"I WANT TO SHOW you something."

Abby heard notes of both pride and uncertainty in her mother's voice that made her feel wary. "You do?"

"Yes." They were standing in the kitchen on a sunshiny Monday morning, the day after the end of their grand-opening festivities. Rachel and Claire had come in to clean just as they'd promised, so all Abby had had to do was stumble out with a smile. The place had been packed with children, children laughing and children screaming; there wasn't much difference between the two sounds. Abby had assembled an easy craft of gluing sand and seashells onto card stock, but as she'd suspected, unleashing glue into a two-year-old's hands was, to put it mildly, unwise. The Hart twins had ingested a good portion of the bottle and she was mopping up sticky spills well into the evening. The toddler mornings she ran every Wednesday would stay toys-only. Crafts with two-year-olds were way too much to handle.

Laura had hidden in the kitchen, making sandwiches and jugs of black currant squash, wincing every time a child let out a particularly ear-piercing shriek.

"You owe me," Abby said when she came in to get the sandwiches.

"I owe you?" Laura pretended to look shocked, a smile lurking around her lips. "This was your idea."

Sunday was a little more low-key, although the queue for the free ice-cream cones snaked all the way past the car park.

"It's a good thing we only offered one hundred free cones," Laura had said darkly. "We need to hire someone to do the ice cream ASAP."

"Or someone in the kitchen, if we're going to offer meals in the evenings," Abby replied. "I know you said we could do it, but I'd rather hire the work out if we could."

Laura paused in her flawless rhythm of scooping ice cream and handing over cones. "Yeah, why not? I'll place an ad."

The world had felt limitless that weekend. Chris had shown up at the party on Friday night, making Abby feel like her blood had just been carbonated. It was ridiculous to get soppy about a guy she barely knew, but she didn't care. She just liked the feeling. And Chris had flirted with her, even if Abby had suspected it was the thoughtless, knee-jerk reaction to an obviously available female.

By Sunday night she'd been exhausted, though, and so had Laura. They'd dragged themselves to bed, groaning and smiling at the same time, both basking in the success of the weekend even if Abby felt like she'd been run over by a truck. She'd come into her bedroom humming, and then taken a second to pause and savor everything about the moment: the fact that she felt pretty, the enjoyment of all the events, and even the simple fact of her bedroom, with its spaciousness and raspberry walls. It didn't feel like her grandmother's bedroom anymore. It had been nearly two months since Mary Rhodes had died, and while Abby missed her—of course she did, every day—she also felt the empty spaces, spaces that had been there long before her grandmother's death, starting to fill up. Thanks to her mother.

She wasn't going to attribute everything to Laura—but she was still grateful. Someday she'd work up the courage and the eloquence to say something of that to Laura.

Now she leaned against the kitchen counter as she switched on the kettle. Every muscle ached and the sunlight filtering through the kitchen curtains was way too bright. They had to open the café in half an hour.

"We should have closed the café today," she said on a yawn, even though she didn't mean it. Now more than ever, they needed to capitalize on the success of the weekend. "So what do you want to show me?"

"I'll wait and explain it at the time," Laura said. She definitely sounded cagey. "How about this evening?"

"What about Noah?"

"He can come along."

"Come along? So where is this thing you want to show me?"

"In the village." Laura waved vaguely with her hand. "It'll make sense soon, I promise."

"Okay." Abby felt too tired to question her mother further. She wanted to go back to bed and curl up under her duvet; Noah had woken her up at the unpleasant hour of five thirty and CBeebies didn't start its programming until six. She'd spent an ungodly half hour playing Snakes and Ladders with him until she'd been able to switch the television on and sneak guiltily back up to bed to snatch another hour's sleep.

Now the thought of a day spent in the café's kitchen made her spirits flag a little, despite the high of the weekend. No matter how pretty the café looked now, no matter how hard they worked, they were still just running a restaurant. She found the realization, obvious as it was, strangely dispiriting. She'd enjoyed her time here, but was this really what she wanted to do for the rest of her life?

The kettle switched off and Abby spooned coffee granules into a mug. "I'm curious now," she said, although she wasn't really. Not yet, anyway. Maybe after she'd had her first hit of caffeine and was feeling more human, more like the pretty, flirty self she'd been on Friday night . . .

"All will be explained tonight," Laura said with a smile. She looked annoyingly refreshed and energized for seven thirty in the morning.

For a woman who drank, smoked—or used to—and pooh-poohed green vegetables, she glowed way too much.

The day ended up being so busy that Abby didn't have time to feel tired. The steady stream of customers might have been up to the gorgeous sunshine, or it might have been the publicity they'd splashed out on, or both, but it was nice to see the queue snaking through the door, even if it meant Abby was racing from till to table and back again all afternoon, with Noah underfoot for most of that time.

"I'm really thinking summer camp," Laura said under her breath when she nearly collided with Noah while carrying a tray of teas.

Abby didn't bother to retort that they couldn't afford it, or that Noah was actually behaving well, considering he had to spend most of the day inside. At that point, with a headache coming on, she was thinking summer camp, as well.

By early evening, with the café locked up and a dinner of frozen pizza consumed, she was feeling a bit better—and a bit more interested in what Laura was eager as well as nervous to show her.

"So where exactly are you taking me?" she asked as they walked up the beach road, the sunlight sending long, low rays across the sheep pasture on either side and making the mud puddles glint.

"You'll see." Laura was walking with an almost manic energy, so Abby and Noah struggled to keep up with her.

"Why do you seem so nervous?" Abby asked, and Laura let out a high trill of laughter.

"Nervous? I'm not nervous."

Yeah, right. It was weird to see her mother acting nervous. She'd seen her in lots of moods, from coolly confident to coldly furious, but not actually anxious. Her mother, Abby realized, was the most confident person she knew.

Right after they crossed the bridge and turned onto the high street, they went down a narrow side street that Abby rarely went down, with two-story terraced houses on either side. Laura stopped in front of the first one on the left and, inexplicably, took out a key.

"Well. Here it is."

"Here's what?" Abby asked. "Do you know who lives here?"

"Yes, actually." It was a pretty house, small and neat, with flower-pots full of clematis under the one downstairs window. Abby watched as Laura put the key into the lock and then opened the door.

"What . . . ?" she said, but found she couldn't finish the sentence. Next to her, Noah had started hopping up and down.

"Are we visiting someone? Are we going to get ice cream?"

"For someone who lives next door to a café that sells ice cream," Laura murmured, "he seems rather excited about that possibility." She opened the door all the way and then stepped inside. "Come in."

"Okay." Abby stepped into the entrance hall, small and pristine, with a stone-flagged floor and walls of a soothing sandy color. A narrow hallway led back to the kitchen, and a staircase with a banister of gleaming polished wood led to the upstairs. Abby could see French doors leading to what she presumed was the lounge. The place was clearly empty of both furniture and people.

Noah poked his head around her, pushing against her back so she was forced to move farther into the house. "Where is everybody?"

"No one lives here, Noah," Laura said in a voice of suppressed excitement. "Yet."

And then Abby put it all together with an almighty clang. *Duh.* She should have put it together ages ago. Her mother was going to move in here. Her mother was going to leave her. She felt two years old again. Of course she didn't remember when Laura had left her back then, but she imagined it felt something like this.

"Let's have a look," she said tonelessly, and walked into the lounge. Laura followed her. Noah was everywhere, rattling doorknobs, pressing his nose against the windows and smearing the glass. Abby let him.

"It's nice and bright, isn't it?" Laura said. She sounded like a real estate agent. "And airy. These doors go right out to the garden. Noah, do you see the garden?"

"Can I go out there?" Noah demanded. "Can I? Can I?"

"Of course." Laura fumbled with the French doors for a moment before she managed to open them. "The garden is walled," she told Abby over her shoulder. "It's perfectly safe."

"Great." Abby crossed her arms across her chest and then uncrossed them; she didn't know what to do with her body, her face. What expression was she wearing right now? Did she look sour, cross? *Hurt?*

She made herself move to the doors to inspect the garden for herself. It was lovely, a small rectangle of perfectly trimmed, lush green grass, the stone walls on three sides covered with purple wisteria. Noah was running in circles, windmilling his arms.

"And a patio," Laura said helpfully, as if Abby could not see it for herself. "For those few evenings when it's actually warm enough to eat outside. Although I shouldn't complain. It's been a lovely summer so far, hasn't it? Weather-wise, I mean." Her mother gave her a guilty, unhappy look, and Abby knew she was thinking about Mary.

It felt like a lifetime ago, walking into the café and seeing Laura. Burying her grandmother. An utter lifetime.

"Yes," she said, and she tried to inject a note of normality, if not enthusiasm, into her voice. "Yes, the weather's been great."

"Come see the kitchen." They left Noah in the garden and went to the kitchen, which was as small and perfectly laid out as the rest of the house. The same stone-tiled floor as the hall, granite countertops, and top-of-the-line appliances. Room for a table for two in a little nook, and a utility room off the kitchen, with space for a washer and a dryer.

"A dryer," Abby said with a rather hard laugh. She'd never had a dryer. She hung the wet clothes out by the bins in good weather, or over the radiators in bad. Some days it felt as if they were living in a sea of Legos and school uniform.

"Do you want to see the bedrooms?" Laura sounded hopeful and yet timid, a combination that was so unlike her.

"Why not?"

Noah thundered up the stairs after them and Abby inspected the bedrooms, one clearly a master with enormous built-in wardrobes.

"And the bathroom's really amazing," Laura said, and showed her the sunken marble tub. Abby stared at it and felt that bitter root of hurt burrow deep into her soul. It was all so *Laura*. She'd found her little haven of elegant perfection in Hartley-by-the-Sea. Of course.

"It really is amazing," Abby said dutifully when they'd gone back downstairs. Laura was locking the French doors; the garden was now cloaked in twilight. "Really top-notch."

"Yes, I couldn't quite believe it when I saw it," Laura said with a little laugh.

"When *did* you see it, out of curiosity?" Abby asked, a hard note entering her voice. She realized she was angry. *All this time I thought we were working together, building something, and you were planning your getaway?* She could already imagine Laura's response, the cool, remote tone, the touch of impatience. *Oh, come on, Abby. We work together. We don't need to live together, do we? No need to be in each other's pockets, for heaven's sake.*

And she was right—that was the truly irritating part. There was no need for Abby to feel abandoned now. No need at all. Laura wasn't actually leaving. She was simply finding her own place. It was a normal, grown-up thing to do. But right now Abby felt like a little kid again, her nose pressed to the glass, pestering her grandmother about when Laura was coming to visit.

"Oh, I saw it last week," Laura said airily. "Not that long ago. But I snapped it up. I doubt there are many places like this in Hartley-by-the-Sea."

"Probably not." Her stomach was churning and she felt her fists clench. She was waiting for her mother to say something, to spell it out. Apologize, for goodness' sake. *Sorry to spring this on you, Abby, but I think I really need my own space. And you'll be able to spread out a bit more, won't you?*

But in typical Laura style, she wasn't explaining anything, and apologies were out of the question.

Abby took a deep breath; the air felt heavy in her lungs. "So when do you move?"

Laura smiled in a whimsical way, as if she'd been waiting for this moment, preparing for it. "Well, that's the thing. I'm not intending to move."

"What?" Noah, his interest in an empty house flagging, had started to rhythmically head-butt Abby in the stomach. She placed her hands on either side of his head, his hair sweaty underneath her palms, and did her best to keep him still. "What do you mean?"

"Well . . ." A small, playful smile flirted with Laura's mouth. She looked like a child at Christmas. "I thought you could move here instead."

Abby stared. The words didn't make sense. The whole concept didn't make sense. "You want me to move out?" she said dumbly, and for a second Laura's expression clouded, a hint of impatience visible in the set of her mouth.

"No, of course not. It's not about you moving out, Abby, or me taking something away from you. It's about giving you something. This." She spread one arm wide to encompass the lovely little house. "I want you to have your own place," she rushed on, the words tumbling over themselves. "Not your grandmother's house or some grotty council flat. I want Noah to have a garden to play in, and a place to invite friends. You were so pleased to paint the walls of your bedroom—imagine being able to decorate your whole house." Laura looked at her beseechingly for a moment while Abby just stared, trying to process this entirely unexpected development. Laura dropped her arm. "If you don't want it, that's okay," she said quietly. "I know I should have run it past you first. I just saw it and thought . . ." She let out a laugh. "Well, in all honesty, I thought I'd like to live here. But then I realized I wanted *you* to live here more. Not away from me," she clarified hurriedly. "But for your sake. For your happiness." Another laugh, and she turned away so Abby couldn't see her face. "And now I'm sounding revoltingly soppy. Just tell me to stuff it. Ask me where I was when you really needed help." Laura sniffed, and Abby felt tears threaten. She hadn't expected this. She hadn't expected this at *all*.

A smile broke through then and she walked over to her mum and laid a hand on her shoulder. It was the closest she'd ever come to hugging her; even now that felt like a step too far. "Thank you, Laura," she said quietly. "It's perfect. I love it. And Noah will too."

Noah, who had been running up and down the hallway, poked his head in the doorway. "What about me?"

"What do you think of this house, Noah?" Abby asked. "Do you like it here?"

He regarded her suspiciously. "What do you mean?"

"I mean, would you like living here? The two of us?"

"Not Nana?" He glanced at Laura, looking even more suspicious, and she smiled.

"I'd stay at the café, but don't worry, Noah. We'd see each other every day."

Noah considered this for a few seconds, his lower lip jutting out in an alarming way. Abby didn't want him to have a meltdown here, in front of Laura, when she'd been trying to do something nice for them both.

"Imagine having a proper garden, Noah," she said, her voice full of enthusiasm. "And being so close to school—you could almost run up to Nathan's on your own!"

Noah's eyes widened. "Could I?"

She was going to regret that suggestion. "Eventually," she said. "Maybe when you're . . . seven."

"He'll hold you to that," Laura murmured.

Abby's mind was starting to race. Living here, she'd actually be part of the village instead of feeling on the fringes of it, down at the beach without any other houses around. She'd have neighbors, and she could plant things. Not that she'd ever really wanted to plant things, but *still*. In this house she'd feel like a proper mother. A proper grown-up, for the first time in her life. She had a bizarre urge to make curtains or bake cookies.

"What do you reckon, Noah?" she asked her son, and he grinned.

"I like it," he pronounced. "When can we move? Can we sleep here tonight?"

24

Laura

TODAY WAS HER BIRTHDAY. Laura was trying not to feel maudlin about it. She and Abby had spent the last week doing up Thimble Cottage amidst shifts at the café; they'd managed, between charity shops and kindly friends, to assemble enough furniture to kit out Abby's new home. Mostly, anyway. Laura had had visions of magazine-worthy interior design, but the eclectic assortment of battered furniture and framed posters would do, for now.

On Sunday, when the café was closed, they'd moved most of Abby's things. Dan Trenton had lent them his van as well as his impressive muscle for shifting the furniture, and Laura and Abby had packed boxes full of clothes and toys and books.

"You'll have to take some kitchen things," Laura said as she emptied out several cupboards. "You'll need pots and pans."

"I don't want to leave you without. . . ."

"Are you kidding? When am I going to use a double boiler?" She chucked it into the box with a smile. "Go wild."

Abby and Noah had spent Sunday night at the flat; Laura had insisted on ordering a takeaway to celebrate. She'd even bought a bottle of champagne and a Fruit Shoot for Noah. The weather had turned, as it often did in August, so the rain sleeted against the windows and the wind rattled the panes. Even so, it felt festive in the kitchen as they toasted each other and Laura listened to Abby shyly outline her plans.

"I'm going to go through the rooms slowly. I don't want to make rash decisions about paint colors or anything like that."

"Regretting that raspberry?" Laura surmised, and Abby looked bemused.

"What? No."

"Ah." She supposed she'd have to keep the raspberry, then. Perhaps she'd move to Noah's room, save the big bedroom for . . . well, for something.

"Are you going to do up the flat?" Abby asked. "It's all yours, now, really, isn't it?"

It didn't feel hers, never mind that she'd grown up here. Thimble Cottage had felt like hers, even as she'd realized she'd rather Abby have it. Her decision had come about on Friday night, after the party, when she'd been outlining her own glorious future and simultaneously realizing she could not leave Abby and Noah in the dust. Now Laura glanced at the peeling lino, the old Formica countertops, and the flimsy cupboards. "Maybe eventually."

"Well, we're really excited, aren't we, Noah?" Abby ruffled her son's hair. "I was thinking we could have a housewarming party, after I've got things the way I like them. Maybe in September."

"Sounds good."

"Lucy's wedding is in two weeks, you know. Are you going to go?"

Lucy had come in a few weeks ago, brandishing invitations and gushing about her wedding plans. Laura had taken a step back. She never liked to get close to that much enthusiasm. "I suppose," she said, sounding doubtful. She hated weddings. All that happiness and hope. She felt like taking the couple by the shoulders and shaking them both. *You have no idea what crap life is going to throw at you. No idea at all.*

"It should be good fun," Abby said. "Alex will keep Lucy from tipping over into total sentimentality."

"That's something, at least." Laura smiled and topped up both their glasses.

Monday morning Dan came over with his van and he and Abby loaded up the last of her stuff while Laura minded the café. It was pouring again, sheeting down so hard Laura couldn't even see the sea. The café held only a few customers gazing moodily out at the rain-lashed landscape.

"Why don't you take the day off and unpack?" Laura suggested. "I can manage alone today. I'll come by later and see how things are."

"Are you sure?" Abby asked, her face suffused with hope.

"Yes, of course I'm sure."

Abby and Noah hurried out, and Laura sank onto the stool behind the till, dropping her head onto her arms. Being a good mother was so exhausting.

That evening she walked to Abby's, knocking on the door before poking her head round, noting the half-empty boxes, the spill of clothes and books across the floor. A sofa sat in the middle of the room, a great lump of oatmeal-colored velour. It had been donated by a mate of Dan's, and getting a new one was, in Laura's opinion, a priority.

"Abby?" she called, and stepped into the room.

"Oh, hey." Abby came out of the kitchen, breathless and smiling. "I'm just unpacking dishes. Noah's in the garden—he loves it. And one of the boys in his year lives next door! They're playing football now that the rain has stopped." Abby delivered all of these statements as if they were miracles, and perhaps they were. Small everyday miracles, but no less precious for it.

"Fantastic," Laura said. "Can I help?"

She spent the next two hours unpacking boxes; Abby threw a frozen pizza in the oven and they ate in the kitchen, amidst all the happy mess.

Laura left when Abby was putting Noah to bed, after cleaning up the kitchen while Abby was upstairs with Noah splashing joyfully in the big sunken tub. She walked home quietly, her hands in her pockets, as she tried to fight off the overwhelming tide of melancholy she could feel was poised to sweep straight through her.

She hadn't told Abby it was her birthday Who wanted to celebrate turning forty-three, anyway? She hadn't celebrated her birthday in decades. In fact, Laura couldn't remember the last time she'd celebrated her birthday, at least as an adult. Those messy birthday cakes and impromptu family parties had ended when her dad had died.

The clouds had gathered again as Laura let herself into the flat; they looked dark and billowy, crowding the horizon. She kicked off her shoes and stood in the hallway that led to the kitchen, feeling the stillness, the emptiness, of the flat reverberate through her. She shouldn't have felt lonely, or at least no lonelier than usual. She'd lived alone for decades. Even for those first few awful years in Manchester, when she'd shared a grotty two-up two-down in a nasty suburb with several girls in similar grim situations, she'd had her own room and barely spoken to them. She knew loneliness. She understood being alone.

But it felt different this time. She pictured Abby giving Noah a bath, blowing bubbles and giggling, making memories. It sent a sharp pang through her and suddenly she craved a cigarette. But no, she hadn't smoked a cigarette in weeks. She wasn't going to go back now.

She walked slowly into the kitchen; even though she couldn't see the spaces in the cupboards where plates and cups had been, as well as that stupid double boiler, she *felt* them.

"This is ridiculous." And now she was talking to herself. Fabulous.

This was what she'd wanted, even if the surroundings weren't quite as elegant as she'd once hoped. But she'd been craving solitude, peace and quiet, *bliss*. Or so she'd thought.

Sighing, Laura kicked off her shoes and headed for the sofa. She'd watch mindless TV for a couple of hours and then go to bed. It was what she might have done any other night, although usually Abby would have been watching with her. They'd taken to watching some really awful reality TV shows, and once they'd both become ridiculously entranced by a documentary on moose on BBC2.

"England does not understand the concept of prime time the way America does," Laura had proclaimed, but she'd been gripped and even moved by the mother moose's journey through the snowy Rockies in search of food for her baby. *She'd* been a good mother.

And you're a good mother too. Finally. But also a lonely one.

She opened the fridge and considered pouring herself a glass of wine, but drinking alone felt pathetic. She shut the door and wandered to the lounge. Mindless TV it was. She had pressed the power button on the remote and was just about to flop on the sofa when a tap sounded on the front door.

She froze, shocked, uncertain. It was half past eight. Who on earth could have been stopping by? Chucking the remote onto the table, she went to the door.

Rob Telford stood there, holding a bottle of gin.

A feeling of relief seized her so hard that for a moment she couldn't speak. "Well," she said when she trusted her voice to sound normal, light and mocking, "you'd better come in."

She stepped aside and Rob sauntered in, all cocky self-assuredness. It should have bothered her, his obvious arrogance, but she was too glad simply to not be alone. And she was also glad for the gin.

"I brought the essentials," Rob said, "but not the extras."

"Tonic water and lime?"

He nodded, his smile slow and easy, and Laura turned away. If Rob Telford thought he'd come here for a booty call, then he could just forget it. Fast. "Fortunately my kitchen is well stocked," she said, and although the words were light, her tone was cool. She moved around the kitchen, taking out the necessary items and two tall glasses with brisk efficiency.

"I thought it would be."

If there was innuendo, she ignored it. Rob cracked open the bottle of gin and poured a measure into each glass. Laura added the rest and then took both glasses into the lounge.

"I was just about to watch *The Great British Sewing Bee*," she said, although she'd been intending no such thing.

"Sounds good," Rob answered as he sat down, sprawling onto the sofa, one arm resting along the back, with such ease that Laura started to feel annoyed. "Although I prefer *Big Brother*."

"Of course you do," she scoffed. "I almost forgot how young you are."

"Really? For a whole two seconds?" His eyebrows rose. "I find it hard to believe."

She smiled a bit at that, in spite of her best intentions not to. "Well." She sat on the opposite end of the sofa, back straight, as prim as a convent girl. Rob's mouth twitched.

"Well."

Silence stretched on for a good ten seconds before Laura broke it. "Why are you here, exactly?"

"Ouch."

"I'm just curious."

"Suspicious, even?"

She met his wry gaze evenly. "You could say that."

He didn't answer for a moment, just slowly rotated his glass between his big hands. "I knew Abby was moving out tonight."

"And you thought I needed cheering up?"

An eyebrow lifted. "Is that so bad?"

Was it? She always resisted the prospect of pity. "Maybe."

He laughed softly and shook his head. "I don't pity you, Laura."

"How did you know that was what I was thinking?"

"It was written on your face." He took a sip of his drink. "In capital letters."

Laura looked away. She didn't want him to see anything else written on her face. She gulped down some gin. She wasn't used to being so transparent.

"What exactly is bothering you?" Rob asked. He angled his body so he was a little closer on the sofa. Laura resisted the urge to move away.

"I just don't know why you're so interested," she said. "I feel like you've . . . you've *targeted* me from the moment I walked through the door of your pub." She semiglared at him, daring him to disagree.

"That sounds a bit creepy and stalkerish," Rob said mildly.

"Well?"

"I'm interested in you," he said, choosing each word with care, "because I think you're very brave to come back to Hartley-by-the-Sea."

His words fell into the stillness of the room, created ripples. "I don't know whether to be offended by that or not," Laura said after a moment.

"Why would you be offended?"

"Because the implication is that I'd *have* to be brave to come back here and face everyone after what I did."

"I didn't mean it like that."

"How did you mean it, then?" She hated feeling this raw. She needed more gin.

Rob didn't speak for a long moment. "I guess I was just thinking that I admire you," he said slowly. "I know how hard it is to come back and face a community that knows exactly who you are and where you come from."

Laura stilled, the feelings of rawness and vulnerability superseded by a sudden, surprising empathy. "Is that what you did?"

His smile was faint and self-deprecating. "You know my story."

"I never should have said that about your mum," Laura half mumbled. She could feel her face starting to heat. "I don't actually know the first thing—"

"It sounded like you knew enough." He spoke without any bitterness; Laura thought she almost heard a touch of humor in his voice.

She opened her mouth to backpedal some more and heard herself say, "Tell me."

Rob paused, his glass halfway to his mouth. "Tell you . . . ?"

"About your childhood." She shrugged, embarrassed she'd asked. "Whatever crap you had to take."

"You really want to know my crap?"

"I'm asking, aren't I?" She held his gaze, waiting, almost breathless. She wanted to know. She wanted to hear someone else's story.

Rob blew out a breath and then he leaned his head back against the sofa and closed his eyes. Still he didn't speak, and still Laura waited. Finally he said, "My mother was a drunk. That's my story. Sometimes it feels like that's *all* my story is." He tilted his head up so he could look at her. "You know what I mean?"

"Yes," she said quietly. "Yes, I know exactly what you mean."

"A lot of days she'd be at the pub at eleven a.m.," he continued. "Twenty quid and a crumpled pack of cigarettes in her hand. That's all she needed. Twenty quid might not seem like that much, but trust me, it buys enough pints, and we could have used that money at home."

"I believe you," Laura said. Her story was different and yet there were painful similarities. The sense of trapped futility, the grinding down.

"It wasn't always bad. Some days, some weeks, she was sober. It was just the not knowing. Coming home from school and having no idea what I'd find."

"Yes." She felt a tightness in her throat at the thought of Rob as a little rumple-haired boy, carefully, quietly opening the front door, his heart in his throat, and then that sense of free-falling when he realized it was one of those days. "What about your dad?"

"He left when I was four. There were a couple of visits to Workington to see him in a grotty flat, and then he got a job on the oil rigs up near Aberdeen and that was that."

That was that. One of the most crucial relationships of childhood just written off. She knew how that went. So much.

"So you left Hartley-by-the-Sea for a while and then you came back?"

"I left for university. I did a course in business down in Manchester. I got some decent A levels, despite all the dire predictions."

Which was more than she'd done. "And what made you come back?"

"Mum," he said simply. "She couldn't cope on her own. She was diagnosed with cirrhosis when I was twenty. She died when I was twenty-four."

"I'm sorry." He shrugged, a response Laura understood completely. "So I have to ask," Laura said, allowing a hint of humor to enter her voice. "Why on earth did you buy a pub?"

Rob let out a tired laugh and leaned his head against the sofa once more. "Firstly because I needed a job back here. And secondly because owning the pub meant I controlled it." He hefted his glass. "I didn't touch a drop of alcohol until I was twenty-four."

Laura winced. "Oh no, am I corrupting you?"

"Nope. I got blind drunk at my mother's funeral. Fitting, eh? But it didn't take much, since I'd been a teetotaler. And then afterwards I decided that not drinking at all meant I was afraid of it. Of alcohol and what it could do. Controlling my drinking, drinking like anyone else without a problem, was the stronger thing to do."

"And it doesn't bother you? Working all hours at the pub? Watching people drown their sorrows?"

"Sometimes, when some no-hoper stumbles in."

Another wince. "I hope you're not talking about me." A horrible thought occurred to her. What if this was all pity? Sod the being-brave spiel—maybe he was trying to *save* her. The thought was abhorrent.

"Of course I'm not talking about you." Rob rested one big hand on her knee; the feeling was surprising but not unpleasant, and Laura tensed, not wanting to offend him by shrugging his hand off, but not quite comfortable with it there. "I told you that you were brave, Laura."

"I think you're the brave one. To spend every day in the pub . . ."

"Actually I think it was the best thing I ever did. I redeemed it and myself. But facing everyone here was hard, especially at first." He removed his hand with a knowing smile, as if he understood exactly how it had discomfited her. "So I suppose that's why I feel like I relate to you." He shifted back to skewer her with an uncompromising look. "So now it's your turn. What's your story, Laura Rhodes?"

25

~

Abby

THE HOUSE SEEMED VERY quiet, even with Noah in it. After his bath he'd begged to go outside again, and because it sort of felt like Christmas, Abby let him, even though she knew it would defeat the purpose of his bath in the first place.

The sky had cleared and fragile sunlight was filtering through the clouds. Abby brought a kitchen chair out to the terrace and watched Noah race around like a mad thing. The garden was nothing more than a wedge of grass, nothing special about it at all, and yet he loved it because it was his. Their neighbor's son, Tom, popped his head over the wall again and as the sun started its lazy descent—it was after eight now—the two boys played football, their laughter echoing off the walls and floating through the air.

Abby was slapping at the midges attacking her bare legs, wondering if she should force Noah back inside, when Tom's mother, Bethan, popped her head over. Abby had seen her at the school, one of those cool mums, often decked out in exercise gear, shiny hair pulled into a high, tight ponytail. Tom and Noah's friendship seemed a much simpler thing than a potential one between her and Bethan.

"Tom's so pleased to have a friend next door," Bethan said. "I don't think I'll get him to sleep tonight."

Abby gestured to the boys playing. "I hope you don't mind me letting him come over again. He was desperate."

"I'm sure." Bethan propped her elbows on top of the wall, which compelled Abby to rise from her chair and walk over. "You lived down at the café before, didn't you?"

"Yes."

"I was sorry to hear about your grandmother. I didn't know her, but she seemed one of those cheerful souls."

"Yes, she was, in her own way." She thought of Mary's easy banter with the customers with a pang.

"What made you move out of the café? You're still working there, aren't you?"

"Yes. I suppose I decided it was time for a change." At least her mother had decided, and Abby was grateful for the dropkick out of the nest. She'd needed it. "I wanted some neighbors."

"That's good to hear. I could use one, as well." The flash of naked need in Bethan's face surprised her. Wasn't she one of the in girls? As if recognizing what she'd revealed, Bethan continued stiltedly, "Things haven't been that easy lately." She lowered her voice. "Tom was a surprise baby. We got married a year after he was born. I was desperate to settle down and start family life, but Steve wasn't so keen." She grimaced. "He's come round, of course, but sometimes . . ." She bit her lip and said nothing more.

"Noah was a surprise too." Abby kept her voice low even though the boys were shrieking and couldn't possibly hear. "His father wasn't so keen, either."

"No?" Bethan's eyes widened. "What happened?"

"He died in a motorcycle accident when I was four months pregnant. I like to think he would have come round, but sometimes I wonder." Ben had been enraged, and then he'd been coldly furious, and then he'd been depressed. What would he have felt next, if he'd been given the chance? A few days before his accident, he'd started to come round; they'd talked about marriage. It had felt fragile but hopeful, and Abby had started to build a life on it that had been snatched away just days later.

"I'm sorry," Bethan said. "That can't have been easy."

"No." Abby managed a small smile. No, it hadn't been easy at all, and Ben's parents, who had never approved of her, had made it harder. A double loss.

Bethan grimaced and rolled her eyes. "I'm stating the obvious there. But seriously, I'm glad you've moved here."

Abby felt something green and tender unfurl inside her. "So am I."

She called Noah inside soon after, with promises from Bethan to have a girls' night sometime. Abby closed and locked the French doors, breathing in the scent of newness and cleaning spray that permeated her home. Her home. "Noah," she said. "What color do you think we should paint the lounge?"

"Black!" Noah cried, and Abby instantly regretted asking her son's opinion.

"Might be a bit dark."

"Purple!"

"How about blue? Blue like the sea, since we can't see it anymore." She didn't mind that, though. The sea was still there, and living here, they'd be protected from the punishing wind, the salty spray.

"Blue," Noah agreed. Despite his hyped-up energy, Abby knew he was exhausted. "Come on, time for bed," she said, and Noah didn't even protest. She'd unpacked most of his room earlier that afternoon, so his bed with its dinosaur duvet was set up, a box of toys and books spilling over the floor. "We'll have to finish unpacking tomorrow."

"Can Tom come over tomorrow? Please? Please? And Nathan? I want him to see my new house." Noah scrambled under the covers before peering at her expectantly from underneath a dinosaur grinning in a ten-gallon hat.

"Tentative yeses to both," Abby said, and Noah screwed up his face. "What does ten-ta-tiff mean?"

"It means maybe." Abby sat on the edge of the bed and touched Noah's silky, sweaty hair. He had Ben's surprising dimple, and Ben's peaked eyebrows. She imagined what it would have been like if Ben had lived, something she didn't do very often, because it was punishing and there was so obviously no point. But now she imagined it differently. Not the happily-ever-after she'd insisted on in her mind, a semidetached on the outskirts of Liverpool, Ben a lecturer at the university and her working as a vet, trips to the zoo or the park on the weekends, a smiling, sunny montage of family life that she'd wanted when she'd been a child.

But what if it hadn't happened like that? What if Ben's fragile acceptance had shattered under the pressure of his studies and caring for a newborn? Maybe he would've insisted on pursuing his PhD with the single-minded intensity he'd always had about his studies, and which she'd once admired. She pictured him blowing up because the baby was crying and he couldn't concentrate to study; she pictured him staring down at Noah's wrinkled newborn face and dispassionately telling her how much raising a child cost. He'd never wanted children. She'd known that from the first. She'd just thought he'd change his mind when she fell pregnant. And maybe he would have.

But maybe, through Ben's death, she'd been spared. Maybe she would have had months and years of tension and hostility, ending with a different kind of heartbreak than she'd experienced when Ben had left one rainy night on his motorbike to go to the library and died.

Abby closed her eyes against the pain of the memory and Noah's hand found hers and squeezed. "Mummy?" he said sleepily. "I like it here."

Abby squeezed his hand back. "I like it here too, Noah."

Noah had just dropped off when a light knock sounded at the

front door. Abby opened it to see Lucy standing there with her usual sunny smile.

"I thought I'd see how you were settling in. And I brought champagne, or at least cava."

"Come on in," Abby said, and opened the door wider.

"This house is the sweetest thing," Lucy said, admiring the lounge with its French windows even though she'd seen it before. "It's so titchy and perfect."

"It is tiny," Abby admitted. "But I don't mind."

"No, of course not. Now, can you open this?" Lucy thrust the bottle at her. "Because I'm hopeless with champagne corks."

"I thought it was cava," Abby teased, and peeled the foil off the top. She wrestled with the cork for a moment—she hadn't had many opportunities to open a bottle of champagne—before the cork exploded out with a large pop and hit the ceiling. "Thank God it wasn't the light fixture," Abby said as she held the foaming bottle over the sink.

Lucy found glasses in a box and held them aloft while Abby poured. "To you and Noah," she said as they toasted. "I know you both are going to be so happy here."

"I know it too," Abby said with unaccustomed firmness, and drank.

They retired to the sofa in the lounge to drink the rest while the evening descended into purple twilight. "You'll need a bit more furniture," Lucy said pragmatically as she glanced around the near-empty room. "Some bookcases and a telly . . ."

"Yes, all in good time. Although Noah would argue the telly's the most important thing."

"You could try eBay."

"I might." For the first time Abby noticed how fixed Lucy's smile looked. "How are you?" she asked. "Everything going okay with the wedding plans? Twelve days and counting, right?"

"Right." And to Abby's shock Lucy's smile started to wobble and slide off her face.

"Oh, no." Abby put down her glass of champagne. "Lucy, what is it? What's wrong?"

"Nothing and everything," Lucy said on a sniff. "Maybe it's just cold feet. Everyone gets them, don't they? Right before?"

"You have cold feet?" It was the last thing Abby would have expected. Lucy adored Alex. Abby found him slightly intimidating; he often seemed to be scowling, but she'd never doubted his love for Lucy.

"Is that terrible?" Lucy asked. "Am I terrible?"

"No, of course not. But why? Did something happen?"

"Just a whole lot of little things. Bella's being a complete pain. A bitch, if I'm honest." Lucy lowered her voice as if Bella could overhear.

"She's what, fourteen? Isn't that what fourteen-year-old girls do?"

"I know, but she shrieked at me the other day that I wasn't her mother. Shrieked in public—we were about to go out and I just told her to go easy on the makeup, you know? Because Alex would make her scrub her face anyway. I thought I was doing her a favor."

"She's likely to be feeling a bit nervous, with the wedding coming up," Abby suggested. "Things will settle down surely, afterwards?"

"Or what if they just get worse, and there's nothing anyone can do about it? Welcome to the rest of my life." Lucy shuddered.

"I suppose that's the risk you take when you say those vows. But you and Alex love each other, Lucy. That's the main thing."

"Yes, but have you noticed how bad-tempered he can be? His mouth goes all thin and he becomes so silent. I have to jolly him out of it sometimes, and frankly it's exhausting. I'm not *that* bubbly, you know."

"Surely you've dealt with this before now? You've been dating for a year and a half."

"Yes, but now I'm facing it for the rest of my life. You know, there are quirks you think you can handle in a boyfriend, but in a husband? It's completely different."

"I suppose it is."

Lucy leaned forward, her face animated now. "What about you

and Ben? I know you didn't get as far as planning a wedding, but you *were* engaged. Did you wonder what you were doing?"

"All the time." Too much of the time. The seeds of doubt and discontent had been sown early, but Abby had been so enraptured, so thrilled and grateful that someone loved her, that she'd pretended they didn't exist, that those weeds hadn't grown up around them and started to choke the good things. They'd had some good times, certainly, and everyone had those weeds. Who could say how it would have ended?

"Did you and Ben ever talk about it? Did you . . . did you think about breaking up?" Lucy made a face. "Sorry. I'm being terribly nosy, aren't I? Tell me to shut up."

"No, it's okay." Reflections about Ben were particularly poignant and raw after her conversation with Bethan and her earlier imaginings. "Yes, we fought. Actually . . ." She took a deep breath. Telling Bethan, who'd shared a similar story, was one thing, but confessing to Lucy, whose life seemed shiny and perfect despite these last-minute doubts? That was scary. It felt like opening a door that would never close properly again, or maybe at all. "Ben didn't want Noah." She spoke quietly, even though she'd left Noah snoring away upstairs. "He wanted me to get an abortion, initially."

"What?" Lucy's mouth dropped open. "Oh, Abby, that's awful. I'm sorry." Abby shrugged some sort of accepting thank-you. What else could she have done? It *was* awful. It had been horrendous at the time. "He came round, though?" Lucy asked. "Didn't he? Eventually?"

"Oh, Lucy." Abby let out a laugh. "Ever the optimist. Yes, he came round, at least a little. He was starting to come round, anyway. We had a talk . . . a really good talk." She paused, holding on to that memory, the last good one. "He'd been so negative about it all and then he felt Noah kick and he got this huge smile on his face. I've told Noah about it. It was lovely. I remember he said, 'Maybe we can do this.' It felt huge."

"I'm sure it did," Lucy murmured, her eyes wide and round.

"It was the start of something, but he died a couple of days later."

Abby shook her head. "So who knows whether we could have done it or not? I was thinking that before you came, actually. I've always wanted to paint a would-have-been-happy ending, for Noah's sake, but maybe that isn't how it would have all gone down."

"Oh no, I'm *such* a dingbat, coming in here and asking you all these questions," Lucy exclaimed. "Sorry . . ."

"It's fine." And incredibly it was. "I think I needed to accept that I don't know what would have happened. No one will ever know. And there are enough good memories to tell Noah about. And Noah himself . . . he makes it all worthwhile." She smiled. "As soppy as that sounds."

"It doesn't sound soppy," Lucy said, but then nothing seemed overly sentimental to her. She let out a shuddering sigh and then drained her glass. "Time for a top-up, I think. I *am* going to get over these jitters."

"I'm not sure you do that by guzzling champagne, but whatever," Abby teased. She topped up both of their glasses. "You and Alex are good together, Lucy. You balance each other out."

Lucy raised her eyebrows. "Are you saying I need balancing out?"

"Doesn't everybody? And Bella and Poppy love you, even if they don't always act like they do. You might not be their mother, but they need a mother again. Trust me on that."

"Speaking of mothers . . ."

Abby rolled her eyes. "Nice segue."

"I thought it was particularly subtle." Lucy leaned forward, looking almost anxious. "But things are good, aren't they? Between you and Laura? They *seem* good. Or at least better."

"That isn't actually saying that much, considering we had a non-relationship before two months ago."

"But you two were getting along at the party last weekend. And before . . ."

"We're learning to get along." It still felt tentative, but Abby was starting to trust it. Trust Laura. "It was her idea for me to move in here," she continued. "I thought she was going to move in here herself, but then she gave it to me."

Lucy's eyes turned starry. "Oh, that's so . . ."

"Please." Abby held up a hand, laughing. "Don't gush."

"Are you going to have a housewarming party? Because that would be fab."

"I was thinking about it." She'd even thought about inviting Chris, and had spun a pleasantly vague daydream about him accidentally on purpose arriving a little early, bearing a bottle of wine. "Not for a while, though. Your wedding comes first."

"I don't want to miss it," Lucy protested. "We'll be on our honeymoon for a week after the wedding."

"It'll be after that," Abby promised. It was rather nice to have something to plan and look forward to.

Lucy unfolded herself from the sofa. "I should make a move. Juliet will be wondering where I am."

"She doesn't seem the type to worry." Abby had gotten used to Juliet's abrupt and sometimes abrasive ways, but it had taken a while.

"No, but she's been rather grumpy lately." Lucy made a face. "Of course, being Juliet, she doesn't tell me what's going on."

"Everything all right with Peter?"

"I think so. He still seems to adore her." Lucy sighed. "But who knows? Everyone's got problems of some kind. Some people are just better at hiding them."

"Very true." Abby thought of Bethan, who she would have assumed had the kind of perfect, glossy life she'd once envied, but it had taken only one conversation for Abby to see the cracks.

After Lucy had left, Abby tidied up the kitchen, enjoying the simple pleasure of cleaning a room that looked good even dirty, with its granite countertops and stainless steel appliances. She stroked the sleek granite, marveling at it, before turning on the dishwasher and listening to the pleasant whir of it starting.

Outside the world had descended to inky darkness, but there was something peaceful about it. The only sound was the hum of the dishwasher; she couldn't hear the sea as she could from the café, that constant whoosh and rush. She stayed there for a few more minutes, gazing out at the darkness, and then with a little smile she switched off the lights and headed upstairs to bed.

26

Laura

WHAT'S YOUR STORY? MOST people wanted to tell their story. Most people were breathlessly waiting their whole lives for that question, desperate to share or brag or grumble. Laura stayed silent.

"Hey, I told you mine," Rob reminded her.

"So?" But she didn't mean it. She knew she would tell him; she could feel it, a pressure in her chest, an ache in her throat. Her heart started beating harder. Fight-or-flight response right there. Too bad she had nowhere to go.

"So fair's fair," he answered, and held her gaze, a faint smile on his lips, in his eyes. Laura held her breath.

"You told me my story," she said finally, flippantly. She was postponing the moment of having to speak, to confess, and she could tell Rob knew it. He wasn't worried that she would put him off; he was just waiting.

"I told you the little bit I knew."

"The little bit everyone knows. Sometimes that feels like that's all there is." She drew in a breath and then plunged on, not waiting for his response. Not needing it now, because she'd already jumped off the cliff and was hurtling through the air. So be it. "In Hartley-by-the-Sea I'll always be the woman who abandoned her two-year-old." She met his gaze, daring him to contradict her. "Always."

"Yes," he agreed, and she stared at him, shocked and ridiculously a little hurt by his ready agreement.

"Yes?"

"You wanted me to say differently?"

She managed a shaky laugh. "I suppose I did."

His expression softened as he said, "It doesn't necessarily mean that's all you'll be."

"Ah." She leaned back against the sofa. "The silver lining."

"I guess."

"Not much of one, really."

"Maybe not."

They were both silent; Laura knew he was waiting for more, just as she knew she would tell it. It was easy now, in a strange and painful way. She felt more tired than anything else. "You know, Abby was a really difficult baby. She wouldn't nurse and she was colicky and she didn't even like to be cuddled much. Not that I was a great cuddler. But she'd always squirm away, arch her back. It was annoying as hell."

Rob stared at her unblinkingly. "That's not why you left."

He left her breathless, how quickly he cut through her prevarication. "No," she agreed. "It's not."

"Her father?" he asked after a moment.

Laura let out a tired laugh. "Isn't that what everyone asks?"

"Has anyone actually asked you?"

"My mother, only once. But everyone wonders."

"True."

She shook her head. "I can't blame them. Who wouldn't be curious? It really doesn't matter." But she could feel her throat getting tighter and tighter, and she knew it did. "He was married. *Is* married."

"You know where he is now?"

"Sort of."

"He didn't want Abby, I guess."

"You could say that." Loudly. You could scream it from the rooftops, you could shout until you were hoarse and desperate, and it still wouldn't get across how much Abby's father hadn't wanted her. Hadn't wanted Laura, all of fifteen years old and frankly terrified, to have something on him. But she wasn't about to explain all that. That was part of her story that Rob Telford didn't need to know.

"And you did."

"Obviously." She shook her head. "Abby's already asked me why I didn't get a termination. What a conversation, trying to tell your daughter why you didn't abort her." She tried to laugh but couldn't quite pull it off.

"I can understand why she asked it."

"Can you? Well, let me ask you something, then. Didn't you ever want to be part of a *real* family? With a dad who was around and a mother who wasn't drunk in the pub by noon?" Rob's expression tightened, and she saw the realization flash in his eyes. "That's what I wanted too. That's what I was trying to create, with Abby. I didn't do a great job of it, I know, but that's what I wanted."

"You mean, because your father died." It was a statement.

"Yes, but not just that. Although that was a big part." Too big. Thirty-two years later and it *still* felt fresh and raw. It didn't feel fair, to lose someone so important when you were so young. Oh, she knew plenty of people, plenty of children, had worse. What about all the orphans in China and places like that, the photographs in the newspaper of crying children in war-torn countries? She was spoiled, compared with them, and yet that knowledge didn't make it hurt any less. "I was a daddy's girl," she explained quietly. "From birth, really. Mum was thirty when she had me—they got married when she was four months gone. They'd only been dating a few weeks, so I was quite the shocker. I think she resented me, but Dad never did. At least he didn't show it."

Rob straightened, his expression of befuddlement almost comical. "Why would your mother resent you? You were the child she was afraid she was never going to have."

"No, that would be Simon. I was the inconvenience that messed up her dating life." Laura smiled wryly. "She was finally just starting to have fun, I think. She'd cared for both of her parents. I think she wanted to enjoy it for a while. Trips to Blackpool, dinners out . . . or at least fish and chips." She'd meant to sound light, but she had a feeling it came out a little snarky. A little sad.

"And the second reason?" Rob asked quietly.

"Because Dad doted on me, pretty much from the moment I was born. I think she was jealous. Which sounds petty," Laura conceded with a sigh, "but I don't know what else to think. Then it got worse after he died. As if she blamed me somehow, although the man smoked a pack a day. Lung cancer," she clarified at Rob's questioning look.

"Everyone handles grief differently."

"I guess." And her mother's way had been to blame Laura for everything and idolize Simon. Well, fine. She was over it. She had to be over it, because her mother was dead. You couldn't stay angry with a dead person. You couldn't blame one, either. It was pointless and bitter.

"Do you miss her?" Rob asked, and Laura stiffened.

"Yes . . . ," she began, but it sounded like a question. As if she was hoping she'd guessed right. "I miss her," she said more firmly. "Of course I miss her. Because no matter how difficult our relationship, she still stayed. She was there, for both me and Abby. And that's more than I did." She tried for a smile, but it didn't feel right. And Rob was looking at her with way too much sympathy.

"Still, it must have been hard growing up."

"Mum had it hard too," Laura said. She was determined to be ruthlessly fair. No giving herself any breaks, not this time. "She worked all hours, and looking back, I think Dad regarded the café as his free lunch. Literally." A small smile that they shared. "He never helped out with it—he probably thought of it as women's work. He worked as a mechanic, but it was off and on. He liked his football and his beer and his cigarettes. You know the type."

"I serve them every night."

"Right." She let out a long, weary sigh. All this emoting was so draining. "So it was hard for Mum. I get that. I really do. And then when I became pregnant . . ." She stopped, amazed at how the words were flowing. Half a gin and tonic must have really gone to her head. Or the more alarming possibility was that she *wanted* to talk about it, that after so many years of silence and suppression, she wanted to get it off her chest, her heart. To Rob Telford, of all people. What was happening to her?

Rob shifted on the sofa. His leg, Laura noticed, was a few inches closer to hers. If he was viewing this conversation as some sort of emotional foreplay to a booty call, she was going to be seriously annoyed.

"So what happened when you got pregnant?" he asked.

"Mum wasn't best pleased. I'd ruined my life, I'd ruined her life, and I'd ruined my brother Simon's life. The *shame.*" She laughed a little, shaking her head. "You'd think I was the first teenager in Hartley-by-the-Sea to get up the duff."

"You certainly weren't that. Why do you think she was so furious?"

All of a sudden Rob's questions were starting to annoy her. What was he, her bloody counselor? "Well, I don't know, genius," Laura drawled. "Why do you think? Why don't you give me some of your worldly wisdom?"

He recoiled slightly, as if she'd surprised him. Hurt him, even. This whole conversation suddenly seemed so stupid. Who was Rob Telford, anyway? The bloody *bartender.* "I don't know," he said mildly. "Which is why I'm asking."

And as quickly as that, Laura's moment of ire evaporated. Who cared, anyway? Who cared whom she told or what she said? It was all ancient history. Her mother was *dead.* "Because I wasn't your normal teen with her pimply boyfriend in tow, the kind of bloke who'd be shaking in his shoes but trying to do the right thing, even if he never quite managed it. I refused to tell her who the father was. I refused to tell anyone."

"Because he was married."

"Yes." Among other things. And thankfully Rob didn't press, because if he had, Laura would have gotten *really* shirty. "In the end she was the one who suggested I leave," she continued recklessly. She could tell she'd surprised him with that one. She half regretted saying anything, since she hadn't even told Abby this. "She wanted to give me more of a life." That, Laura had long ago decided, was being generous to her mother. She suspected her mother had just wanted her gone. "So she arranged for me to have a job at a nightclub. A friend of her cousin's knew someone who knew someone. You know the kind of thing."

"Yes . . . a nightclub, though."

"What?"

"Not the usual mother's dream for her daughter."

You could say that again. "I think she thought I'd have more opportunities in the city," Laura said with tipsy diplomacy. "And if I'm being charitable, I think Mum wanted a second chance. She didn't get it right with me, but maybe she would with Abby." Laura drained her glass. They were, thankfully, nearing the end of her story, or at least as much as she would tell. "I think she did mostly get it right with Abby. She was never the most patient person, but I don't doubt she loved her."

"Do you doubt she loved you?"

"Enough with the psychoanalysis," Laura snapped. "Let's leave it there."

Rob held up his hands, palms towards her. "Fine. I won't ask any more questions."

"Good." It was nearly ten o'clock. Laura knew he should leave, but Rob didn't move. "You're not scoring tonight, I hope you realize," she said haughtily. "I'm almost old enough to be your mother."

"Not quite that old."

"I had a kid when I was fifteen, Rob. I think so."

"You're only forty-two."

"Forty-three, actually. Today." And then she wished she hadn't said that, because what was more pathetic and needy than telling someone, a near stranger no less, that it was your birthday?

"Today's your birthday?" He looked both startled and weirdly a little hurt. "Why didn't you say so?"

"Because I'm turning forty-three. Not much to celebrate."

"You look pretty darn good for forty-three."

She held up a hand, shaking her head, even though the compliment made her want to smile. "Don't."

"Have you had cake?"

"Did you miss the part where I said there wasn't much to celebrate?"

"You can celebrate your birthday when you're ninety," Rob insisted. "Didn't the Queen? You need cake."

He rose from the sofa and Laura watched him, bemused. "There's no cake in this house." Because if there had been, she would have eaten it.

"Fine," Rob called over his shoulder. "I'll look elsewhere."

Laura stayed where she was, listening as Rob unlocked the door to the café, clearly on a mission. She rested her head on the back of the sofa and closed her eyes, feeling tired. She wasn't going to think about everything she'd told Rob, an emotional bloodletting that she had no desire to remember. She was just going to sit here and enjoy not needing to move and not being alone.

"Here we are."

Laura opened her eyes, slightly befuddled, aware she might have actually dozed off for a few seconds. Rob stood in front of her, brandishing a day-old chocolate cupcake from the café.

"We usually throw out the baked goods that haven't sold."

"Thank God you missed this one," Rob answered. "I even found a candle." He brought one from behind his back. "In the kitchen drawer. And fortunately there was also a lighter."

"Seems like it was your lucky day."

"Or yours." With great ceremony Rob stuck the candle in the cupcake; Laura saw that the icing had gotten a little crusty. She hadn't had a birthday cake since her father had made her one. The realization was almost too much to take, on top of everything else. He lit the candle and then held the cake out towards Laura. "Now make a wish."

She closed her eyes, needing to escape the look of compassion in his. *A wish.* What did she want?

"Any day now," Rob murmured, and without opening her eyes, Laura answered, "I'm thinking."

Most of all, she wanted Abby to be happy. She wanted her daughter to fly. To realize her dreams in a way Laura had never been able to. Whatever that meant. Wherever it would take her.

"Laura?" Rob prompted gently.

And so she wished, a single word that encompassed everything she wanted. *Abby.* And then she blew out the candle.

"Excellent," Rob said, and Laura opened her eyes. "We'll split it." She watched as he peeled off the paper and then broke the cupcake in half, showering them both with stale crumbs. "Here you go."

"Thank you." She was trying not to be ridiculously touched by his gesture. All he'd done was nick a stale cake from her own café, after all.

"So," Rob said when they'd managed to choke it down, "what was your best birthday ever?"

"Oh, I have no idea." She spoke too quickly, not wanting to remember. But already a memory was slotting into place, not of gooey birthday cakes like in the photo album Abby had found, but something else. Something so sweet and private it made her eyes sting. She and her dad, her eighth birthday. He'd woken her up early and they'd snuck out, just the two of them, tiptoeing down the stairs so they wouldn't wake Simon, because he would have begged to come along.

It had been a perfect day; she didn't think she was putting on the rose-tinted filter afterwards. It really had been perfect. Sunlight slanting on the beach, lighting up the puddles. Gulls circling and crying above them. The air had been warm, even at dawn. They'd walked down the beach, hand in hand, leaving a trail of footprints behind them in the damp sand. When they were far enough away from the few early-morning dog walkers, her dad had set up a barbecue. You weren't supposed to do that on the beach, only in the barbecue area above, but that hadn't bothered him. He'd never been much of one for rules or even common sense.

He'd made them bacon sarnies and they'd sat on pieces of driftwood, eating their sandwiches, the grease dripping onto their hands, as they watched the sun rise. It had been the best birthday, the simplest and purest celebration, that she could have ever wanted.

"You're remembering something," Rob said quietly. He was looking at her almost tenderly.

"Yes," Laura said, and it came out on a gasp. She could feel a pressure in her chest, as if the dam she'd built inside herself had just now developed a hairline crack, and then another, and another. And the cracks were spreading out like spiders' legs, until the dam was crumbling and the dreaded emotion was rushing through. "Yes," she gasped again, and then the tears came, and not just tears but noisy sobs, awful, tearing sounds that made a distant part of herself think, *Why is that poor woman making noise like that? She sounds like an animal.*

"Oh, Laura," Rob said, his voice gentle. He pulled her into his arms and she didn't resist, couldn't, because crying was taking all of her effort, all of her strength. It felt like a full-body workout, with her shoulders shaking, her chest heaving, and the *tears*. She should really have been embarrassed about those. She had snot on her face. She knew she did, and she couldn't even care.

She pressed her cheek against his chest, that same distant voice telling her she really shouldn't do that, that Rob was liable to get ideas, and she definitely didn't think of him that way. She just wanted— needed—a hug.

But Rob wasn't getting ideas—at least Laura didn't think so— because he simply held her, stroking her back, murmuring to her as if she were a child. And Laura let him, as that distant voice became louder and more insistent, more present, saying, *You are really going to regret this later.*

27

Abby

WHEN ABBY CAME UP to the café the next morning at half past eight, she was surprised to see it was still locked up and shuttered. A woman with two schnauzers was looking distinctly put out.

"Someone told me they did really good coffees here now," she said sniffily. "And that they opened at eight."

"We do," Abby said cheerfully, and unlocked the door. "Just give me a sec."

While the woman waited outside, she hurried about, flipping on lights and firing up the fancy espresso machine, which Laura hadn't yet shown her how to use. Where was her mother? Before she'd left last night, Laura had offered to open the café so Abby could unpack some more. She'd come by at half past eight only because . . . well, because she'd actually missed Laura.

The woman opened the door. "Are you open yet?"

"Please do come in," Abby said graciously. The woman didn't seem like a local. "What would you like?"

"I'll have a skinny latte, please. You don't have soy milk, I presume?"

"I'm afraid not." Definitely not a local, then. The woman plopped herself in a chair even though you were supposed to pay at the till first. Never mind. Abby had more important things to worry about, like how to make a latte on this new machine. Fortunately a few seconds later Laura came into the café, looking bleary-eyed.

"Can you make a latte?" Abby asked, and Laura blinked a couple of times.

"Of course," she said, and moved to the machine.

A few minutes later the demanding customer had her precious latte, and Abby gave Laura a thorough once-over. "You don't look so great."

"Thanks," Laura replied dryly. She went into the kitchen and poured herself a glass of water. Abby followed her.

"Are you okay?"

"Just tired. I didn't sleep well last night."

"I would have thought you'd sleep better, without Noah waking you up at crazy o'clock."

"Yeah, so would have I." She sighed, closing her eyes, and pressed the glass against her cheek.

"Seriously, maybe you should go kip for a few more hours," Abby said. "It won't pick up here for a while."

Laura hesitated, and then shook her head. "No, I'll stay. It's fine. Let me just brush my teeth first." She grimaced. "I woke up with such a start, I just pulled on some clothes and rushed down here. I thought you were staying home this morning, to unpack."

"I was, but my neighbor offered to watch Noah, and so I thought I might as well come down and give you a hand." She felt a strange sort of pride at saying that: *my neighbor*. She was part of a community, a network, more than she'd ever been before, thanks to Laura.

The bells on the front door jingled and they both started. "I'll get that," Abby said. "You brush your teeth."

"Priorities," Laura agreed with a flicker of a smile, and headed back over to the flat.

Abby kept herself busy for the next little while, serving customers, and Laura went into the kitchen to restock the fridge and cupboards and then handle the lunch rush.

By early afternoon the rush had slowed to a trickle and Abby went back to the kitchen to figure out what was going on. It almost seemed like her mother was avoiding her. Laura was leaning her elbows on the kitchen counter, her glasses perched on her nose as she frowned down at a piece of paper.

"Everything okay?"

"You keep asking me that." Laura looked up briefly. "Fine. I was just looking at some specs for the kitchen improvements."

"I thought we couldn't afford those."

"Technically we can't, but there are all sorts of pay-later schemes, and I think we need to go ahead and do it. We need to start offering a wider menu."

"I guess." Her excitement about the café had been, temporarily perhaps, eclipsed by her excitement about her own life. Her house, her neighbors, even her fledgling friendship with Chris. She looked more closely at her mother. "Are you sure you're okay?"

"I said I was, didn't I?" Laura pushed back from the counter. She looked both weary and brittle, and Abby didn't think it was down to a bad night's sleep.

"Is it because of Thimble Cottage?" Abby blurted. Laura frowned. "Did you . . . did you want it for yourself? Because . . ." *I don't want to give it up.* "I'd understand if you did."

"Oh, Abby." Laura shook her head. "No. I'm thrilled to bits that you and Noah are there, really. Thrilled." She sounded so sincere that Abby couldn't refute her. But something was going on, and Abby needed to know what it was. She was worried about her mother, which was an entirely new feeling.

"Then what . . . ?"

"If you want to know the truth, Rob Telford came over last night with a bottle of gin and I told him more than I wanted to."

For a few seconds Abby couldn't speak. "Rob Telford," she finally squeaked. She could feel herself blushing, and Laura noted it with a cynical smile.

"It was purely platonic—don't worry. I'm not going to embarrass you by dating a man who is only four years older than you. Lordy." She closed her eyes briefly. "The last thing I need to do is set the tongues wagging in this place yet again."

"Okay." That was a rather huge relief. "Then why did he . . . ?"

"Come over? I asked him the same question. He said it was because I was brave." Laura's voice caught a little and she looked away. "I'm a stupid old woman, aren't I? I fall for that kind of pointless flattery."

It felt tactless to ask why Rob Telford thought Laura was brave, so Abby stayed silent. Laura guessed anyway.

"You're wondering why he said that."

"No . . ."

"Yes, you are. I don't blame you. I wondered it too. All my life I've felt like a coward."

That surprised her. "Why . . . ?"

"Cowards run away," Laura said flatly. "Cowards *cower*. They hide and cringe and flee."

Abby saw something bitter and hard in Laura's face, but there was a tender vulnerability in her eyes and the set of her shoulders. The incongruous mix touched her. "What were you fleeing from, Mum?"

Laura stared at her, her mouth slightly open, and Abby stared back. *Mum.* For the first time ever, besides that one sneering insult, she'd called her mother Mum. She'd *felt* she was a mum. And yet looking at Laura's gaping mouth, Abby almost wanted to take it back. Apologize or explain. *Sorry. I didn't mean that. That might not be what you want me to call you.*

"Did you mean that?" Laura asked quietly.

Abby gave her a wobbly smile. "Did you want me to?"

"Of course." Laura let out a trembling laugh and brushed at her eyes. "Of course."

This was the moment when the music in the movie swelled, and they both started laughing and crying at once as they fell into each other's arms. Except in reality neither of them moved.

"Well," Laura said, straightening. "Enough of that. I think the door just opened."

Smiling, faintly relieved, Abby turned to go serve their latest customer.

They didn't talk again in that emotional way, by silent, mutual decision. Laura immersed herself in the café, inviting builders to give their estimates, going to the DIY superstore in Workington to get wood and tile samples. Abby didn't mind; she was actually enjoying taking a backseat with the café, and having a little more time at home with Noah. They'd spent a few happy hours in the garden, planting chrysanthemums in the beds by the walls. She'd painted the kitchen a sunshiny yellow, and was thinking about painting the lounge. She and Noah had dabbed a dozen different colors on the walls and voted on each one.

She'd had her girls' night with Bethan, where they'd knocked back a bottle of wine between them, chatting on the terrace while the boys played outside, and then moving indoors when it got dark. Bethan tucked Tom in bed and came back over, topping up their glasses with a grin.

"Steve is listening out for him." She rolled her eyes. "Such a huge sacrifice, I know. Honestly, sometimes I feel like a single parent."

No, you don't, Abby wanted to say. *Not really.* But then she didn't know what it felt like to be part of a couple, to have a husband who was involved even just that little bit. And she felt surprisingly sorry for Bethan—she could see how it might actually feel lonelier with someone than without.

Friday was Lucy's hen night, and a bit uncertainly Abby asked Laura if she wanted to go with her. "It's pretty casual. Just drinks at Raymond's down by the train station."

"I don't think so." Laura's smile was polite but firm. "I'll come to the wedding next week. Anyway, you need someone to watch Noah."

Abby acknowledged this fact with a guilty smile and Laura chuckled. "It's what grannies do. I'll make sure to bring my knitting."

"You don't actually . . ."

Laura rolled her eyes. "No, Abby, of course not. The remote control will do me fine."

Abby was looking forward to going out with the girls, although she didn't know all of Lucy's friends. Still she thought it would be a laugh, to tease Lucy about getting married and listen in on the local crack, which hopefully wouldn't be about her.

"You look nice," Laura remarked when Abby came downstairs in a summer dress with skinny straps, a little cardigan, and a pair of high-heeled sandals.

"Once in a while I make the effort."

"You should do it more often. It's worth it."

Abby might have taken offense at that kind of remark once, but now she simply smiled. She kissed Noah good night, noting how easily he cuddled into Laura, who had one arm around him, and then opened the door to Thimble Cottage and stepped outside.

Lucy was presiding over a table of seven women when Abby arrived at Raymond's, Hartley-by-the-Sea's one upmarket bistro. They were well into their first bottle, and the laughter was already turning raucous.

"You know Juliet, of course, and Claire, and Andrea. . . ."

Abby nodded at everyone and tried to remember the other names of various schoolteachers Lucy mentioned as she sat down at the end, but consigned them all to be forgotten almost instantly.

"Drink up," a red-haired teacher commanded as she filled Abby's glass. "You're behind."

For the first hour Abby was content to sip her wine and listen as the banter was batted back and forth; the old marrieds teased Lucy about what to expect, and the smug singles smiled into their glasses and tried not to act like they wished they were getting married too. Lucy was ebullient, those prewedding jitters seeming to have vanished completely. She had confided to Abby that Bella had had a mini-breakdown, tearfully confessing she was afraid Lucy would get sick of her.

"We spent half an hour in Boots buying makeup and then got huge hot chocolates," Lucy had finished with a happy sigh. "So that's sorted, for now at least, thank goodness."

Abby had drifted into a pleasant wine-induced daze when Lucy's voice carried down the table. "What about that scrummy surfer guy at your opening party? What's the deal with him?"

"Chris," Abby clarified, because prevaricating would have just looked silly. "He's a paraglider, not a surfer. I met him on the beach when I was selling lunches. And there's no deal."

"He's hot," Lucy declared. This was met with a chorus of exclamation of mock scandal.

"You shouldn't be saying that at your hen night!"

"Oh yes, she should."

"Last time she can."

"Maybe not."

Laughing and blushing a little, Lucy ignored them all to focus disconcertingly on Abby. "But you're friends?"

"Well, yes, I suppose." She'd chatted with Chris at the party; she'd learned he was from Cornwall, but he traveled around the country, offering paragliding courses in various locales. A bit of a nomad, he'd called himself, with a pretending-to-be-sheepish grin.

"Why don't you invite him to the wedding?"

"What?"

"He can be your plus one!"

"Oh no, I don't think so . . . ," Abby began automatically, and then stopped. She didn't have a date, and she'd already invited him to the party. Why not take a risk? She'd taken so few in recent years.

"She's thinking about it," Diana, the red-haired teacher, crowed, and now Abby was blushing.

"Maybe a little bit."

"When will you see him again?"

"I don't know. . . ." She was loath to return to the caravan park to traipse around in search of him. The allure of the whole idea was wearing off pretty quickly.

"Didn't you mention a paragliding course?" Lucy said. "Some kind of taster day?"

"Yes, but . . ." She didn't remember mentioning the taster day to Lucy. She wasn't remotely tempted to pay a hundred and fifty quid to take her life into her hands. Well, only a little bit tempted.

"You should go!" Lucy was practically bouncing up and down in her seat. "When is it?"

"Tomorrow. I have to work. . . ."

"Laura can cover for you! You should go."

"Now you've got Lucy sounding American," Juliet remarked dryly. "So she must really be worked up about this. But you should go, Abby." Juliet smiled knowingly. "Take a risk."

And so somehow—Abby wasn't quite sure how—the next morning she was standing on the headland overlooking the beach, shivering in the sea breeze, after having forked over one hundred and fifty pounds and asked her mother to manage the café on her own for the entire day. Noah was at Nathan's. Abby still wasn't sure what had possessed her to make all the arrangements, pay the money, and actually show up.

Chris had been thrilled. "You made it! Awesome. You just need to sign a waiver form. I usually have people do it before."

"Sorry," Abby muttered as she scribbled her signature on a form that promised she would not sue Chris if she suffered some grievous injury as a result of this mad decision. "It was a last-minute thing."

"I'm just glad you're here," Chris said, smiling, and Abby's insides went a little liquid in response. Did he smile at all women that way, as if he were letting them in on a secret? Was she being completely stupid and schoolgirlish about this whole thing, thinking every look meant something?

She didn't have a lot of time to ponder the matter, because within the first half hour, after the safety lecture and the explanation of the equipment had finished, Chris had her and the six others who had registered for the course harnessed and ready to try their first attempt at paragliding, admittedly only a few feet above the ground. They stood there, shuffling a bit, helmets on, some people glancing dubiously at the crumpled parachutes behind them—although they weren't parachutes, as Chris had rather sternly told them. They were wings.

"Now, remember this is not like opening a parachute," Chris said. "Paragliding is actually a very gentle extreme sport." Cue nervous laughter. "The launch happens slowly, from land, and you should feel entirely in control. You *are* entirely in control, from when you inflate your wing to using the brakes. If you don't like what you see, you know how to abort."

Do I? Abby thought, swallowing a bubble of hysterical laughter. All Chris was talking about was running down a hill, but she felt as if she might soar up into the sky and disappear forever, a tiny dot nearing the atmosphere, like a child's lost balloon. What on earth had made her agree to this? She wasn't a risk taker. She'd never been a risk taker.

"Now, this might seem scary at first," Chris continued, and Abby thought he was looking at her in particular. "But most paragliders talk about how peaceful and freeing it is up there in the sky." He pointed to the hazy blue above them. "This is about finding a different kind of thrill."

But what if she wasn't looking for thrills? Abby took a deep breath and adjusted the strap of her helmet, which was digging into her chin. She could do this. She was going to do this.

As Chris continued to give instructions, Abby focused on listening and realized she wasn't taking in a single word. Still, it was all fairly obvious, wasn't it? You faced the wind. You pulled on the wing to inflate it. You took off. And then you pulled on the brake as quickly as possible to get back onto the ground. That was the important bit.

"All right, Abby. Are you ready to take flight?" *That would be a no, Chris.* Abby nodded jerkily. "Okay, then. Three, two, one . . . ready . . . go!"

Abby started walking into the wind, increasing her pace to a brisk stride as she pulled on the wing and it began to inflate. She pulled harder and felt the wing lift; she was, as Chris had explained, kiting. She started to move faster; she couldn't help it, with the force of the inflated parachute—or, rather, wing—pulling on her. She could see it billowing up behind her and felt a shaft of both terror and wonder. And then she realized she was actually off the ground. Her feet were not touching God's good, green earth. Abby let out a little yelp as the wing continued to inflate and lift and she began to move forward, her feet dangling a good eighteen inches from the ground.

"And now brake!"

She braked. Hard, so the wing jerked; she had a sloppy, stupid grin on her face as her feet touched ground once again and she took a few stumbling steps to balance herself. Chris was beaming.

"Excellent, excellent! How did it feel?"

She'd felt like a baby bird tumbling out of its nest and then, at the last second, finding its wings. "Like flying."

"Wait until you really get going. I can tell you're a natural."

As if. Abby moved to the side to let the next person have a go. Her heart was thundering in her chest and she felt as if every nerve ending was tingling. All right, maybe her feet hadn't gotten that far off the ground, but it had still felt amazing. She wanted to do it again.

By the end of the afternoon Abby had had several attempts at paragliding, and on the last one she'd actually gotten about ten feet in the air, soaring towards the sea, before Chris shouted for her to brake. It had felt incredible. She'd gazed out at the sea, shimmering in the distance, and felt as if the whole world had opened up in front of her. Just ten feet in the air and she saw everything from an entirely different perspective, the narrow roads and walls obliterated, replaced by an endless vista of possibility. Her body had been tense, poised to soar. She'd wanted desperately to keep going, as terrifying a prospect as that still seemed, and when her feet had touched back down, she'd almost yelped in protest.

At the end of the course, she was happy but exhausted, and she took off her helmet and harness with both relief and regret. The other attendees were drifting away, a couple from Manchester and a guy in his forties who had seemed very outdoorsy, a grandmother who had been given the day as a birthday present and done it with her hip granddaughter. Abby had chatted with them all.

But now she needed to chat with Chris. Last night, after two glasses of wine and with lots of raucous encouragement, the idea of asking Chris to Lucy's wedding hadn't seemed like such a big deal. Now it felt momentous. Monumental. Monumentally stupid, actually. But she was still going to do it.

Squaring her aching shoulders, Abby walked towards Chris. He smiled at her easily, unsuspecting. "You enjoyed it today, hey?"

"Yes, very much."

"If you want to get your license, I can recommend someone local. It doesn't take that long."

"Local? Where are you going?" She'd meant to sound mildly flirtatious, but it came out sounding alarmed.

"Up to the Hebrides in a couple of weeks. There's some decent ridge soaring there."

"Oh." It was hard not to have her face collapse. The flirty smile, the hopeful eyes. She could feel her muscles going rigid. "Right."

"I never stay in one place too long."

"Well, why would you?" She'd adopted that awful, false jolly note of someone whose hopes have been crushed but who is desperately trying to save face.

"So . . ." Chris raised his eyebrows, a gentle question.

"I was just wondering . . . ," Abby blurted even as a voice was screaming in her head telling her to abort the mission *right now.* "There's this wedding I'm going to on Saturday, for a friend here in the village. It should be a laugh . . . a lot of locals coming . . . and I thought maybe you'd like to go? With me?" The second, the very *millisecond,* that she'd added the awful "with me," she wished she could gobble the words back up. That level of clarification had not been needed.

"Oh. Wow." Chris rubbed the back of his neck. Abby kept her smile in place, and then she tried to change it into a mildly ironic I'm-not-bothered type of look instead of the please-love-me plea she feared she was transmitting, which was annoying because she didn't really feel that way. "That's really nice of you. . . ."

And here came the gentle letdown. Suddenly Abby couldn't stand it. All right, yes, she'd enjoyed flirting with a cute guy, but she had not been building castles in the air. She'd just liked the buzz. And now he was going to back away like she'd been wanting to put a ring on it. Good *grief.*

"Just for a laugh," she said, and her voice came out tight. "Nothing more."

Chris's expression cleared with such obvious relief it was almost comical. Almost, but not quite. "Oh, well then, sure, why not?"

Not the wildly enthusiastic response she'd been hoping for, but somewhat to her surprise Abby found she didn't care. He was going to the Hebrides, and she was . . . she was moving on in a different way. And at least she'd asked someone out.

"I do have a girlfriend," he offered, clearly wanting to put that out there.

"I don't have designs on you," Abby promised. She tried to keep her voice light, but she had a feeling she sounded pissed off. He wasn't *that* much of a stud. "Like I said, it should be a fun time, and I felt like going with someone. I'm in the wedding, so you can just show up for the reception if you'd rather. Okay?" She lifted her eyebrows in a don't-mess-with-me challenge.

Chris grinned, and it seemed the message had finally gotten through. "Great," he said. "See you Saturday."

Abby nodded once, satisfied, and then turned around and started walking back to the café before she realized she was actually heading home to Thimble Cottage. But she'd check in with her mother first; she wanted to tell her about her day. And about Chris—they'd both laugh, Abby knew, at the cringiness of it. Smiling, looking forward to that chat more than any she'd had with Chris or anyone else, she started walking a little faster.

28

✑

Laura

THE ESTIMATE FOR THE kitchen renovation was twenty thousand pounds. And that was the low estimate. The reality was it needed new wiring, and in any case, there wasn't enough space to build an extension, not without burrowing right into the side of the cliff, which required a lot more money as well as more difficult planning permission. After the builder had left on Monday, Laura had sunk onto a chair, dispirited. Sometimes it felt like nothing was easy.

"Of course, you could expand inwards," he'd said. "Build the kitchen out, have a few less tables. That would be cheaper."

Laura had nodded, but the café was small enough as it was. Twelve tables weren't a lot, and fortunately most of them were full, at least on sunny days. The last thing Laura wanted to do was eat into their potential profits. But it seemed like not much eating was going to be happening anyway, if they couldn't get a proper kitchen to make proper meals.

She rested her chin in her hands and watched the raindrops trickle down the foggy windows. Abby had gone to the cash-and-carry to get the week's supplies, and Laura was on her own. It felt like Abby was developing more of a life away from the café, far more than she was, and that was a good thing. A very good thing. It was what she'd wanted, what she'd wished for, for heaven's sake, when blowing out the candle on her birthday cake.

But she didn't want to think about that, or Rob, or the fact that she'd soaked his T-shirt while practically sobbing in his arms. Just thinking about it made her cringe and squirm inside and wish she could press a mental delete button, over and over again. She'd done it before, mostly, so why couldn't she just scrub Rob and the way he'd held and comforted her—ugh—while she'd cried from her brain? For some reason she couldn't. For some reason she kept remembering little agonizing details of that moment, like how Rob had stroked her hair—why that mattered, she didn't know, but it kept popping up in her brain—and how *good* it had felt to cry.

Really cry, not just feel the tears well up and then choke them down again with a hard, forced swallow, or discreetly brush a stray one from her eye. No, it had all come out, the tears and the pain, and it had felt like an emotional colonic. Disgusting, but so worth it, especially when you saw all the crap that was hopefully gone forever.

But then had come the awful afterward, when her sobs had finally quieted down and she felt the awkwardness of actually being in Rob's arms and really not wanting to be there. Well, not much, anyway. Not enough. But disentangling herself and facing the expression on Rob's face was just as unappealing a prospect. Eventually, when it had become *really* awkward, she'd eased away and thankfully Rob had let her go, relaxing his arms and sitting back on the sofa so she had a little space. Except she'd wanted a lot of space. She wanted, quite violently, to be completely alone.

She'd sniffed and wiped at her eyes and then, because she didn't have the energy to pretend, she'd said, "We're going to act like this didn't happen."

"Okay," Rob had said, and Laura could have cried again with simple relief. Fortunately she hadn't. Enough tears had fallen already. She'd gone all brisk and bundled him out of the house as quickly as she could, forcing the bottle of gin into his hands, and then she'd stumbled up to bed, only to lie there, gritty eyes fastened on the ceiling, as she replayed the evening over and over again in her mind, the pause-and-rewind agony of a night's regret.

That had been a week ago. Thankfully Laura hadn't seen Rob since, and she had no intention of seeing him anytime soon. She'd buried herself in the café kitchen, head bent so low over the grill she'd burned her forehead. Abby had gone to Lucy's hen night and then paragliding, of all things, and she seemed happier than ever. Laura was just trying to focus on the café. What else could she focus on? But she needed to figure out a way to make the kitchen bigger that didn't involve a planning permission application that was going to get a big reject stamp on it. Burrowing into Hartley-by-the-Sea's headland was definitely a no-no, what with the regular erosion and the yearly unfortunate ritual of moving the coastal path a foot inland.

But maybe she *could* take a chunk out of the café and turn it into the kitchen. Since the place was mostly empty, Laura took the opportunity to wander around the café, trying to see the possibilities with new eyes. There was the ice cream counter and a few racks of postcards and sweets on one side, and the twelve tables with their colorful chairs neatly arrayed on the other. The till in the middle, the kitchen behind it, and the bathrooms next door.

Laura's gaze swung to the bathrooms. They were two tiny cubicles, one for men, one for women, and then the larger disabled one that the EU had required, which Mary had put in, with much swearing and complaining, when Laura had been seventeen. But surely they didn't need three bathrooms. She couldn't remember the last time they'd all been in use simultaneously, if ever.

What if, she considered, her hands on her hips, they got rid of the separate women's and men's, and used the disabled one for all the customers? They didn't have to cut into the café's customer space, which was already on the small side. Nobody would even notice! It made so much sense she laughed aloud. The woman poring over a guidebook at the table in the corner looked up, startled, and then smiled.

"Something funny?"

"Something wonderful," Laura replied, and hurried back to the estimate the builder had given her.

Abby came in, lugging bags, a short while later. "What are you working on?" she asked.

"I had a fabulous idea about the kitchen extension," Laura said rather grandly. "Although I have to give most of the credit to the builder who suggested it."

"As you would."

"He didn't go into specifics, though," Laura clarified. "I came up with that all on my own."

Abby started unloading prepackaged cheese and ham and tins of tuna. Laura couldn't wait to get a bigger kitchen and be able to cook some decent meals. Or at least hire someone to cook some decent meals.

"Well-done, you," Abby said, and Laura pretended to preen.

"Thank you very much." They were actually bantering—and it was fun. "Anyway, it might still be out of our price range, but I thought I'd get another estimate. And I also wanted to hire someone to work in the kitchen."

"Sounds good."

Abby sounded remarkably relaxed about it. A few weeks ago she would have been tense and a bit snarky, doubting they could pay for it, wondering if it would work. "I thought we'd hire a cook for the evenings when we do dinner, and maybe also some lunches?"

Abby frowned. "Lunches too?" Here came the worry, the doubt.

"Yes, we can expand the lunchtime menu, as well." Laura paused, weighing her next words. The last thing she wanted was to get Abby's back up, but she knew her daughter and Abby needed to be pushed. Often and sometimes quite hard.

Laura paused for a second to savor those words. *She knew her daughter.* "I also think," she said, her voice coming out a little more strident than she'd intended, "that hiring another person would be good for you. It will free you up to spend time with Noah, and do the things at the café you seem excited about, like the toddler mornings or the art showings. Develop the cultural side of things."

Abby made a wry face. "After the debacle with the Hart twins ingesting glue, I'm not sure I want to keep offering toddler mornings on a regular basis. But . . ." She blew out her cheeks. "It doesn't seem fair."

Laura could feel her body tense, shoulders stiffening, drawing up to her ears. Deliberately she lowered them. "Not fair?" she repeated carefully, already imagining Abby's litany of how she was taking over the café, pushing her out, and all because of eighty thousand pounds. Eighty-four thousand pounds, thank you very much. "How so?"

"Well . . ." Abby's back was to her as she slowly stacked a few dented tins of tuna onto the shelves. "You'd be stuck with all the boring day-to-day stuff, and I'd just swan in for the best bits."

"Oh." Now, that was unexpected as well as rather heartwarming. Abby was actually thinking of *her*. "I don't mind. And I want you to be able to do other things. Expand your horizons."

Abby turned around. "Expand my horizons?"

And now came the suspicion. "If you want."

"What do you mean, exactly?"

Laura took a deep breath. "Just that I wouldn't want opportunities to pass you by. You didn't set out in life to run this café, after all."

Abby's forehead wrinkled as she rested a tin of tuna in the palm of her hand. "No," she said at last. "But lots of people's lives take unexpected turns."

"True. All I'm saying is if there was something you wanted to do, a dream you wanted to pursue, I wouldn't want to hold you back. And I wouldn't want the café to hold you back. But I'm not trying to nudge you out," she added hurriedly, just in case Abby was thinking that way. "If you're happy here, then great. Brilliant. Let's make a go of it. Kitchen, cultural events, the whole lot." She was starting to babble.

"So what are you suggesting exactly?" Abby asked slowly. "I mean, are you thinking of something in particular? That you think I should be doing? That I'd want to do . . . besides this?"

"It's just . . . Well, you were training to be a vet. A *vet*. That's rather a big thing, and you must have completed several years of course work. . . ."

"Three." Abby's expression was unreadable, her voice toneless. Laura had no idea if what she was saying was resonating.

"So it seems reasonable to think you might dream about going back to it one day. If you could."

Abby was silent for a long moment. Maybe she'd pushed too much, although Laura had felt she'd been pretty hesitant and tentative. But Abby could be twitchy, although she was certainly less so now. Still Laura waited, determined not to say anything else until Abby gave her some clue as to how she was feeling.

"How can I?" Abby said finally. "I've been away from it for over five years. And there's Noah to think of. He's settled here."

"He's five. He can adapt."

"*I'm* settled here," Abby protested. "I know it might not seem much of a life to you—"

"That's not it at all," Laura cut across her. Were they arguing? It was starting to feel like it. She wanted to do the verbal equivalent of backing away, hands held up, but she wasn't sure how. Anyway this was too important to simply back off as if it didn't matter. "I just want to provide opportunities for you, Abby, if I can, or at least help to provide them. It's what every mother wants."

"Is that what you were doing when you walked out?" Abby returned, and then closed her eyes. "Sorry. *Sorry.* I know I shouldn't keep harping on that. It's not relevant right now, and it's not fair to you after—well, after everything. But it still hurts." She opened her eyes. "I can't help feeling that. If you could explain it somehow . . ."

"Nothing I say would make it acceptable," Laura replied evenly. She should have realized the conversation would take this turn. She'd dared to call herself a mother, after all. "I do realize that."

"But it might *help*. Even if you just said you'd had enough of me and you wanted to live a different life. I just want to know why. How."

"You really want me to say that?" Laura shook her head. "Abby, look. The reason I don't say anything is because frankly it's all rather unpleasant. I'm sparing you—"

"I'm twenty-six. Maybe you don't need to spare me. Maybe knowing would be better than not knowing."

Laura took a deep breath. She supposed she was being selfish, keeping Abby in the dark. She just didn't want her daughter to think worse of her than she already did. "Fine," she said, although she knew she was going to regret this. "What exactly do you want to know?"

"Why did you leave when I was two years old?" Abby asked the question quietly, her face pale, her expression nakedly vulnerable.

"Because it had become very difficult for me to stay," Laura answered carefully. She was dodging bullets with these questions. Tiptoeing around unexploded land mines. That never ended well.

"How so?"

"Because . . . because . . ." She blew out a tired breath. "Because your father didn't want me in the area." She saw Abby flinch and cursed herself for saying that much. How on earth could she get out of this? Any information she gave Abby would only hurt her, and potentially make life difficult for both of them.

"Who was my father?" Abby asked. Her voice had risen loud enough for the clinking of cups in the café to fall suddenly silent.

"Let's not do this now, Abby."

"I've never actually asked you that point-blank."

"I'm sure you've been curious. . . ."

"Yes, but I made myself not be. When I was little, I just pretended I sprang up from the cabbage patch, more or less. I refused to think of you or my father, and it was actually kind of easy, since neither of you were ever around." What, Laura wondered, was she supposed to say to that? Yet another apology? But Abby wasn't waiting for one, because she continued, chin lifted at a defiantly proud angle. "He didn't want me, did he?"

Laura released a breath that came out in a weary shudder. "No."

"Were you dating? I mean, obviously you were in some kind of . . . but was it a relationship?"

Yet another difficult question. How to dodge? How much to admit? "Not really," she said after a tension-filled pause.

Abby's expression became pinched, her eyes fearful. "He didn't . . . he didn't rape you, did he?"

Laura closed her eyes briefly. She hated every second of this. "I wouldn't call it rape, no."

"That doesn't sound very certain."

"It was complicated."

"How complicated?"

Too complicated. "Look, Abby, the whole thing was fairly sordid and unpleasant and the details aren't that important, okay?" Her voice trembled and she pressed her lips together. "He's not interested in you and he never was. He drove me out of the village, more or less, because he was afraid I'd tell someone, anyone, that he was your father. And frankly it terrified me enough to force me to contemplate leaving."

Abby's mouth dropped open. "He sounds like a right bastard."

"He was, although I didn't realize it at the time. At least not as much as I should have." She was saying too much, way too much, but after so many years of silence it actually felt weirdly liberating. Like ripping the plaster off and seeing the scar wasn't quite as gruesome as you'd feared. "When your grandmother found me the job at the nightclub, I took it. More to leave him than anyone else." Although that might have been casting her in too victimized a role. "But I admit it: I wasn't a good mum. I was sixteen and lonely and I didn't know how to handle you. Motherhood felt, to tell you the truth, like a really long babysitting job. I was waiting for the real mum to show up, to give me some relief. I couldn't believe *I* was it. . . ." She tried for a laugh. "The teething and the tantrums . . . I couldn't get my head around how *constant* it was. You're a single mum, so you know. You did far, far better than I did."

"You were younger," Abby said, and Laura could hardly believe her daughter was defending her.

"Yes, I was very young in some ways," she admitted quietly. "And your grandmother was angry at me for getting into the situation that I did, and your uncle, Simon, was furious that the two of us were taking up so much space. It was *hard*. It doesn't excuse it—I know it doesn't—but it was bloody hard." She took a deep breath, waiting for the whiplash retort, but nothing came.

"I'm sure it was," Abby finally said, her voice soft. She looked dazed. "I'm sure it was."

Laura pressed the back of her hand to her eyes for a moment. She'd had quite enough of this. "Let's talk about you becoming a vet."

"I think that ship has sailed."

"Not necessarily. What if you went back to Liverpool? Your course work might still count. You could finish your course and come back here if you wanted, work in a local practice. It would be an adventure, a year or two of city living for both you and Noah." The words poured forth, the picture forming as she spoke.

Abby looked taken aback. "You sound like you've thought about this a lot."

"Not a lot. I just want you to have dreams. Good dreams." She smiled self-consciously. She wasn't used to this kind of talk, but she knew she meant every word. Utterly.

"How would I pay for it?" Abby asked. "We're both skint as it is. And uni's so expensive now, plus living. . . ."

"A part-time job? Grants, loans? It's possible to cobble something together, I'm sure."

But Abby was already shaking her head. "I don't know. It all sounds so risky. And I've lived with Noah in a grotty little flat already. It wasn't fun."

"Who said anything about grotty little flats?" But Laura knew when to back off. "Look, just think about it. All I'm saying is, I don't want you to feel trapped. I know what that feels like, and it's not good." Too late, she realized she shouldn't have referenced her personal experience. Abby's expression had turned tentative, almost afraid.

"My father . . ."

"Excuse me?" Someone had come to the counter. "Could I get some service, please?"

"Of course," Laura called, and hurried out of the kitchen before Abby could work up the nerve to finish asking that question.

That evening she composed an advertisement for the *Whitehaven News* for a part-time staff and cook for the café. Even if Abby stayed around, which was fairly likely, they needed the extra help. And with that little bit of uptick in business since the opening, they could almost afford it.

Laura sat at the kitchen table, the computer in front of her, and propped her chin in her hand as she gazed round at the tiny lounge and kitchen. This was her home now and honestly, it wasn't awful. Why shouldn't she change it up a bit? If she was committing to staying in Hartley-by-the-Sea, she didn't have to be a pointless martyr about it all.

She could refresh the kitchen on the cheap, painting the cupboards and ripping up that awful old lino. And paint the lounge . . . that stained magnolia was revolting. She'd paint the big bedroom too, never mind that Abby had just done it all in raspberry a month ago. She'd leave the smallest bedroom for Noah. . . . Who knew? Maybe he'd sleep over sometimes. The possibility made her smile.

Invigorated now, she pressed send on the advert and then rose from the table, needing to do something. But what? She didn't really want to get out the paint pots at eight o'clock at night or rush into any home improvement project. She headed upstairs, pausing when she saw the curling edge of the flocked olive green wallpaper she'd always hated, even as a little girl. She hooked her fingernail under the edge and gave a little tug. The ancient paper, the glue having long ago dried out, came away easily. Laura let out an undignified crow of triumph. She pried up another curling corner and pulled. *Yes!*

She tossed the long, curling peels down the stairs, eager now to be rid of the wallpaper forever. It felt almost therapeutic, like consigning the past to the rubbish bin, where it belonged. *Begone with you, hideous flocked wallpaper! Begone, and trouble me no more!*

"Umm . . . Mum? Are you okay?"

Laura looked up to see Abby standing uncertainly at the bottom of the stairs, surrounded by shreds of wallpaper. Had she spoken out loud? And had Abby just called her Mum again? Maybe that was going to become an actual thing.

"I'm fine," she called back airily. "Never better. I'm getting rid of this horrible wallpaper that made me feel as if I'd been entombed in the home of a spinster from the nineteen thirties." She tossed another ragged strip down. "Is everything okay? Where's Noah?"

"My neighbor's watching him. I wanted to come by and use the laptop, if that's okay." She ducked her head, as shy and uncertain as a schoolgirl in knee socks and pinafore. What would Abby have looked like, walking to school as a hesitant four-year-old? Why had she let herself miss that? The thought was a lightning sear of pain. "I thought I'd look up the admission procedure for the uni course I was on," Abby said. Laura beamed.

"Of course. It's on the kitchen table." Laura waved her towards the kitchen. "That's great news, by the way."

"Well, I'm only going to have a look. . . ."

"Of course." But that was big for Abby. Very big. She turned back to the wallpaper, determined not to gush. Since when had she ever been a gusher?

"But first . . . ," Abby offered shyly, "do you want some help?"

"What?"

"With the destruction of the wallpaper." Abby nodded towards the walls. "It looks kind of therapeutic."

"Oh, it is." Laura held out a hand. "Come tear a strip off. Just tug. It's brilliant."

Laughing, Abby joined her on the stairs and pulled on a piece of wallpaper. "Harder," Laura urged. "You've got to mean it, Abby."

"I think you have more feelings for this wallpaper than I do."

"Tell me you didn't hate it."

"I didn't love it," Abby admitted, and tugged hard.

Within fifteen minutes, with the two of them tugging and then screaming insults at the wallpaper, and really, Laura thought, acting very silly, the walls were bare, save for some brown streaks of dried paste.

They sank onto the steps, both of them gazing in wonder at the mess they'd made. "Wow," Abby said after a moment of respectful silence. "I'm not sure this is a better look."

"I think I'm going to paint the whole house in something soothing," Laura said. "But not magnolia. That sand dollar color was nice."

"Get rid of my raspberry room?" Laura tensed, but then she saw Abby was smiling. "I knew you never liked it."

"No, I thought it looked like dog's barf, or the inside of my kidney. But you liked it—that's the main thing."

"Right." Abby was laughing now. "Maybe I'll paint my whole house raspberry."

"Go right ahead. And you can come over here to recover from your headaches."

Laura stood up and began to gather the wrecked wallpaper in her arms. It smelled dusty and old and awful, like an old man's cigarette breath. Years of her father smoking indoors, she supposed. It was a wonder they hadn't all developed lung cancer. But even so, the smell, horrible as it was, gave her a little pang of sadness. *I still miss you, Dad.*

"So, laptop," she said briskly to Abby. "Get on it and find out what you can."

"Yes, ma'am." Abby rose and went to the kitchen, and Laura took the wallpaper to the bins outside. It was cold and fresh, September only a couple of weeks away, and the sky was lit up with stars. She dumped the wallpaper in the already-full bin and stood there for a moment, one hand on the concrete wall of the café, breathing in the cool, damp Cumbrian air tanged with salt. Her heart was full, too full maybe, of sadness and hope and wonder.

She thought of herself, sitting on the stairs, arms wrapped around her knees, surrounded by that awful wallpaper, ten years old and terrified while her dad hack-coughed his way to death on the hospital bed that filled the entire lounge, and her mother cried quietly. She closed the lid on the bin, consigning that wallpaper, that memory, to a mental graveyard. She didn't need to be haunted by those memories anymore. She had new ones to make.

Whoever thought she would be back here, running the café, loving her daughter? And her daughter, in her own spiky, self-conscious way, loving her back, at least a little.

Thank you, she said silently, because at a moment like this she felt someone—some force, some *thing*—deserved her gratitude. *Thank you.*

29

Abby

"I LOOK FAT, DON'T I?"

Lucy stared at the mirror, her hands fluttering about her waist like little birds, her usually smiling face pinched into an uncertain frown.

"You look radiant," Abby said firmly. She, Claire, Bella, Poppy, and Chloe, Lucy's best friend from the States, were all crowded into her bedroom at Tarn House on the morning of her wedding. They'd spent the last few hours getting ready, all of them decked out in their bell-shaped bubble gum pink skirts and lace tops, even Juliet, whose expression could have soured milk. But she smiled for Lucy and even did a mocking pirouette.

"Just don't expect me to wear this again. Ever."

"I'm just glad I got it on you today," Lucy said with a grin, her body worries temporarily forgotten. "You should have seen her face at the boutique, Abby," she added. "Priceless."

"That was one word for it," Juliet agreed. "I'm almost forty and I'm wearing something that could be featured in *Girl Talk*."

"I like it," Bella said. At fourteen, she was definitely more of an age to wear pink tulle, and the color suited her dark coloring perfectly. Poppy, as flower girl, was also wearing pink tulle and looked adorable.

Lucy shot Bella a quick, grateful smile. "I wanted something youthful," she explained. "I've never been able to pull off sophisticated, so why try now?" She turned back to her reflection. "But I should have done that grapefruit diet."

"Ugh, nasty," Claire said. "Grapefruit are always so disappointing. You get about a teaspoon of actual fruit, and then all those bits that get between your teeth . . . besides which, you're beautiful, Lucy. Absolutely beautiful."

"As if any of you are going to tell me I look fat on my wedding day," Lucy said.

"I would," Juliet replied briskly. "And you don't. So. Here's your bouquet."

"My mother is going to tell me I look fat."

"Probably," Juliet agreed blithely. Fiona Bagshaw, Abby knew, was driving up this morning for the wedding, and leaving that evening to visit friends in Manchester. Maternal she was not, and Lucy had confessed that the less they all had to endure Fiona, the better. "Don't listen to her," Juliet added. "I never do. Now it's almost time to go— and it's raining, so you might want to swap those amazing heels for a pair of Wellies."

Lucy had, in a typically romantic and un-thought-out gesture, decided to walk from Tarn House to the church along with all her bridesmaids. The weather was, unfortunately, not cooperating.

"We can all wear Wellies," Claire suggested. "We probably should."

"Too bad we don't have pink ones to match," Abby joked.

"I have pink ones," Bella piped up, with a sly look towards Juliet. "I could lend them to you."

Juliet pretended to shudder, although perhaps it wasn't pretend. "Don't even think it. We're all matchy-matchy enough as it is. And I haven't worn this much pink since I was six."

They headed downstairs, Claire and Abby going behind Lucy to catch up her dress. Juliet opened the front door and they gazed in dismay at what was not merely rain but rather a torrential downpour. They were going to get soaked.

"Rain on a wedding day is good luck, anyway," Lucy said with a brave lift of her chin. "But Wellies are probably a good idea."

Abby didn't know whether to feel ridiculous or merely practical as they all exchanged their pink dyed-to-match heels for Welly boots, and Juliet started handing out umbrellas.

"Only in Cumbria," she muttered, but she was smiling. "And only Lucy."

They headed out into the rain, ducking under the umbrellas, everyone grimacing at the thought of the rain wrecking the hair and makeup they'd just spent an hour on. Lucy, however, was in good spirits, laughing as she stepped over puddles, Abby and Claire still holding her train, and her good mood was infectious. Soon they were all laughing at themselves as they tramped up the road in bell-shaped skirts and Welly boots, possibly the strangest look Abby had ever gone for.

It had been fun, getting ready with Lucy and the other bridesmaids this morning. It had made Abby feel a part of things in a way that she was getting used to. And yet she might leave this all behind, just when she was really starting to feel properly settled.

The other night she and Laura had spent a pleasant hour browsing animal science courses and then two-bedroom flats to rent in Liverpool. Then yesterday, her fingers near to trembling, she'd e-mailed the registrar and asked about continuing the course she'd left so abruptly five years ago. No response yet, but the simple fact that she'd had the courage to send the e-mail was something.

"Where did you stash Noah this morning?" Claire asked as they continued to hold Lucy's train aloft. The lane to the church was pitted with muddy ruts.

"My mum has him. She's taking him to the church and then my neighbor Bethan is watching him afterwards." It felt strange to have so many plans, so many people in her life. She'd been alone a long time, she realized. Alone in so many ways.

"You and your mum getting along?" Claire asked hesitantly, and Abby remembered how a few months ago she'd moaned so much about Laura's presence in her life. It made her feel a little guilty now.

"Yes, we are, amazingly enough. Really well." Even though the revelations Laura had dive-bombed on her the other day had shaken her to the core. Laura's terse and reluctant admission about Abby's father had taken the puzzle pieces of the past Abby had stubbornly jammed together and scattered them completely. *He drove me out of the village, more or less, because he was afraid I'd tell someone, anyone, that he was your father. And frankly it terrified me enough to force me to contemplate leaving.*

That admission, reluctantly given, had rattled around in Abby's head since. What kind of monster had her father been? And what unknown hell had her mother had to deal with? The selfish singleton in search of city excitement suddenly seemed like something out of a soap opera rather than real life. The truth was much more complicated, and potentially more distasteful. Abby had started realizing why her mother was so reluctant to say anything—and she wasn't sure if she even wanted to know any more. She hadn't yet asked.

They reached the church, the last few latecomers hurrying through the doors before the bride. Lucy had, in her typically warmhearted way, invited the entire population of Hartley-by-the-Sea to the wedding. It looked like most of them were in attendance.

The last time Abby had been in this church had been for her grandmother's funeral just over two months ago now. A feeling of sadness swept over her like a mist rather than the downpour or at least the drizzle that she'd expected. She missed Mary—of course she did—but her death hadn't left the gaping, glaring emptiness that would have been there a few months ago. She still had a family, and friends, and a life to look forward to. She only wished Mary could have been there to see her daughter and granddaughter reconciled, watch them turn the café into something bigger and better than Abby, or Mary for that matter, had ever dared dream.

A sudden hush fell over the congregation, and as Juliet and Chloe fussed over Lucy for the last time, Abby got into place behind Bella, who seemed the least nervous of them all. The music began in an impressive organ swell, and the first bridesmaid started down the aisle.

Abby hadn't thought much about actually being in Lucy's wedding, perhaps because of the little darts of jealousy she'd occasionally felt for her friend's happiness as well as the latent grief for her own lost hopes of enjoying such a day. Now, as she processed down the aisle, she realized the jealousy was gone. The grief was there—it would always be there—but it wasn't the sharp bladelike pain it had once felt like, the blaze of a raw nerve, an open and unhealed wound. No, the grief had grown into her, dug its roots down and wrapped its tendrils around her memories and her heart, shaped who she was, and she could live with that. She could let the hurt go. She could enjoy this.

And she did enjoy it, every minute, from the way Alex fumbled with the rings, his voice hoarse with unaccustomed emotion as he said his vows, to Lucy's wide, beaming smile and gurgling laugh when a ring dropped on the floor with a loud clang. The organist was a tad too enthusiastic and a few jokers in the congregation, no doubt former students of Alex's, weren't above catcalling and whooping when Alex finally kissed his bride. All in all, it was perfect, the ultimate Hartley-by-the-Sea wedding, pink bubble gum dress included.

And then of course there was the reception to look forward to— and Chris. Abby had reminded herself several times over the last week that this wasn't a date. Not even close. Chris was moving to the Hebrides, had a girlfriend, and had, quite frankly, looked somewhat appalled at the thought of her having romantic designs on him. Definitely not a date. And that was okay. It was a chance to flirt a little in a totally safe way. Perfect.

Everyone walked from the church to the school; fortunately the rain had stopped and sunlight was peeking from behind shreds of clouds, lending a diamond sparkle to the puddles on the road. Laura fell into step with Abby, Noah scampering ahead with Meghan and Nathan, and nodded towards Lucy and Alex, who were leading the informal procession.

"They seem happy."

"Yes, they're a great couple. He's stern and she's bubbly and somehow it works."

"I've never known how that feels," Laura mused. "But I can imagine it. Sort of."

"Can you? Sometimes I feel like I can't."

"What about Noah's father?" Laura asked, lowering her voice a little so those walking near them wouldn't listen in. "You were going to get married, weren't you?"

"Well . . . maybe." It felt good to come clean not just to Lucy, as she had a few weeks ago, but to her mother. To the world. "We never got that far. He was coming round to the whole idea of a family, and I hoped that we might make it official. . . ." She let out a little laugh. "That makes me sound like a bit of a saddo, doesn't it? The truth is, Ben didn't want a baby. A few days before he died, he started to think it might work, but that was as far as it—or we—got."

"Oh, Abby." Laura's face was suffused with sadness. "I'm sorry."

"It's okay," Abby said. "Now. It wasn't for a long time. Today was the first time I looked at Lucy being so in love and didn't feel that awful little sting of jealousy. I was happy just to be me."

"Which is a good thing." Laura smiled, and then with a tremulous laugh she brushed at her eyes. "Honestly, I must be going through some sort of premenopause. I'm welling up at the sappiest things."

"Did you just call me sappy?"

"No, *I'm* sappy. Amazingly. Now, where is this Chris? I want to meet him."

"He's got a girlfriend, you know. And he's scarpering to the Hebrides in about a week."

Laura pretended to pout. "Don't spoil my fun."

Abby laughed. A few minutes later they came into the school hall, the hint of sweaty socks and boiled cabbage mostly covered by the fragrance from the huge displays of lilies and roses. Chris was waiting by the bar; he'd scrubbed up nicely in a navy sport jacket and a blue button-down shirt, open at the throat. Classy but casual. Suddenly, despite knowing in every way this wasn't a date, Abby felt nervous.

"Hey." She walked up to him, conscious that she would have rather picked her own outfit than be seen in a dress that looked like something a Polly Pocket would wear. Laura had promised to watch Noah until it was time for him to be carted away by Bethan. "So, you made it." Obviously.

"Yeah, quite a turnout." Chris glanced around the hall, which was filling up quite quickly. "Seems like half of Hartley-by-the-Sea is here."

"At least. Lucy seems to know everybody and Alex is the head teacher at the school. It's kind of a big deal."

"Yeah, I can see that. It reminds me of where I grew up, actually. Cornwall, a village like this one." He gave a wry grimace. "I couldn't wait to get away."

"I was the same, once upon a time."

"But you came back . . . ?"

"A combination of life events made that happen. It felt like failure, but I've come to realize it wasn't. I really like it here, actually." With no qualifiers. She did like it here. She loved it, and yet . . . "I might be leaving, as a matter of fact. For a little while. To Liverpool."

"Cool . . ."

"To finish my uni course. But we'll see." She shrugged and reached for a glass of fizz that one of the servers—some of Alex's former students—was circulating on a tray. "I'm waiting to hear. But it's all good." And she meant it.

They chatted some more about paragliding and Chris's nomadic lifestyle—Abby wasn't sure where the girlfriend fit into that—and then sat down for a buffet meal and the wedding toasts—given by a friend of Alex's from university and Juliet, whose toast to rediscovering her sister was both tartly funny and poignantly emotional. Fiona declined to say anything, and she left as soon as the formal part of the reception was over. Abby watched her go with a slight pang, grateful—semi-amazing as that was—for her own mother, who was sitting at one of the tables, nodding and talking to Juliet.

As the afternoon stretched into evening and the alcohol flowed, the mood relaxed; Bethan fetched Noah as the dancing started. Out of the corner of her eye Abby saw Chris do a double take and then try to cover it when she said good-bye to her son.

"You didn't know about him, did you?" she asked after Noah had gone. She'd never mentioned him in her few conversations with Chris, and she wondered if that had been subconsciously intentional.

"Nope. But it's cool."

It was all cool with Chris, Abby thought, bemused. He was happy to let life slide—or glide—by. She'd been that way once. Since Ben's death and Noah's birth, she'd been a passive recipient of whatever came her way, a spectator to her own life. She wanted to take control now, in every way.

"Hey," she said, her voice coming out a little loud and abrupt. "How about we dance?"

It took a few songs for Abby to get into it; it had been a long time since she'd danced or even felt like dancing. But after several glasses of champagne she started to loosen up, laughing as she sang along with everyone else to "It's Raining Men," all of them gyrating and prancing around in their wedding finery. Even Alex was dancing, although his sense of rhythm was questionable.

"He looks a little like a puppet on strings," Abby had said to her mother.

"'I'm a real boy,'" Laura murmured, and Abby stifled a laugh. Her mother had remained a wry observer for most of the reception, and Abby felt strangely protective of her now, knowing she'd once had a

KATE HEWITT

difficult time, even if she still didn't grasp, and wasn't yet sure she wanted to grasp, the specifics.

Now, dancing in the crowd with Chris doing the white man's over-bite—Abby had thought he would have some better moves—she suddenly caught sight of her mother making a beeline for the doors, which had been flung open to the damp night. Something about Laura's hurried stride, her lowered head, gave Abby a prickling sense of unease.

"Hold on," she said to Chris, who continued with his low-level gyrations. Abby followed her mother out into the dark school yard.

"Mum?" she called uncertainly, because Laura had moved fast enough to already be swallowed up by the darkness. "Mum?" The distant click of heels stopped. *"Mum!"*

"Sorry I'm ducking out," Laura called. Her voice sounded muffled. "I don't feel well."

"Then you shouldn't be walking back to the beach all by yourself, in heels and in the dark—"

"I'm fine, Abby." Laura's voice sounded sharp now. "Please, just leave me alone."

Abby felt stung for a millisecond before she reminded herself that they'd both gotten way past this kind of snippy to-and-fro. "Tell me what's wrong. And let me see you, at least. I'm going to break a leg out here." She moved cautiously across the dark expanse of concrete to-wards the huddled shape she could now see by the gate. "Something is wrong, I can tell."

"I'm just not in the party mood." Laura straightened, her back half-turned to Abby. "Seriously, Abby. Go enjoy yourself. I'm just go-ing to . . ." For a second Laura paused, and in that breath of silence Abby felt as if the world were teetering on its axis. She groped one arm blindly, trying to find her mother's hand.

"Please, Mum."

Another second, a breath, a hope, and then Laura shook off her hand. "I'm fine," she said, and walked on into the darkness.

Abby stood there for a moment, breathing in the cool air, trying to sort out her feelings. Was she overreacting? On a gut-churning level she felt something was wrong. But maybe Laura was just tired of being an add-on guest at a wedding where she didn't really know anyone. And their relationship wasn't strong enough yet that Abby felt she could push.

Reluctantly, unable to shake the feeling that she was doing the wrong thing, she headed back inside. The party mood had left her and she didn't feel like dancing; even the champagne tasted flat. Lucy had gone to change and it seemed like people were starting to drift away while others stood by their etiquette books and waited for the bride and groom to leave first. Abby knew she would wait, even though she was tired and her feet ached and she'd frankly like to consign her dress to the rubbish bin forever. She and Chris stood around making awkward small talk, both of them clearly ready to move on, until Lucy emerged, resplendent in a magenta skirt and matching blouse. She did like her bright colors.

Alex had pulled the car up the lane to the school, in direct violation of the STRICTLY NO CARS sign posted at the bottom. The groomsmen had decorated it with the prerequisite streamers and tin cans, the back window soaped up with semidirty messages.

Lucy was just climbing in when a siren's scream broke the still air. Everyone froze, because sirens weren't heard all that often in Hartley-by-the-Sea. Abby heard the whispers and murmurs rippling in a wave around her. Was it an ambulance? A police car? Oh God, had something happened to Laura—

"It's a fire engine," someone said, and someone else ran to the side of the school yard to peer over the edge.

"It's coming from the sea."

"The *sea*—"

And then Claire came forward, grabbing Abby's hand. "Abby," she cried, "I think the beach café's on fire."

30

≈

Laura

LAURA OPENED HER EYES to stare up at a strange ceiling, her gaze bleary, the taste in her mouth too awful to contemplate for very long. Not only was the ceiling strange, but the room was too. And so was the bed she was lying in, wearing, she discovered as she ran her hand down her body, only her underwear. Good Lord.

"Don't worry. Nothing happened."

The sound of Rob Telford's dry voice made Laura wince. Four words that brought both relief and incredible shame. What on earth had she gotten up to last night?

A montage of blurry memories from Lucy and Alex's wedding filtered through her brain. The bell-shaped bridesmaid dresses, the swell of pride she'd felt seeing Abby walk down the aisle. Dancing with Noah, laughing and wincing as he'd stomped on her toes, and Juliet's wry yet heartfelt toast. Juliet had talked to her afterwards about the four rounds of IVF she'd gone through with nothing to show for it, lifting her chin, her eyes bright, trying to act like it wasn't breaking her heart into pieces. Laura remembered thinking she could be friends with Juliet Bagshaw. But the last thing she remembered, the very last thing . . .

Oh, yes. The last thing she remembered, *really* remembered, was stumbling from the wedding reception, tipsy and unaccountably terrified, and running smack into Rob Telford coming up the lane. He'd grabbed her by the arms to steady her, his voice filled with incredulity and alarm as he'd said, *"Laura?"*

And she, blithering idiot that she was, had simply sobbed, "Get me out of here."

And so he had. He'd taken her up to his flat above the pub, a messy three rooms filled with tattered paperbacks and dirty dishes, but the sheets, he'd assured her at some point, were clean. She'd knocked back several whiskeys that she definitely hadn't needed and refused to talk about anything. She hadn't been able to stop trembling and she remembered Rob draping an old crocheted afghan over her shoulders.

At some point she must have passed out, or near enough. And now she'd woken up to a stabbing headache, wearing nothing but a lacy bra and pants.

"You want to talk about it?" Rob asked gently.

Laura closed her eyes against the bright sunlight, the strange room, everything. "No."

"Something happened."

"Yes, something happened. And obviously I don't want to talk about it." She drew a deep breath. "I need to get out of here." How many people had seen her stumble into Rob's flat late last night? How many people were gleefully muttering about Laura Rhodes being at it again? And, God help her, *Michael* . . .

The last person she'd expected to see at Lucy Bagshaw's wedding was Abby's father. And he obviously hadn't expected to see her. He'd stared at her, slack-jawed, for several stunned seconds before his expression had hardened and he'd turned away.

Laura had simply stood, her mind spinning like a top, going nowhere, as she tried to fight the feeling that she was fifteen and scared out of her mind, with Michael's car crawling behind her on the beach road as she walked home from school. He had rolled down the window and hissed at her, "Get rid of it, Laura. I'm warning you. I'm a very powerful man and you need to make this *go away*."

Every day for three weeks. She'd been so frightened and miserable that she'd ended up cutting herself a couple of times, just to relieve the pressure. She remembered standing in the tiny bathroom, watching the blood ooze from the crosshatch in her arm, morbidly transfixed. It had felt good for a few seconds, and then it had felt horrifying. She'd been so appalled by what she'd done, she'd decided to quit school instead. Easier all round, because he couldn't get to her then. Except of course he had. *And still was.* Except he obviously hadn't known she'd be at the party, or even in Hartley-by-the-Sea, judging by the look on his face. But now that he knew . . . Was she overreacting? She felt like a little girl again, and it was a horrible feeling.

"Why don't you have a cup of tea first?" Rob suggested, and he pressed a mug into her hands. The warmth seeped into her palms, kick-starting her out of her numb fog.

"Sorry. I'm a bit of a wreck." She tried for a smile, but her lips just trembled.

"Only a bit," Rob returned with a wry smile. "But I don't mind."

Laura took a sip of tea, realizing it wasn't fair to cut him out like this. He'd helped her and taken her in, no questions asked. She couldn't hide behind her high wall of chilly remoteness with Rob. She didn't even want to anymore. At least not much.

"I saw Abby's father last night," she said, the words dropping like stones into the stillness. Rob's eyebrows rose.

"Here? At the wedding?"

"The reception. He came in right at the end. What kind of person comes to a wedding reception for the last ten minutes? Oh, wait. I know the answer to that question." She took a hasty sip of tea, realizing she might have given the game away. Rob might have been able to figure out whom she was talking about. "I felt like I was fifteen again," she mumbled against the rim of her mug, her hands cradled around its warmth. "It wasn't a good feeling."

"No, I can imagine it wasn't." He raked a hand through his hair,

making it stand up in about a dozen different directions. Laura thought
he looked tired, and then she realized she must have taken his bed.

"Where did you sleep last night?"

"On the sofa."

"And who— I mean, did you take my dress off me?"

"I closed my eyes."

She slumped against the pillows, ashamed, heartsick. "I'm such
a mess."

"You had a shock, and you're not a mess." Rob paused, his own
mug raised halfway to his lips. "But what are you going to do, Laura?
Because it seems as if there is some unfinished business between you
and this bloke."

"Of course there is. There's *Abby*." She shook her head. "She doesn't
know. Nobody knows. I made sure of that."

"Did he threaten you?" Rob asked quietly. "Back then?"

She was *not* going to cry. Not again. She was not that much of a bloody
wreck, thanks very much. "More or less," she managed, and then took
another sip of her tea to hide the feelings she was sure must have been
written all over her face. "Because he was—is—married."

"Yeah."

Something about his tone made Laura say sickly, "You know, don't
you? You know who it is."

Rob's smile was slow and sad. "Laura, how many influential mar-
ried men are there in this village who rolled in last night in their GSF
Lexus?" He paused, taking a sip of tea, his gaze steady on her. "It's
Michael West."

She looked away. She was wearing underwear, the duvet drawn up
to her chin, but she felt naked. "I wasn't expecting ever to see him
again," she mumbled. "They moved to London, I thought, years ago."

"Twelve years ago, but they kept the house. They keep it for parties, more or less. Swan back here to throw some do and then they're
off again."

"But Claire lives here."

"Yes, she rents her own place on the high street. And Andrew lives in Manchester and is dating a local, Rachel Campbell. So they have ties here, although you wouldn't know it to look at them. But in coming back to Hartley-by-the-Sea, you must have realized you'd run into him eventually."

"I'd hoped I wouldn't. And I'd hoped that if I did, I'd be stronger. That's the thing that really infuriates me," she admitted with a small, fragile smile. "It was as if, when I saw him, I'd instantly become a teenager again. Scared and stupid—"

"Vulnerable."

"I slept with him, Rob. I did that willingly." She wouldn't pretend otherwise. She remembered making the decision. She certainly remembered counting the cost.

"Hard to say," Rob answered with a shrug. "He had to have been at least forty years old to your fifteen. Technically it was statutory rape, which he must have known."

"It was consensual," Laura insisted. "Unfortunately. I didn't know any better. I . . ." But she didn't want to talk about that. She didn't want to *think* about that. She sighed and leaned her head back again. "I need to tell Abby. I've kept this quiet long enough."

"Yeah," Rob said. "I think you do."

But first she had to suffer the walk of shame, leaving Rob's flat at nine in the morning, dressed in last night's glad rags. Ugh. She'd grown out of this so long ago. Still, there was nothing for it but to pull on her wrinkled dress and finger-comb her bird's-nest hair. Lovely.

Rob made her a bacon sarnie, which Laura wolfed down gratefully, even though her stomach was twisting queasily, from both the excess of alcohol and what was to come.

What was Michael thinking now? Was he putting plans in action to drive her out of town once again? *You're forty-three,* Laura reminded herself as she brushed her teeth with a finger's length of toothpaste in

Rob's tiny bathroom. *You're not fifteen anymore, or sixteen with a baby in your arms. You're a grown woman, and you can handle Michael West.*

Too bad she didn't feel like that inside. And what about Abby? How would she take the news? Laura hated the thought of jeopardizing their relationship. It still felt far too fragile.

"Laura," Rob said quietly as she made to leave. "Remember, you don't have to let one thing define you."

"Right. Words to live by, those." Words that were easy to say. Easy to believe when you weren't staring down the barrel of a very bad memory that had just shot you in the face of your present reality. She gave him what she hoped passed as a smile before stepping out into the street. Hartley-by-the-Sea's high street was quiet on a Sunday morning, save for a couple of dog walkers walking towards the beach. She'd head home first, Laura decided, and shower and change. Then she'd feel ready—maybe—to face Abby.

She hadn't gotten as far as the beach road when a car slowed next to her. Laura tensed, half-poised for flight, the Pavlovian reaction kicking in hard as she heard the car's motor growl behind her, like some menacing mechanical beast, just as it had all those years ago.

"Laura." It was Juliet at the wheel, having rolled down the window, looking stunned to see her. Laura stared back, willing her jacked-up heart rate to slow.

"I know I look a wreck, but you're staring at me like—"

"We thought you were *dead.* Abby's going out of her mind. Where have you *been*?"

It wasn't like Juliet to speak in the italics of melodrama. "Been? Umm . . ." She did not want to say Rob's. "Why is Abby worried? Was she looking for me?"

"Looking for you?" Juliet put the car in park and craned her head out the window, one elbow resting on the doorframe. "Laura, do you not know?"

Laura felt the beginnings of a whole new kind of panic flutter in her soul, a trapped bird she wanted to run right over. "Know what?"

"The café . . ."

The café? Not what she had been expecting at all, although the fears lurking in Laura's mind like dementors had been, so far, formless. But if Juliet was at a loss for words, then something must have been really wrong. "What about the café?"

"It . . . it caught on fire last night. Laura, it . . . it burned down."

For a moment Laura could only stare dumbly. The news was so unexpected, so ridiculous, she almost had the urge to laugh. The café couldn't have caught fire on the same night she'd seen Michael West and fallen apart herself. It just couldn't have. It was too much, too awful, all at once. "What do you mean?" she asked, even though the question was absurd. *It burned down* was fairly self-explanatory.

"The fire engines came screaming down the high street right as Lucy and Alex were leaving for their honeymoon. I'm amazed you didn't hear them—where were you?"

"It doesn't matter." The full import of what Juliet was saying started to hit her, one hammerblow after another. But most important: "Where's Abby?"

"She's at her place, waiting by the phone. Wondering where on earth you are . . ."

"Oh, no." Without saying anything else, Laura turned around and headed blindly for Thimble Cottage. She must have looked a right state now, she thought distantly as she half ran up the street in her heels, still wearing yesterday's clothes, her hair a mess, tears starting in her eyes. She knocked on Abby's door and it was flung open almost immediately; Abby stood there, still in her awful bridesmaid dress, looking like a panda with her mascara-run eyes and pale face.

"Mum."

They fell into each other's arms, laughing and crying, as Noah tackled them about their knees. "You're not dead!" he said joyfully, and Laura managed a very shaky laugh.

"No," she agreed. "I'm not. Not yet, anyway."

Abby pulled back, swiping at her tearstained face. "I thought you'd gotten trapped in the flat. I thought . . ." She gulped, shaking her head. "Where *were* you?"

"I have a lot to explain."

Abby frowned. "You mean about last night. You were upset."

"Yes." Laura glanced down at Noah. "Look, I think we could both use showers and some strong coffee, after which I need to see the café, or what's left of it. And then later we'll talk."

Laura thought she'd prepared herself mentally for the sight of the café's smoking ruins, but she hadn't. She got out of Abby's car slowly, staring at the blackened concrete and the shattered glass, the whole thing cordoned off by yellow police tape. For a second she thought her legs would give way beneath her, and she sagged against the car before she made herself straighten and walk towards the wreck of a building.

"You can't go in," Abby cautioned, her voice wobbling. "It's still dangerous. And hot."

"Yes." Laura stood on the cracked concrete steps that had once led to the little terrace of uneven paving stones, a few picnic tables, and the glass-fronted door to the café. Now it was all gone, nothing but rubble and destruction. "How did it happen?" For a horrifying second she thought Michael might have torched the place, out of sheer spite or perhaps just fear. But surely not. She'd been afraid of him, but not that afraid.

"They're not sure, but they think a faulty wire. The electrics were dodgy—we both knew that."

"But not that dodgy. At least I didn't realize . . ." Laura passed a shaky hand over her face. "We were sitting on a ticking time bomb, then."

"I guess."

"We could have both been burned to a crisp in our beds. And Noah too." The possibility was horrific.

"Or we could have been there to call the fire department and stop it before it got farther than the kitchen." Abby sighed and shook her head. "How often are we both away from the café for that long?"

"Bad or good luck, I suppose, depending on how you look at it." Laura stepped closer to the café. The windows were blown out, the concrete walls blackened with smoke. Inside she could see charred wood, the twisted metal of what she suspected was the remnant of the espresso machine. The firemen, Abby told her, had thrown all the furniture outside so they could pry up the floorboards to make sure there wasn't fire lurking underneath. It was impossible to go inside.

"The good news," Abby said with a determined attempt at cheerfulness, "is that according to the firemen, the upstairs of the flat is generally okay. Everything is covered in soot and ash and my lovely raspberry paint has bubbled from the heat, but they think it's mainly sound."

"Very good news," Laura agreed, unsure whether she was being sarcastic. She felt utterly flattened.

"Of course you can stay with me until things are sorted. Noah and I are happy to share."

Laura turned to look at her. "Sorted? How on earth are we going to sort this? We have no money. We owe the bank twenty thousand pounds—"

"We have small-business insurance," Abby reminded her. "It covers fire damage."

"Even if we had faulty wiring?" Laura shook her head, hopeless. "You have to reduce all risks, carry out safety checks, have certificates for everything—"

"We did. Or at least I did, three months ago. I booked it in for every May. And the builder bloke mentioned the need for rewiring, but he didn't say it was an immediate risk. So I think we should be mainly okay. They'll have to give us some money, at least."

"Oh. Right." Abby's brisk practicality seemed so unlike her. Abby was the one who wrung her hands while Laura made efficient and unsentimental plans. But in the aftermath of everything, Laura felt as if their roles had been reversed. She was the one who was stuck spinning, and Abby was moving forward with a purposeful stride.

"Look, there's nothing to be had here, is there?" Abby asked gently. She touched Laura's arm. "Why don't you come back to Thimble Cottage? You look like you could use a sleep. It will be quiet, I promise."

It wasn't as if she had anywhere else to go. And Laura knew she still needed to talk to Abby. She walked back to the car, dragging her limbs, feeling as if her body were filled with concrete. She was so tired, and it was a tiredness that went past a sleepless night or a sudden shock. She couldn't do it again, she realized. She couldn't start over again, rebuilding from the ashes, facing the past. She *couldn't*.

"Mum," Abby said quietly, and Laura started, blinking her daughter into focus. "It's going to be okay."

Laura tried to smile but found she couldn't come up with a suitable reply.

31

Abby

LAURA LOOKED DIFFERENT WEARING Abby's clothes. She'd changed into a pair of baggy yoga pants and an old T-shirt of Abby's, her hair long and straight without its usual careful blow-dry, her face devoid of makeup. Curled up on the sofa at Thimble Cottage, Laura looked younger and more vulnerable than Abby had ever seen her before.

Abby brought them both mugs of tea and a plate of chocolate digestives, because she had a feeling they were going to need the sugar. After handing Laura one of the mugs, she curled up on the other end of the sofa and took a sip of tea.

"So, are you going to tell me what happened last night? Where were you?"

"I spent the night at Rob Telford's."

"What? Oh." Abby supposed she shouldn't have been shocked—Rob had been flirting with Laura, after all—but she was. He was only thirty, for goodness' sake. Her mother was a *cougar*.

"It wasn't like that," Laura said with a small semblance of a smile. "I . . . I saw your father at the wedding reception. It shocked me, and so I hurried out, as you noticed, and ran smack into Rob. I was in a state and he brought me back to his place." Laura sighed. "And then I drank far too much and basically passed out."

"Wait . . ." Abby's mind had snagged on that first detail. "You saw my *father*?"

"If I can even call him that. 'Unwilling genetic donor' might be a better term." A new and surprising bitterness spiked Laura's words.

"But . . . but I thought . . ." Abby was floundering. She'd assumed her father had left Hartley-by-the-Sea, if he'd ever even lived there. Laura had never seemed too concerned about bumping into him since she'd been back. "You actually *saw* him?" She couldn't get her head around this simple fact. After a lifetime of having her father be no more than an abstract concept, some nether-person who only semiexisted, the idea that her mother had seen him—that Abby herself must have seen him—was extraordinary. Mind-boggling. Thrilling and frightening all at once. "Did he know . . . Did he recognize me? Did you talk to him? Did he—" Abby stopped abruptly as she remembered all the things her mother had told her about this man. How he hadn't wanted her. How he'd pressured Laura to have her aborted. "Never mind," she said quietly. Quite suddenly she felt sick. She had a feeling Laura wasn't done, but she didn't think she wanted to know any more.

"You asked me before who he was, Abby," Laura said quietly. "And I didn't tell you for a lot of reasons. Because I didn't want to rake it all up again, and because I thought, or at least hoped, it wouldn't matter. That neither of us would ever see him again. He'd prefer that, I know."

"You don't have to tell me," Abby blurted. "You don't. I'm not sure I want to know anymore, actually."

Laura stared at her for a long moment and then said, "It's Michael West."

The name didn't mean anything to Abby at first. Then the gears started whirring and things clicked sickly into place. West . . . Claire West. Andrew West. *Michael West.* "You mean . . ." Her voice sounded thin and papery. "You mean Claire and Andrew's dad?"

"Yes." Laura looked calm, resolute, and very tired.

"But he's . . ." *Old.* And married. And he was married when Laura was fifteen—which meant she'd had an affair with an older, married man. For some reason that possibility had never occurred to Abby. She'd assumed her father was some pimply teen Laura had met at school or maybe on the beach—an unfortunate boyfriend or possibly a regrettable hookup. But this?

"How?" she asked. And then—"Why?"

"How is simpler than why. I babysat for Claire and Andrew when they were little. Claire doesn't even remember."

"Babysat . . . and that led to . . . ?" She couldn't put it into words.

"He drove me home afterwards. After babysitting," Laura clarified quickly, and then she let out a tired laugh, leaning her head back against the sofa. "It all sounds so sordid, doesn't it? And it was sordid. I think I knew that even at the time, but . . . I suppose I convinced myself otherwise. Somewhat."

"How did it . . . start?"

"I suppose the start for me was just walking into their house. Have you been there?" Abby nodded. "It's gorgeous. I remember the first time I walked in there. I wanted to curl up on the carpet and go to sleep. I wanted to take a bath in that huge, sunken tub. I wanted to live there, breathe it in. It was so peaceful and perfect and a million miles away from my own life. And as for him . . ." With a jolt Abby realized her mother didn't even want to say his name. "I was looking for a father figure, I suppose. I missed my dad so much, even though it had been five years. You never get over that, you know? The grief becomes a part of you."

Abby nodded, her eyes stinging. "Yes."

"And Claire and Andrew's father was so jovial and sophisticated. You know the type? All booming laughs and expensive aftershave."

"Yes," Abby said after a pause. "I know the type."

"He asked me about myself during those rides home. No one ever did that for me. No one was interested."

"No one?" For some reason she hadn't pictured her mother being quite so lonely.

"No, not really. I worked at the café all hours, and I only had a couple of friends at school. Izzy was a good friend, but we were different. I was different. I suppose I felt empty inside, waiting to be filled up. To figure out who I was. And when . . . when things happened the way they did, I thought maybe that would help." Laura shrugged her shoulders. "Not a very well-thought plan, but I was only fifteen."

Fifteen. And Michael West must have been at least forty. The thought made Abby's stomach churn. "That was statutory rape, then."

Laura sighed. "Yes, I know. But it also wasn't. Because I knew what I was doing."

"How can a fifteen-year-old know what she's doing?" Abby cried. "He must have pressured you. . . ."

"No, he didn't, actually. Not as much as you probably think, anyway. I was babysitting one evening—his wife wasn't there—she was visiting family—and we got to talking. He told me I was pretty, put his hand on my knee. I wasn't stupid. I knew what he wanted. He was a little drunk too—he'd come back from some business thing. He kissed me and I let him." Laura paused, her thumb and forefinger braced against her temple. "There was a moment when I could have stopped it all. I remember thinking that. I remember thinking, 'I have time to get up, walk away, act like nothing happened.' And I didn't. I chose not to."

"Why?" Abby whispered.

Laura shrugged again, her gaze sliding away from Abby's. "I don't really know." She took a breath, swallowed, and then started again. "Because in that moment it felt . . . not good, precisely, but something close to it. Someone wanted me. Someone was making me the center of his world, even if just for a few minutes. I craved that."

"Oh, Mum." Abby could imagine the scene of quiet desperation, and she brushed at her eyes.

Laura gave Abby a twisted smile. "And so I lost my virginity on the Wests' living room rug."

"I'm so sorry." Abby took a gulping breath. "And that was it—the one time?"

"Ha, if only." Laura shook her head, a faint, sad smile on her lips. "No, it went on for a bit. A few months. Sporadically, in different places, when he could get away. I told myself it meant something, or at least it was better than nothing. And then I got pregnant with you."

"And he wasn't pleased."

"To say the least." Laura let out a dry husk of laughter. "I don't think he'd quite twigged that I was only fifteen. When he realized that, he was appalled. He knew he could be done for rape, sent to prison, the whole thing. So he tried to make my life miserable."

"But why? Wouldn't that make you angry at him and think of turning him in?"

"It terrified me into silence, which, since I'd refused the termination, was the next best thing." Laura smiled mirthlessly. "You know, on occasion, as an adult, I've almost felt sorry for him. What a pickle he'd got himself into."

"Got his pickle into, you mean," Abby said sourly, and Laura laughed with genuine humor.

"Yes, that too. Oh, it was a right mess, Abby. He used to drive down the beach road when I was walking home from the bus, hissing at me. Telling me I needed to get rid of you *or else*."

"But you never cracked under that pressure," Abby said with something close to wonder. It occurred to her then that Laura had been a stronger, better mother, protecting her child, than Abby could have ever fathomed. "I wish you'd told me this sooner."

"I didn't think it would help. And I suppose before this summer I wasn't sure you'd even believe me." Laura finished on a sigh. "I wanted to put it all behind me. All the rubbishy, regrettable choices I made. I've been ashamed and trying to act as if I wasn't."

"I can understand that. I've felt the same."

"We're surprisingly similar in some ways, you know," Laura said. "Which is weird."

"Why so weird? We do share some genes."

"True."

They held each other's gazes, both of them smiling with sad wryness. "It's a lot to take in," Abby said at last. "You know he could still be done for rape? There's no statute of limitations on sex crimes in the UK."

"Oh, Lord." Laura shook her head. "I don't really see the point in that."

"You were a victim, Mum."

"Maybe, but I have no desire to drag a whole lot of people through the muck of the press and publicity now. Especially not you."

Abby sighed and nodded. Her mind was still spinning with all this new information. "So Claire is my half sister." She could hardly believe she was saying the words, and that they were true. "Is that why you left? Because he was putting pressure on you?"

"No, he stopped after a while. Just tried to ignore me. But . . . he was a presence, you know? I saw his car sometimes flash by. I felt afraid, although of what I'm not exactly sure." Laura held up a hand to stop her from talking, although Abby hadn't known what she was going to say, if anything. "But as I've said before, don't paint me as too much of a victim, Abby. I made my choices. I left because I wanted to leave. Yes, your grandmother encouraged me, because she felt guilty or fed up or whatever. But I left. I wanted something different. I *chose* that."

"I know that," Abby whispered. For the first time, that stark reality didn't feel like a fist to the gut, a knife in the heart. "But you also chose to come back."

Later, as Laura slept, Abby tidied up and tried to figure out what the future held. Would they rebuild the café? She had no idea how much money they'd get off the insurance. And what about Michael West? Would she tell Claire? Did she want to fling that grenade into the center of her friend's life, of the whole village? Because of course word would get out. For the first time she could understand why her mother had been so tight-lipped for all these years.

They didn't talk about it again for a while; dealing with the aftermath of the fire consumed both of them for several days as they filled out paperwork and spent hours on the phone with the insurance company, then with the fire damage restoration services that the insurance company had recommended. Then there were endless meetings—first with the insurance inspector, and then the restoration people. They walked through the blackened shell of the café while the insurance and restoration guys did an estimate of the damage. They hauled away boxes of their possessions that hadn't been damaged to be professionally repaired and cleaned.

Abby took charge of it all, giving information, details, descriptions. Laura walked along with her, silent and pale, and then went back to the cottage to sleep. Abby let her be; she had a sense her mother was both grieving and healing at the same time, protecting herself from the onslaught of everything that had happened and its inevitable aftermath. She felt weirdly protective and tender towards her mother, almost maternal. She wanted to shelter her, provide for her during these difficult days, and so she let her sleep, and made her tea, and brought her soup Laura didn't eat.

Meanwhile Hartley-by-the-Sea came forward in a surge of warm-hearted, well-meaning determination, with casserole dishes stacked up three high in the fridge, and offers to clean, cook, wash, or iron at any time, night or day. Even more than at Mary's funeral, people came forward to babysit or to simply offer the squeeze of a hand or a hug. Abby appreciated every gesture, every murmured word; more than ever, she felt part of this community.

"I'm not going to tell anyone," she told Laura three days after the fire. Noah was in bed and Laura was lying on the sofa, half-watching some reality TV show.

"No?" She sounded only mildly interested, as if it had nothing to do with her.

"It would only upset people, wouldn't it? And make them look at both of us differently. Maybe that means he gets away with it, and I hate that thought, but I can't face the alternative, and I don't think you can, either."

Laura kept her gaze trained on the TV. "No, probably not."

"Mum." Abby grabbed the remote and turned off the TV. "I know this is hard, but we both need to think about the future."

Laura closed her eyes. "I can't."

"Was it seeing him again? Is that what's made you so . . . inert?"

"Inert? Yes, I suppose that's what I am." Laura leaned her head back against the sofa and closed her eyes. "I can't face it, Abby. I can't face the prospect of starting over. Rebuilding the café. It's too hard. I've done it too many times. Remade myself, my life. I'm sick and tired of it."

"You don't have to remake your life," Abby said quietly. "Your life is here. Your friends are here. They're surrounding you, concerned, wanting to help. The only thing you have to do is cash a big fat check from the insurance company and hire some builders to redo everything. And I'll help with that."

Laura sighed heavily. "I don't think I can stay here."

"Why not?"

"Because it feels too hard."

"You've had hard times before and you've come through. Going through with a teenage pregnancy, raising me on your own, starting over in Manchester and New York . . . Mum, you're a strong person. You can do this. And," Abby added robustly, "this time you don't have to do it alone. I'm here with you every step of the way."

Laura let out a choked sound. "What," she asked, "did I ever do to deserve you?"

Abby smiled. "I could ask the same question. You fought for me harder than anyone else, Mum. I just didn't know it at the time."

A week after the fire, the restoration services had done all the cleaning they could, and Laura's clothes, good as new or almost, were on plastic-swathed hangers, delivered by a professional service. A big check came from the insurance company, a hundred thousand pounds, put straight into the bank. They paid off the business loan and started getting in estimates for repairs.

Laura had started to stir herself a little, taking Noah to the beach, and once to Whitehaven to get his school uniform. He'd grown a good inch over the summer, and school started in less than two weeks.

And then, one sunny Friday afternoon ten days before the start of term, the phone rang for Abby.

"Hello, may I please speak to Abigail Rhodes?"

With one eye on Noah kicking the football out in the garden, Abby answered absently, "Yes, this is she." She'd never known if you were supposed to say "she" or "her." Perhaps she should have just said "Speaking."

"Good afternoon. I'm calling from the admissions department of the University of Liverpool regarding your application for the animal science course."

32

Laura

THREE WEEKS AFTER THE fire, Laura was standing in the café, breathing in the smells of new lumber and fresh plaster, when a knock sounded on the new front door. She turned, about to launch into her explanation that the café wasn't open yet, but would be in a few weeks, when her breath bottled in her lungs. Michael West stood on the other side.

For a second Laura could hardly process it. She felt fifteen again, and then quite suddenly, she didn't. Those first few days after the fire, after Michael, she'd wanted to crawl inside herself and never come out. Thanks to her daughter's persistence, she'd finally emerged from that self-protective chrysalis. Not quite a butterfly, but some fledgling thing with damp and rumpled wings. She'd started helping more with the café, taking an interest in the renovations, which allowed for a bigger kitchen and a more dynamic restaurant space. She'd gone for coffee with Izzy, whose idyllic life and gorgeous farmhouse hadn't seemed quite as shiny and perfect as before; Izzy had been furious at her banker husband leaving their holiday in France halfway through. She'd spent some time with Juliet too, who was going to try IVF one more time before calling it quits.

"You can put your body through hell only so many times," she'd said grimly. "But more than that, you can only ride that roller coaster of hope so many times before you fall off."

She'd slowly but surely been finding a way back to herself, and not just that, but a way forward. And now Michael West was here, and as the fears of her fifteen-year-old self fell away, Laura realized she almost relished the idea of confronting him.

She crossed to the door and flipped the lock, opening it and standing in the doorway to block his entrance, one hand on her hip.

"Well, well, well."

"Hello, Laura."

"So civilized," she mocked lightly. She wouldn't give him the power of seeing her upset or angry. "I half expected you to come in here with an eviction notice or something."

"No. May I come in?"

"I suppose, but you're not staying long." She stood aside and watched as he walked in, a slow, shuffling step. He was older, she thought as she noted the lines on his face, the gray in his hair—signs of aging that she hadn't taken in during that awful glimpse at the wedding reception. He was *old*. "What do you want?" She wasn't going to make this easy. She didn't even want to call him by his name.

"Just . . . just to see how you are." His expression was guarded; he had bags under his eyes now, as well as jowls. He must have put on three stone since she'd seen him last.

"How I am? That's new. I'm fine, thanks very much, and so is Abby. She knows, by the way." Laura lifted her chin proudly. "I kept quiet all these years, but I told her after I saw you a few weeks ago. I thought she deserved to know, and frankly you didn't deserve to have a secret anymore."

His shoulders sagged a little. "I know."

"You know? Really? So you haven't come here to threaten me and *make it go away*?" The words rang out, sharp and clear. "I guess you've changed, then."

"Laura, I'm sorry for the way I acted all those years ago," Michael said, half-mumbling the words, his head lowered. "I was afraid. I stood to lose everything."

"You still do." Laura relished the look of utter panic that crossed his face before she added, "Don't worry. I'm not going to press charges after all this time. I don't really see the point of wrecking more lives."

"I didn't know you were only fifteen," he whispered hoarsely.

"Oh, *okay*, then. Sorted, are we?" She shook her head, scornful now, the fear well and truly gone. How had she ever been scared of this man and what he could have done?

"I wanted to give you this." He withdrew a check from the breast pocket of his jacket. Laura watched him dispassionately. The hand he held out was veiny and arthritic. She had a sudden memory of that hand touching her and she felt sick. What had she been thinking, back then? She knew the answer to that one. She hadn't been. She'd just wanted to be loved, even a little. "Aren't you going to take it?" Michael asked, an edge of impatience in his voice. He might have been retired now, but he still thought of himself as powerful and entitled. No doubt he wanted Laura to be pathetically grateful for whatever he was offering.

"I'm thinking about it," Laura returned. "Are you trying to buy me off?"

"Think of it as you will. A payoff or eighteen years of child maintenance payments."

Laura took the check. It was for a hundred thousand pounds. "Funny," she said dryly. "This is the second one-hundred-thousand-pound check I've had in the last few weeks."

"I appreciate your discretion on this matter."

"Now you sound like you're closing some business deal." Laura folded the check and put it in her pocket. "Are you not even curious about Abby? She's as much your child as Claire or Andrew." Against her will her throat started to close up. "You must have seen her over the years, growing up."

Michael shook his head. "I traveled a great deal for work."

Laura didn't know why she pressed; surely she knew the answer already. Yet for Abby's sake she felt compelled to say, "Still, you must have thought of her."

Annoyance flickered across Michael's face. "No. I never thought of her that way. She was nothing but a mistake to me."

Laura blinked. "Well, she wasn't a mistake to me," she said quietly. "She wasn't a mistake at all. She's been a joy and a blessing and a great friend." Her voice shook and she strove to calm it. "So I guess we're done here."

Michael hesitated, and Laura knew he was debating whether to press for an assurance that she would stay silent. But she wasn't a frightened fifteen-year-old anymore. Let him sweat. "This is my property, Michael, and I'm asking you to leave it. Now." Her voice turned lethal. "Don't come back here ever again."

He hesitated for one final second, and then with a quick nod he turned and left, the door banging behind him. Laura let out a shuddering breath. *Well.* So that had happened.

She'd been planning to spend the night in the flat; the repairs had been done weeks ago and she'd started painting some of the rooms. It still looked unlived in, with a few sticks of furniture and her stuff in boxes, but Thimble Cottage was crowded with three of them in there. Noah needed his bed back, and she felt they could all use some space.

But right now she wanted to see Abby.

She walked up the beach road slowly, savoring the way the sun streaked livid orange and purple across the sky. There was a hint of autumn in the air; Noah had started back to school a few days ago. Life moved on. Even hers.

Thimble Cottage looked cozy and welcoming against the darkening night, its windows lit up and laughter heard from within. Laura knocked once and then poked her head around the doorway.

"Hello?"

"Hey, Mum." The endearment came naturally now, but it still felt like a miracle to Laura. "I'm just chasing Noah up the stairs for bed. What's up?"

"Nothing too much," Laura said lightly. "Just wanted to chat to you about something."

"Nana!" Noah appeared gleefully at the top of the stairs. "Will you read my story?"

Laura glanced at Abby, who rolled her eyes in good-natured defeat. "Sure."

She walked up the stairs slowly; for some reason every step, every action, felt momentous. Like she was walking into the rest of her life. And that was, for once, a good thing.

She sat on the edge of Noah's bed, her arm around his thin shoulders, as she read him three stories about the cowboy dinosaurs who cavorted on his bed. Clearly it was a successful franchise.

After they were finished, Noah wriggled under the covers, looking alarmingly awake. "Love you, Nana," he said with simple honesty, and Laura's heart broke a little.

"Love you too, Noah." She waited until his eyelids were fluttering—which amazingly didn't take very long—and then tiptoed downstairs. Abby was in the kitchen, putting away the dinner dishes.

"Everything's okay, isn't it?" she asked with a hint of anxiety. Laura smiled.

"Everything's fine. I just wanted to give you something." Silently she took the check out of her pocket and gave it to Abby, who boggled.

"What . . ."

"Consider it a lifetime of child maintenance payments."

Abby's gaze moved to the name on the check. "He . . . he gave you this?"

"Yes."

"Why? To keep you from speaking out?"

Laura shrugged. "Who knows? Who cares? It belongs to you, Abby."

Abby was silent for a moment. "We could put it into the café."

"The café doesn't need that much money. And anyway, it's yours. Yours alone."

"You should have some of it. . . ."

"No." Laura was firm on that point. "I don't want it. I don't need it. It's yours."

Another silence while Abby stared at the check. "I got a phone call from Liverpool a week or so ago," she said at last.

"What? You did? Why didn't you tell me?"

Abby shrugged. "Everything was so busy here, and it didn't seem like the time. . . . Besides, it's not as simple as I'd hoped. They've agreed to let me return to the course, but I have to repeat a bunch of classes because of the changes to the system. Getting my degree would take over two years."

"So?" Laura raised her eyebrows. "Did you think it would be easy? Life is hard, Abby. We've both learned that, I think."

"Yes, but I don't want to leave you."

"You won't be. I fully expect you to return for every holiday, or near enough. And come back when you're qualified and set up a practice. Plenty of need for vets in this part of the country. There's more sheep than people, after all."

"I don't know." Abby let out a hiccupy sort of laugh. "I'm scared."

"I know." Laura reached out and squeezed her hand. "Don't do it if you really don't want to, Abby. But don't hang back for my sake, or out of simple fear. That never works, not really." She gestured to the check. "And that just made it a whole lot easier."

"Yes, it did, but I hate accepting his money. Not for him, but because it seems like he's getting away with something."

Laura thought of Michael West's hunched shoulders and shuffling step. "He's not getting away with as much as you think. And why shouldn't you take that money? You deserve it. It's yours by right."

"Maybe," Abby agreed slowly. "A hundred thousand pounds! How did we get so rich?"

"We worked and suffered for it," Laura answered. "And now it's time to reap the rewards."

Abby laughed, her face clearing, hope lighting her eyes. "Liverpool . . . I can't even believe it. The course starts in a *month*."

"Enough time to get a flat, then, and sort out Noah's school."

"But it's so *sudden*. . . ."

"Not really," Laura said quietly. "You've been waiting for this for years."

Abby let out a choked laugh. "Yes, I suppose I have. But what about you?"

"I'll be fine here. I'm going to make a go of the café, a real kitchen, proper meals. The works. It's a challenge."

"You're more than up for it." A sly look, so unlike her daughter. "And what about Rob Telford?"

Laura kept her face neutral. "What about him?" She hadn't seen him except in passing since she'd hightailed it out of his flat.

"He seems interested. . . ."

"I'm not. Not right now, anyway. I have enough to be getting on with. But I consider him a friend." Which was something in itself. She hadn't had a lot of friends over the years, but she had several now, and counting.

"Well, then." Abby took a deep breath and let it out in a rush. "I think this calls for a toast. I don't have any fizz. . . ."

Laughing, Laura watched as Abby searched for a bottle. "I don't mind."

Abby held up a bottle. "Will black currant squash do?"

"Noah would be thrilled."

She leaned against the counter as Abby poured them both two glasses of the children's drink. "We'll have to go down to Liverpool and look at flats sometime."

"Yes, I'll need your advice about that."

"I don't know Liverpool very well, but I'm sure there's good accommodation near the school."

Abby waggled the check. "Budget's not as tight as I thought it was."

"Let's drink to that." Laura hefted her glass of squash and Abby stayed her with one hand.

"No, let's drink to something else."

"Okay . . ." Laura raised her eyebrows, waiting.

Abby lifted her own glass, eyes suspiciously bright, her smile wide enough for both of them. "Let's drink," she said, "to us."

A Mother Like Mine

KATE HEWITT

QUESTIONS FOR DISCUSSION

1. What aspect of the story did you most enjoy in *A Mother Like Mine*? Who was your favorite character? Who was the one you could most relate to?

2. Why do you think Laura came back to Hartley-by-the-Sea? Does Abby's initial response to seeing Laura again seem understandable to you?

3. Abby has struggled with being in a rut in her life in Hartley-by-the-Sea. Why do you think this is? Can you relate to her predicament at all?

4. What do you think are the contributing factors to Laura and Abby's fraught relationship? How did Laura's parents and brother contribute to the dynamics that led to the current situation?

5. Both Laura and Abby must deal with grief at losing a loved one. How do they cope with old and new grief? Did their strategies and feelings resonate with you?

6. The café is almost like another character in the novel. How did Laura's and Abby's feelings toward the café change? What did you like most about the café they run and its possibilities?

7. Why do you think it was important for Abby to have her own house, and for Laura to make that happen? How did this development change their relationship?

8. How were Laura's and Abby's childhoods similar? In what ways were they different? How did the events of their childhood affect them as adults? Is there something from your childhood that you feel has affected who you are today?

9. What appealed to you most about Hartley-by-the-Sea? What would you find the most challenging about living there?

10. At the end of the story, do you think Laura was justified in leaving Abby as a child? What do you think she could have done differently?

11. How do Abby's and Laura's relationships with Chris and Rob Telford affect and/or change them?

12. How do you think Laura and Abby both grow and change through the story? How do they help each other to do this?

13. Which part of *A Mother Like Mine* resonated the most with you? What will you remember about the book long after you've read it?

Continue reading for a preview
of Kate Hewitt's

RAINY DAY SISTERS,

Lucy and Juliet's story.
Available now!

LUCY BAGSHAW'S HALF SISTER, Juliet, had warned her about the weather. "When the sun is shining, it's lovely, but otherwise it's wet, windy, and cold," she'd stated in her stern, matter-of-fact way. "Be warned."

Lucy had shrugged off the warning because she'd rather live anywhere, even the Antarctic, than stay in Boston for another second. In any case, she'd thought she was used to all three. She'd lived in England for the first six years of her life, and it wasn't as if Boston were the south of France. Except in comparison with the Lake District, it seemed it was.

Rain was atmospheric, she told herself as she hunched over the steering wheel, her eyes narrowed against the driving downpour. How many people listed walks in the rain as one of the most romantic things to do?

Although perhaps not when it was as torrential as this.

Letting out a gusty sigh, Lucy rolled her shoulders in an attempt to ease the tension that had lodged there since she'd turned off the M6. Or really since three weeks ago, when her life had fallen apart in the space of a single day—give or take a few years, perhaps.

This was her new start or, rather, her temporary reprieve. She was staying in England's Lake District, in the county of Cumbria, for only four months, long enough to get her act together and figure out what she wanted to do next. She hoped. And, of course, Nancy Crawford was going to want her job as school receptionist back in January, when her maternity leave ended.

But four months was a long time. Long enough, surely, to heal, to become strong, even to forget.

Well, maybe not long enough for that. She didn't think she'd ever forget the blazing headline in the *Boston Globe*'s editorial section: *Why I Will Not Give My Daughter a Free Ride.*

She closed her eyes—briefly, because the road was twisty—and forced the memory away. She wasn't going to think about the editorial piece that had gone viral, or her boss's apologetic dismissal, or Thomas's shrugging acceptance of the end of a nearly three-year relationship. She certainly wasn't going to think about her mother. She was going to think about good things, about her new, if temporary, life here in the beautiful, if wet, Lake District. Four months to both hide and heal, to recover and be restored before returning to her real life— whatever was left, anyway—stronger than ever before.

Lucy drove in silence for half an hour, all her concentration taken up with navigating the A-road that led from Penrith to her destination, Hartley-by-the-Sea, population fifteen hundred. Hedgerows lined either side of the road, and the dramatic fells in the distance were barely visible through the fog.

She peered through the window, trying to get a better look at the supposedly spectacular scenery, only to brake hard as she came up behind a tractor trundling down the road at the breakneck speed of five miles per hour. Pulling behind her from a side lane was a truck with a trailer holding about a dozen morose and very wet-looking sheep.

She stared in the rearview mirror at the wet sheep, who gazed miserably back, and had a sudden memory of her mother's piercing voice.

Are you a sheep, Lucinda, or a person who can think and act for herself?

Looking at those miserable creatures now, she decided she was definitely not one of them. She would not be one of them, not here, in this new place, where no one knew her, maybe not even her half sister.

It took another hour of driving through steady rain, behind the trundling tractor the entire way, before she finally arrived at Hartley-by-the-Sea. The turning off the A-road was alarmingly narrow and steep, and the ache between Lucy's shoulders had become a pulsing pain. But at last she was here. There always was a bright side, or at least a glimmer of one. She had to believe that, had clung to it for her whole life and especially for the last few weeks, when the things she'd thought were solid had fallen away beneath her like so much sinking sand.

The narrow road twisted sharply several times, and then as she came around the final turn, the sun peeked out from behind shreds of cloud and illuminated the village in the valley below.

A huddle of quaint stone houses and terraced cottages clustered along the shore, the sea a streak of gray-blue that met up with the horizon. A stream snaked through the village before meandering into the fields on the far side; dotted with cows and looking, in the moment's sunshine, perfectly pastoral, the landscape was like a painting by Constable come to life.

For a few seconds Lucy considered how she'd paint such a scene; she'd use diluted watercolors, so the colors blurred into one another as they seemed to do in the valley below, all washed with the golden gray light that filtered from behind the clouds.

She envisioned herself walking in those fields, with a dog, a black Lab perhaps, frisking at her heels. Never mind that she didn't have a dog and didn't actually like them all that much. It was all part of the picture, along with buying a newspaper at the local shop—there had to be a lovely little shop down there, with a cozy, grandmotherly type at the counter who would slip her chocolate buttons along with her paper.

A splatter of rain against her windshield woke her from the moment's reverie. Yet another tractor was coming up behind her, at quite a clip. With a wave of apology for the stony-faced farmer who was driving the thing, she resumed the steep, sharply twisting descent into the village.

She slowed the car to a crawl as she came to the high street, houses lining the narrow road on either side, charming terraced cottages with brightly painted doors and pots of flowers, and, all right, yes, a few more weathered-looking buildings with peeling paint and the odd broken window. Lucy was determined to fall in love with it, to find everything perfect.

Juliet ran a guesthouse in one of the village's old farmhouses: Tarn House, she'd said, no other address. Lucy hadn't been to Juliet's house before, hadn't actually seen her sister in more than five years. And didn't really know her all that well.

Juliet was thirty-seven to her twenty-six, and when Lucy was six years old, their mother, Fiona, had gotten a job as an art lecturer at a university in Boston. She'd taken Lucy with her, but Juliet had chosen to stay in England and finish her A levels while boarding with a school friend. She'd gone on to university in England, she'd visited Boston only once, and over the years Lucy had always felt a little intimidated by her half sister, so cool and capable and remote.

Yet it had been Juliet she'd called when everything had exploded around her, and Juliet who had said briskly, when Lucy had burst into tears on the phone, that she should come and stay with her for a while.

"You could get a job, make yourself useful," she'd continued in that same no-nonsense tone that made Lucy feel like a scolded six-year-old. "The local primary needs maternity cover for a receptionist position, and I know the head teacher. I'll arrange it."

And Lucy, overwhelmed and grateful that someone could see a way out of the mess, had let her. She'd had a telephone interview with the head teacher, who was, she realized, the principal, the next day, a man who had sounded as stern as Juliet and had finished the conversation with a sigh, saying, "It's only four months, after all," so Lucy felt as if he was hiring her only as a favor to her sister.

And now she couldn't find Tarn House.

She drove the mile and a half down the main street and back again, doing what felt like a seventeen-point turn in the narrow street, sweat prickling between her shoulder blades while three cars, a truck, and two tractors, all driven by grim-faced men with their arms folded, waited for her to manage to turn the car around. She'd never actually driven in England before, and she hit the curb twice before she managed to get going the right way.

She passed a post office shop looking almost as quaint as she'd imagined (peeling paint and Lottery advertisements aside), a pub, a church, a sign for the primary school where she'd be working (but no actual school as far as she could see), and no Tarn House.

Finally she parked the car by the train station, admiring the old-fashioned sign above the Victorian station building, which was, on second look, now a restaurant. The driving rain had downgraded into one of those misting drizzles that didn't seem all that bad when you were looking out at it from the cozy warmth of your kitchen but soaked you utterly after about five seconds.

Hunching her shoulders against the bitter wind—this was *August*—she searched for someone to ask directions.

The only person in sight was a farmer with a flat cap jammed down on his head and wearing extremely mud-splattered plus fours. Lucy approached him with her most engaging smile.

"Pardon me—are you from around here?"

He squinted at her suspiciously. "Eh?"

She had just asked, she realized, an absolutely idiotic question. "I only wanted to ask," she tried again, "do you know where Tarn House is?"

"Tarn House?" he repeated, his tone implying that he'd never heard of the place.

"Yes, it's a bed-and-breakfast here in the village—"

"*Eh?*" He scratched his head, his bushy eyebrows drawn together rather fiercely. Then he dropped his hand and jerked a thumb towards the road that led steeply up towards the shop and one pub. "Tarn House's up there, isn't it, now, across from the Hangman's Noose?"

"The Hangman's—" Ah. The pub. Lucy nodded. "Thank you."

"The white house with black shutters."

"Thanks so much, I really appreciate it." And why, Lucy wondered as she turned up the street, had he acted so incredulous when she'd asked him where it was? Was that a Cumbrian thing, or was her American accent stronger than she'd thought?

Tarn House was a neat two-story cottage of whitewashed stone with the promised black shutters, and pots of chrysanthemums on either side of the shiny black door. A discreet hand-painted sign that Lucy hadn't glimpsed from the road informed her that this was indeed her destination.

She hesitated on the slate step, her hand hovering above the brass knocker, as the rain continued steadily down. She felt keenly then how little she actually *knew* her sister. Half sister, if she wanted to be accurate; neither of them had known their different fathers. Not that Lucy could really call a sperm donor a dad. And their mother had never spoken about Juliet's father, whoever he was, at least not to Lucy.

Her hand was still hovering over the brass knocker when the door suddenly opened and Juliet stood there, her sandy hair pulled back into a neat ponytail, her gray eyes narrowed, her hands planted on her hips, as she looked Lucy up and down, her mouth tightening the same way her mother's did when she looked at her.

Two sleek greyhounds flanked Juliet, cowering slightly as Lucy stepped forward and ducked her head in both greeting and silent, uncertain apology. She could have used a hug, but Juliet didn't move and Lucy was too hesitant to hug the half sister she barely knew.

"Well," Juliet said with a brisk nod. "You made it."

"Yes. Yes, I did." Lucy smiled tentatively, and Juliet moved aside.

"You look like a drowned rat. You'd better come in."

Lucy stepped into the little entryway of Juliet's house, a surprisingly friendly jumble of umbrellas and Wellington boots cluttering the slate floor along with the dogs. She would have expected her sister to have every boot and brolly in regimental order, but maybe she didn't know Juliet well enough to know how she kept her house. Or maybe her sister was just having an off day.

"They're rescue dogs—they'll jump at a mouse," Juliet explained, for the two greyhounds were trembling. "They'll come round eventually. They just have to get used to you." She snapped her fingers, and the dogs obediently retreated to their baskets.

"Cup of tea," she said, not a question, and led Lucy into the kitchen. The kitchen was even cozier than the hall, with a large dark green Aga cooking range taking up most of one wall and emitting a lovely warmth, a circular pine table in the center, and a green glass jar of wildflowers on the windowsill. It was all so homely, so comforting, and so not what Lucy had expected from someone as stern and officious as Juliet, although again she was acting on ignorance. How many conversations had she even had with Juliet, before that wretched phone call? Five? Six?

Still the sight of it all, the Aga and the flowers and even the view of muddy sheep fields outside, made her spirits lift. This was a place she could feel at home in. She hoped.

She sank into a chair at the table as Juliet plonked a brass kettle on one of the Aga's round hot plates.

"So you start next week."

"Yes—"

"You ought to go up to the school tomorrow and check in with Alex."

"Alex?"

Juliet turned around, her straight eyebrows drawn together, her expression not precisely a frown, but definitely not a smile. "Alex Kincaid, the head teacher. You spoke with him on the phone, remember?"

There was a faint note of impatience or even irritation in Juliet's voice, which made Lucy stammer in apology.

"Oh, yes, yes, of course. Mr. Kincaid. Yes. Sorry." She was not actually all that keen to make Alex Kincaid's acquaintance. Given how unimpressed by her he'd seemed for the ten excruciating minutes of their phone interview, she thought he was unlikely to revise his opinion upon meeting her.

And she was unlikely to revise hers; she already had a picture of him in her head: He would be tall and angular with short-cut steel gray hair and square spectacles. He'd have one of those mouths that looked thin and unfriendly, and he would narrow his eyes at you as you spoke, as if incredulous of every word that came out of your mouth.

Oh, wait. Maybe she was picturing her last boss, Simon Hansen, when he'd told her he was canceling her art exhibition. *Sorry, Lucy, but after the bad press we can hardly go ahead with the exhibit. And in any case, your mother's not coming anyway.*

As for Alex Kincaid, now that she remembered that irritated voice on the phone, she decided he'd be balding and have bushy eyebrows. He'd blink too much as he spoke and have a nasal drip.

All right, perhaps that was a little unfair. But he'd definitely sounded as if he'd had his sense of humor surgically removed.

"I'm sure you're completely knackered now," Juliet continued, "but tomorrow I'll give you a proper tour of the village, introduce you." She nodded, that clearly decided, and Lucy, not knowing what else to do, nodded back.

It was so *strange* being here with her sister, sitting across from her in this cozy little kitchen, knowing she was actually going to live here and maybe get to know this sibling of hers, who had semiterrified her for most of her life. Intimidated, anyway, but perhaps that was her fault and not Juliet's.

In any case, when Lucy had needed someone to talk to, someone who understood the maelstrom that was their mother but wasn't caught up in her currents, she'd turned to Juliet. And Juliet hadn't let her down. She had to remember that, keep hold of it in moments like these, when Juliet seemed like another disapproving person in her life, mentally rolling her eyes at how Lucy could never seem to get it together.

And she *was* going to get it together. Here, in rainy, picturesque Hartley-by-the-Sea. She was going to reconnect with her sister, and make loads of friends, and go on picnics and pub crawls and find happiness.

KATE HEWITT is the bestselling author of more than forty novels of romance and women's fiction. Raised in the United States, she lives in a market town in Wales with her American-born husband and their five children.

CONNECT ONLINE

kate-hewitt.com
facebook.com/katehewittauthor
twitter.com/katehewitt1
acumbrianlife.blogspot.co.uk